THE FORBIDDEN GENERATION

PAUL ISON

THE FORBIDDEN GENERATION

PAUL ISON

THE FORBIDDEN GENERATION

© Paul Ison

Paul Ison has asserted his rights in accordance with the Copyright, Designs & and Patents Act 1988 to be identified to be the author of this work.

Published by:
Wi/\le Publishing
British Columbia, Canada

Email: info@wibblepublishing.com
Web: www.wibblepublishing.com

First published 2018

Legal Deposit: Library and Archives Canada, Ottawa, Ontario, Canada.

13-digit ISBN: 978-1-987860-25-2

Printed in Great Britain

In memory of Raymond Ison, rest in peace Dad.

AUTHOR'S NOTE

With my gratitude to Clare Ison, Arthur Gormley and Rick Holden for their efforts in proof-reading the book and for their input.

Other books by the same author:
A Crooked Sign on Albion Street
The Path
The Diary Man
A Field of Crows
From Ashes we Grow
A Time for Justice
Barlow

PROLOGUE

September 1942

He was determined that this was going to work. Overhead the bombers still droned in the night sky and he could see the concern on the faces of his medical colleagues around the operating table. In their tired eyes and tired faces he sensed a resignation that this war would follow the course that many had predicted and that this small archipelago would fall to the might of Hitler's war machine. Perhaps he could make a difference, perhaps the people here tonight would leave this place with a different perspective, with hope in their hearts.

He had known defeat already in this war, he knew what it was like to see a country crumble in the face of a tyrannical madman and he had been lucky to get away from there. It was his country, the place where he had been conceived and where, as a vulnerable waif he had poked his tiny head into the world. A harsh world he had come to learn.

Life had been easy as far as he was concerned, playing in the woods with his friends, food on the table, a warm and fairly comfortable bed. But, as he grew older, he realised what he had been blind to see as a child. Life was not easy, his mother toiled with the effort of putting that expected food on the table when his father, returning from the shipyards with a liver full of vodka to process, stumbled in out of the cold Northern European nights.

He was a bright boy, he studied hard, he had become a prominent man in the field of surgery and he had a keen eye on medical research. Then the war had come and he had been forced to flee the place he had called home. His parents were not so lucky. His mother had got him the place on the boat, his father he had not seen for several weeks and was in all probability already dead by the time he left.

He had much to offer but he needed to convince his new found paymasters of that. If he succeeded here tonight, with the bombs falling all around them then they would gain faith in him, they would gain hope and he might just get the opportunity to convince them of what he felt sure was medically possible.

The woman on the operating table was dead, the bomb that had devastated her life and those of the people who lived near to her on her, now destroyed, London street had sucked the life out of her and he wondered if they travelled together on their journey to the next world or if they made their own way based on the degree to which they had to make peace with the world and with themselves. What he did know was that there was something here that was his responsibility.

Amidst a sea of doubt bordering on scorn he continued his skilful manipulation of the piece of dead human flesh before him. He would never forget the look on the faces of his colleagues when the child was revealed, when the sound of its crying drowned out the sound of the bombers overhead.

ONE

He had done a lot of thinking recently. He had always been a thoughtful child in fact, ahead of his years, seeking adult company rather than that of his peers. His thirst for knowledge was great and he had excelled at school. For him life had to have a meaning that transcended the banal cycle of sleeping, working, eating then sleeping again.

A self-driven loner; he remembered the words from his school report. It seemed like an accusation, it certainly didn't feel like a compliment. What did it mean exactly? Did it mean he was a non-conformist, was he unpopular with his fellow students and teachers? He hadn't tried to be, he was just what he was, and he had always been like that.

He wondered if other people rehearsed their lives as they lived them. He lay in bed at night and tried to imagine how the next day would be, what he might do if this situation or that situation presented itself and how others might react to his reactions. Was this strange he wondered. If it was, he knew no other way to be, no other way to act.

His life had been a success story really, after an odd beginning. He knew that he was adopted; his stepparents had deigned to tell him as soon as they considered him old enough to understand what it was they were telling him. If they had expected an adverse reaction, dreaded such a response even, then they had not needed to worry. It was, to him, just another fact, something that had shaped the person he was, perhaps it explained something about the way he interacted with the world but if it did, he didn't know what it was exactly.

He left school with good grades and attended Nottingham University where he graduated with a first. Things came easily to him and he wondered why he was so blessed. Was it the analytical mind that he had always worried about? Did his mental rehearsal for all the things that happened to him ensure that all went well? So it had seemed to him.

He did have a dark side, however, a part of him that seemed slightly divorced from the other parts of his mind, a depressing place that when visited, either in sleep or in waking thought, seemed to fill his very soul with despair. What were these thoughts he wondered, why did they beset him from time to time? When it happened he went on a self-destructive spiral, hurting himself emotionally, but never physically, it felt like something he had to do from time to time. It was as much a part of him as all the other things, the more positive things that were, after all, more prevalent.

He got a good job, married and started a family. All of these seemed like normal things to do. By the time he was in his mid twenties he had begun to believe that the things that went on his mind were the same for everyone, he was normal after all.

Of late though, things had turned bad for him. The dark thoughts were becoming darker and far more prevalent he was reassessing his earlier thoughts that he fitted in with society and he felt himself drifting into that familiar downward maelstrom that he was usually able to call a halt to before things got too bad. This time it was proving much more difficult.

The noises of a normal life seemed to be fading away below him and he embraced the moment as they did so. The television set sounded muffled and distant, the occasional barking of the dog as the children teased it coming from another place, a world where he no longer belonged.

For a while now things had been getting him down, sleeplessness – only curable it seemed to him by copious alcohol intake, leading to restlessness and dissatisfaction. There was more to it than that though, and he had tried to analyse it and been frightened by the results. That was why he was sitting here now, upstairs in his study with his family below him in the sitting room doing normal things like conversing together and watching television. For Jim Dowley his reality here tonight was staring into a brandy glass and just occasionally at his reflection in the darkness of the rain soaked window before him.

For no discernable reason, he reached forward to touch the reflection that he saw there. The pane of glass was icy cold to his touch, the outline of his hand superimposed by its warmth. The rain continued to pound out its monotonous rhythm on the outside of the glass, streaming down the window pane in erratic rivulets. The darkness beyond was inky black; impenetrable, much like his mood.

Jim adjusted the focus of his gaze once more so that he could look at his haggard reflection there. The eyes seemed too deeply set in their sockets so that they looked like tiny, dark pearls in deep dark pits. The furrowed brow, the shadows of laziness where he had foregone the razor blade that day, added to his dishevelment. He readjusted his gaze, preferring the concealment of that pained reflection, gazing instead at the rain and the darkness outside, looking but not really seeing anything at all.

He heard the sound of soft footfalls on the stair-carpet and guessed that his son, Darren, was heading for the toilet giving him the excuse to pop his head around the study door and check if his dad was okay, or if he needed anything. Darren, more than his wife Jennifer or their daughter Hannah, seemed to be more sensitive to the changes in Jim's temperament and, whilst he was flattered and grateful for this show of concern, a part of him – his darker side – resented the intrusion on his miserable reflection.

The wind outside threw sheets of the heavy rain against the window, hammering as if to be let in on his reverie. It had rained virtually solidly for the last seven days and the dreariness outside matched his demeanour. He poured some more brandy from the bottle into the glass and watched as the fortified liquid slipped slowly down the inside of his glass in the half-light. He heard the flushing of the toilet cistern and prepared himself for the few moments of sociability he would shortly undergo. A minute passed, then two and he realised with a mixture of emotions that he was to be spared the moment.

Taking a deep swallow of the liquid, in the way that a thirsty man may drink from a pint of cold beer, he relished the burning sensation on the back of his throat, feeling the warmth as it ventured forth to his stomach. How many glasses had he drunk already this night? Was it seven, possibly eight; he couldn't remember the dulling of his faculties refused to allow him to focus on the answer to his self-directed questioning. In a bar the glasses would be considered more than large. Why was he doing this to himself? What was he running away from?

The answer to that question was somewhat easier, he felt haunted and he drank to abolish his demons; or more accurately his *demon;* for his dreams and even now his waking hours were dominated by thoughts of one other. It was not a new phenomenon, all his life deep back into his strange childhood he had been haunted by thoughts of someone else. He wondered what a psychiatrist might make of this. He had read accounts of children who had imaginary friends who they spoke to with little or no embarrassment regardless of who observed them doing it. In his case it wasn't quite like that, he was not given to talking out loud to this companion, it was as though it existed only through his mind but he had no control over when it called to visit him.

The self-analysis was the hardest part of what was happening to him, he was desperate for answers to questions that would not form properly in his mind. How could you get solutions to problems when you weren't properly able to define what those problems were? It was hard for him because the reasons for his predicament were always lacking in substance; unquantifiable. There had, over time, been no discernable trigger that would lead him to this pit of despair, no death in the family, no recurring illness, unless, of course, you considered the affliction itself to be an illness which he supposed was possible.

He drank to forget but forgot what he was drinking to forget and yet he still drank. Jennifer did not nag him, she knew that something was wrong but chose not to be confrontational about it, they were well off, his health was good, apart from this recent inability to sleep without the use of artificial, narcotic means and his family were healthy and happy. So why did he feel he had the problems of the world on his shoulders?

He removed his hand, at last, from the pane of glass, watching as it immediately cooled and his hand-print melted away, leaving just the darkness and the rainwater. Was life like that he wondered, ephemeral, once gone did it dissolve as quickly as water vapour on a window pane? If it was, what was the point in worrying about what was happening to him? He guessed there was no point at all but continued to worry in any case.

His stupor adjusted itself to allow him to glimpse once more out into the darkness, the rain still lashed against the windowpane and the darkness beyond was total. This room and all those on the back of the house looked out over fields some arable and others grazing land for sheep and cattle, before a steady rise in the terrain took the land up to the hills and the forest which grew over them.

He focused his gaze once again on the dim reflection of himself looking out from the cold glass. The indistinct nature of the reflection made it possible to extrapolate what he was seeing, to imagine him handsome and smiling, happy with life. He could pretend that he had shaved that morning, that his eyes were clear and his thoughts lucid. He could gaze into his own sincerity there and not see the lies that reflected back, or the truth.

He tried to focus on the darkness beyond the reflection. Something moved. Outside just beyond where he was looking, he strained his eyes to see what it was. A dim light, like another reflection but just beyond where his had been moments before, seemed to shimmer on the other side of the glass. How the hell could that be? He was on the first floor, yet there appeared to be a face looking through the glass at him, indistinct in features but distinct enough to convince him that a face was what he was seeing.

In a moment of anger he drained the brandy glass of its contents and convinced himself that the house was about to be burgled by a particularly daring burglar. He resolved to open the window and tackle the would-be intruder. Something about the way that the face seemed to continue to look in at him as he made these assertive gestures stayed his resolve and he strained his eyes once more to get a measure of what he was about to deal with.

He suddenly felt fear. This was not an emotion that he was particularly prone to and the feeling of the hairs on the back of his neck prickling into movement was unpleasant. He settled uncomfortably back into the swivel chair at his desk and poured more brandy, keeping the image of the watching face in the periphery of his vision as he did so, watchful for movements. There were none.

On the stairs outside he heard the sound of his family as the two youngsters and possibly even Jennifer herself had decided to turn in for the evening. He thought about their safety and his duty to protect them from harm and found that it was strong in him and that he loved them all. Yet, he remained quietly watching his watcher even as Darren and Hannah called out to wish him goodnight. He replied with as much lightness in his voice as he could but his voice sounded choked despite this and it was only moments later that the door opened slightly, allowing light from the landing to pour into the room.

Jennifer moved across the room in the half-light and placed her hands on his shoulders, stooping down to gently kiss the top of his head. She was going to bed and would read for a while, she hoped he wouldn't be too late and she loved him. He responded by gently squeezing her left hand and producing a thin smile that she took to be a reciprocation of her feelings.

Presently his wife left the room leaving the door slightly ajar making it more difficult for him to reassess the window for the face outside due to the extra light. Despite this he was able to locate it, just beyond the glass once more, looking in, not moving, unblinking. Again he felt the fear and again he doused it in brandy.

He sat there in silence – but for the sound of the wind and the rain and his own shallow breaths – watching, as he in turn was watched. By whom or by what he was unable to formulate in his mind. His eyes were tired, stinging as if complaining at the prolonged concentration of staring, the lack of moisture caused by his own failure to blink, the alcohol.

Something like a memory was forming in his mind and he fought at first to shrug it away, as if its intrusion might disturb this shallow peace he had established with the face behind the windowpane. As his concentration began to wander the thought process turned again to this memory.

A dream perhaps, he contemplated, yes that was it. Vivid; he had been having lucid dreams that might even have coincided with the problems he had been experiencing lately. Hadn't the dreams provided the catalyst that had led to this recent, fairly out of character, slide into absolute despair? He tried to recollect the dream, it had led to him waking, screaming out into the night, he had shouted a name, Marie. His wife had been upset. It had left him uneasy, digging away at his consciousness for days, affecting his work. The drinking, the mood swings they had all followed on the back of that night.

His eyes had strayed away from the windowpane and he quickly adjusted his gaze to the glass at this sudden realisation. His eyes were met only by the indistinct outline of his own reflection and he felt panic rise in him like a tide. The feeling that the face at the window was still watching him was overwhelming and he scanned the room – half expecting this wraith to be standing over him, its icy fingers even now reaching forward to clasp his throat and choke the life out of him. There was nobody there. He poured the rest of the brandy into his glass and raised it to his lips to drink away his demons.

The rain seemed to increase its intensity; the drumming on the window pane was now so loud that he felt as though the noise was inside his own head, deafening him, numbing his other senses. He swayed dangerously on his seat, almost falling off it and onto the floor. Leaden hands prevented this particular disaster as he grabbed the desk-top beside him. His glass though slipped from his hand and fell onto its side on the desk. He watched it idiotically as it rolled slowly out of his reach off the edge of the desk and then into the thin air beyond.

Jim watched it as it descended in seemingly slow motion turning over and over as if savouring its freefall. A hundred intricate movements of the light that reflected on the glass as it approached the floor before landing unharmed on the soft pile of the carpet. He stared at the glass for several minutes, making no effort to retrieve it at all, marvelling still that it had survived its journey intact; his mind wandered away to distant places and the room around him became inconsequential. Then, quite suddenly, he was falling! He wondered if he too would survive his unscheduled journey intact.

**

His head was beginning to clear as the cold, cruel rain was whipped against the skin on his face by the fury of the wind. His progress was hampered by the cloying mud which sucked at his tiring legs, trying, it seemed to him, to drag him down; consume him in its oozing depths.

The trees dark and naked in their winter coats loomed over him and were only a few metres away; the girl was nearer still. It seemed that she ran with less difficulty than he did, her footsteps light as she approached the trees, she was about to be engulfed in the darkness of the woods.

He tried to call out to her but the words seemed muted, snatched away, as they were, by the wind; the very gale that seemed to thwart his advance, to stop him in his tracks.

"Marie!"

The word drifted pathetically away in the storm, torn to pieces by the elements and he watched in agony as she was enveloped by the tall trees, brooding dark sentinels which seemed almost to close ranks as she disappeared within their midst.

The rain cascaded still harder from the dark and moonless sky; his mood deteriorated on a similar scale, tendrils of doubt clawing away at his thoughts. Had she really been there this time; or had he once more been chasing shadows? He fell to his knees in the thick oozing mud, he felt it sucking him down, weakening him still further; his desire to follow his prey weakened and drained. His hair hung in lank rat's tails about his face, his eyes stung from the fierce rain and the salt of his sweat. He felt; no, he *knew* that he had been running for miles, knew also that he was hopelessly lost.

A childish giggle, like a distant melody on a gentle breeze brought him out of his misery and he caught a glimpse, once more, of the girl's flowing white dress as it danced its way through the trees. His doubts were erased and he followed once more.

The darkness which had tormented him before, now seemed almost light in comparison with the inky blackness in the woods; here the mud had less of a hold on him, giving precedence instead to a new hazard; the tangle of weeds and thorny undergrowth. Through the trees he could see her clearly again, skipping through the woods with what seemed to him to be gay abandon, how desperately he wanted to speak with her, to understand her and protect her.

He cursed as he fell to the ground, the tentacles of the long undergrowth clawing him down, tearing his clothes, biting into his flesh so that he bled from the myriad of scratches. Again, though, he heard the giggle and again he righted his weary body and followed, on through the trees, following that white flowing garment which seemed miraculously untouched by mud, gleaming white as it flicked through the undergrowth with ridiculous ease.

Now the wind played games with him, helping him onwards so that he thought he might catch her and; as the hope rose in him, as the adrenaline began coursing through him, so the wind howled like eerie laughter in his face, forcing him back, allowing her to put distance between them again, as she did so, again she giggled, so soft and so melodic. She was the enchantress, the Pied Piper; and her laughter was the music to which he danced.

He had followed her so many times before, would he never learn the futility of the chase, the pursuit always the same, though the scenery changed; he had yet to capture her though, despite all his best efforts.

"Marie!" He knew her name though how this could be was as enigmatic as she was.

His cheeks were numb with cold as the icy rain bit into them, hurting his flesh like the cruel thorns through which he ran; his breaths came in rasping gasps as his lungs begged for the chase to be over.

With alarming suddenness, the trees were gone and his mind was fighting to apply some logic to the change. Had he run free of their boundaries and out into this field of glowing colour over which the sun presided with warm and heartening cheeriness?

He did not look back to find out, he felt unable to wrest his gaze from the girl skipping through the knee-high grass which swayed gently under the persuasion of the, now warm, breeze. He watched, transfixed, as she receded from him, occasionally disturbing swift and swallow, starling and sparrow. Beautiful butterflies basked in the sunshine, their glorious colours blending with the profusion of wild flowers which seemed to cover all the colours of the spectrum and all those beyond. Still he followed her.

His progress was easier now, the wispy tickle of the browning grasses brushed against his now naked legs and the sun warmed his soul and gladdened his heart. The memory of the darkness, of the tangles of thorns, the wind and the rain was a distant one. Barely recalled too, was the fatigue which had so nearly drained his resolve, so that he had feared drowning in the sea of mud and slime.

Faster he ran, as the birds serenaded him with songs the clarity and beauty of which he had never heard before. He rejoiced in their simple beauty as he chased his quarry.

"Marie!" He called out her name once more and, though the voice was his own, the tone seemed melodic, a part of this paradise. As he watched he thought he saw a slight break in her stride, as though she had heard his voice and would stop and wait for him, but her progress through the sea of whispering grasses continued unabated.

His eyes rarely left the girl's running form, such that he was not able to fully perceive the strangeness of the place through which they ran, despite this he had the distinct impression that this field had no boundaries, that it would simply go on forever and that this chase would not be over until forever was reached.

A new sound met his ears now, the gentle chatter of shallow water over shingle, and the splashing of feet skipping quickly and easily through its midst, and no sooner had he heard this sound he found that the refreshing water was beneath his own feet, a crystal clear stream stretched out before him with the field of golden grasses to either side of him.

The cobbled unevenness of the stream bed, seemed to cause him no discomfort at all, his feet seemed almost to skip over the stones with each step forward appearing to happen before he had placed any weight on his landed foot. The gap between them remained constant, as though their strides mirrored each others with perfect synchronicity.

"Marie!"

Once more his voice seemed in keeping with this beautiful, if surreal world, this time he was sure that she had failed to hear him and he pressed on though he seemed not to be able to run any faster. In the stream at his feet, tiny, brightly coloured fish danced their fishy dance as they cut smoothly and easily through the crystal clear water. Strange birds, tall and elegant and with exotic plumage watched him as he ran, like sentinels viewing an oft watched scene. Their elegant heads perched proudly on long swan-like necks turning imperceptibly to follow the chase.

The water deepened, slightly at first but then with an alarming suddenness that startled him. The gentle babble of shallow water flowing over rounded pebbles was replaced by a deeper sound; his stride seemed unaffected his progress unabated but he noticed that the girl's began to slow.

At last he would reach her, he could embrace her small body in his arms he felt elated and ran on. The girl stopped now, half turned towards him and he saw that there was unease in her eyes, the water seemed to be pulling at her, taking her down into its depths. Louder and louder the roar of the water rose, and it was now a torrent which swept around them both, the spray leaping into the air between them so that, for a moment, he thought he had lost her only to catch sight of her again, her flowing dark hair now hanging limply about her shoulders and her face.

Doleful eyes peered out of that face, deep, dark, mysterious and yet somehow sad. They were further away from him now and there was fear in them too, she was being taken away from him by the current, perhaps to a watery grave, torn from his protection.

Alarm and fear filled his heart in equal measure, he felt his feet taken away from under him by an undertow that was fierce and strong, and the feeling was like hands on him as he seemed to be dragged out into where the water was deeper, filled with danger, perhaps to his own death.

His fear was increased as his eyes searched for the bank, looking for signs of the land he had only just left behind, he saw nothing but the water and the now angry sky above him which spewed forth rain once again.

Dizziness overcame him as the whirlpool he had been sucked into increased in velocity and his world began to spin. Specks of colour seemed to merge into great swathes as the vortex intensified; a kaleidoscopic pattern like a richly woven carpet of coloured wools seemed to fill his perception as the last vestiges of consciousness began to desert him.

The world spun faster and faster and grew wilder and wilder, until he could no longer take it in; he thought for a time that death had claimed him. The feeling of falling, so real, he felt he was flying like some great bird of prey. Swooping and circling and drifting on thermals, he felt he had the eyes of a hawk in search of his victim. Over pinewoods and lakes and snow-covered mountains, he swam through the air with power and grace, and there, far below him in a field of brown grasses, a beautiful lady was skipping among flowers of every hue.

He swooped and the rush of air both cooled him and excited him, he felt, suddenly, more alive than he had ever felt in his life and his pleasure intensified as he neared his goal. Down and down he flew; the wind pressing into him as he fell to earth. Trees, grasses lakes and mountains were all as one, a colourful blur, and now here he was just a few feet above her and as he called out her name she looked up at him and her smile was radiant. At last he would be with her; his mystery girl, the girl who he knew was called Marie.

**

The landing was indeed a soft one, the plush pile of the carpet breaking his fall from the chair in the study. Dazed, he tried to focus on his surroundings, the empty brandy glass on the floor beside him; he could make out his reflection in the glass. His head was spinning from the combined effects of his fall, his disorienting dream and the alcohol he had earlier drunk.

Who was the girl in the dream and why did she haunt him so? Why too did her face seem so familiar to him? The sound of footsteps outside the room brought his mind back to the current situation and he looked up as his wife pushed open the door and he registered the concern in her face as she quickly moved towards him.

With an effort he dragged himself onto his knees, and then she helped him to stand. Outside, the rain still hammered persistently against the window pane and the wind howled like banshees as it whispered around the gables of the house.

He was able to assure her that he was okay and he retired to the bathroom on unsteady legs, it was then that he noticed the scratches on his legs and remembered the chase through the woods. Just what the hell was happening to him? What would he tell Jennifer when she saw his injuries?

Jennifer was reading when he returned from the bathroom, she didn't look in his direction until he climbed into the bed. Her smile was thin and she looked tired, he felt a wave of love and pity for her. It probably wasn't very easy being married to him he reasoned as he lay back on the pillows and allowed sleep, and the dreams he knew it would contain, to claim him.

TWO

June 1953

The war had been kind to him in the end. Where misery had ruled supreme, where death and destruction had claimed so many. For him, despite his displacement, there was new hope.

Opportunity had presented itself to him and he had reached out with both grateful hands and snatched it to his breast where he had held it tightly ever since.

His skills with a scalpel had never been called into question, his radical thoughts, borne from keeping an open mind and daring to dream that the impossible could one day be real, had sat less well with them.

The Allies were quick to condemn after the war, a witch-hunt of sorts had been undertaken and was still now in full swing. Many senior Nazi figures had simply disappeared, spirited away with the dirty money that they had in abundance for such a time as that during 1945. But some of the science was not to be discarded.

The Americans had already latched onto the missile technology, they would learn from those German scientists and they would use that technology ostensibly in the name of self defence, a protection against the atrocities that war begot. He suspected otherwise, of course, though like the millions of others that shared his views he would keep his own counsel on the subject.

But what of the other science that the German machine had set in train; was this to be ignored? Where the human body and mind was concerned was the research to be condemned on some high minded moral grounds?

The work of Josef Mengele was ground breaking if controversial. Why was it that rockets were deemed acceptable when all they did was take lives and yet medical research, even unorthodox medical research, was bad even though it could save lives? He had argued this loud and long but he suspected that his arguments would not be listened to.

He was known as the miracle worker. A cult hero amongst his peers for the night he had saved a baby's life, cutting it from the womb of a dead woman. Yet they would not listen to his theories, they threatened to censure him for his beliefs. He was becoming sure that no funding or facilities would be made available to him to allow him to further his research and he was becoming resentful.

He sat on the embankment and watched as a barge pushed its way along the dirty River Thames. It would probably be taking waste out to the brackish waters of the estuary. He remembered his own journey, on a small ship as it sailed away into the night leaving Poland, soon to be occupied Poland, behind.

He felt sadness for his loss, a part of him had died that night and, with the thought of death still in his mind, he wondered about his mother. Had she died like so many others in the death camps, or had she been spared that indignity, perhaps cut down by the bullets of a German machine gun. He hoped for her sake that it was the latter. One thing he was certain of was that she had not survived the war.

He listened as Big Ben chimed out the hour, he had come to love that sound. With a sigh he stood up, he would soon need to make some big decisions in his life. Returning to Poland was not out of the question but somehow his future felt tied up with England and London in particular. In London, even when things became seemingly impossible, ways could be found to do things. Londoner's had taught the world to be resourceful, their spirit was a lesson to everyone.

He climbed the steps to Westminster Bridge and stood for a time looking down at the swirling, dirty waters below, the river itself represented the spirit of the place, powerful, eternal and proud it was the lifeblood of the capital.

He had taken a room in a small house in Lambeth, one of the few streets in that area unaffected by the bombs. From his garret window he could see the river and this, more than anything else, had been the reason for him taking the tenancy. It was also within easy walking distance of St. Thomas' Hospital where he worked.

It was to the hospital that he slowly walked now, crossing the bridge slowly, savouring the calmness of the night. Once he was back inside the hospital wards his life would not be his until he finished his shift. The war had left a legacy of injuries and wounds that still kept the surgeons busy even now.

It was times like this that enabled him to think straight, to prophesise about his theories and their likely successes. It had been that night in the operating theatre back in the war years that had formulated the idea in his mind. Just as his colleagues were calling him the miracle worker and his star began rising he was thinking of other miracles, more wondrous than that he had just performed.

As he walked into the reception area of the sprawling hospital by the River Thames he felt its walls close in around him and he was forced to put his thoughts away for a time. One day he would prove to the world what a genius he really was. One day they would sit up and take notice of him at last.

THREE

The room was in total darkness when Jim Dowley first opened his eyes. They were sore; it felt as though tiny needles were being pressed into their soft tissues. At best, someone had kicked sand into his face.

Beside him the even rhythm of Jennifer's breathing was the only clue that the world was still there in the darkness. He lay there for a time, staring at where he knew the ceiling must be until the first tendrils of the grey morning light crept into the room.

In his mind he ran through the strange events that had beset him the night before, he had been dreaming, of that he was certain, and yet how did that sit with the irrefutable evidence of his own eyes? The scratches on his legs were certainly real, even now in the half-light he was discomfited by them.

Jennifer still slept soundly beside him, he turned to her and watched her sleeping form, so peaceful, her breaths so steady and uniform, he felt a wave of love wash over him and he wished that he could put his strange obsession behind him. Who was the woman in his dreams; how could he know her name? He didn't feel attraction for the girl, just a need to be with her, to somehow protect her; but why?

Jim rolled on to his back and resumed his surveillance of the ceiling no nearer to finding the answers to his odd dilemma. It was affecting his health, and, by proxy it was affecting his work as well. At least he did not need to worry about that today given that it was Sunday. His marriage though, that was a different matter, he valued his wife more than anything else, it was just that his strange behaviour was upsetting her; despite this he seemed to have no control over it.

It had started to get worse about a year ago, at first he hadn't realised there was a problem, just a recurring dream in which the girl was a part, perhaps she was someone he had glanced at in the street or somewhere similar and a part of his mind over which he had little control had stored away her image.

For it to be anything else, something more strange or sinister had seemed far-fetched to him at the time but now, here in this greyness it now seemed possible. Last night had probably been the worst incident so far; he feared he was losing his mind.

Above anything else it was the fear that this affliction might never leave him, that he would be trapped with this strange obsession until he lost his job and his marriage, until it finally drove him to madness.

Beside him Jennifer was beginning to stir, she turned towards him in the bed and her hand snaked across his chest, he wanted then to take her in his arms and make love to her but he did not, for him his demons were too great; all consuming and instead he settled for the warmth of her body next to his own.

The pain in his legs made him think once more of his dream, it had been so ethereal and yet he was somehow convinced that aspects of it were relevant. That the woman in his dreams existed he was absolutely positive but who she was and where she was were questions to which he had failed to find any answers.

He thought of the imagery and concluded that whatever variations of landscape, flora and fauna, three things were constant in all his dreams; the girl, him and the chase. What did the chase symbolise; was something trying to tell him that they were destined to meet? Was it down to him to find her? If it were then he really had no idea of where he might start.

He heard footsteps on the landing outside, one of the kids was up and about, he loved them both dearly, regretted that what was happening to him was having a negative effect on them, he just wanted it all to stop but how could he make it stop?

At first the alcohol had helped, he found that if he drank enough he tended to fall into a dreamless sleep, all thoughts of the girl seemed to be blocked out. Over time though, such was the persistence and strength of the images that even the inside of a bottle of spirits failed to shut them out. There really wasn't anything else he could do; unless he swallowed his pride and took psychiatric or psychological counselling; that was his last resort but, he realised that it might be all that was now left open to him.

Outside the rain began to fall again, he could hear the sound of the raindrops as they hit the window pane. He thought back to the moment last night when he had been certain that someone was outside in the darkness, in the slowly lightening day that now seemed wholly ridiculous, and yet the feeling had been so strong.

As he lay there contemplating everything, he could feel his eyes beginning to water as he contemplated the misery he felt inside and he closed his eyes for a moment to get control of his emotions. He felt so trapped, so much of his predicament was just so strange that he felt he couldn't talk about it and that frustrated and frightened him.

Jennifer, such a good listener and such a good wife, even she struggled with what he was trying to tell her on the few occasions he had tried. If he couldn't talk to his own wife and help her to understand what was happening to him then who could he talk to? He felt helpless and the tears threatened again.

At last Jennifer stirred, leaving sleep behind she opened her doe-like eyes and looked at Jim, he looked a haunted man and she wished so much to help him. She had no real idea what he was going through but her greatest fear was that he was having an affair.

On more than one occasion he had spoken in his sleep, more than once he had called out a woman's name, Marie, but who was she and what part did she play in her husband's life? She had watched his behaviour for clues, a man having an affair might be expected to take excessive care of his personal grooming. In some cases though, like yesterday, Jim could not even raise the enthusiasm to shave.

He might be expected to go out at strange times but she saw no evidence of that. He was, largely, a creature of habit and this hadn't changed much, and he still went to the pub with his mates on a Saturday afternoon, as he had done yesterday. He had even invited her to drop in and have a drink with them, that didn't seem like the action of a man who had something to hide; but still she felt that there was something he was not telling her and it worried her greatly.

Jennifer leaned forward and kissed her husband's cheek, he turned to look at her with bloodshot eyes and she felt a wave of pity that she did not want to feel for a man whom she loved and to who she had pledged her life in her wedding vows.

She tried a smile and he responded in kind though his looked pained and failed to conceal his distress. What was she to do to rediscover the happy go lucky man that she remembered with such fondness? Was that person still inside her husband at all or had it gone forever? She hoped not; as she suggested a cooked breakfast she saw a tremor of enthusiasm in Jim's tired eyes and resolved to get one cooked before he changed his mind.

He was drinking heavily; too heavily, and she made it her mission to ensure that he at least did not do so on an empty stomach. With pretence of a light mood she swung her legs out of the bed and put on her dressing gown, then, after pulling open the curtains to let more of the grey light into the room she set off for the kitchen, she hoped that her efforts would not be in vain.

Back in the bedroom Jim had turned to face the grey skies visible through the window, there seemed little chance of a change in the weather, and like his mood it was solemn and cheerless. Remembering the scratches on his legs he quickly pulled on some jeans and, unlike yesterday, made the short trip into the bathroom to shave. His beard grew quickly and the blade wasn't the sharpest resulting in a couple of nicks where he had pressed too hard to remove stubborn chin hair.

The smell of fried bacon had permeated through the house and he realised just how hungry he was feeling. He pulled on a clean shirt and headed for the stairs, he would do his best today to act the role of loving husband and doting father.

FOUR

Even at the best of times she hated Monday mornings. She supposed that this was a universal feeling, Saturdays were spent getting over the working week before and Sundays were spent preparing for the one to come. A bath, some conditioner on the hair, the washing and ironing of clothes. By Monday it was time for a rest and instead what happened? The bloody alarm clock rang out and it was time to do it all again.

The greyness of the morning matched her mood. Although almost half past eight the night refused, it seemed, to do the decent thing and retreat from the scene. Things were not helped particularly by the lost sleep of the previous evening, and Amanda Fellows resolved to continue the heated discussion with her flatmate when she returned home from work that night.

Kate Harvey, the said flatmate, had come home very drunk from a heavy night out at two-thirty in the morning and that was one thing. Knocking over the table in the hallway was another, but being sick into a saucepan on the top of the cooker and then forgetting to mention the fact was a bit too over the top as far as Amanda was concerned and she had told Kate so.

The worst of it was that Kate had been in such a state that she had just grinned in an inane manner when Amanda had attempted to bring her to task. She seemed to find it funny that the contents of the saucepan prior to its impromptu refill were not dissimilar in appearance and texture to the aftermath. Thinking about it now, as she drove painfully slowly along the rain covered main-street on her way to work, Amanda could finally see the funny side herself.

For all her faults, and there were many on regular viewing, Kate was a good and loyal friend. She accepted Amanda's difficult ways and funny habits with a stoicism that was admirable and, if the truth of the matter were known, Amanda couldn't imagine sharing a flat with anyone else but Kate.

Taking advantage of the slow crawl of the traffic she fumbled in the glove compartment of her elderly Ford Escort for a change of tape for the temperamental cassette player in the car. *The Story of the Clash, Volume One;* that should wake her up a bit she thought. Putting it on, she began humming along to the tune of '*White Man in Hammersmith Palais.*' The Clash were underrated she concluded as she drove along the depressingly dark street.

The traffic lights were turning red once again. It seemed that she had only succeeded in edging forward a couple of car's lengths since they last did so. She glanced out of the window, her attention caught by the movement of a passer by stooped slightly forward as he struggled through the gloom. She continued to follow his progress until he disappeared into the doorway of a newsagent's shop a little further along the street.

She was roused from her reverie by the angry hoot of the horn of the car behind. She had failed to notice the traffic lights changing. She raised her hand in a cross between an apologetic wave and an 'up yours buster' and raced for the lights which promptly changed back to red before she could make it through.

As she waited she glanced out of the window once more, where she saw the man emerging from the shop folding a newspaper up and placing it in the large pocket of his coat. She often saw him and often wondered who he was and where he worked, there was no man in her life at the moment and, in fact, there had seldom been anyone.

As she continued to look at him, he looked up at the same moment and their eyes met. He smiled and she shivered. She had seen him somewhere before, perhaps in a restaurant or a bar, a number of times, but where? The man walked off and Amanda watched him.

From behind, the now angry driver of the car tooted his horn again as the lights had again changed and Amanda once more failed to notice. This time there was no ambiguity in her gesture as she pulled away.

Less than a minute later she was at standstill at the next set of lights. The rain was pouring now and she switched the wipers from intermittent to constant. If anything it was getting darker and she thought once more of the warm bed she had left behind.

Her thoughts turned to Kate again; there was nothing else to think about on this banal journey into the town centre. Kate was fun most of the time but since the breakdown of her relationship with her long-standing boyfriend, Chris, she had become a bit of a sad cow, coming home drunk with increasing regularity. Perhaps she should make the effort to take Kate under her wing for a few weeks until she got herself together again. Make the effort to go out with her, be the friend she was supposed to be.

Amanda and Kate had taken the flat just over four years ago, both girls finding the constraints of living among family, adoptive in Amanda's case, a strain. The big wide world was, so they believed, their oyster, and it called them ever more constantly.

The need to come and go, and to conduct a life-style around strict mealtimes and the like was cramping their style. It was to be their new start in life, the grass was greener. It had not been quite as green as they had envisaged but nonetheless the freedom had a novelty that even now had not completely lost its lustre.

It was fair to say that Kate had gone into the venture with a little more lust for adventure than she had right from the start. Amanda felt shaped by what had gone before her in her young life. That was quite a lot compared to most twenty-nine year old single girls.

She had been born, those twenty-nine years ago to parents she had never known, indeed it seemed that no one had known her parents. She had cried herself to sleep as a young girl turning over theories, none of them pleasant, as to why this might be. Were people protecting her from some dreadful truth? Perhaps no one did know who they were and she had tried to fathom out whether this was better or worse.

She had been told that she'd been cared for by an elderly relative for a short time after her birth, but the arrangement had been swiftly terminated and relatives seemed to be something which Amanda Fellows lacked in any abundance.

The Children's Home came next. This was the place where her earliest memories and nightmares were conceived. The bullying, both by staff and other children formed a small hurt that was neatly filed away in the bookshelves of her memories, to only venture forth at the few times of self-pity she allowed herself. She often used this analogy, her mind as a library, experiences good and bad filed away, acts of kindness, of stupidity and of unkindness, to be retrieved and weighed on her own scales of justice when the need arose.

After the Children's Home came the adoptive parents. Two sets in all. To differing extents, both attempts at adoption had been a catalogue of pretence. A tissue of lies had led to her placement in the first adoption that had been doomed to fail from the outset.

Amanda had been six years old when the Williamsons had been deemed suitable adoptive parents for the shy young girl who, despite being bullied on occasion, seemed balanced and friendly when spoken to.

The Williamsons were, she remembered, though vaguely, loud and extroverted; she imagined that some bright spark had surmised that to place a quiet girl like Amanda with an outgoing family would allow her to come out of her shell. To her mind it had been a disaster from the outset.

Alfred and Susan Williamson, denied the gift of parenthood by the cruel twist of biological fate, had proceeded to smother her with a kind of love that left her feeling empty and alone. Sweets and toys, pets and more toys, she felt she was drowning in a sickly pool of contrived attention.

The Williamsons were so eager to impress the social workers that called periodically to monitor the girl's progress that each toy seemed like another point on some notional scoreboard.

Looking back on this period with the benefit of an adult mind she could only feel sympathy for the first parents she could remember. She felt sympathy because she could see that, though they were fighting against the realisation, they had quite simply fallen out of love with each other. The idea of adopting had been one last throw of the dice to save a marriage that had fallen apart.

The contempt that had grown between the two of them had been noticeable even to a girl as emotionally naïve as Amanda was at the time. She could not quite grasp the meaning of the scowls and secret curses, indeed may have thought they were directed at her, but she felt uncomfortable in the atmosphere she was being asked to grow up and develop in. Whatever, the result had been that Amanda had become increasingly withdrawn, retreating into herself.

The Williamsons were keen to create the opposite impression, especially when the social workers were in attendance. On their infrequent visits, Amanda would find herself cajoled to an oppressive degree, almost 'smile and be happy or pay for it later' only to witness her adoptive parents slump in weary relief when their visitor had departed.

If the social workers suspected anything wrong it was not considered sufficiently bad for her placement to be reconsidered. Not that is, until the night when Alfred Williamson came home late from work having dropped in at the pub with a few friends. He found his wife standing in the kitchen, holding his dinner plate in one hand, her foot placed firmly on the pedal of the bin. He watched as the plate was angled so that the contents slid with dramatic slowness into the pile of household detritus already contained within. Something snapped in Alfred that night, but it was a slow, deliberate snap not a howitzer.

Amanda remembered the smell of the liquor on his breath when he walked over to her and kissed her cheek. Remembered too, how strange his voice had sounded when he had spoken gently to her, the glazed almost rapturous calm in his eyes as he suggested she watch the television. It was late, she had only been allowed to stay up so that she could kiss her 'father' goodnight, and she didn't understand the television programmes at this hour of the night. She complied with his suggestion nevertheless.

She could still visualise, in some sort of slow-motion memory, walking into the lounge and positioning herself on the carpet in front of the television. Her father, who she could see out of the corner of her eye through the still open door into the kitchen, calmly took off his coat. He moved from her sight, slowly, quietly.

The scream had startled Amanda; it was her father, his scream, a scream of fury, and an explosion. It was followed by a loud crash, as something was broken against a wall or the floor. Now her mother was framed in the doorway, she seemed to be smirking. Amanda tried not to watch, tried to leave them to whatever they were doing. Adult things, things she didn't understand, didn't want to understand. She couldn't help herself.

The look of amusement that had teased her mother's face into the smirk, began to falter, there was a change in the eyes, a widening perhaps. The smirk became a blank expression and then turned to something else, a frown; fear maybe? Or was it realisation perhaps, the realisation that this time she may have pushed him just a little too far.

Amanda curled herself into a ball, her hands on her head, knees tucked under her chin. The television, that friendly box of tricks that had delivered to her possibly her only genuine happiness during her time with this family, continued to make its presence known now only a background noise in the unfolding of events.

Susan Williamson began to back into the lounge; a hand gripped the door and jerked it wider open. As she backed into the room keeping her focus firmly on her husband her hip clipped the edge of a small table, the result being the upsetting of a number of trinkets. The photograph of a smiling couple on their wedding day fell to the floor. Those same two faces were not smiling now as the young Amanda tried to make sense of what she was witnessing. Hindsight, the memory of the photograph had created a kind of poetry to that one little cameo, precursor to the main event.

Alfred Williamson appeared in the doorway. The long blade of the butcher's knife he held in his hand glinted in the light. He moved his arm so that the knife cut swathes through the air as he advanced into the room with a deliberation that was more frightening than if he had maintained the fury that his scream of rage had hinted at.

When he pounced, Susan had little chance. She held her hands up in a useless attempt to protect herself. She was a frail woman for her age, out of condition; her reactions slow in the face of this unexpected danger.

Her eyes were now wild with fright and something else; doubt. Doubt that this could really be happening to her, hope maybe that he was just teaching her a lesson, that he would put the knife away, maybe cuff her around the ear and tell her never to pull a stunt like the one she had just carried out. Alfred Williamson is not to be messed with! It didn't happen like that though, it wasn't even close.

Alfred jerked the hand in which he held the knife towards his wife. She moved her hands towards him in a futile parrying gesture. It was a feint a boxer would have been proud of. Alfred used the knife as a decoy, his real intention to get close enough to Susan to make his next actions more certain. With his free hand he reached towards the off-balance woman and grabbed her hair, roughly pulling her head towards him as he did so.

Susan screamed partly in shock and partly in pain, she fell forwards into his grasp and he adjusted his feet so that he was able to turn her such that the back of her head was cradled against his chest. She tried to struggle but he twisted his fist so that her hair was pulling at its roots and her face contorted with an agony that she did not give voice to.

The cowering Amanda looked from face to face. Susan's, a mask of pain, terror and pleading; Alfred's wild eyed, manic. He was looking at Amanda and his face softened slightly. She could recall the words, softly spoken, to her, through this horror show. "It's for the best!"

As the knife was plunged into Susan Williamson's throat and twisted, a spray of blood burst forth, it spattered against Amanda's face hands and hair. She had never appreciated just how much blood the human body contained. Blood was just something that happened sometimes when you fell over and scraped an elbow or a knee. It never looked like this. Mummies and Daddies told you things like, "It's just a scrape and a plaster will soon mend the damage and stop the leak." Blood was accepted by Amanda, it was just there. It leaked a bit sometimes. Amanda had the idea that Susan must be very broken to leak that much.

Amanda wondered why her mum wasn't crying when she was that broken. Her dad was crying though, maybe she was confused, and maybe it was him that was leaking. His whimper became a sob, the sob a moan and the moan a wail.

Amanda joined in, aware that things were not good, but unable to get her young mind to focus on the events to a sufficient degree to make sense of them. In her mind, the experience was filed on the shelf marked 'horror.'

Alfred called the police. The sound of the approaching sirens were exciting to a young girl and the vague flashing blue lights she could see through the thin material of the cheap lounge curtains was like something she had seen on the television once. Then policemen and ambulance men were in her living room!

Amanda found herself back in the Children's Home the next day. She was in the home of foster parents, who were later to adopt her, by the end of the following month.

Anne and Tony Fellows were altogether a better prospect than the Williamsons. They were younger for a start and seemed better able to relate to the needs of the young Amanda maybe because of this. With her previous family she had felt less of a person and more of a pet. Love, or what she perceived love to be at such a young age was not about being given dolls and teddy bears and left to find ways to amuse herself with them. It was more about feeling a part of things.

Amanda felt she could seek and be given attention when social workers weren't banging on the door asking how things were going. Dolls and Teddy Bears still arrived but this time she was helped to invent names and characters for them. All these years later she still took Zizz, her battered teddy and her first present from Anne Fellows, to bed with her at night. At the age of twenty-nine for God's sake!

Hindsight told her that Anne and Tony had been less desperate to have a child than the Williamsons. Also that their relationship was stronger and deeper, the presence of a child in their life an enrichment rather than something to focus on to prevent them kicking lumps out of each other.

For ten blissful years, life with her new parents proved to be the best years of her young life. They supported her in her interests but rarely interfered, openly encouraged her to make friends which for the first time in her life she began to find easy. Kate Harvey had been the first and was still the most dearly loved despite her occasional indiscretions.

They met as eight-year-olds, Kate had moved to the school as a direct result of her parents moving into the area from Newcastle. Amanda had liked the new girl's accent, giggling at the way that Kate had to often repeat virtually everything she said to be understood. The school was still relatively new to Amanda as well, the Williamsons had lived on the opposite side of town; her previous school, a sprawling hotchpotch of classrooms and out-buildings in which she made few acquaintances and found herself bullied and sneered at, consigned to the past.

The two girls, strangers in a new world, had taken comfort from each other's predicament and had been virtually inseparable since then. The new school was much smaller and was in what might be described as the more affluent part of the town. Amanda felt more at home there and less threatened, her learning powers evolved greatly and, by the time that secondary school beckoned her, she was highly regarded as a very bright student by all of her teachers.

Eddington High School was next for the two friends who, by fortune or design, were assigned to virtually all of the same classes; such was the environment that their friendship was allowed to flourish.

Kate had been just fifteen when first she had discovered boys, a hastily arranged bottle-party taking advantage of a parental absence which had quickly turned to a sprawling mass of drunken teenagers.

Beer, cider; more beer and cider were spilled on the carpets mixed with peanuts and crisps. The bedrooms had hastily and shabbily made 'do not disturb' signs on the doors as the mixture of alcohol and hormones resulted in the breaking down of boundaries and a loosening of morals.

Kate and a young man, who she had confided to Amanda that she had designs on, had been the first to take advantage. Amanda had been at the party, of course, she was embarrassed by her friend's indiscretion but excited by it as well. When a young man who she had been casting sideways glances at all evening asked her if she would like to go upstairs for a while she had almost accepted.

Since that night her life had been a long catalogue of almost accepted invitations and propositions. At twenty nine she was beginning to wonder if love and marriage would pass her by. It wasn't that she didn't like men; she could drool over film stars with the best of them. It was a fear of commitment, a fear of losing the control that she had exerted over her life.

No one would describe Amanda Fellows as an emotional person. Perhaps it was a direct consequence of her early childhood but she shunned extremes of emotion. She rarely got truly angry and she avoided situations where she might laugh uncontrollably, for her laughter and tears were but a gossamer thin membrane apart.

Kate, of course, being Kate would often tease her about her lack of a close male friend but she had grown immune to it by now. She knew, after all, that she was attractive and a good catch for would be suitors. Perhaps the right man was just around the next corner waiting to be found. She found that she still believed this even though it was not something she was particularly looking for.

As she manoeuvred the car through a right turn she wondered again about how her future might develop. Was time running out for her; would she end up a bitter and twisted old woman pining for something she never gave herself the chance of enjoying?

She was a little unsettled at the moment, she didn't think that Kate had noticed but something had been bothering her for quite some time. She had become moody and difficult, in truth she was troubled by strange dreams and she was finding it hard to sleep, in fact she almost feared sleep. She would need to sort that out before romance could be allowed to knock at her door.

At last she was away from the main traffic and was able to manoeuvre the car into the car-park beneath the office where she worked. Other cars were already there, covered in rain, but she was not late. Here we go again she thought as she climbed out of the car and headed for the lift. As she crossed the reception area to sign in, a prerequisite imposed by health and safety considerations and a way to check who was in the building in the case of an emergency, she exchanged a few cheery pleasantries with people who looked as pleased to be there as she was. She guessed that like her, no one in the world enjoyed the thought or the reality of Monday mornings.

As she returned to the lift and looked at her reflection in the mirror she thought once again about her life and where it was going. The truth was she had lost her way a little and the hardest thing to take was that she wasn't sure how she could get her life back on track.

FIVE

Outside the rain had subsided, perhaps for the first time since the old man arrived there some hours before. The wind still seemed to cut right through him with its icy tendrils snaking inside his clothes so that he constantly had to pull the long, dark trench-coat more tightly around him.

The old coat, procured from the cancer charity shop provided little comfort for his tired old bones having been thoroughly drenched more than once already that day. He had seen much in his life but weather such as this, so poor and so prolonged, seemed extraordinary, perhaps, he thought, it was just his age playing tricks with his memory. The thing he was certain about, however, was that the elements continued to divert him from his task; such a very important task.

The effort would kill him, he knew and accepted this, maybe it would happen before the deed was done, his head told him that this was very possible but his heart, ever fanciful, told him that he would succeed and right the wrongs of so many years ago.

He had been here to watch the girl's home so many times; had almost risked speaking to her on occasion, though she seemed never to see him, as if the ghost from her past that he had always been was invisible to her in the way that ghosts were supposed to be.

The previous night, Sunday, had been the nearest he had come to finally going through with his plan. The other girl had been staying out increasingly later at night, arriving home in the small hours in various states of inebriation, sometimes hardly able to get her key in the lock of the door.

Last night had been one such night; it would have been so easy to walk up behind her and hit her, then he would have been able to use her key to enter the flat and gain uninterrupted access to the occupant inside. He would have been safe in the knowledge that he would not be disturbed and could have fulfilled his destiny for better or worse. The girls rarely had visitors at their flat and certainly not at that late hour.

His plan had failed; failed because, despite all his years and his great experience of life, his successes and his failures, he was still a coward at heart and he had baulked at the idea of hitting the girl at the last moment. A coward was the last thing he could afford to be at this time but a coward he was and he had berated his reflection in the mirror when he returned home. Next time he was presented with such an opportunity he must take it, he must harden his heart and go through with it.

Tonight had been going to be different but, as he contemplated another failure, another negative result, he had been moved to cry a little in self-pity. Tonight neither girl had gone out after returning from their respective jobs and his lonely vigil in the wind and rain had been pointless; futile.

The lights in the flat had gone out over half an hour ago yet still he waited outside in the darkness, cold, miserable and dying. His features, shrouded by the beard he had grown to hide his shame, were contorted with age and pain, his skin gnarled and sallow hung loose from his bones, the body once well appointed had long ago lost its muscle-tone, all effects of the burden he had carried for so long and which he so needed to alleviate.

The eyes that peered out from deep sockets had long ago lost their sparkle, his hair, sparse and unkempt hung limply across his furrowed brow. Anyone hurrying past him in the night might be moved to pity him, to look perhaps for a cap or a cup in which to throw coins, but he was neither homeless nor penniless; he was just ashamed.

He had been a proud man once, egotistical many had said but his confidence and his ambition could not be shaken and he had persevered where others had fallen by the wayside. That persistence had led to breakthroughs which were startling and exciting but, as he reflected back over his life he now realised that the ultimate cost of his arrogance was a life of shame.

He cast one more rueful glance in the direction of the darkened windows of the flat and then, on weary legs, he headed off into the night to the hovel he had learned to call home.

It was raining again and the holes in the soles of his shoes were prone to let in water if he was careless enough to step into a puddle, he did not, however, have the energy to care very much by now. He cut a solitary figure in the darkened street; his footsteps seemed unnaturally loud for this two o'clock in the morning world, where only an occasional building showed a light to indicate that inside a baby cried, or an insomniac watched television, or perhaps lovers made love in their beds.

The room he had rented was only a few streets away, he had needed to get somewhere close so that he could keep watch on the girl and to allow him to be able to walk the distance each day on his aging legs. His landlord had proved the perfect host, inasmuch that he usually only appeared once a month to collect the rent and to check that everything was okay for his tenant; he hardly seemed to notice the general dishevelment of the old man and his tiny room.

Sleep was a luxury that he could ill afford, his conscience troubled him enough when he was awake, but, when asleep long enough to have them, his dreams bothered him more, filled as they were with thoughts of suffering and sickness.

He fumbled for his key, his hands numb with cold, and succeeded in opening the front door of the large terrace house; then, trying not to make too much sound he mounted the staircase to the first floor where his room was the middle one of three. He rarely saw his neighbours on account of the strange hours he was keeping but when he had chanced upon them on the landing or the staircase they had exchanged pleasantries and he felt no threat from them.

Opening the door to his room he winced a little as the smell of age, dirt and sickness assailed him. He would have liked to clean up but his energy was failing him and he needed to conserve it for the task in hand. The light he turned on was of low wattage and was powerless to take away the seediness of the room, exacerbating the shadows in the corners and lending the pale and peeling wallpaper a sallow complexion.

Closing the door behind him he fumbled with the buttons on his coat, eager to get the damp and heavy garment free of his frail body. His fingers were swollen and failed to work properly on the task but eventually he was able to take off the coat and hang it on the back of the door.

The relative warmth of the building caused him to shiver for a few moments, he hadn't realised just how terribly cold he had been outside. Recovering enough to put the kettle on, he began to undress and, after he had drunk coffee from a chipped mug, he slumped onto the poorly made bed in the corner of his room.

All of his joints were aching, he felt for a moment that he might just close his eyes and drift off to oblivion, a place free from guilt; free from shame but there was a job to be done and he had resolved to carry it out. Ever since he had found the girl the wish to carry out the task had grown in him once again. For a time it had invigorated him and he had felt that maybe he wasn't dying as quickly as he thought he was. God had given him a chance, late on in his life, to right the wrongs of his past.

He glanced once more, for he had done so countless times, at the picture beside his bed of the young girl and her friend, smiling for the camera. Taken so long ago now that it seemed to come from another age; he allowed his lips to curve into a faint smile and closed his eyes. Before too long, sleep had claimed him. The dim light, still shining weakly above where he lay played on his skin, sallow and sick. There would not be much time left for his task to be carried out. Outside the rain continued to fall and the wind made strange sounds as it heaved its way around the eaves of the houses.

SIX

"You stupid, inconsiderate, selfish bloody arsehole; why don't you watch where you're going?" Jim Dowley gestured at the man in the smart Lotus who had cut in front of him in the traffic, only narrowly avoiding an accident. It was water off a duck's back to the driver; he merely gestured back and put his foot down on the accelerator, speeding away into the distance.

Jim sighed; his head felt numb and his emotions were scattered, he had slept very little the night before and, yet again, his eyes felt as though they had sand in them. The last thing he wanted was to go into the office today, there was a management meeting at nine-thirty which he was unable to avoid and the thought of Martin Eaves with his sanctimonious expression and sneering little smile turned his stomach almost as much as the snatched breakfast he had managed on his way out this miserable Tuesday morning.

The traffic had closed in now, the streets narrowing as they pumped their slow flow of metal containers into the heart of the town, each of these metal cans on wheels crawled ever more slowly towards their numerous destinations; offices, factories, the arms of a lover, the arms of a wife or husband after a night with a lover, all the drivers would have one thing in common right now; frustration at the town's traffic system.

Jim watched, with a mixture of mild anger and disdain, as another car, its inhabitant maybe even later for work than he was, manoeuvred his car at such an angle that Jim was forced to let him into the queue of traffic ahead of him. What did it matter; he didn't want to go to work in any case?

This was a mid-sized town, relatively modern and affluent, which still retained some of its character from years before, this is why the traffic solutions were never adequate. Trying to blend narrow streets, intended for nothing more than horses and carriages, with wider, more car-friendly thoroughfares, was never going to be easy. Most mornings, particularly when it rained heavily like today, resulted in a sort of lethargic chaos.

The local council had deemed that a multi-million pound by-pass scheme would alleviate all the town's traffic issues with the result that on average the local residents were forced to leave their homes ten minutes earlier each morning to reach work at the same time that they did before the road was built; such was progress thought Jim as he wiped sweat from his forehead.

For all its faults; mostly self inflicted, the town remained a pleasant place to live, the sort of place where the casual traveller might stop for a while on the way to more exotic or larger places. The park was impressive, with its winding streams and lakes and the imposing war memorial bell tower that dominated its centre. Jim looked at this now through the rain soaked window of the car, it reminded him of another window through which he had looked into the face of a wraith who could not possibly have been there, and he shuddered at the thought.

The traffic lights ahead were changing and he raced the lights, getting through just as they turned to red; why the hell had he done that? The question turned over in his mind as he guided the car right into the centre of the town where a strange menagerie of old and new lived side by side on either side of the street.

Year old businesses, fresh with the enthusiasm of their new and hopeful owners, nestled next to those that had been established for more than a hundred years. Shops, offices, cafes and public houses were all around which gave the place character.

It was a market town, once a week, on a Saturday, the market stalls would arrive. The shoppers would arrive in their droves and, for Jim at least, the place became a no-go area. A teeming throng of crazed old aged pensioners wielding walking sticks and umbrellas would arrive, as if from hell itself, mothers pushing their double-pushchairs through unfeasibly narrow aisles, through a sea of bruised legs and squashed toes. Jim preferred the pub.

He glanced at his watch, hoping that it had been more than a minute since he had last done so, it wasn't, he would be about twenty minutes late. That, in itself did not afford him a problem, through hard work and a very sharp mind he had quickly risen through the ranks in the company and was considered vital to its success.

Even allowing for his state of mind in recent weeks he had made some stunning advances for his employers and a place on the Board of Directors was far more likely than getting the sack for tardiness. Most of his problems were non-work related and he was struggling to cope and to find a way to stop them from destroying the man he had been before being beset with this strange obsession that now dominated his life, whether asleep or awake.

He eased the car into third gear, the first time for several minutes he had been able to enjoy such a luxury, brake lights ahead made it short-lived as the great metal snake slithered once more to a halt.

Stationary in the traffic, his mind began to drift back once again to the strange events of the previous weekend. The grazes on his legs were no longer as sore and, surely by an act of some supreme being, he had managed to shield them from the eyes of Jennifer. What the hell had caused those marks though; were they self-inflicted? Unlikely he thought; his nails were not long and there had not been anything else to hand with which he might have made them. Were they some sort of stigmata then? Maybe, but he wasn't even sure that he believed in such things. But what, then, was the alternative?

The weird dream he had experienced when he blacked out had seen him running through thick brambles but surely that could only be a dream, was it possible that his body had somehow been temporarily escorted from his room to another strange world where he chased an unknown and yet familiar woman? All of the explanations seemed very unlikely but he couldn't come up with anything else.

The loud tooting horn of the car behind startled him back into reality and he gestured with two fingers at the driver as he put the car back into gear and caught up again with the traffic ahead, again the lights were changing and he smiled with a kind of wicked satisfaction as the impatient driver behind was forced to stop at them as he sped through.

As he drove he couldn't help but think once more of the girl in the dream, this was becoming an obsession; how he longed to solve the mystery of why she had arrived in his life. She was so very familiar to him, everything about her seemed to fit some sort of mental template he had, her hair, long and flowing, dark; her dark eyes which seemed to register both warmth and an inner amusement, her olive tanned skin which seemed somehow slightly exotic. Where had she come from and why?

With no answers in his mind, his offices at last came into view, he didn't really know whether to feel relief or despair at the sight of them, at least he would be able to get a coffee and that was something he felt sorely in need of right now.

**

James and Hart Associates Limited were a relatively young company. The founders Anthony James and Gareth Hart, both Oxford graduates, had founded the company on an idea and a shoestring budget. For a time things had looked a little bleak but after a while the incomings finally reached a level where the bank manager was happy and the two of them were free to concentrate on the task of building their business without the threat of an imminent visit from the bailiffs.

Over time, the business had become very successful, a general increase in affluence in the area and in the country overall, meant that their niche as independent financial advisers was suddenly a sought after service industry. Many other companies started to spring up in the town and county but the company's longevity gave potential investors and savers a comfort factor that other companies couldn't match and so business had began to boom.

Jim Dowley had joined the company about two years into its existence, he had a particular flair for marketing and through his innovative ideas the company was able to reach out across the whole county and beyond with a series of road-shows that pulled in a huge number of clients.

The founders had now both left the company, one lazed away his days in a villa in Cyprus, working over the internet, the other had moved further afield and the last Jim had heard he was somewhere in the States. Their departure was on the back of a takeover of the company by an insurance company, Paltergate Limited, and this for Jim had resulted in a huge blow to his job satisfaction.

As independents, the company had not been beholden to any of the companies in the market place. Jim prided himself on taking careful note of a client's personal circumstances, shopping around for a bespoke package and delivering the results to a happy and growing band of satisfied customers.

Since the takeover that research element had disappeared from the job, advisors were simply out to sell as many Paltergate packages as they could without recourse to better deals that might be available elsewhere.

To Jim this was tantamount to misleading clients and he now had moved into a role that considerably reduced his client contact, working in areas that would further the business and its marketing strategies, rather than have to go home at night feeling guilty about the clients he had 'helped' that day.

He resolved that he would leave and look either to join another independent or to have a go on his own but, although this remained a goal in his life, recent events had moved it down on his personal agenda. Given the prevailing economic conditions at the present time, this was probably a good thing. The market had levelled out in the last two years and a few of their rival companies had fallen by the wayside but, largely due to Jim, James and Hart Associates Limited remained at the cutting edge of the industry.

The rain had increased in intensity by the time he manoeuvred his flash company car into its 'reserved' parking space outside the building. The clouds overhead were November grey and angry, they were, however, no match for the grey clouds that Jim felt inside as he climbed out of the car and looked disdainfully at the pristine looking building, refurbished by his new masters following the takeover, which in a town of character and diversity represented neither.

Jim's office was on the fourth floor. A large reception area, with marble floor and walnut furniture dominated the ground floor area where clients and prospective clients were greeted by attractive female receptionists with painted on smiles and false platitudes; maybe he was becoming more cynical with age but it always seemed to Jim to be just the first line of veneer in an elaborate sham.

The array of beverages in reception would have put a small café to shame, with clients offered a choice of Earl Grey or twelve other flavoured teas, filter coffee, cappuccino and an assortment of biscuits whilst they waited on the plush upholstered seats and settees for their 'advisor' to come and collect them and take them to equally plush office suites, most with views over the town. It made him sick to see it, especially when he was wet and had a hangover.

He walked across the reception area towards the lift opposite hoping that his arrival would go unnoticed; with Joanne Beaumont on reception it was never likely to succeed.

"Good morning Jim; how are you this morning?"

He tried to smile, his face felt tight and strained.

"Morning Jo, I'm fine and you?" Of all the receptionists he liked Joanne the best, he didn't want to take his mood out on her but his voice sounded dull and flat.

"Late night was it?" Joanne's face was filled with a warm smile, her manner conspirational; he couldn't help but smile back.

"Something like that Jo, yes."

"Martin asked if you would pop in and see him before the management meeting if you've got enough time."

"Martin can go and jump in the lake in the park!" He winked at her and she laughed, she knew the two didn't get on and she often teased him about it.

The lift doors opened with the oh so familiar 'ting' sound that he had grown to loathe, walking in to its pristine interior he contemplated, briefly, just how many times he had done this very same thing; he would have to put his plans to leave the company into gear before too long, his mental health probably depended on it. Then again perhaps he had already waited too long.

He turned to look back out into reception and through the glass doors that represented the sanity of the outside world as the lift doors began to close, glancing briefly at the passers-by as he did so. It took a few seconds for his brain to register what he had just seen and, by the time it did so, the doors had fully closed.

It was her; he knew it, the girl in his dreams, the one who haunted his thoughts day and night. He frantically tried to reopen the lift doors but the upward motion had already commenced and he swore under his breath in frustration. Pushing randomly the buttons on the control panel he cursed as the display indicated that he had gone beyond the first floor already.

It seemed like a lifetime to Jim before the annoying 'ting' could be heard again and the lift doors opened oh so slowly onto the second floor. Knowing that the lift would continue its ascent to the fourth floor, he headed for the emergency stairwell and began descending two steps at a time. He estimated that almost two minutes might have elapsed by the time he reached the reception level once again.

Joanne Beaumont watched in bewildered amazement as one of the company's most respected managers made an ungainly dash across the marbled floor, tried to push the doors open before remembering he needed to pull and then dashed out into the street beyond, into the pouring rain and the bustle of the crowd.

SEVEN

The office always seemed such a dreary place to Amanda Fellows, situated at the back of a tall building and overlooking what was little more than a narrow alley with equally tall buildings opposite. Even on sunny days there was little light that penetrated through the old, metal framed windows of this former college building. No amount of fluffy bears, cats, dogs and rabbits; no amount of cheery posters or pot plants seemed to take away the drabness of the little room.

On this miserable Tuesday morning, she had been forced to park the car in the multi-storey car park; road works having closed the road to the office and thus access to the car park underneath it, she had got wet through and her coat was draped over the old and temperamental radiator in the vain hope that she might get it dry. Some hope!

The two work colleagues who shared the office with her were both away on annual leave, one in America the other in the Canary Islands and so, this day, her only companions in the export and shipping department of Stark and Rutherford's were the cuddly toys on her desk.

With a weary sigh she turned on her computer, its greeting jingle sounding inordinately cheerful in such surroundings, next she filled the kettle and spooned some coffee; lots of coffee, into her ample sized mug. She needed the warmth of a hot drink, her bones ached and she wondered if perhaps she was going down with a cold or something.

She was still in a miserable reverie when she was startled by a voice behind her; she turned to look at the figure in the office doorway, her heart inexplicably racing. It was David Sullington one of the sales reps; he wasn't a bad sort.

"You look like a startled rabbit Mandy, I only asked if you were okay. It looks like you're on your own in here today."

"That's right, for my sins, just me and the teddies, I'll manage though."

"I'm sure you will," he gave her a reassuring smile as he said it and she returned it; why did she suddenly feel so highly strung she wondered?

"You know where my office is; if things get too hectic give me a shout and I'll do my best to help."

"I will do thank you Dave."

He turned to leave and then paused, "I almost forgot what I came to say to you; there was a call for you earlier, the phone was ringing when I first came in."

"Who was it? Did they leave a number?"

"No number, it was your father he said he needs to meet up with you; I assumed you'd know the number Mandy."

"That's odd; I wonder why he didn't call me at home, perhaps he's arranging something for Mum."

"Perhaps; he sounded a bit uptight though, I should ring him before you get bogged down with work."

"I will do Dave thanks for the message and thanks for the offer of help."

"No problem," smiling again he left her to finish making her coffee.

Amanda's mind was racing as she carried the steaming mug back to her desk. What could be wrong and why hadn't her father said when and where he wanted to meet her? Over the years a certain detachment had entered into her relationship with her stepparents; it wasn't hostile and on her part at least it didn't signify a loss of love and gratitude for the life they had given her, it was just so busy in her life at the moment that she had failed to drop by or to telephone them. With increasing dread she convinced herself that something dreadful had happened and it was with a trembling hand that she reached for the phone and began dialling the number.

She pressed the receiver tightly against her ear and waited as clicks and whirrs indicated the connection was being made. She cursed as she got the tone for number unobtainable and forced herself to calm down as this time she remembered to dial the obligatory nine to get an outside line. Again there were clicks and whirrs and the mounting tension. Finally, after several rings the telephone was answered.

"Hello."

"Dad is that you; it's Amanda?"

"Oh hello darling it's nice to hear from you; aren't you at work today?"

"Yes, I just got in; I got your message about meeting you; why didn't you phone me at the flat? Mum's alright isn't she?"

The words came out in a flood and at the other end of the telephone her stepfather tried to digest what was being said to him, he decided to deal with the last question first.

"Your mother's fine, she's having her hair done this morning, though with the weather as it is she'll do well to get home with it still looking nice."

Amanda started to relax; she pictured her stepfather with his steady thought processes and kindly ways and waited for him to continue.

"The thing is though Amanda, I didn't leave any message about meeting with you; though we'd love to see you of course, it's been too long now."

She was stunned but it seemed important not to seem so on the telephone. Was Dave playing tricks on her and if so why? It was November not April. Gathering her wits she continued with the conversation, hoping that her father would not have noticed her slight hesitation or the exasperated gasp she had inadvertently given breath to.

"I know Dad, I've been so busy. Look, if you can get a message to Mum I could meet you for lunch anyway. I wonder how my work colleague could have got the message wrong, he was very clear that he thought it was you on the telephone, though I did think it a little odd."

"Where would you like to meet?"

"Well Mum likes the Black Swan so how about there; just after one?"

"That would be lovely darling; I'll call your Mum on her mobile, I'm sure she'll be really pleased."

"Okay Dad, I'll see you both later."

"You certainly will; goodbye darling."

The click on the line indicated that the call was over; Amanda stared at the telephone for a few seconds before replacing the receiver. Her mind raced with questions; how could Dave Sullington have got the message so wrong? If it wasn't her father on the phone then just who was it; and why did whoever it was wish to meet with her? None of it made sense to her at all she decided as she took a sip of her still-steaming coffee.

It was several minutes later when Dave popped his head around the door and asked her if she had sorted out a meeting with her father, she told him that she was meeting both parents for lunch at one and he told her he would cover any phone-calls during that time. She had been about to ask him about the call again but didn't, he seemed to have her best interests at heart and she couldn't bring herself round to suggesting otherwise, still she found herself thinking about the strange events for much of the morning.

**

The Black Swan was customarily busy on a week day lunchtime, located centrally in the town and with competitively priced drinks and food it was a favourite with the banking crowd and with locally based civil servants.

By the time that Amanda arrived the place was very crowded and she struggled to see if her parents had got there before she had. Standing in the doorway she scanned the crowd for familiar faces, at first seeing none; presently though her stepfather emerged from the sea of people and she smiled as he walked forward to her and embraced her.

"We've got you a glass of white wine, it seemed sensible given the crowds, we haven't done anything about food yet though; come through we've got a decent table, your mother can't wait to see you."

Amanda allowed herself to be led through the throng of people and she was then duly hugged by her mother who, it seemed to Amanda, looked about to burst into tears of joy at seeing her daughter. Again that little pang of guilt that she had not seen her parents in a while.

The lunch was a simple but pleasant affair, the Black Swan was geared up to serving food promptly and it was always well cooked and presented. Their conversation was kept light and they talked only of day to day things. At one point her father asked about the phone call earlier in the day and, not wishing to worry them, Amanda brushed it off as a silly misunderstanding. The butterflies in her stomach betrayed the fact that as yet she had no idea whether that was the case or not.

By the time it was necessary for Amanda to return to work she had relaxed a little, with hugs and kisses she promised her parents that she would not leave it quite so long next time before arranging a meeting or a visit to their house and then she was once more out into the miserable driving rain and headed back to the office.

As she entered her office she was surprised to see Dave Sullington sitting at her desk, he was looking deep in thought and seemed not to notice that she had arrived until she spoke to him.

"Is everything alright Dave?"

He looked up and his normally smiling features seemed clouded in some problem, he paused before answering.

"I've called the police Mandy, I hope you don't mind; it seemed the most sensible thing to do in the circumstances."

"I'm sorry Dave; I'm not with you, why have you called the police?"

"There was another call while you were out at lunch, I didn't quite get to the telephone in time and so the answer-phone had clicked in by the time I got to your desk, I could have picked up the phone while the message was recording but I could hear what was being said and I didn't think it was wise."

"You're still not making any sense Dave, what was the message and why the need to call the police?"

Again Dave paused before answering, as if weighing up the gravity of what his words might evoke in his work colleague. Finally he sighed and told her what he knew she wouldn't want to know.

"The caller was the same man that called this morning. I knew you were with your parents having lunch so when this guy comes on the phone again purporting to be your father I knew something was wrong.

"The man sounded in distress, almost in pain, and his message was, well, frankly weird. I think you have some kind of stalker Mandy and I wanted to deal with it, the police seemed the best course of action; I hope you don't mind."

Amanda slumped down in the seat opposite still in her wet overcoat; she had dared to believe, during the normality of lunch with her parents, that this morning's events were easily explainable. A wrong number for example, now her disquiet had returned with a vengeance and the thought that the police were about to become involved in her life again was frankly terrifying for someone whose previous experiences of blue flashing lights were as traumatic as hers had been.

"Are you okay Mandy; have I done the wrong thing?"

"What did the man say?"

"I could play you back the answer-phone tape, but maybe we should wait until the police arrive."

"I think I'd like to hear it now please Dave." In fact Amanda wasn't at all sure that this was what she wanted but she couldn't bear the thought of just sitting there and waiting for the events to unfold around her.

"If you're sure Mandy; I warn you though the man sounds a bit deranged, it may upset you."

"Okay, get on with it." She hadn't meant to sound sharp with Dave but he seemed not to mind, or at least to understand why she was snappy as he leaned forward and hit the 'play' button on the answer-phone.

Initially there was a lot of background noise, as if the caller was deciding whether or not to leave a message on the machine finally after what sounded like some deep breathing a voice cut through the otherwise silent office.

"Amanda, are you there? Amanda it's me, your father; listen we have to meet, I have to tell you things you might not otherwise understand, I have to make you see why it had to be this way. I have to see you; time is running out for me, it will soon be time to die!"

The loud clunking sound of the receiver being replaced made Amanda jump; she was trembling and did not know what to make of the day's events. Across the desk Dave Sullington watched her with concern on his face, he had seen the way that the colour had drained from her and could see that she was close to tears.

He wasn't sure whether he should walk around the desks and comfort her or if that would only make things worse; he was, however, sure he had done the right thing by calling the police. He let the silence in the room continue for a while watching his colleague as she slowly began to recover some semblance of composure, finally he felt moved to break the silence.

"Have you any idea who might have made the call Mandy?"

She seemed startled that the silence had been broken; Dave thought that he even saw her flinch. Again she gathered her composure before answering.

"I don't recognise the voice, it sounds rasping as though whoever it is smokes very heavily."

"Maybe the voice is disguised."

She looked at him with an expression of bewilderment on her face.

"Who would go to that much trouble? Why would they do this to me and why do it now?"

"If anyone knows the answer to that Mandy it will be you. Could anyone you know be playing tricks on you?"

"I thought about that this morning. I didn't tell you before that when I telephoned my father he denied having made a call; my flat-mate Kate is a bit of an idiot sometimes and prone to practical jokes but this just isn't her style. She's more likely to try to set me up on a blind date than anything like this. No, I can't think of anyone."

As she said this she hoped that her facial expression would not betray her thoughts. A few unpalatable ideas had been swimming around her mind since she had telephoned her father that morning and she was trying to control them and dispel them as fanciful.

At that moment Amanda's telephone rang; this time she did flinch and Dave noticed as he picked up the receiver; the single ring told him that it was an internal line. Amanda, feeling so highly strung had not realised this and her heart pounded as she waited for her mystery caller to make his third call of the day.

Dave, looking as relaxed as he could, exchanged a few words with the caller and then replaced the receiver; he turned to Amanda and gave a thin smile of encouragement.

"The police are here Mandy; they're on their way up now."

**

WPC Julie Walsh and PC Sean Craig sat in the small conference room drinking coffee. Opposite them sat Amanda Fellows looking pale and drawn and staring at the steam coming from her own mug. She had requested that Dave let her deal with the police officers on her own on the premise that he needed to get on with his own work and also listen out for her phone should anything urgent arise.

On their arrival, the tape had been played to the two police officers by Dave as Amanda sat quietly in the corner of her office trying not to feel the panic that was besetting her. Now, here in this room away from Dave's ears, she would have to reveal elements of her past life that were not known to any of her work colleagues nor even her closest friends. It would be painful but she knew it was going to be necessary.

Amanda had already given them the basic facts; that she had been out lunching with her mother and father when the call had come in from someone claiming to be her father. It was only a matter of time before the police officers asked the same question that Dave Sullington had earlier, this time her answer would be more candid. Sure enough, the moment was not long in arriving.

"Miss Fellows, do you have any idea at all who might be making these telephone calls?" PC Craig showed his compassion for her plight as he asked the question.

"Well I don't recognise the voice at all, but there are a couple of things you should know about me before we go on."

The two police officers exchanged quick glances but maintained their compassionate air which encouraged her to go on.

"I was adopted; the parents I met at lunchtime are my adoptive parents."

"So there is a possibility that the man on the phone could be your birth father?" WPC reached the obvious conclusion very quickly.

"Well it's not quite that simple." Amanda felt and knew she looked uncomfortable.

"In what way is it more complicated?"

"My earliest memory is of being in an orphanage of sorts, I was very young but I was told that my birth parents were dead. That's why I think it unlikely that that's who's making the calls."

"Could you have been lied to? Perhaps your parents were unable to cope with having a child and that story was made up to preserve their identities." PC Craig asked the question and his colleague shot him a look that told him that his line of questioning was not particularly sensitive. Amanda noticed and felt a little sorry for the man.

"I could have been lied to, yes; the thing is it's even more complicated than that." She felt herself tensing up as long hidden memories began surfacing in her, things she had tried for so long to blank out of her mind.

"I can see this isn't easy for you Miss Fellows, do you want to go on?" Julie Walsh couldn't imagine what was on Amanda's mind but she knew turmoil when she saw it.

"Yes; I suppose I must really. You see my adoptive parents; the ones I met for lunch are not the first."

"So you had another adoptive father and you think it might be him calling you?"

Amanda shuddered. "I did have another yes; the thought that it might be him fills me with dread. His name was Alfred Williamson, you might have heard of him." She looked at them hopefully, if they knew the story then it would save her the telling of it. She was disappointed to see that neither showed any recognition of the name; perhaps she shouldn't have been surprised, they were both, after all, very young.

"Alfred Williamson butchered my first adoptive mother in the living room in front of me; her blood was all over the room, all over me." Her eyes were watering as she recalled that childhood horror.

"Oh my God I'm sorry Miss Fellows!" The WPC and, indeed, her colleague looked duly appalled.

"He was convicted of her murder but he was admitted not to prison but to a top security psychiatric establishment. Don't ask me which one, it's a part of my life I have spent the rest of my life pretending didn't happen to me. Is there even a remote possibility that they would let a maniac like that back out onto the streets?" The question hung in the air; the police officers were speechless with horror, Amanda continued.

"If they have let him out then it could be him couldn't it? He's tracked me down and now he knows where I work, perhaps he even knows where I live."

"Try not to upset yourself Miss Fellows; I'm sure we can quickly find out if this man Williamson has been let out. It seems unlikely from what you have said but in this day and age it seems that most things are possible. We need to deal with this one step at a time and finding out if he is still safely under lock and key is the first of those steps. Do you know when this terrible thing happened?"

Amanda looked terrified at the fact that the police officer was unable to give her an instant guarantee that Williamson was not back on the street. It was something that she had never even considered before today. Surely society could not be *that* stupid.

"I was about eight at the time I think; I can't tell you anything about the trial at all, like I said I shut it away in my mind until…."

"It's okay Miss Fellows; take your time, we know this can't be easy for you."

Amanda wiped away a tear from her cheek; she was trying to stay strong but it was just so difficult.

"You say you were eight at the time; how old are you now Miss Fellows?"

"Oh for God's sake call me Amanda or Mandy or something!" She looked horrified at her sudden outburst; the pressure was getting to her.

"I'm sorry, this is not easy; I'm twenty-nine, nearly thirty."

"We understand Amanda."

Did they though? Could anyone understand what it was like to not only witness a brutal murder but also to wear the blood of the victim?

"Have you noticed anything odd lately; such as people hanging around outside here or at your home?"

"No, nothing like that; but then I haven't really been looking."

"And telephone calls to your home; anything unusual there?"

"No."

"Do you live alone Amanda?"

"No I have a flat-mate, Kate."

"And she hasn't remarked on anything out of the ordinary or received strange telephone calls?"

"Not that I'm aware of, but then Kate's a bit off the rails at the moment. She recently split up with a long-term boyfriend and she is going out a lot, looking for another one I suppose."

"When you get home this evening will you ask her and let us know if she has seen or heard anything suspicious?" PC Craig pushed a card containing his contact details across the table; Amanda picked it up and looked at it numbly.

"How will you get home tonight?"

"I have my car."

"Is it parked far away?"

"Further than usual; as you probably noticed the road is closed, I would normally park underneath the building."

"Can anyone walk you to your car?"

"I suppose Dave would; the man you met earlier."

"I think it would be a good idea to ask him."

"Okay."

"It should be possible to find out about this Williamson character by the end of the day, can you let me have your contact details so that we might get in touch with our findings?"

"Of course; I'll write them down for you."

With a clearly trembling hand Amanda wrote down her details on one of the notepads on the conference room table, she tore off the page and handed it to PC Craig. What the hell was happening to her? She tried to convince herself that she was asleep and dreaming, that the persons sitting opposite her were not real but something her unconscious mind had conjured into existence for the purpose of filling a night of otherwise boring sleep and inactivity. She willed that this be the case but the sound of words being directed in her direction, real words, relevant words, shattered her hopes and she looked to their source with tears beginning to well somewhere in her eyes.

"Amanda, we will get on to this as soon as possible; in the meantime I want you to keep your eyes and ears peeled and let us know if anything, no matter how seemingly trivial, out of the ordinary should happen."

With an agreement from Amanda that she would do this, the police officers left the room. For a long time after they left, escorted out by Dave Sullington, she stared at the now cold coffee in her cup, lost in thought, lost in a forgotten past. Was he out of prison, were the do-gooders, the human rights protesters winning their war, were people like Alfred Williamson deserving of human rights? She was finally able to stand up and get on with her day after Dave had returned and given her a long pep-talk. He agreed immediately to take her to her car, it was the least he could do.

He had never seen real fear on the face of another human being before but Dave Sullington reckoned that that was exactly what he was seeing on Amanda Fellows' face at that moment.

EIGHT

Jennifer Dowley looked up from the magazine she was reading as her good friend Yvette Marsden walked into the hotel bar. She smiled despite the feelings that were eating away at her inside; feelings of pain and of rejection.

She had arranged to meet Yvette on the pretext that they hadn't had the opportunity to talk about 'girlie-things' for ages, but the truth of the matter was that Jennifer wanted someone to talk to, someone who was level-headed and whom she could trust. Yvette was the name that had sprung into her mind.

The two old friends greeted each other with a warm hug and a peck on the cheek and they sat in the luxurious leather upholstered chairs and waited for the waitress to take their order. Choosing to be 'naughty' they ordered a bottle of Chardonnay and a number of small plates to share, olives, marinated anchovies, garlic bread, Serrano ham and a Greek salad. Decadent, they thought as they giggled their way through the ordering.

Yvette had just returned from a holiday, a second-honeymoon in fact, on the Greek Island of Santorini and she was keen to relate her experiences both about the island and about her exploits in the bedroom and, indeed, on the beach. Jennifer smiled her way through all this wondering if Yvette was the right person for her to be sharing her problems with, after all, she wanted to discuss what she saw as her failing relationship with Jim and here was her friend talking like a love-struck teenager.

The wine was good, the food good and fun too, after a while Jennifer found herself relaxing a little and the conversation slowly drifted away from the Marsden's wonderful holiday and love-life. When would be the best time to broach the subject of her and Jim though? They were having such a nice time it seemed a shame to spoil it with talk of hurt and sadness. Taking a large sip of wine Jennifer decided that if she didn't bring the matter up now then the opportunity would be lost completely.

"Yvette can I burden you with a problem of mine; something you might be able to help me with?" Her voice sounded suddenly weedy; like a little girl lost she looked at her friend with hopeful eyes.

"Of course you can Jenny; what is it, nothing too serious I hope."

"Pretty serious yes; I think Jim might be seeing someone else."

Yvette seemed to flinch, as if from a blow, and she reached down and picked up her wine glass before making any comment.

"I'm sure you must have good reason for thinking that Jenny, but I hardly think it likely, Jim dotes on you and the kids."

"He did, yes."

"Did?"

"Yes, recently he has become restless, aloof. He's drinking heavily and he seems to want to spend more time in that stupid study of his than he does with me and the children."

"Perhaps he has problems at work; maybe he is suffering a mid-life crisis."

"As far as I know things are fine at work, he would tell me if they weren't. As for mid-life crisis; does that really exist?"

"Apparently it does, yes."

"Well maybe that's it but doesn't that by definition lead to people looking to tear up the script of their lives and start again with something fresh?"

Yvette took another sip of her wine, wishing she hadn't come up with that particular solution to her friend's problem.

"What makes you think he's having an affair Jenny?"

"He's so cool and distant; on top of that he thrashes around in bed at night, and I mean every night…"

"You should be so lucky." Yvette tried to lighten the mood, it didn't work.

"Not when he is so obviously dreaming about another woman."

"Jenny, how can you possibly know that he is dreaming about another woman?"

"Because he keeps calling her name out in his sleep, that's why!"

She had raised her voice and others in the bar looked their way and then quickly away again, though they no longer looked directly in their direction they would be sure to be trying to eavesdrop on the conversation.

"Well that can't be pleasant Jenny; I don't know what to say to that, I really don't."

"Neither do I; I don't want to lose him Yvette, confronting him might lead to that, but if I don't say something I'll go mad with the pain of it all."

"I see your problem; I still wouldn't have believed it of Jim though. Perhaps there is a logical explanation."

"I can't think of one."

Jennifer poured them both some more wine and sat back in the chair; a deep sigh escaped her as she did so. A silence descended upon the two of them as they considered the situation; the eavesdroppers lost interest.

Presently Yvette came to a decision. "You have to ask him about it Jenny, no matter where it leads or how painful it might be, it has to be less painful than not knowing. Perhaps he'll confess, beg forgiveness and then end it. Provided that you can forgive him for his indiscretion then that might restore the situation to what it was before."

"But it might just drive him away from us altogether."

"It might, but if he's being unfaithful isn't it best to be done with it, start again?"

"I don't think it is for the best, no."

"Then you have no alternative but to do what you are doing now, wondering, doubting him, and hurting yourself."

"It's Hobson's choice then?"

"I reckon it probably is Jenny; but it's your call."

"What about Darren and Hannah?"

"Have they noticed a problem?"

"I'm pretty sure that Darren has realised that something is wrong. He actually caught me crying the other day; I had to laugh it off as having something stuck behind my contact lens."

"Do you think he believed you?"

"I doubt it; Darren's too much like his father, too smart for his own good sometimes."

"Well I have to say Jenny; you sure know how to give a girlfriend a good time!"

"I'm so sorry Yvette; I just needed someone to talk to; someone who I can trust."

"I know and don't worry I was just trying to make light of a bad situation, what says we turn that empty wine bottle upside down in the bucket and have another one?"

"I don't know whether I should, I've got the dinner to make this evening, although the kids will be later home, Darren's got football practice and Hannah has gymnastics, my mother picks them up afterwards."

"So get them all fish and chips; the kids will have burned off a load of calories by the time they get home with the sound of it. It sounds to me like you need to let your hair down a bit and have a little fun. What better time to do that than now I ask you?"

"You can be very convincing Yvette. The problem is if I'm drunk and Jim comes home and does what he's been doing then, that is, get drunk too, who will look after the kids? They may be bright and independent but they are both still very young."

"It's up to you Jenny; the offer's there, I'll even stick you in a taxi home afterwards and you can sleep it off for a couple of hours before they come home; take a siesta."

The thought of returning to an empty house, where she would turn over her problems in her mind repeatedly, in comparison to spending more time with her friend was not a pleasant one. Reaching forward, Jennifer inverted the empty wine bottle and began trying to attract the attention of the young waitress once more.

**

It was almost five o'clock when Jennifer was dropped off outside the house by the amiable taxi-driver. She had tried to give the impression that she was not the worse for wear on account of the wine and thought she had made a pretty decent fist of it until it had come to pay, when she had suddenly lost the power of rational thought and taken at least two minutes to retrieve her purse and count out the fare.

The house felt cold and empty when she opened the front door and entered the hallway. She would put the heating on and try to cheer herself up a little. Her mother would be along in about three quarters of an hour with two boisterous children, she wasn't sure she was ready for that. The kernel of a headache was already forming just behind her forehead above her left eye and she recognised the signs

Making herself a cup of coffee to wash them down, she took a couple of painkillers and sat quietly in the kitchen. The dog looked at her expectantly but, seeing no promise of food or attention in the situation, returned to his basket and resumed his afternoon slumber.

She tried to work out where things had gone wrong in their relationship. At what point did things stop being good and start to be a drudge she wondered. When did goodnight kisses become simple goodnights? Romantic walks in the park while the dog got some exercise, when did they become walking the dog in the park? She really couldn't say, perhaps this happened in every marriage, why should she and Jim be any different to anyone else?

What if she was overreacting? Could she be creating a crisis when there was none, reading things into Jim's behaviour that were not really there? Yvette had talked of a mid-life crisis, perhaps she was right but perhaps it was her not Jim that was suffering the malady.

She thought back to her younger self, her school days had been happy, her parents had been supportive in everything she had set out to do and she had done very well at school. When she had first met Jim it had been a meeting of minds as much as anything else, two heavyweight intellectuals trading blows and enjoying every moment of each other's company. What had soured that relationship; what had made it turn bad?

She heard the sound of a car outside and then, after the clunk, clunk, clunk of car doors, the excited voices of Darren and Hannah as they raced towards the front door of the house. She didn't feel ready for this at all, but she had chosen motherhood and she had also chosen to indulge in a second bottle of wine with Yvette this afternoon. She had made her bed and she would lie in it, for the sake of her children she would overcome all of this negativity and get on with her life.

Her mother only stayed long enough for a coffee, she had things to be getting on with before she and Jennifer's father entertained some friends with wine, nibbles and a game of bridge. Mercifully she seemed not to notice her daughter's low spirits and Jennifer congratulated herself on her acting abilities. She wondered if she would feel quite so in control when Jim came home. It was doubtful she concluded as she gathered up the children and headed for the fish and chip shop at the end of the road.

NINE

It was cold, already dark and raining quite heavily by the time that Amanda Fellows and Dave Sullington left the office and headed in the direction of the car park where Amanda had left the car that morning. To her it seemed a lot more than just a few hours since she had done that. She was shaken by the events of the day and felt almost as though she were watching a film with her as the star than actually living through the surreal series of events that had beset her.

Dave had agreed immediately to walk her to the car, even though his own car was parked a quarter of a mile in the opposite direction he felt that he had somehow become a part of what had happened to his work colleague and he was keen to show her he appreciated that fact.

Other workers at Stark and Rutherford had witnessed the arrival of the police officers earlier and the place was alive with rumour and counter-rumour, he had watched from a short distance away as Amanda had slowly withdrawn into herself and become slightly paranoid at what was going on around her and he was determined that he would not let it get to her.

On the walk to the car he had tried to make light conversation but he understood completely why this was not reciprocated by Amanda. She looked around her nervously, staring at strangers, avoiding the shadows and her steps were quick and nervous. At one stage he had put his hand on her arm to slow her down a little, she had flinched and that had hurt him a little, he felt protective towards her and he hoped that she realised that.

Dave was single, though he had almost married once, he was generally considered to be good looking, dark skinned, even in winter, with deep brown hair and eyes to match. He spent time in the gym and he played football on both Saturday afternoons and Sunday mornings, though the Sunday games were a bit of fun really, playing for the local pub team where the whole side tended to be nursing hangovers from the previous night's excesses.

Though he had never really considered making a pass at Amanda, he certainly found her attractive and, as he walked with her and saw how vulnerable she seemed, he wondered why he had never been moved to try to make a date with her. They were certainly friends but there was aloofness about Amanda that had nothing to do with snobbery, he hadn't really thought about it before but now, in this odd situation, he wondered if this was born out of something that had happened in her past. Was putting an emotional carapace around her and avoiding close relationships some sort of safety mechanism that she had devised to cope with life he wondered?

As they climbed the staircase to the fourth storey of the car park; the lift was usually broken and when it worked smelled of urine, he noticed that she had become even more edgy. He supposed that if anyone were stalking her that they would know what car she drove and possibly even where she had parked it that morning. He found that the edginess was infectious and realised with some surprise that both of his fists were tightly clenched. What if some crazed stalker was up here by her car? Would he be armed, with a knife perhaps? What good would fists be against the cold steel of a blade?

Her car in sight, Amanda opened her handbag and fumbled for her car keys, she swore as she dropped them to the concrete floor and stooped to retrieve them. As she did so a man appeared from between two parked cars and she let out a small scream. Dave was by her side in an instant and stared with anger at the man. With a shrug the man pressed the remote button on his key fob and locked the car he had evidently just parked and then headed for the stairs. He clearly had no interest in Amanda. Her heart was pounding despite this and Dave realised with a small amount of embarrassment that he had been primed to punch the stranger.

As he watched Amanda climb into her car he reflected on what had been a very strange day. What had seemed like an innocent, if slightly unusual telephone call had led to this strange state of affairs. Amanda gunned the engine, she had offered to give him a lift to where his own car was parked but he had declined, telling her to get herself safely home as quickly as she could.

He watched as she drove away, her brake lights lending a dull red glow to the scene as she negotiated the ramp to the lower levels. He realised he cared a great deal that she should get home safely and stay safe; it was a realisation that had sneaked up on him, how long had he felt that way about Amanda without realising it? As he headed back towards the staircase he realised he couldn't be sure.

**

The walk back to his car was a time during which Dave Sullington learned a lot about himself. Was it finally time to grow up and become an adult? He had railed against such conformity all his life. He left school at sixteen. He hadn't planned to in fact, he had signed up for three A levels and had selected a few O levels that he considered complemented them after that it would be a university somewhere and after that who cared?

He had returned to school after the long summer break to be told that the O level courses he had chosen were under-subscribed and would not be running. He was told to choose others, he told them he was leaving and they told him he couldn't without parental permission. The next day he took a note from his parents and walked out into the big wide world. He hadn't made a very good job of conforming to anything ever since.

Perhaps now was the time. His job, as a salesman got him out and about and the hotel culture had led to a string of one night stands and failed romances. None of that seemed to bother him much, the idea of falling in love and settling down was as alien to him as particle physics, but suddenly he felt a shift. The tectonic plates of his existence were stirring and threatened to change the beast forever.

What was it about Amanda that had stirred his interest and why had he only just noticed? She seemed vulnerable on some level but on others she seemed strong and fiercely independent. Perhaps it was this contradiction, this paradox that attracted him.

He was thoroughly wet by the time he reached his car. A status symbol that he had brought to nurture the carefully crafted image he had of himself. As far as he was aware, his was the only Triumph Stag in the town, perhaps it was also time to trade this in and get something a little more staid, a grown up car for a grown up man.

He drove home via a local Indian takeaway and picked up a bottle of wine from the off-licence near his smart penthouse flat. As he sat and watched a documentary about irrigation in East Africa he ate his food and drank the whole bottle of wine. As much as he tried he couldn't get Amanda Fellows out of his mind.

Just why he had acted the way he did today was a mystery to him. Calling the police was a pretty odd thing to do with hindsight, but, when he heard that voice he had felt something. He had never considered malice or evil before, not to the extent that they could actually be tangible in someone's voice or mannerisms. That, though, was what he felt as he listened to the man on the other end of the telephone, the man who claimed to be Amanda Fellows' father but who could not have been.

All things considered he felt he had been right to involve the police, and, though she was obviously not that enthusiastic to speak with them, he believed that Amanda thought he had done the right thing too. It was funny just how much it mattered to him that he got her approval for his actions, he had never much cared before what people thought about him one way or another. Somehow, what Amanda thought mattered one hell of a lot, times were changing and so, belatedly, was David Sullington.

TEN

"For God's sake Jen can't you tell the kids to fucking shut up?"

Jennifer Dowley, still a little hung over from her 'naughty afternoon' with Yvette looked at her husband with something like disdain.

"You shouldn't swear in front of the children Jim; they'll only pick it up and learn bad habits."

"I'll stop fucking swearing when I get some peace around here; I've had a shit day at work and the last thing I need is Armageddon in the bloody kitchen!"

He noted the hurt expression on her face and wished he had been more tactful and less forceful, he watched as she disappeared into the kitchen and groaned inwardly when the dog joined in the cacophony, barking excitably at her arrival.

On the television the news told of further conflict in the Middle-East, the *Daily Telegraph*, strewn on the coffee table in front of him warned of more economic gloom for the country. Speculators were driving down the value of banking shares across the globe and stock markets were fearful and falling fast. He mused on this for a moment or two; the world had become a cesspit of greed and corruption, war and more war, by virtue of his job he was a part of that, it depressed him still further.

Jim took another long swallow from the can of beer he had opened a few moments before, two others sat emptily on the coffee table beside the newspaper. One further large gulp and this one, too, was empty; he reached for a fourth. The beer tasted bitter-sweet; it was very much like his mood tonight. Jennifer was no nearer to quietening the kids, the dog too was not for settling, he was miserable and there didn't seem to be anything he could do to shake the mood.

He had made an utter fool of himself that morning; his mad dash from the offices out into the pouring rain and the throng of people had been ill-advised. People newly prised from their comfortable beds and their loved ones' embraces, thrust into the cold and damp of a November morning by the lure of paltry pay packets, were not particularly conducive to be pushed and shoved around. He had headed off on his fruitless chase, trying to anticipate where his quarry might be heading for, any number of offices and shops looked likely destinations.

Frantically scouring the street ahead with its mass of miserable bodies he ran through the crowd and the puddles, stumbling past exasperated people, mumbling apologies and ignoring curses as he went. He had run almost half a mile when he finally conceded defeat. The damp air and the thin film of sweat which enveloped his body, slowly cooled him as he trudged back in the direction of his office, making him cold and uncomfortable, he had started to shiver.

He had encountered a few stony expressions as he proceeded, from the people he had bumped into, tripped over or stood upon, he had returned their glares with interest. His mood at the time was one of bitter disappointment mixed with a little anger; no one spoke to him, his expression warning them away.

He had been so close, almost caught up with her; the woman who, until now, had only existed in his dreams and drunken blackouts. Or had he imagined it, had his eyes only seen what his mind wanted them too? Had he been chasing someone who simply wasn't there? Was he, now, so obsessed with this mystery woman that his waking eyes would deceive him?

Even now, hours later, his thoughts were ramshackle, annoying scenarios; he was no nearer to solving this strange riddle now, than he had been when it had first begun. As he sat there he tried to remember exactly when that had been, what might have triggered it to happen but, as with everything about the girl, an answer eluded him.

Things had only got worse when he returned to the office, he had been late for the meeting and had sat there wet and bedraggled, feeling both cold and stupid, his contribution was minimal, his thoughts anywhere but on what was being discussed. Only near the end when it was announced that due to the economic downturn the company would be tightening the purse-strings and that company cars were to be withdrawn and the fleet sold, did his attention finally focus on the events in the meeting room.

So all the financial consultants would be oiling the chains on their bicycles; that would be good for the corporate image wouldn't it he thought? Walking back to his office afterwards he recalled the incident in the traffic that morning when he had considered crashing the car just for the hell of it. If he saw the idiot in the Lotus tomorrow he might just go for it.

In the kitchen, Jennifer had finally managed to calm the kids down, she'd either interested them in some game or other, or maybe she had put the portable television on, it had a video slot built in and Jim suspected that she had bribed them to silence with a particular favourite. The alternative was that she had strangled them both and bundled them into a cupboard. He tried to relax but it just wasn't happening; even the beer failed to calm down his system that seemed to be in overdrive.

He was as convinced as he could be that that morning he had been close to something special, like a believer who had a religious experience; he had almost found the answers he had sought for these past, miserable weeks. Why was fate playing a game with him in this way? Was fate involved at all; was it simply that he was playing games with himself, some strange psychosis that would interest the psychiatrists?

The news, depressing, finally finished and with it the dog finally stopped barking in the kitchen, dog biscuits had probably done the trick there. Jennifer really was a wonderful wife to put up with him and his strange moods and with her patience with the kids and animals in the house. As he thought this he glanced towards the kitchen door and was startled to see that she was standing there watching him, he jumped as if he had seen a ghost.

"You shouldn't sneak up on me like that Jen; you scared the shit out of me!"

"Don't swear Jim, you never used to swear." Her face wore a troubled expression; Jim felt the usual guilt feelings kick off inside him. She looked like she wanted to talk; he was not in the mood for a lecture.

"What's wrong Jim? You've changed so much, you're not the man I married; you used to be so content, so happy."

He wanted to explode, wanted to rail against her observations and against the world at large, he restrained himself, he loved his wife very much.

"I'm just tired Jen, I've had a really bad day at the office, they're taking the car away."

"It's not just today though is it Jim?"

He felt suddenly that Jennifer had been planning this conversation for some time, she was too calm, and Jim felt threatened and defensive.

"Well work's been getting me down for quite a while now, perhaps I need a change."

"To hell with work Jim, to hell with the car as well, this is not about those things is it? It's about us, our relationship, me, you, Darren and Hannah!"

He was shocked by the sudden edge to her voice, behind the mask of normality, that Jenny always wore, a great unhappiness was revealing itself, he saw anger there too and he felt threatened, he did the worse thing possible, he snapped back at her.

"Jen, what the hell are you shouting about, you'll start the kids off again?"

The dog needed no further encouragement to begin barking once more, it was louder than before and was trying to get into the lounge, its paws playing against the closed door.

"It's time to stop taking me for a fool Jim. It's time for some answers, some truthful answers, who is she Jim?"

The question took him completely off guard; his expression must have shown his confusion. Jennifer though chose to misread it and took his silence for an admission of guilt.

"You bastard Jim Dowley; you dirty rotten filthy bastard!"

"Jennifer...."

"How the hell could you do that to us? What about the kids? Did you think of that when you were inside her knickers Jim?"

She lunged forward, slapping his face with both hands, the hysterical tears that had been welling up inside her during this short exchange now burst out, tears of pain and frustration, tears of loss.

The beer which remained in the can now spewed forth as Jim put his hands up to protect himself from the further blows that his angry wife rained upon him, as he tried to push her away the coffee table overturned, Jennifer almost fell with it.

"You're a bastard; bastard; bastard; bastard!" Each word was accompanied by another blow, Jim began to worm free of her attentions leaving her with flailing arms.

The sudden presence of the dog told Jennifer what she didn't want to know; half turning she glanced towards the kitchen door where Darren and Hannah stood looking at the chaos in the room. Darren was crying Hannah simply sucked her thumb, altogether the six years old she was.

Jim surveyed the mess, Jennifer now lay slumped against the settee on which he had been sitting, her body limp with exhaustion; she was sobbing still but not as violently. Beer and tears formed rivulets across the grey surface of the settee, the dog began to bark once more.

"There's no one else Jennifer," Jim said quietly, the words brought no response at all.

"Jennifer, I promise you, there's no one. I'm a bit messed up right now that's all. I'll give up the drinking, it might help I suppose."

Still Jennifer did not move, her gentle sobs the only indication at all that she was hearing him. He turned to the children.

"Darren, Hannah come over here please, Dad wants to talk to you."

Hannah dashed for the stairs, Darren stood his ground. A deep and frightening feeling of hurt suddenly overwhelmed Jim as he realised he had lost the trust of his children.

"Darren, please…" He looked pleadingly at his son who continued to view him with suspicion; finally Darren plucked up the courage to speak.

"Why is Mummy crying Daddy?"

He was taken aback by the question, Darren was eight years old but he sounded so lost he could have been five or six, how long had it been since Jim had spoken at length with his children? He found he couldn't remember the last time. When had he last praised them, told them how much he loved them? Same answer.

"Your Mummy's a little upset at the moment Darren, I think she might just be a bit tired, people sometimes get upset when they are tired."

"Are you tired Daddy?"

"A little bit Darren."

"Are you upset too?"

"I think I probably am, yes."

"Oh!"

Jim held out his arms and Darren trotted over to him, their embrace felt good to Jim, again he wondered when the last time he had felt these feelings had been.

"Don't be upset Mummy; why don't you go to sleep if you're tired?"

Jennifer stirred at last and looked at her son in the arms of his father. She tried to smile for his benefit but the feeling of hurt was too deep. She didn't believe Jim; knew he had been seeing someone for quite some time. She had lain there beside him in bed weeping softly as he called out the name of another woman in the darkness. She had taken it for so long but now some serious talking had to be done.

"Mummy's alright now Darren. Will you and Hannah be good and go to bed now please so that Mummy and Daddy can have a talk?"

"Oh Dad!"

"Please Darren!"

"I suppose so."

"Will you read us a story?" Hannah who had been crouching on the open plan staircase watching the events below now called out to her mother.

"I'll come along in a while and tuck you in; if you're still awake I'll read you a story, okay?"

"Okay Mummy, will it be the Billy Goat one?"

"If you like Hannah, anything you want."

Satisfied Hannah climbed the remaining stairs; Darren kissed both his father and mother and then headed for the staircase.

"Can you read me a bit of the Hobbit please Mum?"

"We'll see Darren, off you go now I'll be up in a while."

"Thanks, goodnight Mum," then, as an afterthought, "goodnight Dad."

"Goodnight Darren." The words almost stuck in his throat such was the upwelling of emotion in Jim, he could still feel the place on his forehead where his son had kissed him goodnight; how long had it been?

Jim and Jennifer watched as their son climbed the stairs and listened for the sound of the bathroom door, when they were sure he was out of earshot they turned to face each other.

"I want to know everything Jim."

He looked at her, her eyes were puffy and bloodshot and tears continued to slide down her flushed cheeks.

"There really is nothing to tell Jen."

"Don't call me Jen, my name is Jennifer, just tell me the truth."

"I am doing, there is no other woman Jennifer."

"Let's start with Marie shall we?"

"Marie?" Jim looked genuinely puzzled, was it possible that he had continued to call out that name in his dreams? Wasn't that the name that he had somehow subconsciously assigned to the woman he kept dreaming about? How could Jennifer know that unless he was repeating her name? His puzzlement was misread by his wife.

"Don't treat me like a fool Jim, God alone knows how long you have been doing that." Her voice was firm but she did not shout this time.

"Jennifer, I don't understand any of this."

"You don't understand any of this? Listen to yourself Jim Dowley, listen to your own lies and be embarrassed. By God you've got a thick skin. What happened to the man I married? You used to be a caring man Jim, God knows; I even thought you loved me once."

"I do love you Jennifer."

"Go and tell it to the trees!"

"Jennifer…."

"Jim, I'm almost past talking to you, I just want to know who she is and how long it's been going on. Then we can get down to more mundane matters like divorce and custody of the kids."

"Divorce; Jennifer you can't be serious."

"Oh yes I can and I am."

"But I keep telling you, there is no one else!"

"Marie?"

"Who the hell is this Marie?" Jim was starting to lose his composure now; he tried to keep his voice down so that the children would not hear.

"Jim, you call out her name in your sleep; almost every night. Do you have any idea how much that hurts me; how demeaning it is to me?

"I've been dreaming a lot later; I can't explain it."

"What is there to explain Jim, you practically give me a running commentary of what is happening every night."

"I don't know who Marie is; Jennifer you have got to believe me."

"I don't believe you Jim and I thought, wrongly obviously, that you would be a big enough man to come clean about it all. How could I have ever loved you Jim?"

"Don't say that Jennifer."

"Hurts does it? I'm surprised!"

"Of course it hurts, you're my wife, and I love you."

"Is that what you tell Marie Jim?" That you love your wife, love your children, and could never leave them? Is that the sort of talk that excites her Jim? Is that how you get her to drop her knickers for you?"

"Stop this…"

"Or do you tell her that your wife doesn't understand you? That's what they say isn't it, my wife doesn't understand me? Is it? You tell me Jim; how does she like it?"

"You're just being stupid Jennifer, stop this."

"No Jim, I've spent the last God knows how long being stupid, I've had enough of listening to you pining for your fucking whore every night whilst trying not to cry. I've had enough of sitting in this bloody living room, reading, knitting, watching television, playing with myself because you won't touch me anymore, whilst you sit up there in your bloody 'no go area' getting pissed. No Jim, don't tell me I'm being stupid!"

"Jennifer, you're shouting, you'll upset the kids again."

"Since when have you worried about the kids?"

The jibe cut deep into him, the feeling surprised him in its intensity.

"Jennifer, can I speak? Will you let me talk to you for just a minute or two without interruption? Even mass murderers get the chance to speak at their trials."

The sullen silence which greeted his plea encouraged him to continue.

"You've convinced yourself that I'm having an affair…."

Jennifer motioned to interject but he quelled her by raising both hands as if to ward off her anger.

"An affair; what is an affair Jennifer? Is an affair furtive sex between a married person and another married person? Is it sex between a single person and a married person? You appear to believe that sex has to come into it at some stage."

"Your point is?" Jennifer needed to say something; she didn't want to feel like she was being lectured to.

"What I'm trying to say is that if I was having an affair I would need to see this woman to have sex with her."

"Marie!"

"Okay Marie, Sarah, Emily, whatever you want to call her. The question is when do I meet this mystery woman? When do I have the opportunity? By your own words I am drinking too much, spending too much time in the room upstairs, if I were having an affair wouldn't I be taking every opportunity to get out of the house rather than staying in it? If I had fallen out of love with you, shouldn't I be trying to put some distance, geographical distance, between us? When do you believe I see this woman?"

"Lunchtimes I suppose."

"Jennifer, are you serious?"

"Why not; you do have lunchtimes don't you?"

"You know that my lunchtimes are virtually non-existent, we are expected to eat at our desks."

"I don't Jim; I don't know anything about you anymore, you're lost to me Jim. God knows we used to be so close, you loved me once, I know that as much in my heart as I know that you don't love me now."

"You're wrong Jennifer, I love you very much."

"I don't think you know the difference anymore!"

"I'm mixed up at the moment but about that there is no doubt."

"You drink too much; you spend too much time in that bloody room of yours."

"I know, but, Jennifer I swear this Marie is not real. I keep dreaming about this woman who I don't even know, almost every night it's the same, I seem to be chasing her through all sorts of strange places. Places I can't describe properly; like fairy tale places.

Jennifer looked bewildered, for the first time she hadn't a riposte ready for him.

"Look I know it sounds really strange but it is the truth. I don't know who she is or why I'm chasing her. I don't know why she's haunting me or why I keep having the same dreams over and over again. Maybe it's some kind of relief from the humdrum of work, some kind of psychological thing. Jennifer I just don't know but I swear to you I am not having an affair with anyone."

"I had to wash the sheets today Jim, they were covered in dry blood, can you explain that to me?"

What could he say to that? Jennifer had slowly mellowed as he had recounted his explanation, maybe she was beginning to believe him; if he were to tell her his theories as to how his legs came to be scratched then that would surely spoil any credibility that he had so far managed to give to his story.

Suddenly and inexplicably his hold on the situation was lost, he collapsed onto the settee with an overwhelming feeling of nausea, as he did so he burst into tears. These were not the tears of a grown man but those of a frightened child.

"Jim what is it? What's wrong with you?" Jennifer's anger was replaced by concern at this sudden and frightening deterioration and she moved to his side. As he embraced her and sobbed on her shoulder the hot tears trickled down the collar of her blouse and tickled her soft skin. She realised that she still loved him, even if the bastard was seeing another woman she loved him and she always would do. The realisation scared her; she resolved to believe his strange story at least for the time being.

"Mummy, is Daddy tired now?"

Hannah stood at the bottom of the stairs, a look of innocent concern on her tiny young face.

"I suppose he is a little tired sweetheart."

"You said you would tell me the Billy Goat story Mummy."

Yes, Hannah, you go back up to bed and I'll be up to you in a minute alright?"

"You promise?"

"I promise sweetheart."

Satisfied, Hannah mounted the stairs once more and disappeared from view. Jennifer stood, righted the coffee table and picked up the empty beer cans. Before leaving the room she surprised herself by planting a gentle kiss on Jim's forehead.

His sobs continued long after Jennifer had disposed of the debris of the night and climbed the staircase. Hannah was sitting upright in bed playing with one of her dolls, she smiled as her mother came into the room and the smile was so innocent and free from the pressure of adulthood that Jennifer almost cried again, she stopped herself though, too many tears had already been cried on this day.

"Will you tell me the Cinderella story please Mummy."

"Yes sweetheart, of course I will."

ELEVEN

His breath swam before him in a cloud of water vapour, forming strange patterns in the air. Beneath his feet the detritus of fallen leaves and litter made soggy by the persistent rain. Above him the sky was darkened by the night and the rain clouds that had, mercifully, for now ceased their bombardment of the land below.

The small park area had been useful for him; situated as it was in the centre of a square around which tall terraced buildings were situated. Most of these old houses had now been converted to flats and it was in one of these that the girl lived with her erratic friend. From the relative cover of the trees and bushes he had been ideally placed to view the comings and goings from the flat without attracting unwanted attention.

The bench on which he was seated was weathered and old, coated in moss and wet from the downpours. He felt its coldness as it seeped through the thin material of his trousers and, so it seemed to him, into his very bones. Still, sitting was the only option for him, he was weak and growing weaker by the day, when he tried to stand still for any length of time he swayed on his feet in an alarming manner, time was growing short for him.

Tonight he must make his move, he must confront the girl and tell her everything; what she did then was up to her but he would at least have settled his debts with her, he could then die with a modicum of dignity.

He looked at the face of his watch, barely discernable in the half-light, it was almost six-fifteen; the girl should be home soon, the other one, the drunkard, rarely showed up at the flat until seven-thirty and sometimes much later so he figured he would have a small amount of time at his disposal before they were interrupted; he hoped it would be time enough.

He shivered against the cold and damp; he had been there an hour already, his obsession with the girl impelling him to come here long before any prospect that she might turn up. He huddled himself into his coat as a man walked by, an excitable dog on the end of a leash sniffed at his old boot as it passed by, the young man tried to look apologetic but he couldn't make out the old man's face, probably some down and out drunk he concluded as he walked on his way in the gloom.

The old man wanted to melt into the shadows, to carry on his vigil unnoticed and ghost-like but there were certain practicalities to consider. The best concealed hiding places did not correspond to places from where he could view the entrance to the flat; therefore, over time it was possible that diligent neighbours might notice his continued presence.

In some ways it would have increased his credible reasons for being in the park if he were to have a bottle of spirits in his hand. The simple thing was that he was so pre-occupied with his quest that he had not even considered such a simple disguise.

He liked this little park though; it had come to represent all the things that mattered to him. A number of small pathways criss-crossed through the trees which were now mostly denuded of their foliage by the winds and rains, a small pond with a fountain that had long ago ceased to work formed the centrepiece. The whole thing was surrounded by black iron railings and there were gates at each of the four corners.

Everything in the confines felt weathered, old and comfortable, the smell of rotting leaves and wet grass felt right to him, perhaps, he had thought, he would continue to come here after he had spoken with the girl; after all, he reasoned, it was better to die here amongst nature than to die in the tiny little room he was staying in. That debate would be for another day though he told himself as he continued to peer through the naked trees, through the railings and out at the front door of the girl's flat.

He caught a movement out of the corner of his eye and turned to see another dog walker on one of the other pathways in the park; this one was a long way away and had not appeared to notice him. Not many people used the park at this time of day and at this time of year but tonight seemed to be busier than in recent days. Typical, he thought as he considered the resolution he had made to himself that today would be the day when he carried through his task.

Those that did use the park and happened upon his crumpled form looked at him with undisguised distaste, probably appalled by his unkempt condition, possibly frightened although he doubted that he looked capable of any kind of violence, maybe they feared catching some terrible disease from him.

The old man had felt their distaste; at first he had tried to allay it by smiling but this had only seemed to make things worse. Steps had quickened; a woman walking past with her two children had pulled them closer to her as she bustled by with almost comical haste. Their reactions hurt him; he still had feelings, still had pride but he had to confess that his place in the social hierarchy was assisting him in his mission. If people gave him a wide berth then they would not be able to describe him very well; that could only be a good thing.

Not for the first time he allowed his mind to wander to a different time, a different place, a time when he had been a handsome man, talented and with a string of female admirers. He had little or no time for this though, such was the import of his work; his dedication to what had been ground-breaking research, the demands of that work. Now the only demands on him were moral ones, his mission in life was now all that mattered to him.

The street outside the park was quiet; the square was only a short way to the town's main thoroughfare but was an oasis of calm. The houses that were not sub-divided into flats were occupied by professional people, doctors and lawyers attracted by the square's close proximity to the town centre, its opulent looking houses and the peace and quiet.

The town had a large student population and entrepreneurial property developers had brought and renovated many of the houses. The renovations had been done with profit in mind and large properties had been sub-divided for multiple-tenancy which accounted for why there were so many flats in the town. All in all the micro-community worked very well, the presence of a tramp in the park had been noted and discussed among the more affluent members of the housing committee members but no action had been decided upon.

The murky night was cast aside for a moment as a swathe of light cut across it like searchlights in a wartime sky; the old man sank lower in his bench-seat. A car had turned into the square from the main road. The old man felt his heartbeat quicken as the car began to slow as it approached the girl's flat. It was difficult to be sure in the dim light and mist but he felt a frisson of certainty that it was her.

His ageing eyes strained to make out the scene; the car pulled up right outside the flat and the engine was turned off and the lights cut throwing the scene once more into a gloomy orange darkness picked out by the sodium street lights. He held his breath as he waited for something to happen; the sudden silence seemed palpable, the tension he was feeling was heightened.

After what seemed like an age, the inside of the car was illuminated as the driver's door was opened; he willed his eyes to adjust quickly to the scene and see if his instinct had been right; it had. He watched as the girl locked the car and climbed the few steps up to the front door of the flat, the urge to call out to her almost too much to overcome.

She seemed to fumble for her key as she reached the door and it took her a couple of attempts to find the key hole; was she drunk he wondered. On finally getting the door open she stood for a moment on the threshold and scanned the street in both directions, then her gaze fixed on the park and it seemed to the old man that she was looking right at him.

He shrunk back into the shadows, irrational considering that his whole reason for being here was to see the girl and speak with her. Finally, as if having satisfied herself of something, she closed the door, returning the street to its dark and brooding silence.

He knew he would have to make his move straightaway but his heart was racing and he felt light-headed, he would first need to compose himself. He tried to take deep breaths to steady his heart rate but his lungs seemed almost to groan with the effort, he wiped a thin film of sweat from his brow despite the weather and marvelled at the effect that this was having on him. He must, though, be strong; he must carry through his plan, it was, after all, his destiny.

**

The carpet of leaves concealed the sound of his footsteps as he approached the gate to the park. Outside, the street was deserted, there were few lights showing in the windows in the houses, most people presumably not yet home from work, or, in the case of the students, probably enjoying the 'happy hours' offered by a lot of the town centre bars. He guessed he would have plenty of time before the drunken flatmate put in an appearance and the thought cheered him.

As he walked, he marvelled at the steady purpose that rose in him, for the first time he was confident that he would fulfil his mission, he would be free at last, all those years of hell; all those years imprisoned with his own guilt. His hand flicked quickly and skilfully into the pocket of his old overcoat and felt for the object concealed there. It felt reassuringly cold in his grasp.

The old man paused for a moment in front of the small flight of concrete steps that would take him to the door of the building. From here he could see the doorbell with her name on it; he had never been this close before. He could see now that the name of the other girl she roomed with was Kate Harvey, how she had got in his way with her erratic behaviour; bitch he thought.

With new resolve he began to climb the steps, determination taking hold of him as he did so, he would make the girl see it his way, and she would have to see the sense of what he had come here to tell her.

The click-clicking of heels on the slabbed pavement could suddenly be heard in the stillness of the night; he must have heard them earlier he reasoned but he had been so involved in what he was doing that he had failed to register them. He turned on the doorstep, feeling cornered like a frightened animal. It was the bitch; Kate Harvey, what was worse was that she had seen him, her footsteps slowed as her face turned into a mask of revulsion.

"Who are you; what do you want?"

Kate held her ground, her body language spoke of a determined woman prepared to fight her ground. The old man ran. He pushed her as he stumbled past her; she fell awkwardly, grazing her elbow.

"You filthy tramp bastard!" Kate screamed after him in the gloom as he staggered away.

The old man had not run for many years, not even to catch a bus; his heart screamed in his chest, his legs and lower back were demanding that he stop; he ignored them. He made it back into the camouflage of the park, but even here, in his haven, he did not stop, he knew he must get right away from the area before the bitch girl called the police. He had made a grave error of judgement and he cursed himself for his folly as he stumbled along.

Back at the flat, a shocked Kate Harvey had picked herself up from the pavement and dusted herself down. She let herself in and closed the heavy front door behind her with a sense of relief. Her pulse was racing and she was sweating; she shivered as she recalled the look in the old tramp's eyes.

TWELVE

March 1959

He had been angry when he had been forced to leave his homeland. Anger had mixed with sadness as the ship had left the shore and he had waved to his mother with the hands that were numb with cold. Her only wish was that he got away from that place and made a life for himself elsewhere; she was convinced that he would have a long and illustrious career as a top surgeon in England.

Until now he had honoured her bravery, he had saved countless lives and he had been a rising star in the field of surgery and also in medical research. All that had changed today though.

He was walking across Westminster Bridge without really taking in the world around him. The River Thames, his precious River Thames, swirled and churned beneath where he walked and he did not even glance towards it. Big Ben chimed out its hour and he failed to hear it at all. They had failed him and they were all fools.

All week he had felt uneasy, he had tried to dismiss it as a mild case of paranoia, the way colleagues looked at him, the way too that other members of the research committee seemed to shun him or find excuses to be elsewhere when he was around. He suspected he knew exactly why but he had wanted to be there at the meeting. He had wanted them to tell him to his face what their decision had been.

He was a little out of breath by the time he crossed the bridge and reached the turn into Whitehall. He was heading for the Red Lion, it wasn't a pub he frequented often but he felt the need to drink heavily, to sit and to think about what he should do next.

His first reaction had been to walk out on his job, there and then, something had held him back and he needed to analyse within himself exactly what that was and why. The misty March evening was pushed out of his mind as he entered the smoke filled saloon bar of the pub. Here civil servants and politicians drank as they discussed their day, the MPs drank and smoked knowing that the division bell would ring and summon them to the House when required. It was easy to be a face in the crowd in such a place and that was all he wanted to be; anonymous and with the time and space to come to terms, or to try to come to terms with his disappointment.

They had refused to fund his research project, even when he had suggested compromise they had thrown it out; they deemed what he was proposing to be ethically wrong. How could they be so short-sighted? Did they have no imagination? Most medical advances had been made by being brave and pushing back perceived boundaries. Only through taking risks could advances in medical science be achieved.

The vodka reminded him of home and he thought back to this now. Poland, a land gripped by fear, an industrial landscape coveted by the tyrannical Adolf Hitler, a seaboard that was strategically important. So many had died trying to defend his homeland but he had fled here to a land where opportunity was supposed to be rife. He had not expected them to bury their heads in the sand; he had not expected them to question his motives and his morals.

He knew he was right though. Whatever they thought of him and his methods, he knew it was possible to achieve what they believed to be both impossible and ethically bankrupt. The question was how far was he prepared to go to prove to himself that he was right?

The kernel of a plan was beginning to form in his slowly relaxing mind by the time he ordered his fourth large vodka. The noise in the pub, loud at first had settled down to a comfortable background mumble that soothed him and he felt unobserved and able to think clearly for the first time since he had stormed out of the meeting room at St Thomas' Hospital.

He could not do it alone but who could he possibly trust to help him? Who would even want to help him? He thought he had an idea on that. He thought too, that he would need to use his charm and, perhaps, a little deceit to make it work. He was aware of his effect on the ladies who made his acquaintance but it was not a romance he was looking for, it was a competent assistant. Perhaps by pretending to offer the former he could acquire the latter.

By the time that he walked back out into Whitehall, it was quite late and he was fairly well drunk. He would need to cross Westminster Bridge once more to get to his room in Lambeth. This time he crossed with less purpose of stride. He paused halfway to look at the river and watched as a tug emerged from the bridge beneath his feet and headed towards Charing Cross Bridge, across which a train was leaving the station, probably heading for the coast in Sussex or Kent.

The plan was fully formulated in his mind by now and tomorrow he would return to work and try to pretend that nothing was wrong, that he was over his disappointment. He would bide his time, after all, he had the rest of his life to prove that he was right.

THIRTEEN

It was almost nine-fifteen that evening when WPC Julie Walsh and her colleague PC Sean Craig rang the bell marked 'Amanda Fellows/Kate Harvey.' As they stood atop the steps outside in the gloomy night they could see their breath snaking out as vapour before them. It was raining again and the wind had increased in the last hour or so. Before climbing the steps they had done a brief reconnaissance to see if anyone was loitering in the area; they had seen no one lurking in the murky shadows of either the street or the little park opposite.

Craig stamped his feet on the stone of the top step to try to warm them a little, inviting a sarcastic comment from his colleague, she being of Northern stock, about what a Southern softie he was and what he would be like when the snows arrived. Despite his Scottish sounding name Sean Craig was a local and was teased accordingly. He was known at the station collectively as either Jock or Haggis though the latter seemed to have stuck more due to its comedic value.

**

Inside the building Amanda and Kate had been deep in discussion for some time. Kate had been badly shaken up by her encounter with the 'tramp on the doorstep' her rambling monologue recounting exactly what had happened had been barely decipherable at first and Amanda had felt the need to pour her friend a stiff drink to calm her down and get her to tell the story slowly. The whiteness of her normally ruddy cheeks told its own story and Amanda wondered just how her own demeanour had been noted by her frightened flat-mate.

Amanda sat in silence throughout Kate's re-telling of the story; allowing her to get it out of her system, her previous rambling had slowed with the relaxing effect of the alcohol and some calming words of encouragement and a more measured account of the incident had slowly emerged.

As she sat there and listened to her friend, it seemed to Amanda that the incident itself hadn't amounted to very much but she tried to sound and look sympathetic. If her own day hadn't been so disconcerting and raised the prospect that she was being stalked by a man who might fit with Kate's description she would have dismissed the incident as nothing. The fact was that as she herself had not even begun to calm down despite her own large glass of wine, she couldn't help wondering if there was a connection between this incident and her own strange day.

As Kate recounted her story the question that Amanda had wanted to ask her had been stewing in her mind, burning a hole there and she had longed to get it off her chest and get some answers.

Contrary to her thoughts earlier in the day, Amanda now hoped that Kate would confess to a practical joke with regard to the telephone calls earlier in the day; she was now very willing to forgive her friend absolutely if only Kate would mutter the words, "It was only a joke Mandy!"

When she was finally able to ask her question, Kate failed spectacularly to oblige. Her friend had been mortified; the very suggestion that it might all have been one of 'Kate's little jokes' had upset her flatmate even more than the incident with the old man. Amanda had ended up apologising for even suggesting that Kate might have been behind the telephone calls and, for a short time, a hostile air had prevailed in the flat; Amanda feeling more wretched than ever.

The wine, at least the second bottle, was having an effect on proceedings and eventually an uneasy calm descended during which Amanda did something that she would never have believed she would ever do, even to Kate. She talked about her past.

Amanda held nothing back, telling Kate everything she could remember about her troubled life, Kate had sat in stunned silence as the story unfolded, wondering just how it was that she could have lived with someone and felt so close to them without even really knowing them at all. She looked at Amanda and saw a vulnerability there that she had never seen, or cared to see, before.

Throughout Amanda's painful story, Kate ran a gamut of emotions, upset, amazed and sympathetic all at once; how could

Amanda have kept such dark secrets? A psychopathic stepfather murdering her stepmother in front of her; how must that feel? She had known that Amanda was adopted but had always assumed that her friend had moved directly from the children's care home into the custody of Anne and Tony Fellows, after all, Amanda had always allowed her to believe that.

The whole episode seemed to explain a few things for Kate Harvey; Amanda was prone to odd moods and depressions from time to time, they had always seemed inexplicable to Kate, seemingly having no bearing on day to day events in Amanda's life, was this the reason; did Amanda occasionally find the gravity of her past too much to live with, too hard to conceal; the memories too painful to harbour?

There was the man thing too; Kate had always found it odd that a 'prize catch' like Amanda had failed to form a lasting relationship with the string of potential suitors who had come her way over the years, was this some kind of throwback; a latent memory of what men were capable of that made her shy away from them when things started to get serious?

Did this also explain why Amanda was having so many nightmares of late? Amanda had tried to play this down but Kate knew her well enough to know that something was amiss. There were dark bags under her friend's eyes that no amount of make-up could conceal, there was nervousness in her mannerisms, her fingers tapped out imaginary tunes on table-tops, and she had stopped singing in the shower; perhaps that at least was a good thing.

After Kate's mood had mellowed, Amanda's telling of her story had become easier; she related the fear she had that her stepfather might have been released and what that might mean for her. The telephone calls today appeared to lend a possibility to this and the police had so far been unable to give her the reassurances she craved. Kate had been amazed at first that the police had even become involved given the loose nature of what had happened but on reflection she considered just how such a scenario might have played out in her own life.

What if she had settled down on the lounge floor one night to watch the Flintstones on the television only for Jack Harvey to come and say hello to Helen Harvey with a ten inch long knife; would she sleep in her bed at night if she thought that such a person might be loose in the streets once more? She thought not and had shivered at the thought.

The look on Amanda's face when Kate had described the old man on the steps outside had told its own story about her state of mind at the moment; what little colour that had flushed the cheeks of her friend had visibly drained away. Kate hadn't really considered it as she told her story but now, with the benefit of hindsight, she recalled that expression.

Amanda looked suddenly older; much older in fact, the lustre that always seemed to light up the face of Amanda Fellows, and which was her most attractive feature, seemed to drain away in an instant as soon as Kate had mentioned that she had caught a 'weirdo' on the steps outside, that look had been simply torn away from her with those few words.

There was no need for Amanda to say anything more; the description of the man obviously tied in with a description; or at least Amanda's childhood recollection, of Alfred Williamson.

A debate had ensued; Kate had been adamant that the incident outside the flat should be reported to the police; Amanda was equally adamant that it should not; she felt that to involve the police in her life twice in one day smacked of 'crying wolf' and she had confidence that PC Craig would keep his word and get back to her if there was anything to worry about.

In fact, all night Amanda had convinced herself that the police would ring at any moment, as they had promised, and that PC Craig would tell her that her un-beloved stepfather had escaped from a secure hospital armed with a machete and an address book with her name in it. Calling the police again, she thought, would only bring forward this scenario. Kate had won the argument though and now, as the doorbell rang downstairs, she felt her pulse begin to race all over again.

**

Kate pressed the button on the intercom system connected with the outside door to allow the police officer's entry to the building and went to the door in the hallway to look through the spy-hole, leaving Amanda sitting in the lounge. Amanda caught sight of her reflection in a mirror, it didn't look good, and the woman sitting there staring back at her looked frightened and vulnerable.

The sound of Kate's voice, calm and indulging in pleasantries with the recognisable voice of PC Craig, eased her fears a little but the fluttering in the pit of her stomach failed to disappear, her butterflies continuing their dance with renewed vigour. She felt like a vulnerable animal caught in the sights of a fearsome predator; perhaps that was what she was.

As three people entered the room, immediately crowding the small lounge in the flat, Amanda had stood up and stared out into the darkness through the window, she should have drawn the curtains; shut them to lock out that scary world outside and she wished now that she had done so. It was just that it was the last thing on her mind when she had got home and it now seemed irrelevant, it wasn't as though anyone could look in; not up here surely; shivering, she closed them anyway.

As she closed them, she couldn't help looking at the little park opposite, the leafless trees, stark black against the orange glow of the street lights beyond. Something about the park made her uneasy, it was as though there was a presence there that was taunting her; waiting for her. Amanda shuddered and turned to greet her visitors.

The two police officers smiled at her and sat on the two-seater settee, Kate and Amanda sat on the armchairs either side. Amanda noticed that Sean Craig looked tired. Perhaps he had a day like hers; perhaps worse; was that possible, she wondered?

"I was sorry to hear about your spot of bother earlier Amanda." He addressed her directly which caused her to blush. Obviously the message that had been conveyed to the visiting police officers had been lost in translation somewhere along the way.

"It wasn't actually me that had the bother it was Kate, she caught some old man in the process of standing on our doorstep, when he saw her he ran off but not before sending Kate flying and shaking her up."

"It was my idea to call you," Kate interjected, "especially when Amanda told me what had happened earlier in the day. It might have been the same man who was making the calls."

"You did the right thing to call us. We would have been here earlier anyway but we've had a bit of a hectic day."

Amanda wondered if this was why he looked so tired but said nothing; she felt a little guilty to have contributed to that 'hectic day.'

"Have you seen the local news?" PC Craig seemed to want to share something.

"We haven't put the radio or television on, there's been too much to talk about," Amanda answered.

"There was an armed robbery at Blakeley's Furniture in the town. It went wrong, we have one dead and one critically injured. It's been a hell of a day."

"Jesus!" Kate found this a little too close to home; she had worked at Blakeley's as a Saturday girl when she was still at school. Blakeley's was a local furnishers specialising in top quality furniture, mahogany dining suites, woollen carpets, office furniture and the like. It had a good reputation for quality.

"Who was it that got killed?" Kate was still taking in the shock.

"It was old Mr Blakeley himself, I'm afraid."

"William Blakeley dead; I don't believe it!" It hardly seemed possible to Kate; the man had been so unlikely to die, larger than life, full of fun, he had dished out sweets to all of the children that came into the store with their parents, a truly nice man.

"He'll certainly be missed." WPC Walsh seemed embarrassed when she realised just what an understatement that was. "The telephone at the station hasn't stopped ringing since the news broke; the duty sergeant is having kittens trying to deal with all the calls."

"Was he trying to stop the raiders?" Kate was curious to know.

"It would seem so, yes."

"It doesn't surprise me; he was a bit of an old soldier."

"Yes, I gather he was."

Kate looked at the austere looking policeman; he looked vaguely silly sitting on the settee, the springs had long since lost their tautness, the result being that any unsuspecting person who perched there ended up about a foot lower than they were expecting to be. This had been the source of much amusement over the years but tonight no one had cracked a smile when the two police officers had learned the secrets of the furniture.

"I'll make some coffee, how would you like it?" Kate took the order and disappeared into the kitchen, returning to stand in the doorway after she had put the kettle on.

Amanda had been grateful for the distraction afforded by the talk of the robbery, though she too knew William Blakeley and was saddened by the news. Now though, there seemed no other excuse to put off the inevitable conversation, the reason why the police officers were visiting tonight, whether Kate had encountered the tramp or not.

"Have you managed to find out anything about my ex-stepfather?"

The question seemed to hang in the air between them for what seemed to Amanda an age; long enough for her to realise that the voice she had used to ask the question sounded more like that of a frightened child than her own.

PC Craig sighed and his already serious face seemed to become even more so.

"We have something for you; it's not an equivocal answer and probably won't do much, if anything, to allay your fears."

"That doesn't sound very promising, go on officer." The nerves that danced in her stomach were worse than ever, in the kitchen the kettle had boiled but Kate did not leave her place in the doorway.

"As you may well know, Alfred Williamson was found guilty of murder on the grounds of diminished responsibility. The original hearing had to be adjourned for psychiatric reports and these showed that he was suffering from a form of schizophrenia, a type, it seems, that can lie undetected for years. It is believed, apparently, that people can suffer this and yet live their entire lives relatively normally, die and be none the wiser."

"So the judge let him off lightly; is that what you are saying?" Amanda's voice was choked with emotion as she asked the question.

"No Amanda, he didn't." It was Julie Walsh who answered the question; she had seen how tense Amanda had become and felt the need to try to make this difficult situation easier for her. Sean Craig smiled appreciatively before continuing.

"The very ferocity of the attack appalled judge and jury alike. Alfred Williamson was sentenced to a life in custody with the recommendation that life, in this case, was to mean just that."

Amanda took a deep breath and took in this news, she compared it to the policeman's opening comment and wondered how the two fitted together; she had a theory, it was one she hoped would go away. She couldn't help herself though, she gave voice to it.

"So along comes some goody two-shoes doctor who gives him a nice clean bill of health, declares him cured and no longer a threat to society. This pillar of society then convinces a mental health board that all the marbles are now in their correct place and, hey presto! Alfred Williamson is back on the streets after all, leaving room in the prison system for some violent maniac such as a seventy year old pensioner who refuses to pay his council tax!" Amanda shocked even herself at this sudden outburst; Kate was stunned and the two police officers looked uncomfortable. Amanda's eyes were watering but she was determined not to lose it completely.

"Miss Fellows; please don't upset yourself." Julie Walsh climbed out of the settee with some difficulty and placed her hand on Amanda's shoulder in a gesture of comfort.

"He is out though isn't he?" Amanda said quietly.

"Well that's where we have a problem." Sean Craig was talking again; Kate had abandoned any thoughts of making coffee and returned to her seat.

"I know I'm upset, but I just can't see where this is leading." Amanda sounded desperate even to herself; the grip on her shoulder was firmed.

"You are wrong about the medical board Amanda, Williamson was never considered for parole and the likelihood is that he never would be."

"What then?"

"Alfred Williamson was a hopeless case after his imprisonment. His schizophrenia became a lot worse and he was subject to violent rages, he had to be sedated frequently, he attacked other inmates and damaged furniture. He was moved to a number of different establishments; top security hospitals mainly, under the constant care of psychiatrists. Five different psychiatrists dealt with him in all; they were each of the same mind; that Williamson should never be let out.

"So why was he; because that's what you are getting round to telling me isn't it, that he's out?"

"He never was let out."

"So he escaped, what is he the Birdman of Alcatraz or something?"

"There was a fire; a bad one, you probably saw it on the news."

"Carlton; he was in Carlton?"

"Yes, he was in the wing that was totally destroyed."

Carlton had been national news fairly recently, hundreds of patients and hospital staff had been killed or injured, and the fire had burned for almost twenty four hours.

"So the bastard's dead!" Kate sounded triumphant.

"We don't know for certain; it is the most likely outcome."

"But surely…"

"His remains were never found. He was in a ward right at the centre of the blaze; the heat was so intense that nothing survived in that area. There were five people unaccounted for from that ward, three of them were prison staff."

"Is it possible he got out?" Amanda's voice was almost a whisper now.

Sean Craig had never wanted to say the word 'no' more in his life than he did now. The chances were that Williamson had perished in the flames along with everyone else but, whilst there was a possibility that he had not, he found he was unable to reassure this vulnerable woman who looked so childlike, who had endured such pain in her short life.

"I'm afraid that the possibility has never been ruled out Amanda, nor is it ever likely to be."

The tears wouldn't stay back any longer and the WPC tried her best to console the stricken woman; Kate merely observed this madness in stunned silence.

Amanda cried for several minutes, Kate went to make the coffee after all, she needed to get out of the room for a while, Julie Walsh battled gamely to bring Amanda out of her despair whilst Craig sat and looked embarrassed whilst feeling terrible. What made things worse for him was that he now needed to exact more information from Amanda; it really had been one hell of a day.

The coffee seemed to work and some ten minutes later a modicum of sanity had been restored to the room, Kate had foregone the coffee and had poured herself another glass of wine, Amanda sipped a little coffee but her enthusiasm for the task was absent as was plain for all to see.

Finally, with trepidation, Sean Craig felt that he could wait no longer before he pushed matters along again; he knew that

Amanda would probably hate him for it but it was, after all, what he was paid to do.

"The man outside the flat tonight, did Kate describe him to you Amanda?"

"Yes," her voice a mere whisper.

"Did her description fit that of your father?"

"Don't you ever call him my father! What that bastard has done to my life only I know, he is not my father, was never my father!" no longer a whisper.

"I'm so sorry Amanda, I didn't mean to infer that he was your father, it's been a long day. I want to help you but you need to help me too. I think you know what I was asking you even if I made an arse of asking the question."

"I'm sorry. It's been a long day for me too. Kate was sketchy on detail, it was dark, the man looked like a tramp, height and build though, colour of hair, other little things she said. It could be Alfred Williamson."

"The psychiatric reports show your ex-stepfather to have shown great remorse for what he had done during the calmer periods of his internment that seemed to be a big problem for him, coming to terms with what he had done. If the man outside is Williamson then it is just possible that he doesn't want to hurt you at all, he may just want to speak with you."

"Is that supposed to make me sleep this evening?"

"Of course not; and it is purely theoretical on my part based on what I have learned. We need to be practical about the situation, so now it's time to talk about what we can do about this."

"I'm listening." Kate was too; another glass of wine was poured, however, to help her concentrate.

PC Craig felt that he hadn't handled this particularly well but then again he had never had to talk to a woman who, as a child, had bathed in her own stepmother's blood. He needed to push on to the end now and hope he didn't put his foot in it again.

"I think that for safety's sake we must assume first and foremost that the man outside tonight is Alfred Williamson. My boss probably won't be too happy about that, deployment of officers is a political minefield at the moment so the idea of preventing a possible crime when we have unsolved crimes to deal with will be tough for him to swallow, but I believe it is the right assumption to make.

"Secondly, despite the theory I've just put forward, it would be prudent to believe that if it is Williamson then he hasn't come here to talk about the weather with you. We have to assume that he means to hurt you. I conclude, therefore, that the best course of action would be for us to keep the flat, and indeed you Miss Fellows, under police observation."

"Guard the door? Is that what you mean?" Amanda looked both shocked and appalled at the suggestion.

"My boss will have to sanction it, of course, but I think a marked police vehicle parked outside in the square should provide a sufficient deterrent to any would-be intruder."

"But what about the other people who live here; do you propose to stop everyone who tries to enter the building?"

"Why not; if their intentions are innocent they won't have anything to worry about will they?"

"But it's such a good neighbourhood; we were lucky to get a place here in the first place. Tony Chadwick, the local MP, lives three doors away, what will he think about having a police car parked outside all day and night?"

"Frankly, and please forgive me for this, I don't give a shit what Mr Chadwick thinks, he's a lousy MP in any case."

"Well we're agreed on that at least." Kate toasted the air and then drank some more wine.

"I'll see that everything is arranged Amanda, in the meantime if either of you should hear or see anything suspicious or if you receive any more strange telephone calls I want to know immediately." For the second time that day he handed a card to Amanda.

"My mobile number is on the back; don't be shy to use it."

"Thank you officer; I hope I won't need to." Despite everything and the turmoil of thoughts that beset her, she was grateful to this man who had become her port in this particularly unusual storm.

"Miss Fellows?" WPC Walsh had spotted the red flush that had formed on Amanda's cheeks.

"Yes."

"It really is no problem, you shouldn't concern yourself."

"It's just that it all seems so unbelievable. Yesterday everything was fine; today my whole world has turned upside down."

"I understand; perhaps you should get an early night, try to get some sleep."

"I'm not sure that I could sleep."

"Well, promise me you'll try."

"I promise; perhaps if Kate leaves me some of that wine it might help!" She looked at her friend with compassion; Kate grinned back.

"Don't you worry now Mandy; there's another two bottles where this came from."

**

It was almost two hours later when Amanda finally pushed open her bedroom door and climbed into bed. The wine hadn't helped much; she thought that sleep would prove elusive tonight, still it had helped inasmuch that she and Kate had managed to have a proper talk. How long had it been since they had spent a night in together in the way they had tonight? She simply couldn't remember; it certainly pre-dated Kate's last boyfriend.

That was the thing about Kate though, her friendship was total, she was as loyal as a young puppy and heart to heart conversations were not what their friendship was about. Amazing how quickly they just slipped back into comfortable conversation even though neither of them could be feeling particularly comfortable about the day's events.

She tried to sleep but it was hopeless; climbing out of her bed in the darkened room she made her way to the window which looked out over the square. Pulling back the curtain she looked at the park opposite, it looked even more ominous at this time of night, the darkness within even more impenetrable. He could be in there she thought, waiting for the right time, waiting, watching, brooding waiting to remake the acquaintance of his darling stepdaughter. She shuddered at the thought.

The street light below barely penetrated the darkness, positioned as it was on the other side of the street to that inky black wilderness that represented the park which she had loved so much when she had moved into the flat, now everything had changed.

A sudden flare of light caught her attention, her pulse raced as she sought its source down below her on her side of the street.

The flare of the match receded and was replaced by the tiny dull orange glow of a cigarette. The policeman was talking to his colleague, the car in darkness; Amanda's own personal sentinel. Reassured she closed the curtains; maybe she would sleep tonight after all.

FOURTEEN

The street was a jumble of people; business people trying to out-jostle each other, rushing this way and that in their individual quests to get to the office on time. How many angry bosses would there be on this morning she thought.

Amanda stood still in the crowd. The throng moved at her like waves, she felt suddenly nauseous; felt the need to sit down somewhere and collect her thoughts. The sound of footsteps sounded like thunder in her ears, a heartbeat of sound which she needed to escape; but which way to run?

Her pulse quickened, panic rising steadily within her, something didn't feel quite right. She looked around her, seeking refuge, but she saw none. Her head felt light; too light, she seemed to be floating in and out of consciousness, her feet barely seeming to make contact with the pavement beneath them.

She swayed on her feet, dangerously, almost falling. The loud honk of a car horn alerted her to her proximity to the road. Strange, she had never seen a car like that before, and such an odd colour too. The shock of hearing the car horn had brought her into a more coherent state, she stared at the people rushing by. Amanda almost giggled; they were all wearing bowler hats, even the women, with a copy of the *Daily Telegraph* in one hand and a dapper black umbrella tucked methodically under the opposite arm.

Now she was laughing out loud; the woman with the moustache and goatee beard bustled by without seeming to see her. A Dalmatian passed by, black bowler hat on its head, *Daily Telegraph* between its teeth. "You've forgotten your umbrella," she called after it; she received a wag of its tail by way of reply.

Amanda felt drunk, light headed, almost drugged, but the feeling had ceased to be an unpleasant one. She found that she could walk in a straight line once more; the waves of crowds subsiding, thinning out, the pounding of their feet reduced to a whisper. She looked down and saw that they were all wearing candy striped bedroom slippers. She giggled again, like a child, putting her thumb in her mouth as she did so. She felt like the carefree young girl she had once been.

The buildings in the street down which she walked had changed too, bright colours, strange shapes she realised with sudden glee that they were all made of children's building bricks, some of them numbered, some with letters. A clockwork policeman chugged past her whirring and clicking as he went.

"Good morning madam; welcome to dream world."

"Good morning," she called after him.

He whirred towards the edge of the kerb and promptly fell over. Amanda moved to help him but was distracted by the sight of something familiar; a face in the crowd, or had she just imagined it?

She peered through the masses whose numbers appeared suddenly to have been replenished. The characters in the scene had grown still more bizarre. She cursed their multitude as she again sought the face in their midst.

"Excuse me please," she wailed at them as she tried to push through the crowd, her voice sounding ethereal, like someone else's, a child maybe.

"I need to see!" The strange voice again, was she saying these things?

The array of freakish beings paid no heed to her pleas, they were now moving around like demented dodgem cars, buffeting each other, showing no signs of cohesion.

"Please!"

She was shouting now but still eliciting no reaction from the people around her, it was as though she wasn't there at all. Through the crowd she caught another glimpse of that familiar face, the man in the crowd, this time she was sure it was him. She started to move in his direction, he seemed to start to move away at exactly the same moment. She cursed him; again the schoolgirl voice.

"Come back here damn you!"

The man showed no signs of having heard her; she started after him, trying to rush but being hampered by the weird dream characters around her. She began to push them, to fight her way through them but they seemed to rebuff her efforts as if trying to prevent her chase.

"That's the way to do it!"

A Dachshund on a moped intoned these words as it passed by on the edge of the road, she was about to try to cross the road but was startled once again by the sound of a car horn, the car responsible seemed even stranger than the one before.

"Damn you all!"

Amanda screamed the words as she tried once more to cross the road. At that moment it seemed as though hundreds of these strange folk crossed the road as well, all walking in her direction, she pushed some more but she was getting nowhere fast.

"Can I interest you in the latest and best anti-dandruff shampoo madam?"

A tall, bald headed man offered her a bottle; on its front were the words 'Tomato Ketchup' in big black letters. Amanda rolled her eyes in disbelief, pushing a second bearded lady out of the way as she did so.

With a suddenness that alarmed her, she was free of the crowd and on the edge of an adjacent road, she could clearly see the man she was following from here, he had made it to the other side. He turned to her and winked. Encouraged, she stepped out and suddenly found herself immersed to the neck in creamy liquid; her senses spun madly and then she realised what it was; milk!

Amanda swam for the far kerb. The man had turned away from her and begun to climb a gentle slope, he no longer seemed aware of her pursuit of him or if he was he didn't seem to care one way or the other.

"Come back…" She tried to call after him but the sickening taste of sour milk in her mouth made her gag and the words came out as a garbled choking sound. With an effort of will, she traversed the milky road and hauled herself out onto the far kerb. A toot-toot from behind her startled her and she turned to locate its source; a small boat chugged by manned by a third bearded woman.

She felt her own chin, half expecting the rough sensation of whiskery hairs there; there were none. Her swim had slowed down her progress and the man she chased had significantly increased the distance between them. She scampered up the slope her feet squelching inside milk-filled shoes.

Ahead of her the man had reached the brow of the hill where he paused for a moment and turned to look back in her direction.

He waved. She waved back, feeling silly and hopelessly exposed to the scrutiny of others, her heart was racing though and she knew more than ever that this man was important and that she must follow him whatever the cost.

As she watched he began to walk again, slowly disappearing from view, first his legs, then his waist, finally his bowler hat; down-slope she thought and quickened her pace. Her pace was unfeasibly quick, she had never moved so quickly in her life as she negotiated the dusty track which wound its way up the hill. Strange how easy it felt to run up hill, it was like her body was no longer her own but that of a finely tuned athlete.

At last, she reached the top of the hill and toppled over the other side, finding herself, amazingly, on a huge water slide. The water that ran down its length was cool, clear and fresh. Forcing herself into an upright position as she slid, she frantically searched for the man in the bowler hat. He was nowhere to be seen.

She cursed once more; what if he hadn't fallen onto the slide? His descent over the brow of the hill had certainly been more dignified than her own; she might be heading in completely the opposite direction but the speed of her descent meant that she could do nothing about that at all, she would not be able to stop herself without seriously hurting herself such was the watery smoothness of her descent.

Amanda realised with some trepidation that she could not see where her journey was taking her; she appeared to be heading into a bottomless world. She gasped as a cloud passed by, was she in the sky?

Strange birds soared and swooped around her convincing her that she was, as impossible as that seemed to her. The sky, she concluded, was impossibly blue, so bright that it hurt her eyes to look into it.

Amanda screamed, loud and long, as the slide suddenly disappeared from beneath her bottom, her arms were flailing as she came to terms with the fact that she was in freefall. Far, far below her she saw what looked like a large lake or a small sea surrounded by pure white sands. Crawling out of the water onto the sand she saw the man she pursued, the bowler hat still perched on the top of his head.

Her fear subsided a little; he had obviously fallen down the slide after all, and looked none the worse for his fall into the sea.

Still Amanda floated down out of the impossibly blue sky; it seemed like hours to her since she had felt the reassuring firmness of the slide beneath her but it no longer seemed to matter to her.

The sea below still seemed miles away, her fall felt akin to slow motion. She forced herself to look up, it wasn't easy, and she almost expected to see a parachute up there. Instead all she saw was the crystal clear sky; of the waterslide there was no sign at all. Bizarrely, she began humming a tune, suddenly enjoying her predicament; she had never felt so free.

"Yankee Doodle came to town." Her voice still sounded like that of a young child.

"Riding on a pony..."

"Damn!" What was it about that song; she could never remember the next line? She knew it was something about ravioli or macaroni but what?

She glanced down once more and was shocked by how near she had come to the water; much of the sandy shoreline had disappeared from view. Amanda tried to remember where the man had crawled ashore. Satisfied she had a general idea she braced herself for her imminent immersion, at least this looked like water; that had to be better than swimming in milk.

When she hit the water she was profoundly shocked, she had expected the stunning sensation of icy cold water but what she got was a feeling of having climbed into a tepid bath. The crystal clearness of the water, though, filled her senses as she plunged to a depth of maybe twenty feet, though it could have been twenty miles, she didn't care, the water was invigorating.

Her descent finally halted, she began to swim for the surface, out into the freshness of the air which seemed excessively clean. Looking skywards she saw the end of a water slide not more than ten feet above the water's surface.

Toot-toot! She looked around for the source of the sound and waved to the bearded lady in the strange little boat she had seen earlier. The woman waved back then sounded the horn once again.

Amanda swam for shore, confident that she would at last find the man that she had chased in so many dreams of late. Her strokes were powerful and confident, she powered through the water at a pace that she would not have thought herself capable of.

Raising her head a little, she tried to see the land but was unable to. Her pace quickened still more, as she turned her head occasionally to breathe, it seemed to her that her arms had become threshing windmill sails cutting through the crystal clear water.

As she swam she drank from the sea. It tasted cold and clear which lent a lie to the temperature she felt the water to be. Once inside her it seemed to invigorate her, sharpening her senses, a sparkling wine of most mysterious origin.

She cried out in shock as the white sand of the beach was suddenly all around her, the speed she had been travelling had literally caused her to run aground rolling idiotically around as she did so.

"Hello."

The man's voice was somehow familiar to her, his face even more so but she had no name to put to either. He no longer wore a bowler hat, in fact all he wore was a pair of boxer shorts that had the words 'jingle balls' on them, a sprig or two of holly had been added for good measure.

"I was just making some soup; would you like some?"

"Soup?" She was bewildered.

"Yes; don't you like soup?"

"Yes…I do like soup."

"Would you like some then?"

"I suppose so, yes."

Soup? Was this man crazy? They were in the middle of nowhere, he had presumably arrived by the same route that she had, how the hell was he going to make soup?

Amanda watched as he rubbed two sticks together, within seconds a small fire was burning. How the hell had he done that she wondered. Then she voiced the question. He shrugged, apparently this was nothing unusual.

"You took a long time to find me; it's been a long time." The man spoke in a relaxed manner, as if they had met in a train station not in the bizarre manner that had brought them together.

"A long time," she repeated idiotically.

"So very long; perhaps it wasn't the same for you."

"The same; I'm sorry I'm not following you."

"Oh but you are."

"I am?"

"Yes, you've followed me for as long as I remember."

"You knew that?"

"Of course I did."

"Then why didn't you stop; why didn't you let me catch up with you?"

"I couldn't."

"Why not?"

"My feet; they just kept moving, I wanted to stop, wanted you to catch up with me but it was like something prevented me from allowing it."

"But now we are here; what does it mean?"

**

The room swam senselessly around her. From a few feet away she thought she saw a dim light source but, that apart, she struggled to make sense of her surroundings. Even as the white light played on her eyes and the concerned voice of Kate Harvey cut across her senses, Amanda was still unable to comprehend that she had awoken from a dream.

Kate had been roused by Amanda's loud cries. Her first thought, at least after she had pushed away the effects of the wine, was that Alfred Williamson had somehow gained entry to the flat and was assailing her flatmate. She had moved with a speed not usually associated with her and she was at Amanda's door before she had even considered the implications of her actions.

Amanda's room had been empty except for her friend who was tossing and turning under the sheets and still calling out to the night. Who the hell was Phillip, Kate thought as she sought to wake her friend from what she guessed was some kind of nightmare?

Perhaps she had called it wrong. When Amanda had started to become coherent after her sudden awakening she seemed somehow disappointed that the dream had been curtailed. Kate felt guilty for panicking and a little silly too. Amanda was a grown woman and, on the whole, a lot more in control of her herself and her life than she was.

She'd retired to the kitchen and made them both a coffee and then sat on the end of Amanda's bed as they drank the hot brew and dunked *Malted Milk* biscuits into their cups. They talked about mundane things; they were just, quite simply, there for each other.

By the time that Kate rinsed out the coffee cups and returned to her bedroom she was quite convinced that meeting Amanda was the best thing that had ever happened to her in her life. She railed at the thought that anyone could want to hurt her friend. Amanda did not have a bad bone in her body.

As far as Kate could remember, her friend had always tried to see the good in people and her kindness was almost a fault. Certainly she had put up with a hell of a lot recently from Kate. As sleep threatened to take her she resolved to try to be a better flatmate, a better person too, Amanda was the ideal role model, and perhaps it was time for Kate to take the hint.

FIFTEEN

September 1959

He had moved into a house in North London, the move was not ideal; for one thing it took him away from the river. The river, as it rolled lazily by on its route out to the estuary and the sea beyond helped him to reflect on things, to get a measure of where he stood. He would have to learn to live with it, to find other ways of finding the space to gather his thoughts together.

It was important that he lived in an area where he was not known to anyone, and so he had made the decision to leave the hospital. His employers were devastated and had tried everything within their power to get him to change his mind. He'd been flattered but not in the mood to reverse his decision. Eventually, reluctantly, they had accepted the inevitable and he'd worked out his notice period with the same degree of professionalism as he'd carried out his entire career. He saved more lives during that time.

His plan had worked out quite well; he would not be spending the rest of his life alone. His research was, to him, the most important thing that he could turn his abundant talent to but he knew he must have assistance. His charm had done that for him, with the hint of a romantic liaison in the air he had succeeded in getting a like minded researcher to join him on his quest for the knowledge that he believed, could revolutionise medical science.

He was quite well off by post war London standards and he had made the house comfortable for the two of them to live in. He'd ensured that they had separate rooms which had seemed to disappoint her at first, but with time she had grown to accept that just sharing a house with him was better than not.

The two of them kept a very low profile. It was important not to draw attention to themselves for fear that the authorities might get an inkling of what was going on in that large house in Leytonstone.

Equipping the laboratory and obtaining the necessary chemicals was always going to be the difficult part and for this he had been forced to break the law. He did so with no compunction, his research was vital and nothing must be allowed to get in the way of it. The bureaucrats had tried to derail him but it would take more than them.

Just three months after leaving St Thomas' he and his colleague were able to begin some preliminary work. He had never felt so alive, so positive and excited about his life. Those dark days in the War when he had waved goodbye to his mother and his old life seemed like a different man, a different dimension. Now he was, at last, free to prove to the world that he was right.

The weeks following the theft of the lab equipment from the hospital had been a bit stressful. He was considered as part of the police enquiries as he suspected he would be. During this time he had retained the tenancy of the small garret room in Lambeth. The house in Leytonstone was not mentioned and, as this was where the stolen equipment was housed, that had been his plan all along.

He had deliberately cut a sad figure for the benefit of the police inspectors, drinking quite heavily he had managed to convince them that he was suffering from some kind of post traumatic stress. A reaction to the war and all the horrors he had witnessed during and after. His career as a surgeon was over, he could barely hold a vodka glass without tremors in his hands.

They had soon lost interest and he had fallen off their radar, he left it a few weeks longer before quietly paying off the outstanding rent and melting away into the night. London was a big city and it was easy to lose yourself in it if you didn't wish to be found. That was exactly his wish and he appeared to have been successful.

He was working from sunrise until sundown, driven by a passion that burned brightly inside him. They thought it couldn't be done, they thought he was borderline mad to even think it might be. He needed no other incentive, they were narrow-minded, and they lacked the mental ability to look beyond the obvious.

Medical research was not about tiny advances in knowledge, proving things that most people already knew were almost certain to be provable, that was not the best use of resources. Risk was what brought reward, calculated risk. Did they really think that he had not thought this through in detail? They were fools and he would show them to be fools.

Things were going slowly though, he had to admit that, at least to himself. The lack of a steady flow of the things he needed led to frustrations and he had been forced to take a step back from his obsession and afford some care towards his partner in the venture who, wearying of his moods and short-temper, was showing signs of abandoning both him and his project. Thus it was that he capitulated and allowed her to sleep with him. This seemed to have alleviated that problem at least but in its stead he now found he was not sleeping well and this was clouding his thought processes. He supposed that over time he would grow used to the changes in his routine, but he was a man who wanted to get where he was going in a hurry and it frustrated him.

It was just before Christmas 1959 when he achieved his first significant breakthrough; and, looking back on the nine months or so since he'd decided to leave the hospital he had to admit that this represented rapid progress of a sort. Thus it was that he'd allowed himself the luxury of enjoying the festivities that year.

SIXTEEN

It had only been a week since the company car had ceased to be part of his life, the sense of loss, minor at the time, had steadily increased and it now represented just another disincentive to getting out of bed in the mornings.

Getting to work by car in this town was tedious and difficult, getting there by public transport was purgatory. He'd decided to hire or buy a second hand car but so far nothing suitable had come to light.

The last few days had disappeared in a depressing tide of bad moods and sleepless nights; work had been a pain in the neck, his lack of interest upsetting the few clients he still had in his portfolio and who were usually too polite to question his application to their financial affairs. He seemed unable to break the mood, swimming in a deep pool of self pity and confusion.

It was only a matter of time before he started to lose those clients, losing clients would mean less commission, less respect from his superiors, maybe even the loss of his position. If things continued like this he would do the decent thing and resign, he had contemplated it often enough in recent months; Jennifer wouldn't be too pleased with him though if he did.

He cast his mind back to their terrible row of around a week ago; to him it felt much longer, a distant but uncomfortable memory. They had made love that night, passionately and with genuine love for each other, something that they had not done for a very long time. For a while afterwards they lay side by side enjoying the silence; enjoying being with each other.

Their love-making, coupled with their violent argument earlier, had numbed them and a healthy tiredness had descended upon them. Sleep had taken Jennifer first, then shortly afterwards Jim succumbed to its clutches also. It was the most restful night he had experienced for months. Not so the nights since then though. That night had offered him genuine hope, perhaps they could reclaim the deep love they had for each other, rebuild the things that had started to fall apart at the seams.

As he ate the cooked breakfast the following morning, probably the best cooked breakfast that Jennifer had made him in a couple of years, things still had an optimistic feel to them. By dinner time that same day though he had started to feel uncomfortable with the over-friendliness that had come between them, it felt brittle, like it might crack at any moment.

By the following day things had reverted back to how they were prior to their spat. They had not made love since and, although he was trying hard to hang on to the memory of that night, he felt that things were slipping away from him again, with it perhaps his marriage was going too. Now he felt dejected, a part of him empty, he couldn't explain why that should be and that didn't make it any easier.

The dreams, too, had come back, clearer and stronger than before. The woman in the nightly images his mind created, she seemed so real but was she? He had thought he had seen her in the street but had he been mistaken? He was no longer sure. Maybe she was real and he had seen her as a face in the crowd without realising it months ago, perhaps he had registered her face subconsciously and then dreamed about her. But to the point of obsession; how did that work; was he losing his mind?

The whole scenario seemed nonsensical, illogical, how the hell could he explain it to himself let alone to Jennifer? He was quite sure that she had sensed the steady decline in him during the last week; she hadn't said anything yet but that was probably only a matter of time. Was he still whispering or even calling out the woman's name in his sleep he wondered? Marie… why Marie; how come he had a ready made name for his dream character and why did she haunt him so?

He punched his large walnut desk with the side of his fist; a release for the frustration that welled inside him and threatened to consume him, the dull thud was satisfying, the slight pain barely relevant, he stood up and walked to the window.

Below him, the town went about its business in the rain, a humdrum town, humdrum people with humdrum lives, was this what life was supposed to be about? He continued to look as he watched mothers pushing children around in tiny, weather beaten pushchairs, old ladies pulled shopping trolleys towing home tonight's supper or tomorrow's breakfast perhaps.

The people looked like ants, all intent on some hidden purpose, scurrying around, each and every one of them with some place to go, some objective to achieve. A visit to a relative perhaps, or a tryst with a lover, maybe a business meeting, he felt alienated from them all and guessed that the reason was that at the present time he lacked any purpose at all in his life.

He continued his self-analysis, why was he never satisfied with his lot in life? He had been moderately successful in everything he had tried but had always felt the need to move on just when things were getting good, as though he was forever depriving himself of the ultimate glory, running away from his own success. There was always the need for change, for betterment, a new challenge, but why? Was that what was wrong with his marriage? Did he feel the need to rip it all up and start again?

He considered this for a while as he watched the driving rain outside and decided that it wasn't; he loved Jennifer immensely he just wasn't making a very good job of showing it at the moment. He continued his reflection; pretty, intelligent wife, nice, healthy kids, nice house with only a small mortgage, no car at the moment but enough money to buy a decent one, good job with employers who rated his abilities; so why was he so unsettled, what more could he want from life?

Did all this discontent stem from the dreams; who was this Marie, was he in love with a character which only existed in his dreams? He thought not, in fact he thought the link between he and Marie went deeper than love but that didn't lead to any answers in his mind. Who was she and why was she destroying his life like this?

Jim adjusted his gaze, seeking his reflection in the glass, he looked tired and stressed, his thoughts went back to the night in the study when, through a drunken haze, he had been sure that someone was looking in at him; was it possible he really was losing his mind? He didn't think so; he had cut down on his drinking and nothing had changed in terms of the thoughts that were dominating his conscious thought, whatever was afflicting him he didn't think it was madness.

Glancing at his watch he plucked his jacket off his 'top of the range' office chair and pressed the *on* button on his top of the range answer-phone. The Green Man was only two streets away, they did a nice range of bar meals and, more importantly, the beer was good. In the days before the current management regime had taken over the company, many a good lunch hour had been spent in that particular establishment and he hoped a good one was in store today as well. His improving mood was bettered when Joanne, the leggy and fun receptionist asked if she might tag along for a swift glass of wine and a chicken tikka masala.

**

The warmth emanating from the glowing embers of the fire were a welcome contrast from the November chill outside. The smell of fresh and stale beer was partially cloaked by the appetizing smells emanating from the tiny pub kitchen. Jim and Joanne approached the bar where the smiling face of Jack Smithurst, the proprietor of this popular establishment, greeted them in the way that only good pub landlords can manage.

"The usual is it Jim?"

"Yes please Jack and a glass of dry white wine."

Jim was surprised that his visits to the pub had been sufficiently frequent for the landlord to know his drink but dismissed the thought, a good landlord probably studied the drinking habits of all his clients whether frequent visitors or not.

He smiled at Joanne; an attractive girl and good company, he tried not to let her know that he fancied her but in truth she probably knew damn well, after all, all of his male work colleagues had an opinion about Joanne and she probably knew it and milked it for all it was worth.

"I'll grab a couple of seats and take a look at the menu just in case there's something on there that grabs my fancy more than the chicken tikka."

Joanne, probably sensing his sudden discomfort did the diplomatic thing and left him at the bar. He watched her as she walked across the room admiring her poise and, in particular, the shapeliness of her legs.

The cosy lighting and warm, inviting open fire coupled with the friendly banter of working people set the Green Man apart from the other town centre pubs at lunchtime. It was a good place to come and just lose oneself in thought and beer, looking around he saw plenty of people doing just that right now.

As he carried the drinks over to the table where the radiant smile of his work colleague awaited him, he realised that he felt on edge. It was as though he anticipated that something was going to happen, or that someone would walk in and change his life; was that Marie? He couldn't be sure of anything anymore and he was frowning by the time he reached the table.

"A penny for your thoughts Jim; you look unhappy."

"Waste of money Jo; I'm alright."

"Yes; and I'm Nicole Kidman."

"Hello Nicole. Really I don't want to bore you with my problems, that's not why we're playing hooky from work is it?"

"It's not a problem, you've just bought me a glass of wine, and I'm putty in your hands now." She smiled and he relaxed a little.

"My marriage seems to be failing, I don't like my job anymore, and I'm obsessing on a woman I've never met. I'm drinking too much, my feet smell like old Camembert cheese and the dog's got fleas. That just about sums it up."

Joanne smiled and took a sip of her drink.

"Pretty impressive I'd say," she said at last.

"Have you decided what you want to eat?" He changed the subject.

"I'll stick with the tikka masala. Now what's this about a woman Jim?"

"I'll go and order the food." He stood and made for the bar; Joanne watched him go, intrigued, she hadn't taken Jim for that kind of man, she knew he liked her but she felt safe with him. Was he looking to play away from home? She hoped not, she knew Jennifer and liked her. If he was though, she would be pretty flattered to be the recipient of his attentions.

Jim returned, eventually, clutching two sets of knives and forks wrapped in green napkins, he hoped that Joanne might drop the subject; no chance.

"Who is this mystery woman who you say you're obsessing on Jim, please tell?"

"If I knew I would tell you, trust me."

"You're not making too much sense."

"Fine; none of it makes any sense to me, why should you be immune?"

"Where did you meet, or see this woman?"

"I told you before; in my dreams."

"You are, of course, joking."

"In fact I'm not. I dream about this woman virtually every single night, I'm obsessed with her but I don't know who she is. I thought I saw her about a week ago, in the flesh, but when I tried to follow her I lost her, or more accurately, she lost me."

"Bizarre; is that why you ran out of the building that morning a few days ago?"

"Yes it was, and you're right it is bizarre. I even have a name for her, Marie. Unfortunately I periodically call out this name when I'm asleep. As you might imagine Jennifer is not best pleased."

"I can imagine."

"Perhaps you can; it's not a comfortable situation."

"So your marriage; is it over?"

"Not yet; not quite."

"I like Jennifer."

"Yes, well I love her but this is not good. I'm trapped; I have no control over what is happening to me."

The meals arrived and they both stopped the conversation while the pleasant waitress attended to them. Jim wished that the conversation had never happened; his earlier sense of well-being had diminished, not quite gone altogether though.

What happened next stunned him. Joanne; gorgeous Joanne who every man in the company coveted in their dreams told him something that knocked him sideways.

"If your marriage does go tits up Jim, I want to be the first to know. You can dream about some ghost woman all you like but if you and Jennifer split up I want to know about it. Do you understand what I'm saying to you?"

He didn't. She spelled it out to him and he was shocked that someone like him could possibly attract someone like Joanne. He even managed to think about something other than the woman in his dreams for the rest of the day.

Was he simply undergoing some sort of middle age crisis he wondered? Was it that simple; that he simply needed to feel that he remained an attractive proposition to the opposite sex? He thought about it but failed to convince himself that this was the solution. Still, if nothing else, it was highly flattering and good for his ego that Joanne saw him as a good catch.

SEVENTEEN

Even the memory of that night was painful; the tightening sensation in his chest had been frightening, so intense. His breathing was laboured, his whole body trembled, it seemed he was incapable of taking in enough oxygen to compensate for that he had used during his unexpected exercise.

On reaching the dingy hovel that he called home, he had propped himself up on the bed using the two grubby looking pillows provided by his landlady. She had heard him come in; she would have had to be profoundly deaf not to in fact, like a frightened animal he had fumbled with his keys, noisily mounted the stairs, still at a half-run then; reaching his room he had locked the door behind him.

Just seconds later she was at the door asking him if he was alright, could she get him anything. Through clenched teeth and with considerable effort he had managed to convince her he was fine, it was long seconds though before she left the door, apparently satisfied, and he heard her heavy-footed descent of the stairs.

Several minutes had passed before he was finally able to convince himself that he would survive his ordeal; the pain in his chest subsided very slowly. He turned his mind to the girl, Kate Harvey, why had she chosen that particular night to show up early at the flat? It had taken him so long to come up with the courage to do what he knew he must do. He spat in frustration, the green phlegm landing with a nauseating plop on the threadbare carpet beside the bed.

Now all this seemed like an age ago, something that happened to a different person in a different time and place. Reaching for the half-empty bottle of vodka beside him he took a long swallow wincing at the pains that wracked his tired old body as he reached out for it. The liquid relaxed him, he needed to relax, he had gone out on a limb this time and he was panicking a little.

Thoughts returned to that night, what a bloody fiasco it had been, so much planning just wiped out in an instant. He had been so sure that it was the right time, the night when he would finally get to speak to his little girl, get the chance to tell her what had happened, clear his conscience, right the wrongs of the past; his past.

One thing was certain, time was very short now, soon he would die and his guilty conscience would travel with him to his pauper's grave, which was why he had to do what he was doing now, whatever the cost. He winced at his pain; the cancer was eating him alive now.

 He contemplated, not for the first time, just collecting his things and returning to his hovel to die, and then dismissed the idea, he had to do this; he had to speak to his girl. A tear had begun an uneven descent through the stubble on his cheek and was quickly followed by more. His body must not fail him now, one last effort, and if the girl, Kate Harvey, got in his way again he would despatch her to her maker, he felt the knife in his pocket. This was his insurance policy.

He had killed before; war did that to a man, but never a relative innocent who happened to be in the wrong place at the wrong time. He hoped it wouldn't come to that.

Now, as he sat in the gathering darkness of Amanda Fellows' flat, the vodka bottle in one hand and the knife in the other he allowed a smile to form through his tears of pain, soon, at last, it would all be over and he could die in peace.

**

They had no bloody right to turn him down all those years before; he was the best in his field, the very best. If those faceless bureaucrats had possessed the courage to endorse his research then it would all be different, none of this bloody mess would have ever happened and he wouldn't be sitting here in her flat with feelings of contrition.

The vodka bottle, now empty, lay on the floor beside the chair on which he sat and waited for her to come home. Why had she chosen tonight to be late? The smaller, whisky bottle that he had retrieved from the inside of his overcoat was now half-empty too, but the alcohol was not having the effect it should have, he was too highly strung, too focused on the job in hand to let it get to him. He took another swig and relished the heat in his throat, for seconds at least he could forget the pain created by those growing cells in his body as the cancer slowly choked the life out of him.

It was really quite dark in the room now; it had been broad daylight when he had broken in to the flat. It was easy for him to do; he'd broken into many places during his life. He'd needed to steal the laboratory equipment so that he could continue his research after the faceless bastards withdrew his funding; that was one of the times he'd had to use his skills. Bloody hypocrites; what was moral about test-tube babies? What he was doing was similar but far more ground-breaking. He had always known that he could bring his project to fruition but they had deemed it unlikely to work, a waste of government funding and morally bankrupt. He had made it work despite everything, his only crime was to be years ahead of his time.

It was just after the Second World War when Vladimir Kowalski first conceived his plan, a highly respected surgeon, his work in the field of genetics was ground-breaking. Towards the end of the war he had been in the field with the allied troops as they advanced through Europe towards their ultimate victory.

In those days he had witnessed horrors which had been almost inconceivable to a man dedicated to the preservation of human life. How could men live with themselves after doing such things to their fellow men? He had no answer to that even after all these years; in fact things were even worse now.

The war left an indelible impression on him, a festering scar, and a voracious nightmare that devoured him when he thought about it. Many nights he had spent sitting upright in his bed with the light on, too afraid to reclaim the sleep which were the resting place of those terrible times, those war induced atrocities.

After the war had ended he settled in England again and worked at St Thomas' Hospital, he continued working as a surgeon but his vocation lay in innovative medical research. The day he had told his colleagues at the research institute what he intended to do was like a still photograph, to this day he could picture their looks of amazement, in some cases embarrassment, but he knew he could do it, he had done the science.

Many of his colleagues had been visibly horrified, others visibly intrigued, none particularly visibly enthusiastic; his idea had been thrown out unreservedly and Vladimir had resigned unreservedly. At that time he brought a large terraced house in Leytonstone, he converted one of the four bedrooms into a laboratory where he could begin work on his ambitious project.

The two children, born some twenty years later were the result of his research, of trial and error, much failure and little success. But in the end he had been proven right, the faceless bureaucrats that denied him would never know but he had prevailed against all the odds.

He had not worked alone though; the very nature of his work required a colleague, a female colleague, a guinea pig of sorts really. Phillipa West had been his more than willing protégé, she had been a colleague at the institute and had been intrigued by Kowalski's ideas.

Not least influential in her decision to leave the institute and help him was her desire to become his lover as well as his colleague, he knew of her interest and he used it, trying as best he could to keep her at arm's length, always encouraging her but never really taking it to the next level, she wanted to marry him but it was not for him.

Twenty years she had worked for him, twenty years of undying support until, at last, he was successful. Vladimir Kowalski, surgeon and Polish exile, had proved it was possible to fertilise a human egg outside of the womb and to maintain the subsequent embryo to full term by replicating the conditions that it would be party to in the womb.

The egg, though, had split, two embryos developed, this was almost too much to hope for; would they both survive? Would they develop into normal human beings or would he be presiding over a freak show? If they did survive, what would be the consequences for the children born of such an experiment?

Phillipa had wanted to tell the whole world when the two children were successfully brought into the world; Vladimir had begged her for restraint. "Let us see what happens before we boast about our prowess," he had cautioned. She was not for listening to him, here was a proud 'mother' one who had experienced no morning sickness, no labour pains, no bulging waistline and no craving for cottage cheese, and she was not to be denied.

The two of them argued; it was not pleasant; a scuffle had ensued resulting in Phillipa losing her balance and tumbling awkwardly down the stairwell.

His medical knowledge was sufficiently sound to diagnose a broken neck, indeed a layman might have suspected her fate on seeing the impossible angle at which her head was positioned in relation to her body. He had thrown her body in the Thames, sufficiently weighed down with rocks from the garden to ensure that she would be permanent company for any fish which survived the pollutants in the capital's liquid lifeblood.

Guilt was a hard thing to live with for him; he had known, perhaps for the first time, just what a man felt like when he took a life for some other reason than a senseless war being thrust upon him.

At the moment when a trigger is squeezed and a man ceases to be a man and instead becomes a soldier seemed almost comfortable by comparison. His life was forever altered, he supposed that in a way he had grown to love Phillipa in the same way that he knew she had always loved him. What seemed like a lifetime later he had learned to live with the guilt, he had also learned to accept that the man he had been before had ceased to exist that night.

His drinking had become heavier following that period in his life and his wartime nightmares had returned with a vengeance, he had become very reclusive, only leaving the house to buy essentials and more drink. His only regular visitor was a fellow Pole, Anna Karpok who had married a soldier during the war and settled in London with her husband afterwards.

Vladimir had proved very supportive towards her when her husband had been killed some twelve years before, returning home from the pub one evening he was hit by a bus, incidentally the only time that particular bus had run on schedule for days.

Anna had never forgotten his kindness and visited him occasionally; she knew of his experiment, the only person left alive who did, she asked no awkward questions about Phillipa's sudden absence and eventually became his only contact with the outside world.

He thought again about the experiment; remembered the excitement of the early months as the embryos began to resemble human beings, ten toes, ten fingers, two seemingly healthy babies, one male, one female, the most unique of twins.

And then the 'birth' he had almost lost the girl, ironic that would have been, death at child-birth given a whole new meaning.

The thoughts that passed through his mind that night, that Phillipa was actually giving birth three months after her death, that what he was doing here wasn't just unique, it was possibly morally bankrupt too, had the institute been correct after all to reject his research? Who, after all, could bring these children up; him?

Both children survived, they cried, they slept, cried again, drank the baby milk he had given to them, filled their nappies, then filled them again. It was almost a month after their birth that he finally began to accept his experiment had somehow created two perfectly healthy children.

He had named the girl Marie and the boy Phillip; Marie had been his mother's name and Phillip, well; he felt he owed his colleague that at least. There would still be many problems to overcome, would the children have reduced immunity to disease and infection on account of their means of conception? Only time would tell him that. Would they be mentally brilliant, sub-normal, would they be geniuses or fools or would they die before he got the answer to any of these questions?

Anna loved the children, doted on them in fact; she provided nappies, baby clothes and food for the delightful offspring of such an unlikely birth. Her visits became considerably more frequent. Vladimir himself, marvelling at her natural maternal instincts, had found himself falling in love with his Good Samaritan.

She brought a pram and would often walk the children late at night so as not to arouse suspicion among the neighbours as from where the two young children had materialised. Though Vladimir suspected that the neighbours knew perfectly well that there were children in the house, after all, both had a particular talent for expressing their desire for food in the early hours of the morning, he indulged Anna's wishes.

The children were just under a year old when things started to go wrong; Phillip had had colds and recovered, Marie had had measles, miraculously failing to pass on the infection to her twin brother, she too had recovered from her infection; it seemed that the immune systems in both children were working perfectly well.

Unfortunately for Vladimir, his own aging body was not in such pristine condition; the stroke he had was frighteningly sudden, he hadn't seen it coming at all. He had not felt particularly well for a couple of days but nothing could have prepared him for the crushing pain that ensued, the world had swirled around him as he crashed to the ground in agony.

Faces, memories flashed before his eyes. The soldier in the trench in France with only half a face, others with limbs missing, his own father's face the last time he had seen him, a broken man, drowning in vodka. The look on Phillipa's face as she had lain at the foot of the stairs, her expression one of surprise mixed with pleading and the agony of a sudden death. The worried face of Anna Karpok standing over him, her partially naked body seeming to be in another world, one that he had left behind, the memory of their love-making seemed equally distant, then there was only darkness.

It was more than six weeks before he was well enough to sit up in bed. Anna had visited him, even bringing the children on occasion. He was unable to hold a conversation with her; indeed he was barely able to comprehend what she was saying to him in their one-sided conversations. Those early weeks after his stroke were dark days from which he feared he would not recover. But recover he had, to a fashion at least and that was how he had come to be here today; sitting in the darkened flat, watching, waiting.

It was as he was beginning to see progress in his recovery that Anna stopped visiting him. There was no warning. On her final visit she had brought the children with her and had told him how much she loved him and how she hoped that they might one day marry when he got out of the hospital; then, nothing.

He found he missed her immensely, her kindness, her frequent visits when he had no-one left in the world but her. Her rugged, if unspectacular, beauty had endeared her to him over the many years he had known her. Then she was not there any more; what the hell could have happened to her?

Anger turned to disappointment followed by grave concern, it wasn't just Anna he was missing, what had happened to the children, had she kidnapped them and if so why?

It was three more months before he was able to leave the hospital and it was with considerable trepidation that he visited first his own home and then, reluctantly, Anna's. She had evidently not been to his home for some time, the preponderance of junk mail and bills were evidence of this.

It was several years since he had visited Anna's terraced home despite the fact that it was located less than a mile from his own. He was out of breath by the time he got there. The sight of the windows dirty and without curtains was the first sign of something being wrong, a look through the glass at the bare room beyond, devoid of furniture and carpets was the second.

"Anna died." Those words had been stored in his mind ever since, the neighbour who said them could never have known just what those words meant to him. Where were the children she was looking after he asked, his question answered with a shrug. Where was he to start looking for them; what was he to do?

The words had come from Anna's neighbour who had turned out to be a kindly old lady named Emma Beckett. He remembered her from his previous visits as someone who was frequently seen twitching the curtains, watching the world at large from the shelter of her own cosy little home. She invited him in for a cup of tea and, despite himself, he had accepted, he wanted answers and perhaps she might have them after all.

Anna, it turned out, had not shared the resilience that he had when dealing with a major medical trauma; she had been out shopping, the children with her at the time when she collapsed. She was dead before the ambulance even arrived, a massive heart attack apparently.

Again he asked about the children, trying not to show his anxiety lest he invited difficult questions from Mrs Beckett. The truth was he was feeling strangely paternal, the children were, after all, his offspring even allowing for their method of conception and development.

Despite his gentle probing, even the formidable fount of knowledge that Emma Beckett was, she seemed to genuinely have no idea where they were. The slight frown lines around her eyes told him that she was growing curious at his concern and that it was time to leave.

For a crazy moment he had contemplated killing her, he had done it before to protect his secret and he didn't doubt that it would be easier a second time, but nonetheless he dismissed the notion, thanked her for her time and for the tea and biscuits and left.

As he left she suggested he might contact the local authority to determine the whereabouts of the children but wouldn't that only draw attention to him? In any case they could be in foster care, perhaps a children's care home of some sort. London was a big city and he was a weakened man for his recent health problems.

Mrs Beckett was right about one thing though, the local authorities were the most likely source of information. How could he approach them though? What would he say to them? He couldn't say he was the children's father, there were, of course, no birth certificates; in fact no evidence at all that Phillip and Marie had ever existed. And who was the mother they would ask; it would be difficult to explain that their mother had died three months before they had been born now wouldn't it?

It was hopeless. The only thing he thought he might be able to do was to break in and try to locate the records; another needle in a haystack situation.

His raid on the municipal building had been successful in that he was not caught in the act; unsuccessful in that he had found no records of where the children might be. He knew it was hopeless but he kept trying anyway. Through the yellow pages he had located two children's homes in the area.

He spent many hours outside the gates of one of them; his instinct told him that they were in there. The moss covered bench just beyond its perimeter wall became his regular spot as he watched the comings and goings from the large Victorian building pretending to read a newspaper.

His vigil proved futile, when the winter set in he had been forced to abandon it, returning to his house in Leytonstone, which, like him, was falling into a state of disrepair. He concluded that he had lost the children for good; they were not just his offspring, they constituted his life's work and his obsession, how cruel fate had been to take away all that mattered to him in his life.

The depression into which he sunk was almost the finish of him; on dark and often drunken nights he toyed with the knife which he had removed from the body of the soldier near Paris and which he had kept with him ever since; it reminded him of the futility of war, the importance of life but it also reminded him how simple it was to end one.

He reflected on his life, a hotchpotch of mercy and compassion interspersed with arrogance and even cruelty. He thought back to the moment that Phillipa had fallen down the stairs, how callously he had dealt with the situation, so cool and clinical like the surgeon he once had been.

Since that sorry chapter in his life story he had never quite been able to see himself as a complete human being; he had lost something of his very substance that night and the loss of Anna and the children had removed more of him.

Those dark days that continued for almost four years were his nadir, until now of course. He decided he had to leave London and its strangling grip, the choking nature of the city he had once so loved, the city now exhausted him. He had wearied at travelling to and from the small café where, against all the odds he had secured a part-time job, he the great surgeon serving tea and coffee with shaking hands, sneaking a mouthful of vodka on occasion to stay the tremors, or so he believed.

This was a man who had made a breakthrough that would have stunned the scientific world had he been able to tell that world of his achievement and now he went home each evening smelling of cooking oil. His self-pity was painful but an inevitable consequence of his situation.

The bed-sit he acquired in the village of Woodburn was ample for his few needs, his life had become very simple, no longer the fanatical desire to discover the undiscovered; attain the unattainable.

He managed to get a job as a postman. He had been very lucky to get it in fact; being out and about helped him to rediscover a relish for life. His tired old body and slight frame was perhaps not suited to the position but the only other two applicants for the position had both had noteworthy criminal records and the pressing need to fill the post prior to the Christmas rush had secured him the posting.

For two years Vladimir had found contentment in his life that had been missing for years; leaving London had been the key. The nightmares that had beset him there were now infrequent and the hurt of losing his children, though it never went away completely, was now manageable in the way that all bereavements can be over a period of time.

The newspaper that had sat poking out of his letterbox one day when he returned home from work had looked normal enough as he pulled it free. He made a pot of tea and grilled a couple of slices of toast before he spread the newspaper out and began to read its contents; it was to change his life again.

'Local Man in Horrific Wife Murder,' even that hadn't seemed too earth-shattering, living in London for years provided a certain immunity to such headlines, the denseness of the population there led to stresses and tensions not always present elsewhere. Here it was not so prevalent but the horror factor passed him by at first.

The story had been sensationalised, after all that's what sells newspapers; there were a wealth of statements from shocked neighbours stating what a mild mannered man the perpetrator had seemed. There were pictures too; Alfred Williamson did not, Vladimir had to agree, look like a maniac, his wife was girl next door pretty, and the daughter…

Adrenaline pulsed through him causing his chest to tighten and he worried that his medical condition was returning to claim him. The girl was Marie, he was certain of it; in fact he had no doubt whatsoever the more he looked at the grainy newsprint, even the small but barely detectable mole on her tiny chin which both of the twins had.

They had changed her name to Amanda, he couldn't expect anything else really, after all when Anna died who was there to correct them, and it turned out that the family lived in a small town only an hour and a half away by local bus. He had rushed out of the room, grabbing his coat off a peg as he went, his tea barely half drunk and the toast virtually untouched and headed for the bus station.

In hindsight his journey was as futile as his vigil outside the children's home back in London, the house wasn't hard to find, the newspaper had revealed the street name in its coverage of the story but the house was boarded up, police tape marked the site as a crime scene and a lone police officer kept a vigil outside, perhaps the scene of crime officer's were inside, he couldn't get close enough to tell without drawing attention to himself.

A few neighbours, Mrs Beckett wannabees peeped around their curtains as he walked as nonchalantly as he could down the street. None seemed to pay much attention to the old man who walked along; still wearing his postman's uniform as he went.

His daughter had, of course, eluded him again. He had even less chance of finding his daughter here in this strange town by asking questions than he had following Anna's death; and so for him the chase continued throughout the years, it had been nineteen years before he was lucky enough to find her again.

Once again it had been a local newspaper that had assisted him; her photograph appeared amongst a crowd of people who had gathered to wish a fond farewell to a retiring member of staff at the company where she worked.

The name under the picture had been Amanda Fellows. Did that mean she had married he wondered; or could it be that she had been adopted and her surname had changed to Fellows on account of that? He certainly hoped it was the latter

If she were to marry and try to start a family who knew what would happen? He certainly didn't, that was why he had to find her, and it was in the lap of the gods as to whether she could give birth to healthy children, just as her very own birth had been all those years ago.

He vowed to find her, to confront her and tell her what she was, who she was and how she had come to be and, well, he so wanted to see her again, the fruits of his labour, his research, to hug her as he had when she was tiny and vulnerable.

What if she knew where Phillip was; would he get to see both of his offspring before he succumbed to the cancer that was slowly eating him away? The hairs on the back of his head stood aloft as he considered the thought.

But now it had come down to this, sitting here in the dark and lonely flat that Amanda Fellows called her home, full of the liquor he had consumed in the name of courage and he knew she would be home very shortly from the clock on the mantelpiece, which he could just make out in the gloom by the light of a streetlight outside.

He had found another bottle of whisky in one of the cupboards, there was a lot of booze here in fact and he found himself worrying in a paternal way that his daughter might be drinking herself to an early grave. It was an ironic thought given the amount he was drinking to take the edge of the pain he lived with night and day.

If the bitch girl, Kate Harvey, came home first, this time he would not hesitate to use the knife on her, the knife of a slain soldier retrieved all those years ago. He just could not allow himself to fail again, his end felt very imminent indeed.

**

The sound of footsteps on the landing outside the door stirred him; despite the drink, his senses reached a high level of alertness. A key was being inserted into the door of the flat and was being turned.

Vladimir was seated in the armchair that he had deliberately positioned so that it faced the door into the hallway so that she would see him as soon as she entered the room; would she remember her father; the man who had hugged her as a tiny child the father whose brilliance was responsible for her very existence?

Would it be his Marie though or would it be the bitch? As the door to the flat was closed and he heard the click of the hallway light he tensed his body in expectation. He seemed to know the answer even before the door swung open, light from the hallway beyond pervading the darkness and hurting his eyes, the light in the flat clicked on to add to his discomfort and sudden disorientation.

For a moment she looked deep into his eyes and he was sure that there was a flicker of recognition there, or at least something, pity maybe. He was sobbing, wracking sobs that hurt him with their body wrenching intensity; it was as though in that moment a lifetime of mental agony had been removed. He could feel the warmth of his tears as they poured down his grizzled cheeks, for just a moment he felt preternaturally alive.

Still Amanda did not move, how the hell had he got in here with a police guard outside was all she could think of. Even when the old man, whose tears she could not tell were of joy or pain began to clutch at his chest and the agony appeared on his face, she still stood watching and silent.

For Vladimir Kowalski these moments represented the ultimate disappointment in his life, he knew he was dying; and that his daughter would never hear the tale he had to tell; that he would never find out if Phillip had survived and that his time on the spinning ball they called the Earth was over.

A crazy thought passed through his mind as he leaned forward in agony and fell from chair to floor. He was the second parent that this poor young woman had seen die in front of her but this time she would not know it, she would not be covered in the blood. It was a lot for anyone to take. He hoped, desperately, that she would be strong enough to deal with it and live a happy life.

Amanda looked at the slumped, dishevelled body on her floor for quite some time after his battle to stay alive had been lost, the scream which had locked in her throat when she had first seen the figure in the chair finally filled the room and reverberated through the whole building.

EIGHTEEN

He was cold; the wind was turning and was now blowing from the North East. He had a good knowledge of such things, his time in the army, post war national service, had taught him survival techniques that he retained to the present day.

He had found some berries to eat, blackberries on the brambles by the side of the road down which he walked. They were a little bit overripe but he knew their nutritional value. The British Army trained its men well and he knew what he could and couldn't eat from the terrain around him. His feet were hurting, the boots he had salvaged were ill fitting and his toes were cramped inside them. That wasn't good, he still had a long way to go and, although time wasn't a factor in the grander scale of his plan, the sooner he got where he was going and began to make plans the better.

It was raining again, did it always rain? He had been away too long and little things like the weather were of no concern to him where he had been. He tried to remember what it was like before but great swathes of his memory seemed to be missing, as if the things they had done to him had somehow wiped his memory banks clean.

What things they had done; the electrodes, the injections, the medication that made the world visible only through a foggy mist that threatened to swallow him in its embrace. His head felt stuffed with cotton wool and it was only now, after some days, or was it only hours, on the road that he was starting to feel sensations that had long ago been suppressed.

Ahead the country road down which he walked seemed to bend a little; it was hard to tell by the occasional light of the moon which poked through the rapidly moving black clouds only from time to time.

Although he wore no watch little clues were telling him that dawn was not too far away, as soon as the grey light began to show he would need to find a place to stay and see out the *daylight hours, not that there was likely to be too much in the way of light judging by the weather conditions that prevailed.*

In the near distance he could hear the sound of dogs barking. The likelihood was that there was a farm nearby. An old barn would be an ideal place to hang out for the day but the dogs would be a problem, he might be forced to sleep rough again as he had the night before.

Sleeping out in the open had a multitude of problems attached to it. For a start it made him more likely to be discovered by some passer by, perhaps a dog walker, which would present problems that he hoped he would not have to deal with. On a more practical level, it further exposed him to the wind and the rain which were working in tandem to weaken his spirits and resolve for the task at hand.

That task, for the time being at least, was nothing more than avoiding detection and maintaining what little strength he had. There was more to it than that, of course, a lot more, but he was trying not to think about that lest it take his concentration away from getting to his destination.

He heard the sound of a car, its engine noise carried on the wind to where he walked, it was probably as much as a mile away and he would have ample time to find a position at the side of the road from where the vehicle could pass by without seeing him. He found a gateway into a field, the ground beneath his feet was sticky with the mud, implying that the livestock that grazed in the field were herded through the gate and along the road at some times.

He crouched low down next to the gatepost and waited as the sound of the vehicle got louder. He watched as it sped by, a police patrol car, but that was just a coincidence, they weren't looking for him, they were probably heading into the next village to pick up a newspaper, a cup of tea and a bacon sandwich.

For a moment or two, he continued to crouch there, listening for the sounds of other vehicles, but, at this early hour, there were none. The dogs were barking again as he rejoined the road, trying to scrape the thick mud off the bottom of his boots as he walked. The dogs were not barking at him, perhaps a fox stalked the farmyard looking for a hearty breakfast of its own.

The rain was now more of a persistent mist as the first light of dawn made the terrain through which he walked slowly visible. The sound of the barking dogs was now a distant one and he looked around him with only shelter in mind as he trudged along the road.

Soon more traffic would be about and by then he would need to be out of sight. To his left, beyond the dry stone wall that was endemic in this part of the country, the ground dipped away and in the resultant valley, through which a small stream was running, a farm was nestled among a small outcrop of trees. The barns to the right of the grey stone farmhouse looked very run-down and he pictured a farmer that had fallen on hard times.

This place had possibilities he decided and took the risk of leaving the road and descending the slope in such a way as to remain invisible to anyone who might look out of the windows of the farmhouse.

So it was that he found the barn, relatively waterproof and, mercifully, out of the wind where he would be able to spend the day. There were even bales of straw on which he could settle down and try to get some sleep. Above all, if the farm had a dog, it hadn't been alerted to his presence.

Eating a few of the berries he had saved from earlier, he settled down and, draping the overcoat over him, nestled down in the straw to a dreamless and undisturbed sleep.

NINETEEN

The near silent but monotonous ticking of the carriage clock on the mantelpiece which Jim had brought her on their second wedding anniversary seemed like thunder to her ears. For over an hour this had been the only noise to pervade the air in the room where Jennifer Dowley sat in miserable reflection.

The knitting, a sweater for Jim, lay discarded on the arm of the chair in which she sat; a half-completed crossword sat on the coffee table in front of her, filled with errors where she had been unable to concentrate.

By the fire, even the dog hadn't bothered to raise its head from its warm slumber. Outside, the rain that had been incessant for days had finally stopped and the wind which often made ghostly sounds as it blew around the eaves of the house had also dropped and the world seemed to be unnaturally still, as if, like her, it was waiting for something to happen.

The children were asleep upstairs, they had wanted to stay up until their father had returned home from work, a few bedtime stories read in the half-light afforded by the light on the landing had quelled their young protests and cajoled them to sleep; it wouldn't have done to let them stay up. Jennifer had serious doubts as to whether Jim would come home at all tonight or any time soon.

Jennifer hadn't really wanted to find out about his infidelity, after their argument the other night she had realised that she would always love Jim no matter what he did, he was a part of her. She hadn't believed his story, of course, how could he have expected her to? She was, after all, an intelligent woman, despite the crossword, and that was one of the reasons he had been attracted to her in the first place.

She had made up her mind to forgive and try to forget. She had stupidly hoped that his conscience might force him into ending the affair but the phone call to his office this afternoon, made in innocence to ask him to pick up a loaf of bread on his way home, had served to quash any hopes she had of that.

Jim had left the office at lunchtime and had not returned, she had been told by the receptionist who added for good measure that she thought he would have returned home hours ago; but he hadn't had he?

It was now nearly midnight and she was out of her mind with worry. He had never been this late before, at least not without warning her by telephone beforehand. Was he alright; was he even alive? Despite everything she hoped he was both of these things but how could she tell; who could she contact?

Jennifer thought about calling the police but what would they make of that? She didn't think they would take her seriously, not yet at least; just another wayward husband out with his mates or courting a lady; another broken marriage in the offing, police priorities, budgets and all that jazz.

Her eyes felt hot with welling tears; tears she was determined would not be shed in either grief or anger. She pondered their marriage once again trying to focus on the happy times; the early days of their union had been all she could possibly have hoped for.

She met Jim at a New Year's Eve party held at the home of a mutual friend, and though she had thought herself brazen at the time she had marched right up to the attractive man who her friend had failed to introduce her to; though Jennifer had been willing her to all night. A few too many gin and tonics had done the trick, giving her the courage. Despite all that had gone on in their lives since that night she had no regrets about doing that.

Jim had already drunk a fair amount himself and had been struck by her forthrightness. They had chatted incessantly, toasted the New Year and sang Auld Lang Syne then chatted more, until four o'clock in fact; by which time most other guests had either left or fallen asleep after their over-indulgence.

They had arranged to meet for dinner at a local restaurant, Rafferty's, the following week, such was the instant rapport they had struck up. She always remembered that first date, she had chosen to go by bus so that she could have a drink with her meal and had missed it; she used public transport so rarely her timetable was hopelessly out of date, by the time she had reached the restaurant she had fully expected Jim to have left already. He had waited though, and that spoke volumes to her. She gave credence to her initial feelings for him, after all she wasn't in the habit of throwing herself at a man.

He had been the perfect gentleman; which also impressed her, he wasn't out for all he could get like some other men she had dated and been hurt by. The meal had been wonderful and they had returned to Rafferty's many times in the early days, it had become 'their place.'

Her whole life had changed after meeting Jim; he seemed to have a God given talent for making her feel good about herself and about her position in life, she felt important but most of all she felt loved. Prior to meeting him she had not been confident in company, especially crowds, the world now seemed a different place, and it was like her life had just begun, as if she had morphed into a different person.

Her old life seemed dull and grey, or black and white perhaps, now it had colour in it, it was a kaleidoscope. Jim had given her that and she loved him for it; she would always love him, he was a very special man despite his faults.

Now, for whatever reason, Jim had decided that he no longer wished to be her knight in shining armour, but why; when had things started to change?

The children; she had often wondered whether the children had been the beginning of the end of their special relationship. Had he hinted that he didn't want to start a family at a time when she had been mad keen to do so? She tried to think back but didn't think so. He certainly had not been a natural father though, sometimes she had winced at his efforts even though she knew he was trying his best and the children didn't seem to notice.

For all the things he excelled at; and that was a lot of things, paternity did not sit easily with him. She loved her children desperately but there were times when she tried to imagine how her marriage might have been without them.

It was soon after the birth of their first that Jim had begun to drink heavily; she'd tried to stop him but nagging about it only seemed to make matters worse. He seemed always to have things, major things, on his mind and resented her interference.

If only he would share his fears or whatever else it was that led to the long silences and brooding then perhaps she could help; she certainly wanted to. Slowly, but perceptibly a divide came between them, a divide that became a gulf and now a chasm; but why?

Then his wretched dreams had started and the talking in his sleep, his health was deteriorating and he seemed either not to notice or to not want to do anything about it. His face had lost its fullness, those dark pools that were his eyes lost their lustre and, on days when he didn't have to go to work, he often failed to shave.

Her feelings were mixed; her concern for the man she loved tempered by his persistent mention of another woman in his dreams, Marie, she had grown to hate the name. That name represented all that was wrong in her life; it filled her with anger and resentment and was the reason why she had finally confronted him a few days ago. Had she done the right thing or should she have swallowed her pride; grinned and dealt with the pain?

Jim had always been so intense, everything about him seemed important; his attention to detail, his integrity, his thoughtful love-making, sometimes this was frighteningly good. She had loved all of these things about her husband and more, and, despite everything, right at this moment all she wanted was for the door to open and her husband to walk through it, looking sheepish, contrite even, but still in love with his wife.

The dog raised its head and lazily looked in the direction of the window, his ears pricked up and his head half-cocked. Jennifer looked in that direction, at the long ago closed curtains for evidence that the dog had sensed Jim's return. There seemed to be none.

Disappointed, she sat back in her seat, the dog, however, stood up and stretched wagging his tail and headed for the hallway. Seconds later came the sound of a key in the lock of the front door; Jim was home at last and she ran a gamut of emotions.

Standing up on stiff legs and walking into the hallway she tried to suppress a whole array of reactions. He looked alright if a little pissed, what the hell; or who the hell had kept him out until this time of night? She spoke first; her voice sounding weak when she wanted it to be stronger.

"Darling are you alright; I was worried, you're very late?"

"Yes, I'm okay, listen we need to talk."

What did that mean she wondered; was this the end of their marriage?

"Talk? Yes okay come into the lounge in the warm. I'll put the kettle on."

Jim did as she requested without question, entering the lounge and sitting in his usual chair, not even bothering to remove his coat. He seemed to be swaying slightly as he walked, perhaps he had just been on a bender and everything would be alright after all she thought as he perched precariously on the edge of the chair.

The business like manner of his first words, despite the alcohol, and the fact that he still wore his coat worried her as she busied herself with the kettle. Afterwards, sitting opposite him and trying to get a clue to his mood from his eyes she noticed that he seemed to be avoiding eye contact, something that he rarely, if ever, did.

He appeared to be contemplating what he had to say; Jennifer who had endured too much silence this night already felt the need to fill the void.

"You're home very late tonight darling; is there something wrong?"

He sighed but did not answer straightaway.

"Jim what's wrong?"

"I have to leave Jennifer."

"Leave; what do you mean?"

"I have to Jenny."

He hadn't called her that for an age and it shocked her; this was serious.

"But why; why do you have to leave Jim?"

"I'm no good for you anymore; no good for you, no good for the children."

"Jim I love you; we can work this out." She sounded as desperate as she felt.

"Jenny, I know you love me. Right now I wish you didn't love me. I don't want to hurt you Jenny; I know I already have done but I can't keep hurting you this way. I have to leave."

"Is this something to do with Marie?" She couldn't help herself; the question was out before she could stop it.

"In a way I suppose it is, but not in the way you think. I need to get away from everything Jenny; I think I may be cracking up and I need to try to sort myself out."

"You're not alone on that score Jim." She sounded fiercer than she wanted to be; she was a human being for Christ's sake.

"I know Jen, I'm sorry."

She looked at the man sitting opposite her through dispassionate eyes and marvelled at just how much he had changed in such a short time. He looked in a pitiful state; maybe he was close to a nervous breakdown.

"Jim I want you to stay."

"I can't Jen; I'm ruining your life."

"Where will you go?"

"Away."

"What you really mean is away with her; with this Marie woman don't you?"

"No; I told you, there is no her."

"This is not making any sense Jim."

"I know it's not Jen; my life has stopped making any sense."

"Then tell me about it; don't shut me out of your life."

"I don't know where to begin." He looked her in the eyes for the first time since he arrived home. Then he continued, rambling, pouring his heart out.

"Look Jen, I don't know what's happening to me. I seem to be having some sort of breakdown. I seem to be having moments that I don't remember, no matter how hard I try. I seem to be doing things that I don't believe I am doing, dreams are becoming reality, and I don't know where reality begins and where it ends anymore. I swear though that I have never been unfaithful to you and I don't know who Marie is. I can't go on living here, I need to get help."

"Then how does this Marie woman end up in your dreams?"

"If I knew that then I wouldn't think that I'm going mad. Marie is just there, until recently a figment of my imagination."

"You just said until recently?" The words hung in the air, they hadn't been said in a nasty way but this was a development that Jennifer wasn't sure she wanted to hear about.

"Yes, well now I know she exists, she is a real person though I swear I still don't know why the hell she is inside my head."

"So how do you know she exists?"

"I saw her in a crowd, I tried to follow her."

"Why?"

"I wanted answers; I wanted to know why she is inside my head."

"You do need help; what did you say to her when you caught up with her?"

"I didn't."

"So you just stood there and gazed into her eyes?" Her voice now had an edge to it; she tried to control it, after all, it was her that had asked him to tell her everything.

"I didn't catch up with her; I lost her in the crowd. Jennifer I can't put you through this, I can't take much more. There's something happening that's beyond my understanding or my control. The other night in the study; when you found me on the floor, I had an incredibly vivid dream that I was running through woodland after this woman; this Marie."

"You asked about the blood on the sheets; I dreamt that I was running through sharp brambles, that they were tearing my legs as I ran. When I woke I had blood all over my legs. Jennifer how can I explain that to anyone, let alone my wife? I have to be going mad don't I?"

"Then stay the night and we'll get you an appointment with a doctor in the morning." She was suddenly seriously worried for the mental health of her husband; these were ramblings bordering on insanity, even allowing for the drink in his system.

"Jennifer you don't understand, I am out of control, I'm having blackouts, and who the hell knows what I might do when these things happen to me. I have you and the children to consider, I'm not safe to be around." His mind made up he stood and prepared to leave.

"Jim!" The tears she had vowed would not be shed poured forth now in abundance.

"Jim don't leave us, please don't leave us."

"It's for your own safety Jen, perhaps I'll sort this thing out and be able to come back." He was crying too. All signs of drunkenness gone, he made for the door. She chased him and grabbed his arm as he walked into the hallway. He turned and just for an instant she thought he might have changed his mind. Then, kissing her lightly on her brow to avoid the salty taste of her tears he headed for the door, opening it he didn't turn round and was quickly lost to the darkness beyond.

"Where's Daddy going?"

The children crouched at the top of the stairs, their innocent, cherubic faces uncomprehending the scenario enacted below them.

"Daddy has to go away for a little while." The words almost stuck in her throat as she said it.

"Mummy, are you tired again?"

"Yes, it's very late, please go to bed now."

Jennifer returned to the lounge, not bothering to check if her request had been complied with, and sat once more in the chair that had housed her for so long this evening. The dog had returned to his slumber in front of the fire. The carriage clock continued its monotonous refrain, but this time it was not the only sound in the room, this time Jennifer's sobs contributed to a lamentable duet.

**

Outside, a thin film of light rain fell on Jim Dowley as he turned one final time to look at the house that had been his home for so long. At this moment he realised just how easy it must be for Jennifer to be content within those four walls; realised too that he had not known contentment on any level for months.

For Jennifer, life had been stable and safe, she had not wanted for anything more than she already had, he envied her for that, envied and loved her but he knew what he was doing was the right thing to do. He was out of control, had almost succumbed to the advances of Joanne earlier in the day, well yesterday now actually.

Tonight would be spent sleeping in the car he had hired earlier that afternoon after he had decided not to go back to work and which he had been far too inebriated to drive home. It would be uncomfortable, but then, at this time, so was most of his life.

Tomorrow he would try to decide what to do. He hadn't been entirely honest with Jennifer, it was, of course, true that he had followed Marie and lost her in a crowd. But that had been before hadn't it; today he had found her again, just after he left the Green Man.

He knew where she worked and, after hiring the car he had followed her home. He had been sitting there deciding what to do when all hell broke loose and the building where she lived had suddenly been crawling with policemen and blue lights and sirens had filled the night. Just before he decided it would be prudent to leave the area when an ambulance had arrived on the scene. He couldn't make any sense of what he had seen and he was no nearer doing so now.

He had made his decision to leave Jennifer and the children over his sixth pint of *Guinness*. It would have been all too simple to go home and pretend that nothing had happened, go to bed in his nice warm bedroom and snuggle up to his nice warm wife. But he couldn't live a lie; now that he knew where she was he had to get to the bottom of why this stranger had come to dominate his thoughts, in fact his life.

Right now though as the fine rain became a steady downpour and the wind began to add to the general chill of the night he thought of that nice warm bed, of the woman who was his wife who he knew he had hurt so badly and wished that this whole scenario would just go away.

The fact was that despite her dominance in his mind, he had never considered the mystery woman that was; he was certain, Marie to be a potential lover. He knew in his heart though that he would never be able to convince Jennifer of this and so, as he climbed into the back of the freezing cold car and tried to pull his soaking wet coat around him for warmth, he fell into a troubled sleep convinced that he had done the right thing.

TWENTY

Police Constable Bill Carter could actually feel his face getting redder and redder; could feel too the anger that welled inside him approaching explosion point. Okay, so he and PC Harry Maden had screwed up pretty badly on what should have been a straightforward surveillance job but the last thing they needed was some smart-arsed Detective Inspector reading the Riot Act.

The girl had been bloody hysterical by the time they had got there, and who the hell could blame her really? Somehow the old bastard had got into her flat; how the hell had he done that? How could he have possibly got past them?

The man was dead now, but by the look of him he must have been well on his way when he broke into her flat. They had been vigilant, ultra-vigilant in his opinion, they had observed everyone that had walked down the street that day; anyone, young or old that acted the least bit suspiciously. In Carter's experience, most people did when the police were around and had been approached and spoken to in the nicest possible way.

How long had the intruder been in there waiting for her? God alone knew the answer to that now that the old guy wasn't around to ask, the old bastard had obviously run rings around him and now he was under the cosh; there would be no commendation for his police work this evening.

"Reading the newspaper were you Carter? Or have you got something a bit more titillating in the car? Because whatever you were doing you certainly weren't doing your fucking job were you?"

Carter hoped the question was a rhetorical one; if he were forced to answer he might regret his response to the sanctimonious superior officer.

"How long was he in there Carter; minutes, hours?"

"I don't know sir; we didn't see anyone like him in the area."

"You didn't see him! From what I've been told he looks about a hundred years old for God's sake; are we dealing with the invisible man here?"

"No sir!" The DI was having a field-day.

"Then what exactly happened here PC Carter; how could you possibly have missed him?"

"I don't know sir."

"You don't know. It's your job to know, a job that I can't guarantee you will still have in the morning."

"Yes sir."

"Is the girl alright?"

"She has a WPC with her now; she's pretty shaken up actually."

"Actually, I'm not fucking well surprised. Is she upstairs?"

"Yes sir."

Turning, the DI headed for the stairs. "I'll deal with you two later," he said over his shoulder, Carter gave him the 'V' sign and hoped there were no mirrors around.

Amanda Fellows' flat was on the second floor, the door was ajar, and, tapping on it gently, he entered. The inside of the flat was a hive of activity, SOCOs were doing their thing, the body of the old man had been covered and two paramedics were preparing to remove it from the premises.

Amidst the maelstrom of activity Amanda Fellows, looking ashen, was comforted by WPC Julie Walsh. He went first to the old man and pulled back the shroud that covered his face. It was true; he did look a hundred years old.

"Is he our man?" DI Jones asked the young police constable who was loitering in the room looking slightly embarrassed, probably by the incompetence of his colleagues.

"Alfred Williamson? We're not really sure at the moment sir. He had no ID and the lady who lives here hasn't seen Williamson for years, she was a small child at the time. The old man had a bloody big knife on him though so it might be him."

"So the woman doesn't recognise him at all?"

"She's in a state of shock sir; Julie is trying to calm her down now, getting her to think clearly."

"I shouldn't think that she has a lot of faith in us right now."

"No sir; it was a complete balls up."

"Bill Carter has been on rocky ground for quite some time now. I can't say what will happen to him after this latest cock up. How did the dead man get into the flat?"

"The SOCOs are working on that at the moment sir, there are no signs of a forced entry; it's starting to look as though he somehow managed to use the front door, we found some sort of instrument, skeleton keys probably."

"Why would an old fart like that be walking around with skeleton keys?"

"It beats me sir."

"There were a few things in the kitchen that were disturbed according to the victim. No signs of anything broken though. It looks like the old man just got hungry. We think he had been drinking heavily, we found an empty vodka bottle, scotch too; he must have been pretty plastered by the time Miss Fellows got home."

"It looks like he's been here for some time then?"

"Judging by the alcohol sir; he might have been here for several hours."

"He could have been here before Carter's watch then. Who were on duty before Carter and Maden's watch?"

"It was Bob Taylor and Tony Chapman sir."

"Get in touch with them; see if they saw an old man hanging about, he might have slipped in when the shifts changed."

"Yes sir." Sean Craig turned and began reaching into the inside pocket of his jacket.

"Oh and Craig..."

"Yes sir."

"Do you have any preliminary thoughts on cause of death?"

"The paramedics think a massive coronary sir."

"Thank you Craig."

Turning once more to the body, he surveyed the grimy looking individual just before the paramedics re-covered his face. The old man looked as though he should have died years ago; what had caused him to carry on living; and how the hell had he got past the police guard outside? Why, if it wasn't Williamson, was he here at all?

"Sir!" His thoughts were interrupted by a woman's voice and he turned to see WPC Walsh.

"Yes Julie; what is it?"

"Miss Fellows sir; she has recovered a little from the shock, she doesn't think that the man was Alfred Williamson."

"Then who is it?"

"She doesn't know, she said he looked slightly familiar but she can't place him, can't be more specific."

"Will she speak to me do you think?"

"It's possible, she's coming out of the initial shock now; she seems a pretty tough cookie."

"I'll give it a try."

Together they approached Amanda who had stopped crying now and looked stoically in their direction.

"Miss Fellows, I'm Detective Inspector Andrew Jones." He shook her hand and sat on the chair next to her. I'm sorry you had such a nasty shock tonight, the officers who allowed this to happen will not go without reproof."

"Do you think sorry is good enough?"

Jones took in the other woman who he had not really taken a great deal of notice of, this must be Amanda Fellows' flat mate he concluded, Kate Harvey.

"You will be Miss Harvey I guess; in answer to your question no sorry is probably not good enough but it's all I have to give."

"Leave it alone Kate."

Amanda's voice was cool and firm, she didn't think that Kate, acting the loose cannon, was going to help anyone.

DI Jones turned once more to Amanda.

"Do you feel you can talk about it?"

Amanda nodded.

"WPC Walsh informs me that you don't think the intruder is Alfred Williamson."

"No." Her voice was now more of a whisper, her heart raced at the sound of the name.

"And you don't have any idea at all who he might be?"

"I don't think so; there's something familiar about him but it feels more like a long-distant memory than anything I can bring to mind. The funny thing is that I had the feeling that he didn't mean me any harm."

"He had a very large knife on his person; we have reason to believe he had been drinking heavily."

"I know, I saw the knife when your officers removed it; all the same I didn't feel threatened, it was as though; well I know this sounds odd, but it was as though he cared for me, like he had feelings for me in some way. The look in his eyes; oh I don't know I can't explain it."

"Fortunately for you Miss Fellows, we'll never know whether you are wrong about that. In my experience people who carry knives, big knives, don't do so without a reason in mind."

"Whatever!" Amanda had her opinion and she didn't feel swayed by this policeman.

"My people will be trying to get an identity for our intruder; in the meantime I suggest you try to get some rest Miss Fellows. I don't think we'll be much longer here and we'll leave you in peace."

"It was the man who knocked me over the other night!" Kate was feeling chastened by Amanda telling her to shut up earlier but she felt that she had to say this; after all she lived here too, perhaps the mad old man was after her and not Amanda.

"Do you recognise him then Miss Harvey; perhaps you've seen him around, maybe he's a stalker?"

"I only saw him that night; I don't know him and, looking at the old fart I wouldn't have wanted to either. What the hell could have motivated a man of his age and in his state of health to break in here, and with a police guard outside as well? It just doesn't make sense."

DI Jones could only shrug by way of reply; he had been wondering the exact same thing. Thanking them both for their help and reiterating that they should both get some rest he left, most of the rest of his team doing so at the same time.

"Do you need anything?" WPC Walsh and PC Craig were the two left behind, Julie Walsh asked the question.

"A stiff drink I suppose," Amanda answered, trying to sound lighter than she felt.

"That old shitter stole the whisky before he pegged it."

"There's brandy in the cupboard over there." Amanda pointed.

"Are you a secret drinker Mandy?"

"It's left over from last Christmas; there's Port and Sherry in there as well."

"Well we'll leave you to it then; don't get too drunk; you need to keep your wits about you. For tonight at least, the car will still be outside, hopefully my colleagues will be a lot more vigilant than before."

"I don't understand!" Amanda looked horrified.

"You said that the man here tonight was not Williamson; we can't take the risk that he might be out there, that what happened here tonight was completely unrelated."

Sean Craig hoped he looked sympathetic as he said this, but the thought that her nightmare might not, after all, be over was a crushing blow to Amanda. After they left she burst into tears, she couldn't take much more of this.

"Do you want a doctor Mandy?"

"No Kate, the police woman asked me that at least half a dozen times."

"Well come here then and let me hug you." Amanda did, she needed love right now.

"You know Kate; I felt so sorry for him."

"How could you; the man was a criminal?"

"He didn't feel like a criminal."

"But he broke in didn't he? He stole my whisky, he had a knife."

"He wasn't stealing anything when I got home; he was just sitting there waiting."

"Waiting for what though Amanda?"

"Waiting for me, I think."

"To kill you no doubt; remember the knife."

"I don't think he wanted to kill me Kate."

"But how can you know? If the bastard hadn't croaked it might be you in the morgue now."

"It was just the way he looked at me. I know that face from somewhere Kate, he looked so old and tired now but there was something about him that I associated with happiness not pain; not murder. He was crying."

"Crying; why the hell would he be crying?"

"I don't know Kate; he was crying but they seemed to be tears of happiness not pain; and then it all changed, suddenly he was in agony, it was written all over his face, and I just stood there dumbstruck.

"Perhaps I could have helped him, saved him even, but I was just too bloody shocked I couldn't move. And then he died; just died in front of me and I did nothing and a part of me died too. I felt strange, a sense of loss that I can't explain; even now I'm feeling something that feels more like grief than shock."

"Are you sure you don't want me to call a doctor Mandy?"

"The next person that asks me that question is going to get a punch on the nose." She giggled. Kate joined in and soon they were holding their sides trying to recover from the affliction. Finally though, they regained their composure.

It was some time later, they had settled for wine, the brandy saved for another Christmas, probably the one after next. They had the stereo on low and had made a meal of sorts from what they found in the fridge. The wine had calmed them both down and Amanda was actually feeling quite mellow in the circumstances.

"You know Kate, I have a theory, and I know you'll laugh at the thought but I'm going to tell you anyway."

"Go ahead Amanda, I'm agog with anticipation." They giggled again but for not as long as previously.

"I think it was my father."

"You said it wasn't!"

"No Kate, I said it wasn't my first stepfather. I think it was my real father."

"Are you serious?"

"I think I am yes."

"Why?"

"An instinct I suppose. What were your impressions of the man Kate?"

"A down and out."

"I'll agree he looked down on his luck. I was thinking more of his features, he had a distinctive face. Didn't you think he had an ethnicity to him at all?"

"I suppose he might be Northern European, he had that look about him I guess."

"I thought that too Kate."

"And your point is what exactly?"

"It was just something that my parents mentioned when they told me that I had been adopted."

"Go on, tell me."

"Well, apparently, the officials at the children's home told my current stepparents that I had probably been born in London. The home itself was in the city. The woman who had been looking after me when they found me was apparently Polish. She died and there didn't seem to be any next of kin, nobody came forward to claim me. I guess I was 'left luggage.'"

"That's a terrible story Mandy."

"Do you see what I am getting at Kate? The man who broke in here tonight could well have been Polish. A part of me wants to believe that he came here tonight to apologise for deserting me. Perhaps when my mother died he didn't feel he could take care of me anymore. Perhaps he thought that I had a better chance in life if I stayed in the children's home. Maybe he was very poor."

"But that makes the story even more terrible."

"Terrible it may be but also quite likely to be true. I think it's time to ask my stepparents a few more questions."

"But that could open up a lot of old wounds Mandy; are you sure you want to go ahead and do that?"

"I'm not really sure of anything but it just feels like it's something I need to do."

"Well, try not to hurt your stepparents okay. Remember that they have always been there for you and that even if the old guy who died here tonight is your real father and even if he had good reason, he wasn't there when you most needed him. If he hadn't forsaken you then Alfred Williamson would never have featured in your life."

"I know you're right Kate, I love my stepparents and I would never do anything to hurt them."

The conversation was over for the evening; at least the heavy conversation was anyway. Kate was apparently satisfied with Amanda's undertaking to tread carefully though she remained perplexed by her friend's belief as to the identity of the old man. As they settled down to watch an old film, whilst they drank the rest of the wine, she considered the strange events of the last few days and tried to make sense of them.

**

The weekend followed and the next day Amanda explained to her employers just what had happened and had taken a day's compassionate leave. Dave Sullington had agreed to man the telephones; his star was rising as far as she was concerned.

The drive to her parent's house was, if anything, even more traumatic than the events of the night before. What would they make of her questions? She had plenty to ask. They had greeted her, as always, like she was the most precious person on God's earth, perhaps that was what they really thought, she sincerely hoped that they would feel the same way by the time she left.

**

"The people at the children's home told us that you had come from London. Leytonstone actually, at least that was what they thought; though they never elaborated on that. The woman who was looking after you when they found you died in the street, a heart attack, she was Polish, her name was Anna but she was apparently not your birth mother."

"You went into care with a young boy, they were quite sure that he was your brother; your twin actually, though in those days they didn't have the technology that they do today; with the DNA testing and all that. We would have adopted him as well to keep the two of you together but he had already been adopted."

From the slow and deliberate way that her stepfather delivered this speech, it was quite obvious that he was finding it very difficult. All these years he had lived with the knowledge that one day his beautiful and precious daughter might start asking questions about her real parents. That she might seek out her past and reject him and his wife, who had loved her as their own.

"I have a twin brother? Why didn't you tell me this?"

"It seemed best not to; we didn't know where he was, I'm sorry."

"Will they have records? Can I find him?"

"The home closed down about eighteen years ago I think. I would imagine that records still exist though. I wouldn't know where to tell you to start looking Amanda."

"I have to find him; I have to know."

"Sometimes it's better to leave the past alone Amanda. Your brother may know nothing about you; finding him now could present all sorts of complications. Perhaps he has never been told that he was adopted. If he found out now he might reject his adoptive parents; you could end up destroying his life."

"Dad… is this why you never told me about my past? Did you think I would reject you and Mum?"

"That was part of it I suppose."

"You and Mum will always be very special to me; as far as I am concerned you are my parents whatever I may find about my past." She embraced him and realised that he was shaking with emotion. Her mother who had been silent throughout the conversation and had cried a little now joined in the embrace.

"I am going to find my brother; my twin brother."

"That is your decision darling; we will stand by you and we hope that you are doing the right thing," her mother finally spoke.

As Amanda drove home she wondered if this latest revelation in her life explained anything. She thought it probably did, she had always felt that something was absent in her life; she had never suspected that she had shared a womb with it though.

TWENTY ONE

The sun was startlingly bright when he opened his eyes, sudden pain registered in his sleep dulled mind. It quickly subsided; the heat of the sun comforted him, lapped his sun-tanned body and invigorated him.

He sat up; before him an endless sea of turquoise water lapped gently onto the impossibly white sand on which he had slept. How on earth had he got here? He had no recollection of that but he knew *why* he was here; where was the girl?

He looked around, behind him a tropical jungle filled with palm trees and strange plants the like of which he had never seen before, ahead of him the sea. No sign of the girl; hadn't they eaten soup together? It was a hazy memory. With a small cry of excitement he noticed the small footprints in the sand, heading towards the trees.

He stood up, naked except for the ridiculous boxer shorts that Jennifer had brought for him, as a joke, last Christmas. Wiping at the thin film of sweat that had formed on his brow he headed across the hot sand in the direction of the jungle. The sand was painfully hot away from the water's edge and so he ran to minimise the contact with it. Ahead he heard the musical sound of her laughter. The chase was once more underway.

On reaching the tree cover, the contrast in atmosphere was marked, here the air was hot and heavy with moisture, he followed the noise that was coming from ahead of him, so far he had not seen the girl but he had heard her and this was encouragement enough to continue deeper into the depths of the trees. His body became sticky with the sweat of his exertions and with the humidity in the air.

Just ahead, a small clearing gave him his first sight of the girl, she was completely naked and he almost blushed at the sight of her. Who was she, why did he feel the need to be with her? His pace quickened and hers seemed to do so too. Why; was she scared of her pursuer? Another giggle and he convinced himself that she wasn't.

She disappeared from his view, the clearing crossed and the bright green undergrowth swallowing her once again; another giggle, he ran harder still. He wanted answers from her; he should have asked her when he had the opportunity, now he was determined to learn just what this elusive creature wanted from him.

With astonishing and frightening speed, day became night and the so recently green paradise became a place of shadows and darkness. It was a foreboding place; his pace slowed but not much, there was a fear factor here now.

The jungle that had seemed silent apart from the noise of their progress in the sunlight now throbbed with a living cacophony of sound. Creatures, unseen, rustled in the undergrowth all around him, his foot landed on something slimy and he squealed like a small child might at its clammy touch. He felt it writhe beneath him before it exploded, the wetness on his feet and lower legs told him he was covered in blood. Not for the first time he thought.

The silver coating of moonlight aided his progress as his eyes slowly adjusted to the change in light intensity. Occasionally he caught sight of her, beautiful in this silver light; she didn't seem to have slowed down at all and had consequently increased her lead on him.

The noises around him seemed to be reaching a crescendo; it was now so loud that it hurt his ears. He felt fearful for his safety; and for the girl's of course, the rustling in the undergrowth had become a crashing sound, indicating large animals were involved in this pursuit.

A strange manic chuckle off to his left made him shudder with fear; there was something altogether evil about that voice, the voice of something not quite human. The sweat which trickled slowly down his face was no longer the sweat of honest endeavour, it was the sweat of fear, and he felt its cold embrace.

There were more voices now, whispering voices that came from the trees all around him. Quickening his pace didn't seem to make any difference; his pursuers seemed to keep pace with him anyway. In fact he suspected that they were getting closer all the time.

Suddenly the tree cover disappeared and he almost ran straight into the large, moon-bathed lake which spread out before him. A short distance away, the girl continued her flight, her feet skipping through the shallows at the edge of the lake as she circumnavigated it. He continued his chase.

Behind him the creatures kept pace with him. On the lake itself strange water-birds swam on the crests and troughs created by the breeze which was cool and fresh and turned the sweat on his body cold.

A large bird, which resembled a swan except that it had two heads atop two slender necks called to the night, its call was ghostly but strangely enchanting. He marvelled at its grace as it joined a further bird, this one with three heads.

High above, a solitary cloud briefly enshrouded the moon, subduing its silver brilliance. In the darkness he heard movement behind him, much closer than before, and he increased his pace still further.

The moon regained its superiority in the sky and, as it bathed the lake in its silky glow once more, it became evident that the water was frozen. The previously imperious water-birds now skated clumsily around often falling over and squawking their disapproval.

The temperature had plummeted and he shivered as he ran. Beneath his feet he could hear the crunch of freshly fallen snow and the icy coldness of its touch shocked him; it felt like only minutes ago since the heat of the sand had burned the soles of his feet.

Just how long had he been running; hours, days? What did time mean in this strange place anyway? He had no sense of time, just an overwhelming desire to catch up with the elfin like figure that skipped and danced through the snows ahead of him; it mattered not, how long that quest might take.

He focused on her again, her previously naked body was now clothed in flowing white robes, the material looked silk-like, its luxurious quality reminded him of the milky white flesh beneath it.

As quickly as it had arrived, the coldness was now receding; with consternation he realised that he was fully clothed. Where the hell had the clothes come from; when had he put them on? Had he had another blackout? He really needed to see a doctor.

A blood freezing howl filled the icy white landscape; it came from the snow capped mountains which had come into view ahead of them, far beyond the valley through which they ran. What kind of creature could make such a noise he wondered, and what kind of animal was following him through this ethereal landscape.

The howling seemed to hang in the air for an age in the still of the night-time air, echoing around the valley, bouncing off unseen rocks or cliffs, it would be heard by unseen creatures who would cower in their nests or lairs, feeling protected from the wrath of the creature who had called out to the night.

"Marie; please wait for me."

His voice sounded small, almost pathetic, after the roar of the beast. The girl, Marie, had certainly not heard him, her light stride continued unchecked. Her waif-like figure seemed the perfect accompaniment to such a beautiful setting. If the chase were to end here it would be the perfect place. Marie, or whoever she was, seemed to have other ideas though; the chase showed no signs of ending here.

For the first time he managed to avert his eyes from the figure of the girl; allowing him to glance over his shoulder to investigate the scuttling sounds behind him. Something was certainly following him, quite what it was was impossible to discern from just a quick glance and he had no intention of slowing down for a more thorough look. The low guttural sound it made didn't lend itself to geniality.

He tried yet again to increase his pace, hoping to lose his pursuer and close the gap between him and the girl but his legs felt heavy with such sustained exercise and refused to respond to his needs.

A further change in the light intensity caused him to look skywards once more; there were now two moons, one a crescent, one full, dark patterns seemed to move about their surface like huge animals scurrying around. Then, yet another change in light and now there were three moons, this one gibbeous, then four, five, six and more until the whole sky was filled with their light and it became as daylight once more.

The lake had become a field of tall grasses, a long and seemingly eternal pathway snaking its way through the tall stalks some of which must be at least eight feet tall. A warm breeze caused the grasses to whisper in an almost melodic manner, a whisper of strange music that caused the hairs on the back of his neck to stand to attention. It was a symphony of nature, a celebration of this wondrous place.

The gap between him and the girl which had been growing had narrowed considerably, perhaps she was tired too, and she seemed for the first time to be taking in her surroundings, the wondrous surreal beauty washing over her as it had Jim Dowley.

The path had taken them over the brow of a hill over which the tall grasses gave way to fields of flowers. They were flowers of the most stunning beauty, Jim gasped at the sight of them, a kaleidoscope of colour that took the breath away.

What type of flowers were they he wondered as he ran on through them? Certainly they were like none he had seen before, huge butterflies, invisible until they took to the air, on account of their equally magnificent colourings hovered busily around the flower heads and birds, brightly coloured, which in shape resembled swallows but in colour were more like parrots, swooped here and there emitting a call that sounded like music. He felt as though the whole world had become an orchestra in which the sounds of his own footsteps were the percussion.

The music was so beautiful it was beyond his wildest imaginings, no composer he had ever heard could replicate such a sound and he revelled in its magnificence as he continued to run. The pain in his muscles was a distant memory, he felt as though he could run forever. The girl, too, seemed to be in ecstasy as she ran, she ran so fast she appeared to be floating above the ground, her perfect white dress flailing out behind her like a super-hero's cloak.

Just beyond him a rabbit crossed his path, turning its head inquisitively towards him. Apparently satisfied that he posed no threat it continued onwards, its oversized feet seeming to impede it as it hopped clumsily about.

Huge and beautifully green mountains, with no sign of snow caps, loomed above the foot of the path along which they ran. Cypress trees, deep green, rich and majestic stood like sentinels, interspersed with other, less recognisable, but no less spectacular species.

The girl had reached the first slopes and he noticed for the first time the huge cave which loomed just beyond her, its vast gaping mouth open like that of a hungry predator, the drops of water that fell from the cathedral like interior still furthered the analogy, resembling as it did saliva as the great chasm relished and anticipated the small but beautiful meal it was shortly to devour.

He wanted to warn her about entering the cave, wanted to scream out his warning, but a sudden panic and an incredible fatigue seemed then to overwhelm him and he found he couldn't speak let alone shout. The warning came out as a hoarse croak that was barely audible above the sound of his slowing footfalls.

As he watched in awe, he saw the girl run into the cave which instantly seemed to shrink in size like a great mouth preparing to swallow a morsel of food. Jim tried again to quicken his pace but his legs were leaden and he stumbled and fell on to his hands and knees like a supplicant kneeling before his God. He tried to crawl but, like his legs, his arms were suddenly useless and he fell forward, his face landing in the dirt of the track, grit and sand in his mouth. Finally he lay there, panting, exhausted and beaten.

He became aware that whatever had been following him was now almost upon him, he forced himself through a great effort of will to turn and face his fate. The creature which approached him, shambling along the track was like none he had seen before, by now that no longer surprised him. The nearest thing he could think of to describe it was spider-like, though its six legs and unsteady gait lent a lie to this.

As he watched, the creature emanated a strange sound like a mischievous chuckle; it came from one of the two heads which perched on short stubby necks on the top of the creature's bulbous body. The faces looked human but only just, both were old and male; a fearsome malice burned in the eyes of the one that had made the strange sound, the other remained silent and still, the glazed look in its eyes giving Jim the impression that it was dead.

There was something vaguely familiar about this second head and he tried to recall some long-lost memory as the creature advanced upon him. It wouldn't come to mind, his fatigue and his fear overwhelming him.

The beast was alongside him now and surveyed him with a measure of disdain; a further menacing snicker came from the mouth of the malignant looking head and its features morphed into a grotesque mask of something between rage and cruelty. Jim had the time to notice that its mouth did not move at all though.

A quick glance at the second head, just to make sure that it was not preparing to devour him, resulted in him catching a slight flicker of movement in its dead-looking eyes; just for a brief moment he had the impression that those eyes were heavy with sorrow, a deep and painful sorrow, maybe a regret of things that had gone before and couldn't be changed. It was a strange thought to be having at a time like this but a thought nonetheless.

The creature stood over him for what seemed like an age, it appeared to be confused, as if some internal dilemma prevented it from being decisive and doing what, presumably, it had followed him all this way to do. The huge pincers which waved menacingly close to his head looked as though they might kill him at any moment, Jim didn't doubt their capability to do so. Yet the beast refrained from killing him, for some reason. Jim became sure that this was due to the will of the sorrowful, dead-looking head, as if it exerted its will over its more malevolent twin.

With a speed that seriously alarmed him, the creature moved onward, hissing in a most terrible manner as it did so. Jim cowered away from it as it moved expecting instant death, watching it through the fingers of his hands which he had used to shield his face in a useless gesture of resistance.

As he watched it go he noted that the sorrowful looking head had rotated through one-hundred and eighty degrees and was regarding him with its doleful eyes. Once again Jim felt an inexplicable feeling of recognition and with it, just for a moment, a feeling of the creature's torment.

The relief he had felt as he realised that the creature was not going to kill him; quickly changed to despair as he realised its new intention. The cave entrance that had completely disappeared after the girl had entered suddenly began to open up once again and allowed its strange, beastly visitor to gain access.

"Marie; be careful!"

He cried out uselessly. The words were thick in his mouth, barely intelligible, he tried to rise; tried to be the gallant knight to this damsel in distress, but strength and resolve failed him and he collapsed back down to the ground, another mouthful of grit his reward for his effort. He gagged as the dirt filled his mouth and filled the gap between his tongue and his teeth but he was unable to raise his head and he merely dribbled onto the path as he lay there, shattered.

A thunderclap signified the commencement of a downpour the like of which Jim had never before had the misfortune to experience and, the dusty ground on which he was lying turned into a moving quagmire of sticky quicksand, he tried to swim in its filth, his movements as uncoordinated as a newborn child and useless in the swampy ooze.

He knew he was drowning; sinking further and further into oblivion, further into the darkness, closer to his impending death. Somehow, he heard the girl scream, even from the depths of this slime, and the noise created in him the fresh resolve he needed. Strength seemed to pulse back into his body and he began thrashing through the semi-solid mixture into which he had allowed himself to sink and prepare to die.

Ahead of him he saw a light, a most glorious light, and beyond that he sensed life and a new resolve. He had to survive, he had to save the girl, and he was all she had. How could he have allowed himself to almost die when she needed him so desperately?

As he opened his eyes once again, he winced at the sudden pain that began pulsing in his head, it pounded like an incessant drummer, the thunderous roar of the torrential rain hammered overhead so that he thought that the very sky might collapse, the rain was relentless as it crashed against the roof of his car.

This had been the most real of all Jim Dowley's nightmares, as he lay there in the gloomy confines of the car with pain in his head and in his lower back he tried to order his thoughts. Time was running out he thought; but time for what, he didn't know. It was all to do with the girl; Marie, but why? Were their destinies somehow entwined; did he have to fulfil some duty to her?

He adjusted his position on the car seat and winced, once again, at the pain in both his head and his back, if nothing else came out of this crazy day and night there would certainly be one hell of a hangover when the sun deemed to rise above the horizon and start the next one.

Settling back in the seat, which was both cold and damp from his earlier drenching, he stared through the window of the car at the snaking rivulets that formed patterns which were random but somehow beautiful in the half light created by the street lamps. He was still trying to make some kind of sense of the dream.

He thought the girl was in danger, but from whom and why? He thought that somehow the dream he had just been through, so vivid and so frightening, was, in some way, a message to him, but from whom and why again? Why him; why the girl and why now; he hadn't asked for this and now his marriage lay in ruins about him. Right now it felt as if his whole life did. Was this some retribution for something he had done wrong in this life or maybe the last one? The thoughts hung heavily over him as he somehow managed to reclaim sleep despite the pounding rain and the pounding in his head.

TWENTY TWO

The weather was turning decidedly nasty; in late November she supposed it was to be expected. Already snow was falling on upland areas. The weather forecasters had predicted a cold snap for the whole of Britain with temperatures set to plummet to well below freezing-point by midweek.

Tuesday mornings, like Mondays had never been a great favourite with Amanda, and so as the wind driven mixture of rain, sleet and hail hammered against the bathroom window she longed even more for the comfort and warmth of the bed she had just left.

Work was not going to be easy today, the first day back since the incident with the old man. There would be many questions to answer, some from genuinely concerned people like Dave Sullington, others from sensation seekers, wanting her to relive her ordeal for their entertainment, she had a good idea who would fall into either camp as she savoured the hot and powerful shower and tried to shut herself away from what was to come.

She had insisted that she return to work today; even though her parents had advised against it and so, too, had Kate. Kate was not returning to work yet, but then Kate was Kate. The friendship that had weathered the rigours of childhood; and the tantrums of their teenage years had truly stood the test of time though. Kate had rallied following the incident, providing everything that Amanda could have possibly wanted or needed over the last few days. A shoulder to cry on, a laugh when she was feeling low; Kate had been her 'rock' on whom she could rely.

As she turned off the shower and emerged from the cubicle, a squally wind hammered the hailstones against the glass so hard that she feared it might shatter. Indeed, she found she had involuntarily taken a step back from the window in anticipation of such an event. She was still jittery, jumping at her own shadow almost, perhaps her parents were right, she thought again of the bed. She tried to fight the feeling.

She looked at the window, it was dark out there and somewhere in the street was a police officer who was there for her benefit, she felt like a charity case despite everything, but then again that darkness looked foreboding, filled with menace.

She thought about the previous night; her dreams had become troubled again, she still dreamt about the man, so familiar and yet so elusive, and last night there was another man, an older one, gnarled and bitter, but what did it all mean?

The tree branches swayed violently under the increasing wind, it must be close to gale-force she thought, the movement created strange shadows in the eerie orange glow of the sodium light outside when she turned off the bathroom light. She shuddered as her imagination dreamt up claws and sharp teeth, reaching towards the glass; those thin but cruel hands coming for her.

Before showering she had put the kettle on and she now poured hot water into a pot that contained a tea-bag. She headed next to the toaster and, despite the fact that she felt sick with worry and nerves; she put two slices of bread into the slots.

As she sat down to eat them she considered the last few days. The death of the old man had made the local paper but no names had yet been mentioned. Police enquiries had apparently proved fruitful in identifying the man. She had received a visit from WPC Walsh that had revealed that he was a Polish man, a former surgeon. This had not come as a shock to her; hadn't her stepfather revealed that when she had been taken into care, the woman with her had been Polish. Perhaps, as she had suggested to Kate, the old man had been her biological father after all.

The thought both excited and, in a strange way, depressed her. If only the man had been able to say what he had come there to say she might have had a clue as to what had happened to her twin brother. Like this she might be left to wonder about that for the rest of her life.

If she ever did find him; would he be in a position to verify whether the old man was her father or not? And if it was her father why had he come; did he want absolution for abandoning her? She would have given him it, there were always good reasons for life turning out the way it did; but now he would never know that.

Her father was flesh and blood; her flesh and blood, and that ran deeper than anything. People who were kin never really stopped loving each other no matter how harsh the words or actions that might come between them. That was what Amanda believed and had always believed; perhaps it was a coping mechanism for dealing with the fact that she had started her young life alone.

She slurped noisily at her tea and looked at the clock on the kitchen wall; it showed the time to be twenty past seven. She would need to leave soon; the weather was so terrible that if she left it any later she would be caught in the interminable traffic jams that snaked their way into the town centre each day. Collecting her coat from the peg in the hall, she paused briefly to reflect on the day ahead. She knew it wouldn't be easy and she tried to steel herself against the thought of that. She was startled by a voice from behind her.

"Good luck Mandy!" Kate had popped her head, sleepily, around the bedroom door.

"Thank you Kate. Go back to bed; I'll see you tonight."

"No problem." Kate didn't need any further encouragement to find her cosy bed once again.

Amanda reached for the door-handle, a slight tremble, and then she was out into that world once more. The world where bad things happened, without fail, every day; would today be her turn in the badness that had beset mankind?

She descended the stairs, each of her steps feeling unsteady, her resolve waning, her fear going the opposite way at a faster rate. Then she was out into the street, into the terrible weather; the terrible world. The sleet was icy cold, its ferocity shocked her; it felt as though needles were being driven into her flesh. She noticed that there were snow flakes amongst the driving onslaught and guessed that a blizzard might be close at hand.

She pulled her coat more tightly around her as she descended the stone steps in front of the building. Her car was parked a little way along the street. Kate had used it on Saturday evening when she went out to collect a Chinese take-away they had ordered on a whim. In this weather and in these circumstances, she suddenly regretted that decision.

The umbrella she had unfurled when going outside; quickly proved to be useless in the wind, she should have known, but she still wasn't thinking straight. A man began to walk towards her, a shadowy figure in the half-light; his head bowed against the wind or, just maybe, so that she wouldn't recognise him. In his hand was a leash, on the end of it a fine looking, if bedraggled, dog.

She told herself to get a grip as the man passed by with barely a nod; even the most ardent dog-lover might regret having to take their pet for a walk in weather such as this.

By the time she reached the car she was almost paralysed by her fear. She hadn't seen a police guard; were they so short of manpower that it had been removed and she had not been told? Everything that was bad seemed possible in this darkness, in this weather; it was now snowing heavily.

It should have been getting light by now she thought, but the angry sky above and the snow, enabled the darkness to cling on to the world in which Amanda had to exist; the fear knotted her stomach, she had chest pain and, despite the weather, she found that she was sweating too.

Driving in these conditions wasn't easy, the snow wasn't actually settling on the road surfaces yet, although the pathways were looking white and pristine, and as she drove behind other cars a sea of slush was kicked up behind them.

The snow was being driven even harder now and it was difficult to see despite the best efforts of the windscreen wipers. Despite this her mind would not leave the events of the last few days. She toyed with her recent memories but the disquiet she had felt from the first day when Dave Sullington had fielded the telephone calls would not be acquiesced.

By the time she reached the edge of town, the snow was really beginning to take hold, where the wind blew, small drifts were already forming; it threatened to be a chaotic day.

When it snowed here it usually hung around for a while. She thought once again about the warm bed she had left behind, was she just being stupid, trying to walk before she could run? She thought that this was exactly what her work colleagues would think when she arrived at work.

Almost inevitably her thoughts now returned to the old man who had died in her flat. How he had come to be there was still a bit of a mystery and certainly a source of acute embarrassment to the local constabulary.

There had been a hell of a stink kicked up and the press had got hold of the story. They seemed a lot more interested in the failings of the local constabulary than by the fact that she and Kate had an intruder in their flat.

The reporters were more than a little interested as to why there had been a police presence outside the flat in the first place, but, to their frustration, no one was telling them. They weren't about to give up trying to find out though.

Had the old man been her father? She thought that maybe he was; in fact she was now quite sure about it. The Polish connection seemed to be a vindication of her thoughts.

As she drove, a memory stirred inside her; a memory so distant it was scarcely a memory at all, more an image, like a freeze-frame on the television set. The image was that of the old man, only he hadn't been so old and tired then. His eyes had burned with a passion, he had been an intensely proud and driven looking man but she recognised the image all the same. What hellish kind of existence could he have lived to turn him into the broken man who had collapsed under her gaze, what torment might have broken him, drained his passion dry?

Perhaps the torment of some guilty secret had caused his decline; perhaps that guilt came from the loss of his family; quite clumsy that, she thought inanely, losing a whole family. He had been very drunk on the night he had died, apparently; was he an alcoholic; had his guilt reduced him to that? The man had been a surgeon once, the man in her flat wouldn't have been able to hold a scalpel she thought. It seemed to her, such a decline; such a waste of a life.

She hoped that other things had contributed to his demise; the thought that it might have been due to the loss of his daughter filled her with something like remorse; she felt somehow responsible. What about her brother; her twin? Where was he; how did he fit into this riddle? She had to find him and ask him; she had to chase her unknown past, to blow away the dusty cobwebs of time and find out who she really was and why her life had taken such a rocky route to where she was now.

London was the place to start she thought; that was, apparently, where this had all begun. But in London, where would she even begin in a place as vast as the capital to find out about events that had happened such a long time ago? She may look forever and never find the answers, but she knew she would have to try, it felt like her destiny.

She was near the very centre of town now; the snow-covered suburban houses had been replaced by snow-covered shops and offices. There were a lot of people around for this time in the morning, perhaps like her they anticipated a nightmarish journey to work. The darkness was finally subsiding leaving behind a miserable grey sky and slush covered roads. The brilliant white snow on the pavements and the trees and rooftops lent a certain addition to the light but it felt like the very heart of winter was upon them all despite the fact it was still November.

Here, amongst the taller buildings of the town centre, the wind, which seemed to have been increasing incrementally throughout the journey, was less of a problem. The snow flakes, very large ones, now just settled gently on the ground, whereas before they had literally been driven into position.

She could feel something approaching panic rising in her as her journey continued. Amanda had not informed anyone at work that she would be coming in today; instead she had allowed herself the luxury of changing her mind if necessary. Dave Sullington had telephoned her a couple of times the day before to check on her welfare and advised her to take as long as it took to feel better about things. Dave she decided was not the person she had assumed him to be. She had considered him a bit of a lad, a boy racer who had never quite grown up, but she had reassessed her opinion of him following the care and friendship which he had shown her in the last few days.

Seeing Dave was just about the only thing she was looking forward to about today. She had vowed to thank him warmly for his continued concern. That was quite a sea change for her; was she starting to feel something for him that amounted to more than just being a work colleague? Times were certainly not dull for Amanda Fellows at the moment. When was the last time she had any inclination towards starting a relationship? She realised she couldn't actually remember and the thought bothered her for some reason.

The office came into view at last as she rounded a bend in the road, at least the bloody road works had concluded so she would be able to park in her normal place. The anxiety that had barely lain under the surface for the entirety of the journey now threatened to overwhelm her. She considered, briefly, just driving on by, it wasn't as if anyone would know she had tried to come in to work today, but she managed to steel herself to her situation and continued on, only pausing once more when she had left the safety of the car and pressed the call button for the lift.

After leaving the basement where the car park was housed, the lift came to a stop on the ground floor; the company operated a policy whereby all people on site should sign a register so that in the event of fire, all staff and visitors could be accounted for.

Entering the reception area where a number of staff-members were hanging around she felt suddenly the centre of attention; it made her even more uncomfortable, she had never been an attention seeker; just how much did these people know about what had happened?

Amanda did the only thing she could think of to break the tension; she wished them all a good morning with a voice just slightly tinged with irony. It was enough to break the tension and her colleagues descended upon her with a mixture of sympathy, horror and surprise at her unexpected appearance.

Through the crowd she caught a glimpse of Dave Sullington emerging from the lift that she had just vacated; she was pleased to see him and it probably showed; she didn't care right then. She followed him with her eyes as he approached the reception desk, signed in and then turned to look at her.

"We didn't expect you back at work so soon," he said, as he chaperoned her away from the small crowd and back into the lift. She was more than grateful to him for this; she had despaired of being able to get away from the throng in reception on her own.

"I couldn't stay at home any more; I wanted to get back into a routine, put all this behind me."

"I suppose that makes sense but I'll be keeping my eye on you."

Amanda found that to be reassuring; she wondered how she might have felt a few weeks ago. As the lift climbed through the building she found herself sneaking surreptitious looks at him through the mirror in the small compartment. He really was quite a good looking man she concluded, and she tried not to blush, scared that he might somehow be able to read her thoughts.

"Thank you for your concern Dave, I really appreciate it."

They parted company at the door to her office and he gave her a warm smile as he walked off to his own little room, a bolthole for when he was not on the road doing his salesman thing.

Amanda's office, which had always seemed to her to be dull and dreary, looked almost homely; this was a return to normality and she wanted to embrace the feeling. She allowed herself to glance at the inane posters on the walls, they looked familiar, safe. Pictures of exotic holiday destinations were interspersed with pictures of famous male celebrities; David Beckham competed with Brad Pitt and Tom Cruise. She began to relax a little.

On her desk was a large pile of work which needed her attention. Dave had done his best but this wasn't really his field, perhaps it was just as well that she had come back today. She thought about Dave again and found that she was smiling; what did that mean; was she falling in love with him?

She launched herself into her work and had already dealt with a good deal of it by the time that Caroline and Susan arrived to take up position at the other two desks in the office. Fending off their repeated questions was as harrowing as anything she had been forced to endure so far.

The two girls who had holidayed and only returned to work the day before and so had missed all of the events of the last few days had obviously heard snippets of information on the grapevine and now wanted all the details of what had happened to her. They had bombarded her with questions, eager to compare her answers with the rumours that their work colleagues had fed them the day before.

There was no choice but to give them a potted version about what had happened. They would not leave her alone until they had got their pound of flesh. She felt slightly sick as she recounted the telephone calls, the break-in and the death throes of the intruder, it was like living through it all again and, as a result, no more comfortable than before.

They asked if the intruder had meant to kill her. What could she say to that? He had a knife; a big knife but she didn't think that he had meant her harm. The two girls had exchanged quizzical looks in response to that answer; she hadn't expected anything else really.

By the time that Sue had decided that cups of coffee were required, Amanda had had about as much as she could stand. The butterflies in her stomach and chest would not be quieted; she was sweating again, experiencing mild panic attacks.

She decided that the use of diversionary tactics were her best bet and moved the conversation away from her and onto the holidays of her colleagues. It worked; the next hour was spent discussing drink, sunshine and young men. Amanda was bored stiff by it all but at least she was no longer the focus of attention.

The pile of outstanding work which she had looked upon with relish when she had first come in that morning, didn't look much smaller, it was not sorted and prioritised and it screamed at her to end this banality and get on with it.

It was, of course, much the same for Caroline and Sue and by late morning Amanda doubted whether her decision to come in today had much benefited her employers. The talking done; the gossip exchanged it was almost eleven o'clock by the time she could refocus her attention on her work. She had planned a twelve-thirty lunch; she would need to make inroads into her backlog.

If her lunch had been taken at midday, as she often did, things might have been very different for Amanda Fellows. Fate being fate, decreed that the telephone would ring at twelve twenty-five and that Amanda would answer it, Caroline and Susan having just left for their lunch breaks.

There was no warning, no premonition, not even any hesitation on Amanda's part as she reached for the receiver and picked it up with well-practised élan. She put it to her ear.

It was a bad line, a lot of hissing and sounds which could have been, to Amanda's sudden heightened senses, heavy breathing. She dropped the receiver as if she had been burned by it; it landed on the desk top with a loud clunk. Good, she thought as she imagined the caller clutching his ear in pain at the loud and unexpected noise.

Even as the receiver lay harmlessly on the desk top she could hear his voice, that harsh rasping sound which still seemed to have a deadpan delivery, it didn't sound as though she was listening to a human being.

Was her real father talking to her from beyond the grave? Don't be stupid she thought to herself but she felt at that exact moment anything was possible.

Like the naughty schoolchild that impelled by some inner devilry to do something which it knows to be stupid and will have dire consequences eventually, Amanda reached out and picked up the receiver once more. Pressing it to her ear she listened to the barely coherent monologue.

"Amanda, please Amanda, I must speak with you. It's your father calling. I must make you understand why I did what I did... Amanda?"

His voice degenerated into a blubbering sound; was he crying; who the hell was this; Williamson? She had to find out.

"Who is this; what do you want from me?"

"Amanda? I told you before, it's your father."

"You're not my father you complete bastard; my father is dead, I watched him die!"

"Is that what you really think Amanda? You know you don't, the police have brainwashed you into believing what they want you to hear. The police had no right to do what they did to me!"

"If you are who I think you are; they had every right you fucking moron!"

"Amanda, please don't say such things."

There were more sounds like crying and a cruel part inside Amanda, a part she didn't know was there, was glad she had hurt him somehow.

"Please don't shout at me Amanda, I love you so much, you know that don't you?"

"I know you need help; perhaps the hangman's rope will sort you out."

"Will you help me Amanda?"

What was he asking here; should she say yes and tell the police, and end this nightmare? She found she was terrified.

"Look, will you please, please leave me alone, let the past lie, I don't want to see you."

"But I'm your father Amanda."

"I've told you once already; my father's dead and you are just a lunatic!"

The man's tone of voice turned to one that scared her even more than before, he was raging, out of control.

"You don't know anything you fucking spoilt bitch and unless you meet me you never will. Things were alright until you came on the scene. I loved Susan." His voice softened again as if he were remembering better times in his life.

"But you killed her!" Amanda, if she had ever had any doubts, knew exactly who she was speaking to now.

"You, Amanda, made me do it!"

"I was just a child; how can you say that?"

"You were a demon in disguise; you invaded my dreams and made me crazy. I never meant to kill Susan. We were childhood sweethearts you know?"

"Please leave me alone." Amanda's voice was sounding less assured, her anger spent; she was like a child once more.

"Never; God has told me that you must be made to pay for what you forced me to do. You must be made to face the punishment that is your destiny. You will thank me and God in the end for giving you redemption."

"You are a mad man; I will never agree to meet you."

"Mad! Well there's something you finally got right, bitch. I'm certainly mad at you. I'll make you pay. If you won't come to me then I'll come to you; count on that. You had better be looking over your shoulder Amanda Williamson, because your daddy is going to be right behind you sometime very soon. You can avoid that; all you have to do is to agree to meet with me.

"If you won't come to Daddy then Daddy will come to you and, trust me, I will punish you for all your sins you little bitch!"

Alfred Williamson began to laugh; it was the laugh of madness not humour, perhaps he had forgotten what humour meant.

Amanda slammed the receiver back into its cradle and raced to the window in her office; there was a public telephone box opposite the office, was the bastard ringing her from there?

The snow-covered kiosk was empty. She ran towards her office door and out into the corridor beyond. Behind her she heard the sound of the telephone ringing again. Susan had just returned with an armful of shopping and some fast-food; Amanda ignored her.

"Hello Stark and Rutherfords can I help you?" Her only reply was that of a click as the caller hung up.

**

Outside the snow was now deep, her efforts to run were clumsy, bordering on comical, this, and the fact that she wore no coat in such inclement weather, attracted the attention of passer's by who would otherwise only have been concentrating on getting from one place to another as quickly as possible.

A kindly old man reached out to her to ask her if she was alright and stepped back in stunned silence at the look and scream of terror she emitted when she avoided him. The scream, of course, attracted still more attention, soon it seemed to Amanda that everyone she passed was looking at her, as she continued her aimless flight.

"Has she been attacked?" An old woman asked the question of a passer-by as she battled to pull her shopping trolley through the worsening and increasingly deep snow. The young man she asked merely shrugged and continued his own blundering advance through the worsening conditions.

She had created sufficient attention that a crowd of people, curious and with nothing better to do on such a terrible day, had begun to follow her in the hope of discovering just what was going on.

Amanda was crying; it was hard to tell, the tears which welled from her eyes were lost in the snow that coated her face as she ran straight into the wind. The snow stung her face and melted on her cheeks; she failed to notice, she was out of control, not knowing where she was going or why she felt the need to run at all. There were, after all, more rational responses to what had just happened to her.

In her mind, she accompanied every running step with the mantra; bastard, bastard, the emotions that she had managed to lock away for all these years, since that evening when she had watched the television but then become part of an unfolding horror story, a night when she had showered in her stepmother's blood, suddenly threatened to engulf her completely.

Suddenly that night seemed like only yesterday, the look on her stepmother's face was frozen in her consciousness, the terror and then the agony. The look of horror, the knife, the blood; horror, knife blood, horror, knife and blood. The images would not go away.

Amanda slipped and fell to her knees, the tights she was wearing, already drenched and dirty were now torn as well; she didn't care, glancing over her shoulder she expected to see the face of Alfred Williamson, manic and hate-filled, right behind her. He would be wielding that same knife, wearing the same expression and the outcome would be the same.

"Come to Daddy Amanda." The words were in her head but to her they sounded real enough. She tried to regain her feet but slipped again, she was exhausted, wet and cold.

She noticed for the first time that she had now become the focus of everyone's attention, and, possibly for the first time since she had received the telephone call, she succumbed to rational thought. Trying hard to resist the temptation to run on, she began trying to brush herself down. It was hopeless and she was now sobbing.

"Are you alright lady?"

She looked deep into the eyes of her questioner, looking for some clues as to his intentions. He didn't look like a knife-wielding maniac and she thanked him for his concern as she said that she was okay. She climbed to her feet and proceeded to walk on. She could feel a multitude of eyes watching her go and was suddenly glad, despite how cold she was feeling, that the snow was getting still heavier. She wanted to hide in its icy-white embrace.

It was only now that she was walking that she realised that she had not got her coat with her. The wind was bitter and she shuddered with the cold, it was as though the wind could just chill the very blood in her veins; perhaps it could, she was in danger of succumbing to exposure. Recognising both the need to calm down and get in a warm environment, she began to look for a place to do it. The door of the Red Lion looked inviting; it was the only encouragement she needed to step inside.

The contrast in temperature took her breath away, a hearty fire burned in the hearth, its warmth bathing her in its rosy glow, even before she was properly inside the building. Just the sights of normality around her made her feel better though she knew that once again she was the focus of everyone's attention. She walked towards the bar on painful legs, her feet squelching inside her shoes; she cut a despairing figure and a mumble of low conversation attested to that.

Smiling the very best smile that she could manage, she ordered a large gin and tonic and looked longingly at it as it was dispensed from optic to glass as she began to shiver with both the cold and the adrenaline that had coursed through her body in the last few, what, minutes; hours?

The landlord looked almost embarrassed to be serving her as he stated the cost of the warming liquor; he managed a warm and friendly smile though. Amanda reached for her handbag and her now thin smile evaporated completely, it was not draped on her shoulder as it should have been; of course it wasn't, like everything else it was back in the office.

"I'm afraid I've lost my handbag."

It was the only thing she could say as she turned and left the pub. She knew that every eye watched her sad retreat.

TWENTY THREE

When Jim Dowley awoke again it had been hard to tell just what hurt the most; the remains of the hangover that pounded in his forehead or the pains that coursed through his back and legs. Beneath his aching head came his stiff neck, the position he had found himself in when waking would have impressed an amateur gymnast.

During his restless night the rain had turned to snow. It was daylight and the blinding brilliance of the snow hurt his eyes. Looking at his watch he was astounded to find that it was ten-thirty already. He'd overslept, he had meant to rise early and to try to seek out a bed and breakfast, and then go into work. Work would have been out of the question in any case, he concluded, as he tried to wipe the sleep out of his eyes.

He tried to think about the night before, but there was more emotional pain there than he could deal with at the present time; he had enough with the physical pain. He supposed he ought to telephone the office and report in sick, but for some reason he decided to let them stew. He had given that company so much and all the reward he got was to have his company car taken away; fuck them!

Groaning as the various pains kicked in, he pulled himself into an upright position and pushed open the door of the car. The snow was surprisingly deep here, where the strong wind had blown it against both the car and the large wooden fence that surrounded the pub car park where he had parked the car the previous day.

He trudged across this now, through his tired eyes and pounding head he had noticed that the sign above the door stated that the establishment did bed and breakfast and that a vacancy was available. It seemed as good a place as any, at least for the short term.

He was lucky, the landlord recognised him as an occasional visitor to the establishment and remembered that his potential guest could sink beer with the best of them; he tried not to appear too keen as he agreed to take Jim in. The two exchanged pleasantries as he was shown to a clean and functional little room with views out over the car park which looked good only due to the snow cover.

When Jim mentioned that he had been forced to spend the night in the car, the landlord had suspected marital strife as the reason for this and agreed to cook him a breakfast there and then for a small consideration.

For some reason, a good fry up had always sown the seeds of recovery to a hangover for Jim Dowley. With food inside him and the chance to freshen up in the shower, he began to feel slightly human once more. The shower water was hot and steamy and he could feel the aches and pains and the coldness in his bones drifting away with it as he stood there and let the shower pummel him.

He knew he would have to go back to the house at some stage to pick up a few things, he knew too that he would need to start searching for a more permanent place to stay. The room at the pub was, apparently, only available until the end of the week, after which a brace of builders had booked it for a six-week stint. He would try to go to the house when Jennifer and the kids were not there, perhaps when she was doing the school run. A repeat of the emotional trauma of last night was something he didn't feel he could face right now.

Jim had built up a few useful contacts through his work; he had certainly helped a few influential people out of some tight spots and he thought it was time to call in a few owed favours. There were a lot of clients who had invested in property in the town for subsequent letting to the plethora of students and young professionals who were found here in abundance. He would make a few calls and try to get a decent place at a decent rent. He had a couple of candidates for a phone call in mind.

It was as he had been tucking into his breakfast that Jim made the decision to resign from his job. There were too many reasons to leave and nowhere near enough to stay. Not least of his worries was Joanne who had virtually expressed her love for him yesterday, he didn't want to hurt her, Jennifer or himself by making life even more complicated than it already was.

It seemed like a good reason among the several others. He had been flattered at her attention but he could not let it become anything more than that. He still hoped above anything else that he would be able to save his marriage.

It had come as a great shock to find that he was thought about in a sexual way by Joanne. She was a good six years his junior and in any case he had never really considered how other women might perceive him, such was the solidity of his relationship with Jennifer. It was, somehow, ironic to find out that his wife had been right to be concerned as to his capacity for an extra-marital affair when he himself had considered himself to be beyond such things.

Jim headed into town shortly after his shower, thanking his host for his kindness. He had walked into his offices expecting to see Joanne on the reception, she wasn't there and he thanked God for that. When he revealed his intentions, his boss had been astounded that Jim was taking this course of action, he was the most valued member of staff he was told, but he had been firm about his intentions, he felt reckless and it felt good, at least for now.

He had to give only a month's notice; that was their problem, he thought, they should have given him a better contract, he was owed four weeks leave, so he walked out of the building without a job and more happy for it. As with the incident with Joanne, it was enlightening to see the shock waves that his decision created in the company. He had been so lost in his own confused world, so convinced that his performance at work was suffering as a result, that it had amazed him how highly he was still regarded there.

Jim felt great as he walked back through the reception and back out into the snow. Joanne had still not been there and he had enquired where she was; a dental appointment he was told. Good that meant that her absence was nothing to do with the embarrassment of spilling her heart out to him the previous day.

It was another reason for him to feel good, it wasn't as if he had broken her heart or anything was it? A quick recollection, an uneasy one, of the pain on Jennifer's face as he had taken his leave last night, tempered his spirits a little, but not too much. It felt like he was removing clutter from his mind that would allow him to think clearly, maybe face his demons and rebuild his life.

As he walked along he considered the change in the weather. The snow was getting quite exciting really, it certainly showed no signs of stopping and he tried to remember when it had last been this heavy and prolonged. He couldn't recall, though he seemed to remember building a snowman in the garden with Darren not all that long ago so perhaps it was more recent than he thought.

The memory of the snowman gnawed away at him as he walked; what would the children make of his absence and what would Jennifer tell them was the reason for it? He tried to push such thoughts out of his mind; he needed to focus on the here and now not the past or the future.

What would he do now? A drink to celebrate his new found freedom of course; what else? He would sit and drink and think about all the things that had made his recent working life so miserable. It wasn't like he wasn't wealthy. It was funny how it is so important to work all the hours that God sends even when you have enough money to last a lifetime. How deadlines and making other people richer than you are seem so important.

Perspective, he concluded, was something that you lost when you became embroiled in your work to the extent that he had been. People were starving in Third World countries, earthquakes and bush fires devastated lives and left people homeless, wars were raging all over the globe. Jim had been in a sour mood because he had lost the use of a company car, something that had been offered back to him this morning when he handed in his notice. It all seemed so pathetic now.

He got to the pub at twelve-thirty and he was already on his third pint by the time the girl staggered in out of the snow. Through the mirror, he had stood at the bar and watched in stunned silence and disbelief as she walked in, bedraggled, and obviously in distress, and made her way to the bar where she stood beside him. She was wet, pale and dishevelled. Her breathing was heavy as though she had been running. She became the focus of attention in the pub and the conversational buzz had noticeably lowered on her arrival.

Was he asleep and dreaming again? He could no longer differentiate between fantasy and reality. Perhaps he was still asleep in the car, still in a full time job. If she was real, from this distance he could reach out and touch her, but he daren't take the risk, he didn't want to make a fool of himself in public and in her bedraggled state he was equally worried that she might scream.

It was only as the vulnerable woman realised, with obvious embarrassment of her own, that she had mislaid her handbag and had no money that he was spurred into action. After all, what had he got to lose? If this was reality he would be deemed gallant; if fantasy then it didn't matter a jot in any case.

As she turned to leave, he had offered to stand the lady her drink, the landlord heard and looked pleased; the girl, however, had not heard the offer and she made for the door. Jim watched her leave, she looked so vulnerable, almost frail, he had chased her for so long and yet he stood there transfixed and watched her leave. It was as though he was caught between two dimensions, unable to think properly or move in either of them. He forced his mind to focus.

The landlord told him the cost of the drink and then watched in bewilderment as the man, who had seemed so affable and who looked set for a good drinking session which would benefit his cash till considerably, suddenly turned on his heels and headed for the door of the pub. Moments later he was through it and out into the cold.

It had been that kind of day really. The landlord left the drink on the bar next to the man's unfinished pint of bitter just in case. At least there were plenty of people in the pub today. With a shrug he moved along the bar and served a young, professional looking couple with food and wine. At least they held out some cash to him when he had dealt with their requirements and they showed no signs of legging it out of his pub either.

The door to the pub opened once more and he glanced up, hopeful that the odd couple were returning. A group of four young women laughing and trying to brush the snow off their coats walked into the warmth of the bar. He knew the sort; food and wine and a few more quid in the till.

TWENTY FOUR

He knew he had scared the girl and he was glad, he'd relished every moment of their conversation. He knew he must make her pay for what she had made him do; knew too that she must share his pain; all those wasted years in incarceration, she had to pay for that didn't she?

When he was inside the various institutions, nobody had listened to him when he had told them that it had been the girl, Amanda, who had influenced him, had made him do what he did, by way of strange dreams that she had put into his head. It was Amanda that had caused him to murder his wife; his precious childhood sweetheart.

He had led a rational and happy life until that scheming little bitch had entered their lives. Childhood tantrums that took away his concentration, his peace of mind; all that crying, being sick all over everything and shitting everywhere, all those sleepless nights. This had affected him, his life was rattled by the presence of her, and he became moody and depressed.

Susan had never argued with him before the girl had invaded, but as soon as the poisonous child was in the house things had started to go wrong and that, more than anything else, was why the girl must die now.

He would cut her; that was a certainty, long, slow cuts. He would see to it that she died slowly and painfully, in agony and screaming for mercy. He knew he would laugh in her face when she screamed for his mercy; he would mock her, play with her mind as she had played with his when she was a child.

He had hoped that he could persuade her to come to him but his anger had pervaded his thoughts just a little too much for her to trust him. Her voice had sounded so innocent, like the young girl he remembered, but he supposed that all demons could speak like angels when the need arose, when it was in their interests to do so.

As a teenager he had read all about demons, they could take on a multitude of forms to trick people, the whole subject had fascinated him and he felt he was as expert as anyone on the subject. All things occult or unexplained had interested him; ghosts, flying saucers, the Bermuda Triangle, he had become obsessed by a book written by Aleister Crowley which, he considered, had changed his life; changed it for the better of course.

Through this book he had developed a greater understanding of life and how things worked. Crowley was an occultist who had gained a formidable reputation during his lifetime. Alfred didn't agree with everything the man had to say, for one thing Alfred was a staunch believer in God; but he believed that much of Crowley's philosophy, coupled with the teachings of *The Bible*, could explain the world around him.

Susan had never been very interested in that sort of thing; she had been a sweet, tender and kind woman; a loving wife who he adored. He had met her in the playground at primary school and had fallen for her straightaway. The other boys had picked on him at school; hardly a week went by without some sort of beating being inflicted on him. But he had Susan and she loved him.

Susan and her friend Rebecca had been his only true friends. Becky had been plump and plain; his Susan was slim and pretty. He had loved her so much it hurt his insides when he kissed her at the school gates each evening and then walked home to his parents' house.

Alfred was an only child; his mother had almost died in labour and was not prepared to take the same risk again. She refused to even contemplate sex after his birth. His father was a drunk; possibly due to the removal of his conjugal rights, Alfred hardly ever saw him. His father worked in the steelworks and would make a point of visiting the Forge Public House straight from work with his work colleagues. It was quite often past midnight when he staggered into the house and demanded his dinner.

The few nights when he came in not demanding his dinner he usually reeked of whisky and perfume, having sought some kind of sexual relief in other places. "In the beds of whores," Alfred's mother used to say. On the few occasions that their paths did cross, Alfred was often soundly beaten and despatched to his room. Alfred assumed that his father blamed him for his mother's frigidity and was out for revenge. It was just his life and he accepted it as it came.

Alfred often turned up at school with cuts and the occasional black eye, once even with his arm in plaster. When he was at school he would be beaten some more and Susan and Rebecca would be there to console him, to nurse his wounds, make him whole once more.

He left school and did some National Service which toughened him up and, in fact, by the time he left the army he was as big a bully as anyone. He had grown considerably in his late teens and the propensity for people to pick on him had declined.

When he left the army he got a job in a local shop, selling carpets and furniture. He hated it but was determined to stick at it to earn enough money to be able to rent a flat for him and Susan. When that day finally arrived there had been hell to pay. His mother had screamed at him in her disapproval and had even hit him. So what; just add another protagonist to the list he had thought; he knew he could crush the woman in any case.

He was accused of walking out after afflicting so much pain in the house. Why was that he wondered, he was guilty only of having been born. Susan was, of course, referred to as the whore.

For, perhaps, the first time in his life, Alfred had lost his temper; he had punched his mother square on the nose as he defended Susan's honour. The tide of red liquid that accompanied the act surprised him. In the past, before the army, it was usually his own blood that he saw, it had elated him and he had hit her again and again until she had lain in a pool of her own blood on the kitchen floor.

After making sure that he hadn't killed her he collected his things and headed out of the nightmare building that had been his home but felt like a prison for so long, home was now with Susan in their own little place. He had kicked his mother in the stomach for good measure on the way out.

Living with Susan was a different world to the one that he had dealt with for so long. He could do exactly what he wanted and do it exactly when he wanted to. Sex had been a problem at first, but once he had taught Susan what his special needs were, things picked up considerably.

Susan was kind and understanding, he figured that he would not find many women who would be able; or willing to put up with his little foibles; but then Susan was a very special woman. Her only fault was her maternal instincts; she so badly wanted a baby. Alfred did not want that kind of responsibility in his life; he had endured a miserable childhood and didn't wish to put another youngster through the same ordeal.

Still at the shop, he had worked his way up to the position of assistant manager; only the owner, William Blakeley, outranked him. He had wanted to hurt Blakeley, he was treated as slave-labour, and he wanted to punish the man for not paying him enough money.

Alfred had planned to kill Blakeley when he had finished with Amanda, but the old bastard had got himself killed in an armed robbery a few days ago, at least it saved him the bother, but he had so wanted to chop the man into little pieces. God was his guide though and Alfred accepted that He made all things happen for a reason, his priority was the girl and he was determined not to fail in his quest to kill her.

Alfred had long suspected that Susan could not have children, long before she finally conceded that there was something wrong. They had sex every night for years but Susan had never had so much as a late period in that time. A few medical tests had confirmed her worst suspicions and Susan had sunk into the depths of a long and painful depression.

The sex had stopped abruptly; reminding Alfred of his parents who, by this time he had not seen for years; his needs were great and Susan had stopped pampering to them, he felt cheated and angry. For a time he tortured himself with thoughts of what he could do to return their relationship to what it had been before Susan had got her devastating news.

Ridiculously, it had been his suggestion that they consider adoption, he had said it more or less in desperation but Susan's reaction was instant and the woman he had known came, once more, into his life.

Their sex life returned to what it had been before, the two of them were registered to an adoption agency, and Susan strutted around as if just doing this had impregnated her. It was worrying for Alfred but at least part of his life had returned to the stability that he so yearned. Amanda arrived eighteen months later and, for Alfred at least, that was when the problems really started.

Their sex life again fell victim to this monumental change in their circumstance; their attempted liaisons were invariably met with a loud and wailing response from the next room which would result in Susan immediately leaping out of his embrace to cater for the child; that poisonous demon spawn that had been sent to hurt him and destroy his life.

The night when a young Amanda had wandered into their bedroom to find Alfred tied to the bed and Susan sitting astride him had been the beginning of the end. Susan would only indulge in what she called 'normal' activities from that night forwards. "It's not healthy for a young girl growing up in a place like this." The words had been like a dagger to his heart.

Susan was sounding more like his mother every day; Alfred began to stay out later at night, just a small modicum of sympathy for his father's plight entering his consciousness. The Rose and Crown was a homely place, it felt more homely than home; that was for certain. Some nights he would just come home and go to bed leaving his dinner untouched. He was losing weight; he didn't care.

The dreams he had, had started just after the girl had come to live with them; that couldn't be a coincidence now could it? They became more and more ethereal and resurrected his interest in the supernatural; he was almost afraid to sleep and took to reading books on the subject until the early hours of the morning. Susan seemed not to notice, or not to care, she doted on the young demon in their midst, the spawn of Satan himself.

Alfred became resentful of the attention that his wife gave to the child at his expense and they had begun to argue, sometimes violently. In his dreams; the girl resplendent in gowns of deep, red velvet trimmed with gold and wearing a crown on her head which writhed as the snakes that constituted it moved around her poisonous head; carried a red velvet cushion on which was placed the large knife which should have been in the drawer in the kitchen.

She had presented it to him and he had taken it and walked to the huge stone altar on which was tied the prone and naked body of his wife, black candles burned in the vault around him. The girl, Amanda had smiled at him and he had killed Susan, he was bewitched, how else could he have done such a thing? The warm blood engulfed him, as her heart pumped it out of her body through the huge slit that he had made in her throat.

So, it had been the girl's fault, entirely her fault, on the night that he had come home to find his wife pouring his dinner into the bin, he had been early by the standards of the time, but the girl's influence had made him do what he did. The Satanic influence that she exerted over him was impossible to resist. How could he, a mere man, fight against that kind of power? He had killed his bride; his childhood sweetheart and it had all been the fault of the innocent looking angel devil who watched it all, who had bathed in his wife's blood.

The days afterwards were all a blur, the nights sleepless, he was interrogated by policemen, analysed by psychiatrists then interrogated again. He remembered little of the trial; they had decided he was mad, a crazed creature who should never again see freedom, but they had been wrong, all of them, it was they who were mad. The girl too, she was crazy, he had even told them that but they showed no intention of listening to him; maybe she held some Satanic spell over them, maybe her powers were greater than even he had imagined. They sent him for a time to a place with padded walls; why had they done that? The girl's influence again probably.

The cell had been a place of nightmares, but also a place of safety, maybe the padded walls protected him from the girl and her mischief. It was a place where he could sit and contemplate revenge; the girl could not get to him in this environment. There were no windows and even the door was padded. Here her evil could not affect him.

In his deliberations he concluded that the girl would have to die in torment, she would plead with him for her life; oh yes she would plead but he would be strong and he would carry out God's will; with God on his side he would surely triumph over the demon and the world would come to realise that they had done him a disservice, that he had been blameless and they would thank him for his help in purging the world of the girl's influence, her lies and arch trickery. He would at last be free; free to look for another woman like Susan who would tend to his needs.

**

The fire at the institution had surely been a gift from God Himself. The alarm bells sang out and to Alfred it was a song of beauty, the nurse who had opened the cell door had been terror stricken, easy to deal with for a man with Alfred's passion for revenge. His skull had split open as Alfred threw him backwards against the corridor wall, he felt no pity as he watched the blood start to form on the floor around him.

The place was chaotic, which suited his needs; the corridors were filled with the cloying smoke, creeping through air vents and under doors.

The main electricity supply had failed and the dull light provided by the emergency lighting was useful to him but also eerie as it tried to push back both the blackness and the smoke. To his left he saw flames for the first time as they licked away at anything that was willing to succumb to their devouring embrace, to his right, an orange glow in the distance told him that the fire was completely out of control, but it was, nevertheless, to the right that he turned and ran.

His legs were stiff; lack of exercise due to his confinement was responsible for that, but the smell and the fear of death were in his nostrils and adrenaline coursed through his blood-stream. He had no idea of the layout of the building but then he was sure that God would guide him, He would help him to fulfil his mission in life, a God given and important mission.

He almost missed the door. He had run into a wide area which was ablaze, the flames dancing around, and the heat ferocious, the surfaces on which they cavorted were charred and cracked. The smell of cooked meat confirmed Alfred's suspicion that men had perished here. He didn't intend to add to their number.

The door was beyond where at least two of them lay; here the flames were at their fiercest. He would not be able to get through, the heat was overwhelming, the smoke acrid and becoming unbearable. His eyes streamed, it felt like his eyes were actually baking; the back of his throat was sore from the taste of the smoke he was being forced to take in. He felt light-headed.

The sparse grey clothes, standard issue for the inmates who didn't actually need straightjackets, which he was wearing, were crisp and, he thought, on the verge of bursting into flames. He looked back the way he had come and saw that the flames were advancing, he was trapped. As he looked a great chunk of the burning ceiling came crashing down and more flames appeared, the wave of heat that accompanied it almost knocked him off his feet. The door was his only chance. Turning, and feeling like a frightened animal, which he supposed was exactly what he was, he dashed past the burning bodies and to the door beyond.

The flames bit, cruelly, into his flesh as he rushed through them, he had put his hands up to his face to protect his eyes, but he felt the skin on his cheek blistering and then sizzling as he advanced through the inferno.

He screamed; it was the scream of a frightened beast, but also one of determination, he wanted his revenge; God's revenge. His clothes were now on fire but he had made it to the door. He steeled his mind to the imminent pain; the agony that he knew he would have to endure, he would use his left hand, the one he used less, and he reached for the metal door handle; would it be locked? If it was he was dead.

His flesh sizzled immediately as the red hot handle cut into the palm of his hand. He must be strong; he forced himself through the tears, the flames, the heat and the smoke to concentrate on turning that handle. With a superhuman effort, the like of which can only really be found in such life-threatening situations, he turned the knob and pulled at the door, which was now ablaze, it opened, God was clearly watching over him.

The darkness beyond the door was refreshing, cool, he cried but his tears were too cooked to fall, through the darkness he could see one of the many fire engines approaching the building, he ran out into the night, rain played onto his shrivelled skin and he wanted to cry out with the agony or the ecstasy of it, he needed to be invisible, he must make no sound.

He ran out across the expanse of lawns which surrounded the old, red-brick Victorian building, it had the appearance of a stately home but Alfred Williamson knew differently. Its appearance disguised the misery within those walls. He knew he had to find cover, to get as much distance between himself and the building before he was missed; though looking at the building once again, it was clear that that might be a long time from now.

A large area of woodland lay beyond the wall that surrounded the grounds, the darkness within looked safe and inviting. He scaled the wall with considerable difficulty; his left hand was practically useless, such was the agony he felt from it. He ran into the trees, tripping and falling over several times, cursing the night but in a whispered voice. His muscles were tightening by now and the effects of his burns were becoming more and more painful.

He was standing in the stream before he had even realised it was there. Using his right hand he spooned the cooling water into the smoke burned interior of his mouth and then allowed it to trickle slowly down his throat. This he did several times, the sensation was wonderful. Here he was, by God's hand no doubt, free and drinking water from a stream in woodland. It was a world he had not seen for many years; how many years; had he a clue or had he stopped trying to count? It didn't seem to matter to him. He could only guess; in his cell, day and night had been all one.

Contentment and tiredness overcame him in equal measure and he sought refuge from the rain which dripped through the overhead canopy of trees. His eyes were becoming accustomed to the dark though they still stung painfully. He found a tree which afforded some degree of shelter and collected some relatively dry bracken to act as both cover from the cool night and camouflage against a casual passer-by. Then he slept, it was a long and dreamless sleep.

When he awoke it was daylight, but a fading one, he had slept almost right through the day. He felt refreshed though he was still in considerable pain from his injuries. He marvelled that he had slept through the pain and once again attributed this to God.

It was good that it was this time of day he reasoned, he would have to travel by night until he had put some miles between him and the institution. It wasn't probable, but by now the authorities might have noticed his absence, at the very least he needed to achieve his mission before he was returned to custody.

The skin on his cheek and his left hand felt taut and unreal, the excruciating pain had subsided to a throbbing ache, as he tried to flex the fingers of his hand he immediately regretted it. He yelped in pain, his voice echoing around amongst the lengthening shadows and it seemed to linger in the early evening air for an age. He felt exposed, he was probably being observed by hundreds of unseen creatures, sitting in the shadows, watching, listening.

The hollow feeling in his stomach identified for him one of his top priorities. The search for food in this tree-bound wilderness, and in fading light, would not be easy. He had found the stream again and he stooped to spoon some more of the crystal clear water into his mouth which was still sore and dry. He marvelled at how it invigorated him, was this yet another gift from God?

His thirst slaked, he set off; he had no idea where he was but he knew that the institution was on the other side of the stream so he headed away from it in the opposite direction. He walked all night; the first indication that dawn was coming coincided with his first sight of civilisation. The trees had thinned gradually and, as more and more of the surrounding countryside came into view in the half-light, he had seen the small village about a quarter of a mile away tucked into a valley.

He covered the distance quickly; he wanted to be back in the relative safety of the woodland before full daylight. His movements were furtive. The last thing he wanted was to make a noise and possibly disturb a dog which might bark and give away the fact that he was there. Until he had put a lot of miles between him and the institution he was vulnerable.

The authorities and, indeed, the local population would be fearful that during the chaos of the fire inmates may have escaped both the flames and their captors and be on the loose in the area. He had to be very careful; God would help him though, he was sure of it.

The first dustbin had been disappointing, nothing particularly edible there, he had scooped a little cat food out of a tin and sampled it with trepidation. The meat had been so rancid he had almost been sick into the tin. The second dustbin had been much better; here the remains of the previous night's dinner nestled invitingly at the top of the bin. He ignored the empty deposits from an ashtray which lay beside the fare and scooped the food up noisily with his good hand.

The washing on the clothes-line had been a real bonus, a shirt, a pair of trousers, some socks, even a woollen sweater. They were all still wet, the residents of the semi-detached house having left their washing out all night in the damp night-air, but anything would be better than the fire and dirt stained attire he was wearing at the moment. It would make him less obvious; more acceptable despite his unshaven skin and burned flesh.

By the time the pale and watery sun had crawled into the grey and dismal sky, Alfred had been safely hidden in the golden but still leafy foliage of the woodland floor. As he lay there trying to see out the day, he resolved that he would really press on that night.

The road signs he had seen revealed that the village he had visited was called Anstle. He knew where Amanda was, being incarcerated didn't mean that he couldn't keep an eye on the outside world. The town where she lived lay less than one hundred miles away; what good fortune God had bestowed upon him that even his prison should be so close to where she lived. His childhood sweetheart's murder would shortly be avenged.

Eventually he had slept well during the daylight hours, his ordeal and the walking of the previous night had exhausted him, and, by the time he woke, it was again to the sight of lengthening shadows. Now clad in the more acceptable attire he had purloined from the clothes line he pressed on with his journey immediately.

The new clothes were, eventually, a lot warmer than those he had now discarded. He had taken a long time to put them on though, his damaged hand proving a great hindrance and the source of much cursing and swearing. He had been very sensible, given the ferocity of the fire, to use his left hand, which had shown real foresight and a calmness of nerve.

He decided to keep to the roads, to do otherwise would slow his progress down too much, he moved away into the shadows when occasional headlights threatened to reveal his presence. The muscles in his back and legs were getting stronger all the time; he had been able to cover the first seven miles without stopping for a rest. By the time that daylight began to return once more, he found he was standing on a hill, a good place from where to look for a suitable place to hide during the daylight hours.

Somewhere in the busy little town he looked at, would be a place to lie low, a place to eat. Soon he would get the chance to look down at another town, a town in which there was a girl; or, more accurately, a demon that he must vanquish. She must feel the cold steel of a blade in the same way that Susan had done all those years before. He knew this was his destiny; God Himself had told him.

Alfred was not in a great hurry. The deed would be done in God's own time; planning was everything. He would first find out about her; then he would need a knife, in the meantime he needed money. The knife, he fantasised, would have a serrated edge, he hoped that there would be lots of blood.

It was a few days before he reached the town where Amanda lived, he had to conserve his energy on the journey which had not sounded long at first but had been difficult. A few days had passed by before he had raised enough courage to be seen in the town during daylight hours. As before, he had lived out of bins, the one near the fish and chip shop a particularly rich source of food.

It was amazing really just how much got thrown away. In the town people stared at him; that was unpleasant, perhaps they recognised him; maybe his description had been circulated through the press. After a couple of days he had dispelled this fear. He now had a beard, he was burned, and he bore no resemblance to the Alfred Williamson who had been imprisoned for a crime he could not have prevented.

The mirror in the public toilets was his only friend, in moments of doubt he would visit the little building and stare at the stranger that peered out at him from the murky glass. Patches of his skin had been horribly distorted by the heat of the fire, he appeared like something from a low-budget horror film and this, of course, was why the people stared at him in the street.

Finding the girl had been easy, he knew her surname was now Fellows, she was in the phone book; how very convenient he thought. God moved in mysterious ways. Things were to get better; when he had first seen the brown leather wallet on the kerbside amongst a pile of wind-blown litter, he had almost been too nervous to pick it up. What if it had been discarded by a thief and it lay there empty? It wasn't, the one hundred and twenty pounds it contained was truly an offering from on high. He bought a coat from a charity shop and, more importantly for his task, he bought a knife; a big knife.

He watched Amanda's house from the small park opposite, a park which was nearly always deserted apart from the old tramp who had often sat on the dilapidated bench and who would drink from a bottle on occasion, it could have been vodka, gin, maybe even meths, Alfred didn't care, the old man was harmless.

Amanda; the demon, had done well for herself judging by the neighbourhood, she must be earning a fair wage to live in a place like that. He had seen her a few times; he had followed her once when she had popped out to the local shops.

The temptation to run up to her and just butcher her there in the street was almost too much to resist. But resist the urge he had. By pure fortune, or divine intervention, he had found out where she worked, he had happened to see her driving into Stark and Rutherford's one day as he walked past. As before, it only took a telephone book to find a way to get to her. He was truly blessed by God.

He would torment her on the telephone he decided, he wanted her to know fear, he wanted her anxious and sleepless, he wanted to revel in her terror, it was what she deserved after all. He wanted her to piss herself like she had on the night when she had forced him to end his precious Susan's life.

She would always be that demon child to him, the new length and shapeliness of her legs, the subtle curve of her hips, the hidden secrets beneath her blouse were all lost on him, she was still the demon, a changeling, this new carapace she wore was just another façade.

Some robotic machine had answered the telephone the first time he rang Stark and Rutherford's. Such things had not existed he thought, before the days when he was incarcerated, he didn't know how to deal with it. He tried again a few times, all with the same result before he finally plucked up the courage to do what the automaton said and left a message.

He hadn't left nearly enough, he had practised his monologue the night before as he slept beneath the bandstand in the park. He had worked really hard on it, but the machine took away his concentration, the next time he called was the same.

Then there was the time when a man answered the telephone. Who was he, a work colleague perhaps, or maybe her lover, he had left a vague message but had been heartened by the fact that on this occasion he had spoken to a real person and not a robot.

But then, at last, he had made a call that she had answered personally. The conversation had gone better than he'd planned, a thousand times, it seemed, he had practised that monotone voice, and a thousand times it had not sounded as eerie, as menacing, as it had that morning.

Amanda had panicked so early in the conversation that he had felt like a puppeteer pulling her strings, making her jump, wince, and squirm at will; his will or God's; he wasn't sure. He had enjoyed it though, by God how he had enjoyed the thought of her shitting herself in fear.

The knife which he kept in an innocuous looking paper bag was the best he could buy using his unexpected windfall and leaving enough to buy hot drinks and, occasionally, food. The blade was sharp and cruel, the perfect implement for the perfect execution. As he had hoped, he had managed to get one with a serrated edge from a shop that specialised in fishing tackle and outdoor pursuits. It had been easy and, despite his appearance, the young man in the shop had asked no awkward questions of him.

The time was close at hand; the time to strike was up to him and God to decide but he knew it would be soon, he would be the conductor and the demon girl would dance to his tune at last. Then, the whole world would know that Alfred Williamson was God's avenging angel, they would recognise their mistakes and they would thank him; whether he could forgive a society that had spurned someone as important as he was would be in God's hands, as was everything. Beneath the bandstand in the park, he fell, contentedly into a dreamless sleep.

TWENTY FIVE

When he dashed out into the snow to follow her Jim Dowley's emotions were all at sea. He had left his pint on the bar, half full. She had looked terrified when he called out after her using the only name he had for her. Recognition had triggered in her face and she had relaxed a little but a puzzled expression had formed on her face.

Their meeting had been like neither of them had imagined. The dreams that they had shared about each other had only conveyed a part of the message; their own subconscious additions had clouded the reality. He had taken her hand and led her back into the pub, out of the snow and the cold. Despite her state of fear she had allowed him to do so, somehow she knew it was alright; that it was the right thing to do.

The silence between them as she had turned to face him had felt pregnant with expectation. It was almost as though the air between them was crackling with static electricity; it was unseen but very intense. They approached the bar where they had stood before both vaguely aware that they were the centre of attention in the busy pub.

The landlord was just about the most confused man in town at that time, he had poured a drink for a girl who looked as though she had been through some terrible ordeal. Then he had watched as she turned tail and fled and then watched as the quiet man at the bar, who had showed no signs of knowing her at first, had raced off after her leaving his beer behind.

As the two of them returned to the pub, covered in snow, he had been about to pour away their drinks. Now he returned them to where they had been before and waited to see what might happen next. He wondered if the man would keep his word and pay for the lady's drink; he was gratified to find out that he did.

A couple of business types came to the bar and he served them both with gin and tonics but he kept his eyes on the silent couple, who stood at the bar, pretending to ignore each other as they contemplated some inner thoughts. He'd been in the trade a lot of years now but this was a first; perhaps he'd have a drink for himself as he watched the drama unfold.

It was fully ten minutes before the spell was broken and the couple engaged in any kind of conversation; it was Amanda that spoke first.

"Thank you for the drink; I certainly needed it."

"You lost your handbag; shouldn't you report it to the police, maybe cancel your credit cards?"

"I left it in the office; it won't be a problem."

"You obviously left the office in a hurry then."

"I wasn't thinking clearly; I was panicking."

"Do you want to tell a stranger about it?"

"You don't feel like a stranger to me."

"I know what you mean but I can't explain it; look, why don't you find a seat and I'll get us some more drinks."

"You're being very kind; I know I look terrible."

"Don't worry about it, just go and sit down and I'll be with you in a minute."

There was an empty table near the door and Amanda headed for it, her mind racing. What did this mean; the man in her dreams was flesh and blood and he was here with her now? She looked at him as he collected the drinks from the bar but averted her gaze as he turned to bring them over to the table. She was still aware of eyes on her; the ripped tights would have to be dispensed with as soon as she could get to the ladies' room.

When Jim got to the table she excused herself and headed to tidy herself up as best she could. A glance in the mirror made it painfully apparent why she had been the focus of attention in both the street and the pub. She would just have to do the best she could. Meanwhile, back in the pub the landlord studied the pensive looking man who looked as if he had seen a ghost, such was the look of bewilderment on his face.

After around five minutes Amanda returned, she looked a lot better for ditching the torn nylons but still looked like a woman who had been through quite an ordeal. At least she wasn't attracting as much attention as before. Her comfort level was far from restored, however.

There was a silence between them again, this time it felt more companiable than previously. They were both lost in their own thoughts and not sure how to advance the conversation. Once again it was Amanda who broke the ice.

"Do I know you from somewhere; you seem so familiar to me, like I've known you once but then almost forgotten you?"

"It's possible; I was thinking of asking you the same question; I just didn't know how to ask it without it sounding trite."

"So where might we have met or seen each other before then?"

Amanda was trying desperately to recall a long forgotten party or a meeting with a counterpart from another company in the town or surrounding area. She wasn't really prepared for Jim's answer when it came.

"You won't believe me; I think the place that I've seen you before was in my dreams."

He knew this might sound like a corny chat up line and he waited for her to either laugh or walk out. She did neither and her face became suddenly serious.

"It was the same for me; I had no idea who you were but I kept dreaming about you."

Jim took a few moments to digest this. Was it really possible that the last few months had been the same trial for her, that the dreams had been the same only in reverse? He knew he needed to respond in some way and he realised that he had no doubts that she was speaking the truth. He gave voice to the question that had formed in his mind.

"So why has this happened?"

"I was hoping you could tell me."

"But I wasn't even sure that you were real; it makes no sense to me."

"I think I always knew that you were real. I just didn't understand who you were or why I dreamt about you all the time."

"I had to leave my wife; my dreams were becoming so overwhelming I was calling out your name in my sleep."

"You know my name?"

"It's Marie isn't it?"

There was a flicker of recognition in Amanda's eyes but she told him the truth and his puzzled expression was enough to tell her that he really had been dreaming about her.

"I'm sorry about your wife; what happened?"

"She couldn't take it anymore; neither could I, I left her for her own good. I thought it was the best thing to do."

"And was it?"

"It's too soon to say."

"How long ago was it when you left her?"

"Last night."

"My God; you must be pretty devastated."

"That's probably a pretty accurate description."

"I'm sorry I contributed to that. I didn't know you; what could I do?"

"You didn't do anything wrong."

"Are there any children involved?"

"Two I'm afraid; our arguments weren't doing them any good either, obviously."

Amanda looked suddenly thoughtful; she looked at him as if to ask him something but then appeared to change her mind.

"What is it?"

"I have a name for you too; from my dreams, is your name Phillip?"

"My name is Jim Dowley; it was rude of me not to tell you."

"That's strange; I was so certain."

"I was too; sure about your name being Marie. I mean, if it's any consolation to you."

"Meeting you this way is not at all how I had imagined it would be. The places in my dreams were always so ethereal, beautiful but somehow unreal. Seeing you here, in a pub, with me in this state, well I just never imagined it would be like this that's all."

Amanda took a sizeable swallow from her glass, savouring the burning sensation in her throat, feeling the life flowing slowly back into her. She had made a decision, perhaps a rash one, but a decision nonetheless.

"A few days ago I watched my father die. He was a broken man; he died right in front of me without getting the opportunity to say goodbye."

"I'm very sorry Amanda; it must have been awful for you." He could see the pain writ large across her soft features; he wanted to comfort her but something held him back.

"I know you might think me mad Jim; I can't help how you will react to this. I think he was your father too."

Jim was taken aback by this; how could this woman, a woman he was sure he had never met except in dreams, possibly know that he had no idea who his real father was? For all she knew he could have had a pint and a game of darts with his father the night before. This was all a bit too much to take in, and yet, he had been expecting some kind of bombshell from the moment he had retrieved her from the snow and led her back in here.

Would what she said make sense of what was happening to him; why his life had been turned upside down? He had to admit that it possibly did, that he might be looking across the table at a sibling. As the thought formed in his mind he noticed the tiny mole on her chin; it matched his own but that was just too much of a coincidence wasn't it. He failed to find the words to reply to her.

Amanda looked suddenly embarrassed and once again very vulnerable. She regretted being so forward. Things suddenly felt awkward between them when before it had seemed the most natural thing in the world to open up to him and tell him all that was on her mind.

"I'm sorry Jim; I shouldn't have said that," she managed.

He looked at her, there had clearly been nothing malicious in what she had said, and she obviously believed there was a weird logic to it.

"Why did you; why did you say that Amanda?"

"Because it's what I believe. Until a few days ago I was happy to accept that my father died years ago; things have changed for me. I think I have the only rational explanation for why I dream about you and, from what you have told me, why you dream about me."

"You think we're brother and sister. Why; how can you know anything about me? How do you know that my father isn't alive and well and about to come in here in a few minutes' time?"

"I don't know; but I feel that I do; my guess is that you were adopted like I was."

It was Jim's turn to take a long swallow from his glass; this was all too weird, how could she know? Was there a modicum of truth in her words? He didn't know why, but he was prepared to go along with her theory; at least for the time being. He was moved to ask her a question.

"What was he like?"

"My father; he was old and tired and he looked like he had lived a life of hell. I think he had come to my flat to explain himself; I think he had come to make a confession."

"To make a confession to you; about what exactly and why?"

"I think he had come to justify himself, to account for why he deserted me; why he deserted us, perhaps. He never got that chance; he suffered a huge coronary before he could say a word to me."

"What was he doing in your flat if you didn't even know who he was?"

"He broke in!"

"An old man; he broke into your flat?"

"So it seems; I think that, despite everything, he cared about me. Coming to my flat was his dying act, and that must mean something."

"I would say it did; why do you think he was my father?"

"We seem linked; it's obviously a very strange link. My stepfather told me what he knew of my history, he told me I was one of twins and that my twin was a boy."

"This is a lot to take in; you are suggesting that we are twins?"

"I don't know for certain but I think we are, yes."

"Why would they separate us if we were twins?"

"That I don't have an answer for; it seems like madness. All I know is that my stepfather knew that I was one of twins but that you had already been adopted before he and my stepmother located and adopted me."

"Twins," Jim said the word out loud whilst he contemplated the consequences of such a strange discovery after all these years. Amanda wasn't finished yet; she was still working things out in her own mind but the more she thought about this strange sequence of events, the more it made sense to her.

"Jim, think about it for a moment. Here I am an apparent stranger to you, a person who you are meeting for the first time. Why have you had recurring dreams about me and why have I dreamt about you too? You sit here and I tell you that I think you were adopted and you confirm that you were. It wouldn't make any sense at all unless we had some kind of filial link. We are connected psychically; look at me and tell me that you don't feel that."

He felt uncomfortable under her gaze but he had to admit that she had a point, however bizarre it all seemed to him.

"Amanda; before today, at least as far as I am aware, only my adoptive parents and myself knew that I had been adopted. I have read stuff; things about twins having a psychic link, but to find yourself being confronted by a sister you didn't know about suggesting that this is what is happening to me, is a bit of a tough one to digest without a lot of thought."

"I understand; I'm sorry, I shouldn't have said anything about it." Again, Amanda looked vulnerable, Jim felt protective, and perhaps she was actually right.

Jim smiled at her and the thin looking reciprocation that she offered told him that he had not, at least, hurt her feelings too much. It was just that it was all too much to cope with, on top of leaving Jennifer and the children, resigning from his job and spending a night sleeping in the car in freezing conditions.

He suggested another drink and Amanda accepted, both of them grateful for a lull in the conversation that was bordering on the bizarre but was, nonetheless, feeling like it might have a thread, or more than a thread, of truth flowing though it.

Amanda watched him as he approached the bar, the man from her dreams, alive in the flesh. She recalled that despite his omnipresence in her night time thoughts, that there had never been a hint of anything sexual about her dreams. She was becoming more and more convinced that she was right about this; she hoped that Jim would sense that and, eventually, agree with her.

Their conversation turned to more general things when he returned with the drinks; they gave brief histories of their lives but Amanda pointedly did not mention her first set of stepparents and the problems thereto. She might, after all, be wrong about Jim and to pour such troubling secrets into a relative stranger seemed like a crass thing to do.

They seemed to have a good deal in common, their personalities, the way that they looked at life. The longer they talked the more credibility Jim was attaching to Amanda's strange theory. It was odd, looking at her now, at her identical birthmark that it had never even occurred to him in his dreams. He had never noticed any family resemblance as he chased the woman in his dreams and yet, seeing her in the flesh it seemed almost obvious.

"Why do you suppose that in our dreams we were both adults; when presumably we haven't seen each other since we were very small children? Jim asked the question and Amanda took some time to respond; perhaps it was something that she had never considered before.

"I really can't think why. Maybe at some subconscious level we knew that by now we were adults."

"I never considered the fact that I had a sister; in my dreams you were a woman who I chased, knowing that I had to catch up with you."

"Why did you follow me?"

"I never got to find out."

"Do you have a theory?"

"I sensed that you were in some sort of danger. Maybe that's why you were running; perhaps you sensed that I was a threat to you in some way."

"It wasn't you who I was running from."

"Then who was it?"

"I'm not sure; I think someone wants to kill me."

"That's a bit extreme isn't it?"

"Perhaps I am losing my mind."

"Is that why you are here now, why you didn't bring your coat, your handbag?"

"In a way it is; yes."

"Was he chasing you, this person you think wants to kill you?"

"You said he; why did you assume it was a man?"

"I don't know; something about my dreams, I felt there was someone else, chasing both of us after a fashion. I can't really explain it. Am I wrong then, is it a woman that wants to hurt you?"

"You're not wrong."

"So you think there is a man who is trying to kill you. I'm surprised you are speaking to me then."

"It's not you; I'm certain of that, I'm equally certain, now, that you are my twin brother." She looked up at him and he thought he saw tears in her eyes, he was sure he saw stress and fear.

"Have you told anyone else about this Marie?"

"Amanda," she corrected him.

"A few people know about it."

"Do the police know?"

"Yes they do, sort of."

"I don't think I understand."

"There were telephone calls; someone purporting to be my father, when an old man broke into my flat and died there, there was an assumption perhaps that this was the end of the matter."

"And it wasn't?"

"No, I got another telephone call today; it was threatening, I didn't know what to do, I just ran and ended up here."

Jim reached forward and squeezed her hand. She looked at him through doleful eyes and decided; that if anyone on Earth should hear her story, it should be her brother. Jim listened in appalled silence as Amanda recounted the horrific tale of her first stepparents.

By the time her tale was fully told, Jim had made a decision. After finishing their drinks they left the pub; Jim wrapped his coat around her to keep her warm in the continuing blizzard. The police station was only two streets away and, once they had got there, Jim had done all the talking.

As soon as he mentioned the name Amanda Fellows to the desk sergeant, they had been afforded the very best of attention; everyone in the station knew of the botched surveillance operation. They were seen almost immediately in a private room. As luck would have it PC Sean Craig was available and his face looked pale and drawn as he greeted them. He noted the dishevelled state of Amanda and his pulse started to race. Had they got it wrong again?

Her story told; the young policeman agreed to continue the surveillance on her flat, though he didn't tell her so, the purse-strings were dictating that it be called off until this latest incident. Amanda's telephone at Stark and Rutherford's would also be tapped so that should the perpetrator dare to call there again they might be able to trace him. He also offered to give them both a lift home but they declined this. Jim and Amanda had already planned to call in at a local Chinese Restaurant for a meal. It was a tentative celebration towards the possibility that long-lost siblings had found each other.

**

It had only been around eight-thirty when Jim and Amanda arrived, covered in snow, but in fairly good spirits, at the steps that led up to the front door of the building where her flat was. She still didn't have her bag, she had used Jim's mobile to contact Dave Sullington and advise him about the telephone call and the fact that she wouldn't be back that day. He had been very understanding; her handbag would, by now, be in the office safe.

The police officers, not the same ones, had spoken to them as they walked past the prominent car and, apparently, satisfied that Amanda was not in mortal danger from the man who accompanied her, had bade them a goodnight. Looking at the steps it was clear that a few people had been coming and going from the building, their footsteps clear in the continuing snow.

Amanda felt much calmer now; on top of her afternoon drinks, they had shared a bottle of wine at the restaurant, and, despite the weather, she felt a rosy glow about her. The walk from the restaurant to the flat was not a long one but for Jim it had been cold and wet; he was feeling just a little sorry for himself.

Amanda glanced in the direction of the small park; it still gave her the creeps. What if that monster, Alfred Williamson, was lurking in its darkness even now, watching her arrival from the camouflage of the trees? Was he there waiting for his moment; waiting to pounce; waiting to snuff out her life? She shivered; but it had nothing to do with the cold.

Reaching the top step she pressed the button for the intercom to her flat. Long moments seemed to pass; it was filled with silence as the large snow flakes fell around them. She tried again with the same result.

"Damn you Kate!" Amanda called out to the air; of all the nights for her to choose to go out. Where the hell had she gone anyway, certainly not to work?

She took a step backwards allowing her to look up at the window of their flat; a light burned there.

"She's probably in the bloody shower; or else she has the stereo on so loud that she can't hear the doorbell."

Jim couldn't help but smile at her indignation; faced with the same scenario he would have behaved exactly the same. The intercom maintained its silence and so, in desperation, Amanda tried that of one of the other residents, Margaret Jones, who also acted as the liaison to the Resident's Association, which entailed having a master key to the building. This time there was a response.

Amanda explained their dilemma; Margaret, her voice sounding tinny and robotic sounded a little unsure about opening the door at first. All the residents were understandably on edge following the events of the previous week.

Eventually she had answered enough questions for Margaret to be sure that she really was speaking to Amanda Fellows and the click and buzz of the intercom's lock release system gave them egress from the cold and snow.

She glanced at Jim. He looked cold, wet and very tired. Perhaps Kate would agree to let him sleep on the settee tonight, the thought of him walking from here to the pub where he had told her he had secured a room didn't seem fair to him after all he had done for her today. She wanted Kate to meet her brother; was quite excited at the prospect in fact.

She was very sure now; the longer they had spent in each other's company; the more they had relaxed, they seemed almost to know each other's thoughts. Was some kind of filial telepathic link the reason for the mutuality of their dreams? She thought it probably was.

The hallway was well lit and warm, a welcome contrast to that white world outside the front door. As they ascended the stairs and reached the first floor landing Margaret gave her first warm smile and then a quizzical look as she set eyes on Jim. Her eyes were full of fun as she handed over the master key and berated Amanda for being silly enough to lose her own key. Amanda did not wish to go into lengthy explanations so she merely put on her best smile. It probably wasn't very dazzling but it would have to do.

As Margaret returned to her own room she tried to make sense of what she had just seen. Her neighbour wrapped in an overcoat that was a few sizes too big for her and obviously belonging to the man she was with; the man, wet and bedraggled though obviously very gallant to give the lady his coat. Had Amanda finally found a man to share her life with? She hoped so, the poor girl deserved it.

Reaching her front door, Amanda fumbled with the key and was surprised and a tiny bit disconcerted by how easily it turned in the lock. Inside the flat was illuminated but the stereo certainly wasn't on. Amanda was suddenly troubled.

"She must be in the shower, or else she forgot to turn the lights off before she went out."

Jim, who had heard a little about Kate and her erratic habits, just shrugged his shoulders; he was feeling suddenly uneasy and didn't know why. He sensed the unease in his companion; his sister, his twin?

There was a small dark patch on the light coloured carpet, just inside the door. It looked like spilled wine, red wine; Amanda was suddenly pissed off with her flat-mate. They had a nice flat; why couldn't Kate be more careful?

"She could be asleep; she drinks a bit too much sometimes."

Amanda felt herself apologising for her friend, and resented it. She failed to notice the other stains on the carpet which were dotted around.

"Kate; I've got someone here who I would like you to meet!" despite her growing anger she still felt excited at introducing Jim as her long-lost twin brother. What would Kate make of that?

Amanda's mood changed as she took in the scene around her; how many times could lightning strike; she thought insanely as she looked at the carnage? The mutilated face of her near life-long friend stared at her from across the room, the second time in a week that she had been forced to endure such a nightmare scenario. The body had obviously been placed in the chair for maximum effect.

On the wall behind her friend's body, smeared writing in the copious blood that she now saw was splattered all over the room, were the words; "Enjoy the view; you'll be next devil woman!"

TWENTY SIX

For the second time in a week the flat was awash with Scene of Crime Officers, there were more this time due to the blood and gore. Amanda and Jim were away from the bedlam, sitting in a state of shock on the large settee in Margaret Jones's flat.

Amanda looked as ashen as the snow outside which continued to fall unabated. She appeared to have retreated into herself; she hadn't even screamed when she first saw Kate's body; it was as though she was remembering another time and place and Jim was pretty sure he knew when and where. He had watched her as she began to shake as if with a fever and he tried to work out whether it was anger, shock or repulsion that was causing this malaise.

Amanda's face was a mask of misery and shock, she had cried but not sobbed; that would surely come later, perhaps a lot later. Jim had tried to comfort her but, in reality, she remained a relative stranger to him and he couldn't find the words of reassurance he wanted to. He felt isolated sitting there, the woman, Margaret, was being very kind and supportive but she was a stranger to him. As he sat there he considered the strangeness of a situation that saw a neighbour knowing more about the woman beside him, who might well be his twin sister, than he did. It seemed bizarre to him.

There was the added problem that he knew virtually nothing about the dead girl. He really only knew that she and Amanda had been childhood friends and that she had been a fun loving if slightly erratic character. Her love of fun was over for good now though and it had been on a day that had promised such good things. Finding the right words was never going to be easy in a situation such as this and he resigned himself to making appeasing noises and holding Amanda's hand from time to time.

Jim had not been as measured in his reaction to the sight in the flat as Amanda had been. The remains of his chicken chow mein would be just one more thing for the forensic team to sort through and catalogue; deposited, as it was, on the carpet by the door. Unfortunately he had vomited so much and with such gusto that his stomach and his throat hurt a lot. He needed to be strong for Amanda but he could barely stand up by the time he left her flat. To see a sight such as he had seen was not something that happened to most people in their lifetimes and he wondered what twist of fate should have brought him into this situation simply by virtue of meeting Amanda after all this time.

Kate had still been in her night-gown when she had been murdered; maybe Amanda was right and she had showered a short time ago, but, to Jim's untrained eye, it looked as though she had been dead for some time.

Much of the blood, at least where it was less profuse, looked to by quite dry. Probably the maniac had got into the flat earlier in the day, before Jim and Amanda's trip to the police station; the police were thus either not there or possibly on a reduced state of vigilance, believing that Alfred Williamson was elsewhere, stalking his prey.

Well they had their work cut out now, Jim thought wildly. If the murder had been carried out this morning the maniac might have only just missed Amanda's departure for work, he shuddered at the thought and then felt guilty about his selfishness. There was a body in that flat; a vital and well-liked person had occupied it at the start of the day. Why should he be relieved that it was Kate's and not Amanda's unless he really did feel a kinship with her?

Behind the deadpan expression; Amanda's mind was racing, it was struggling to come to terms with what she had seen, what had happened. This was new horror; she had dared to believe that she had seen enough of that in her life and now she had this new nightmare to deal with. First her murdered stepmother, then the old man in the flat that might have been her real father and now this terrible crime. What had she done to deserve to be surrounded by such horror?

Amanda had always considered Kate to be a permanency in her life; just took it for granted that she would always be there. She had loved her friend; just how deep was her affection for her wayward flatmate was only now becoming apparent to her; was that always the way? Did human beings who care about each other never get round to telling each other how much until it was too late to do so?

She was thinking now of all the things she had wanted to say, should have said; now the words would be empty and meaningless. Kate was gone and a void in her life had opened up on the very day when one had been filled.

There were so many adventures left to be had, so many places left to visit with Kate; so many girls' nights out; or quiet evenings in with a pizza, some decent wine and some trashy television programme. These things were all gone; just like her wonderful friend was gone.

The regret she was feeling at these things was dwarfed by the guilt she felt that her messy and chaotic early life had impacted on Kate; that Kate's own life should have been tainted by the maniac that was Alfred Williamson. There was no doubt in her mind who the perpetrator was, the police were 'keeping an open mind' for the time being at least. She knew that was police speak and it bugged her that they had even suggested that anyone other than her former stepfather could be considered as a culprit.

The anger that Amanda felt that Williamson had involved Kate in what was, quite frankly, her war and her battle was one more of the several conflicting emotions raging inside her. This was her fight to fight, her past that had re-surfaced, her problem to overcome and now that bastard who had destroyed so much of what Amanda was and might have become, had gone and murdered her best friend in the world. What possible grudge could he have towards Kate Harvey; how did the twisted maniac's mind work?

Amanda knew it was pointless to blame herself for this but her negative thoughts were on a rampage of their very own. Why couldn't the mad bastard have killed her so that it was Kate who returned home from work to witness the carnage? At least that way Kate would still be alive; she might, in time, get over it.

She concluded that there was only one reason for what had happened here today; Williamson wanted to make her suffer; the bloody writing on the wall was proof enough of one thing as far as Amanda was concerned, the man was clearly still deranged. How many others would be killed to get at her and who would they be; her parents, the man beside her on the settee, work colleagues?

She thought back to when they had arrived at the top step and pressed the intercom; how she had shuddered at the sight of that little park opposite. Was he in there, gloating, looking and revelling in the pandemonium he had created? Could he sense her pain; feed off it perhaps, like some kind of parasite?

A multitude of images of Kate now occupied her mind which, behind that mask of calm, was going into overdrive. The first day at school when the two of them had met each other, she remembered at how she had smiled at the strange accent, two strangers together, helping each other; just being there.

That same week, when Sally Golders had stolen her bag of sweets, Kate had hit her on the nose so hard that it bled. Nobody stole Amanda's sweets after that. Kate had been punished; a whole week of not being allowed out of the classroom at playtimes but she had never held that against her new friend.

Kate was tough but to her credit she had never been a bully. The incident in the playground had given her respect and Amanda often wondered if her friend was, in fact, the toughest in the school. She had many other facets to her though including a warm heart and unstinting loyalty.

Another image sprang into Amanda's mind, the night that Kate had broken up with her boyfriend. It had been a long relationship; Kate had been devastated. Amanda had never seen her friend cry before; a plethora of false illusions came to her as she saw the vulnerable woman inside that tough exterior.

The crying hadn't lasted too long. Kate pulled herself together, at least to the outward eye, and suggested they go and fetch some fish and chips. Amanda had needed to try not to laugh at this sudden change in her friend. Looking back this had been when Kate had gone off the rails a bit. She had a string of short-lived flings with unsuitable men; Amanda felt sure that this was a deliberate attempt by Kate to get back at her long time lover but she had never interfered.

Where had that got her; what did it matter now that she was dead? She was dead because she shared a flat with Amanda and again that innocent young face in the playground flashed back into her mind. How had it come to this?

An irrational thought came into her mind, just one of many in the soup of her emotions. What if she could avenge Kate's murder; had she got the guts to seek him out and pay back not only Kate's murder but that of her first stepmother? The thought frittered away in a sea of frustration; Kate was stronger than she was and yet she hadn't been able to stop the maniac. In any case, she concluded, killing him would make her no better than Williamson was. Where did killing for revenge rate in comparison to killing for other reasons? She considered this and decided that killing was killing, however it was dressed up.

Despite her conclusions, could she really say that given the opportunity to get him; that she would not take it? She thought not but searched the deep pools of her emotions, trying to find something to cling to, could she find pity there, pity for the monster that had caused this mayhem? She didn't think she could but her thoughts were like a raging sea, unpredictable and wild.

She came to realise that there were other people in the room around her now. Where the hell was she anyway? All seemed to be a blur, she wasn't in her own flat, that was just about all she could grasp, her own flat was filled with horrors. She managed to focus enough to see that the other people in the room were police officers, and also Margaret Jones, and beside her on the settee the man called Jim that she had only just met and she thought of as her twin brother.

She recognised two of the police officers as the ones who had attended before but couldn't remember their names. The first words she registered came from the man beside her; his voice sounded edgy but kind.

"Amanda; the police would like to speak with you; do you feel up to talking to them?"

She turned to look at him, the expression on her face remained dazed, barely a flicker of emotion showed there now; he wondered what his own must look like and decided he didn't care. He asked the question again, this time a little frown showed that she had at least heard him.

"Yes, I'll speak to them." Her voice sounded surprisingly strong considering her obvious trauma.

"Are you sure Amanda; we can wait until you're ready."

It was the policewoman Julie Walsh who spoke and Amanda recognised her properly now. She nodded that they should proceed.

Seemingly satisfied the WPC sat on a chair beside Amanda, her colleague stood behind, not wanting to crowd her but needing to hear what the distraught woman might say.

"We know this must be terribly hard for you Amanda, but we need to catch this lunatic before he strikes again. We will need your help and cooperation for that, do you understand?"

Amanda simply nodded.

"We just need to ask a couple of questions first; if it gets too much for you then just say and we'll stop and do it another time."

"Okay, I understand." Amanda's voice still sounded forceful, as if anger was welling only a short way from colouring her choice of words.

"Could you tell us what time you left for work this morning Amanda?"

"I don't know exactly; I think it was around seven-twenty, I was trying to beat the traffic, and with the weather like it is at the moment…"

"Was your flat-mate Kate awake when you left?"

"Not very awake, but she popped her head around the bedroom door as I was going out and wished me luck."

A tear snaked down her cheek.

"This was because you were returning to the office?"

"Yes."

"When you got outside, did you see anyone hanging around?"

"No, I did look, I was nervous, but the snow was heavy, there was a man walking his dog but he just seemed hell-bent on getting back in the warmth, I think the dog was too. I didn't see anybody else."

"Do you recall what breed of dog it was Amanda?"

"Not really, it was quite small but the snow was very heavy. The man walking the dog though, he was heavily wrapped up against the weather, I got the impression that he was a fairly young man; it couldn't have been Alfred Williamson."

"We're still not sure that it was Williamson who did this to Kate; we have to keep an open mind for now. Did Kate have any enemies, ex-boyfriends perhaps?"

Amanda looked at the young WPC as though she might be mad but answered the question anyway.

"Kate was always full of fun; I don't think she had any enemies, no."

"Think hard Amanda; no nights in when she mentioned something or someone bothering her?"

"No; there was nothing like that."

"Alright Amanda; let's go down the route that puts Alfred Williamson at the scene. What time was it that he telephoned you at work? You told us earlier I know but that statement is at the station and we're just trying to build a picture whilst we are at the crime scene."

Amanda nodded, "It was just before I was going to take my lunch; around twelve-thirty."

"So there are about five hours from when you left the flat until he made his call?"

"Yes; I'm pretty sure."

"When he called, did Williamson sound excitable; as if he might have done something terrible prior to the call?"

"He sounded erratic; he made no mention of Kate though."

Once again a tear left her eye as she said her friend's name. Julie Walsh placed her hand on Amanda's in a show of sympathy and support.

"We won't know the exact time that this happened until the pathologist has completed a thorough investigation. On the face of it though, it looks like he struck just after you left for work.

"He might have been waiting for you to leave. There was no sign of forced entry, but there was blood by the door. It could be that the perpetrator was already in the building when you left and knocked on the door as soon as you were out of sight. Kate might have opened it thinking it was you, perhaps thinking you had forgotten your keys. Are you sure you saw nothing unusual when you left?"

"Yes I'm sure." Amanda looked hurt that the question had been repeated; another tear.

"Are you sure you're okay to carry on with this Amanda? We could do it another time."

"It's alright, I'm okay."

"When you left this morning, were all the doors that were supposed to be locked as you would expect them to be?"

"Yes they were."

"Amanda, is it alright if one of my colleagues from CID has a little chat with you?"

"Yes."

Amanda looked at the men standing behind WPC Walsh and picked out the plain clothes man among them. She remembered him but only vaguely from the incident with the old man in her flat the previous week. He looked suitably sympathetic, and

Amanda prepared herself mentally for the next part of her ordeal.

DI Andrew Jones replaced the WPC on the chair beside Amanda and sighed as he sat. He had seen a lot of bad stuff in his time, but the scene in this vulnerable woman's flat took some beating. She was holding up pretty well but how might she take what he thought he was going to propose? He knew he would have to tread carefully but, despite his experience, there didn't seem to be a clear way forward without being open about his intentions.

He looked at her old, young face and felt pity, tears still welled in her eyes but she was making a fist of her situation. He hoped dearly that he wouldn't spoil that now.

"Miss Fellows; you appear convinced that this crime has been perpetrated by your former stepfather Alfred Williamson. As my colleague told you, we cannot make that same conclusion until we have some kind of evidence to support it. In fact, due to the ferocity of the fire that burned down the institution he was being detained in; we cannot even be certain that the man is alive.

"I can see the conviction in your face when you suggest that he may be the perpetrator though; and I can see from that that you genuinely believe this. Therein lies my problem."

Amanda looked at him through tear-laden eyes but did not make a comment; she seemed to be shrinking back into herself once again.

"Miss Fellows, putting it in its simplest terms, given the circumstances, if it is Williamson, I am going to need your help to catch this man. He might kill again at any time, given the nature of today's crime, and again I stress that if it is Williamson, not that it might be another, unconnected perpetrator, he seems to want to hurt you, punish you, perhaps for something he perceives is your fault in some way. If that's so, then he could strike anywhere, your work colleagues, friends and family, or he could just go for you."

"We can't place surveillance on all of these people; the logistics are way beyond our capabilities and manpower. Do you get an idea of what I'm suggesting here Amanda, and if you do, what would be your reaction to that?"

"You want to use me as bait in a trap?"

"I wouldn't have put it so succinctly but, in essence, that is what I am suggesting yes. We have no way of tracing this man but he is in contact with you, he wants something from you, or maybe, in fact probably, he wants to kill you. You are our only route to the killer if Alfred Williamson is our man."

"What do you want me to do?" Amanda's voice was suddenly full of determination.

"I feel sure he will try to contact you again; either on your home telephone line or at your place of work. We can arrange to divert telephone calls to a single source; it doesn't even have to be in the buildings in question. When he telephones you the next time, I want you to agree to meet with him."

"This man killed my stepmother and now my best friend. Is that wise?" Amanda's question was rhetorical but DI Jones answered in any case.

"Wise is probably not the best description for such a course of action; but I can see very little alternative; time seems to be critical here. We would, of course, be monitoring everything, if you did meet him, we would be there with armed police, we would do all we could to keep you safe Miss Fellows."

"You can't guarantee her safety so easily; look what has happened here tonight. The man's a maniac, he will stop at nothing!" Jim spoke for the first time, his voice wracked with emotion.

"Sir; Jim isn't it?" Jim nodded.

"Jim, I can't guarantee that the sun will still be in the sky tomorrow, or that I will be alive to see it if it is. I can only try my best.

"The only alternative is that this lady will spend the rest of her life looking over her shoulder, sleepless nights, maybe more nights like this one. Remember too, that the perpetrator of this crime today could be someone else; Williamson may have perished in the fire."

Jim didn't think that had happened; he shared Amanda's reservations and convictions on the subject of keeping an open mind as to Kate's murder. He allowed himself to be acquiesced for the time being at least.

"I'll take the risk!" Strong emotion was infused in Amanda's body language and her voice as she said this. "I want that bastard for what he has done to Kate, my stepmother and me; he has always been there, haunting me, my dreams, my waking hours and now he is stalking me; I don't know why but I am so sure of that, it's time to end it or die trying."

"Are you quite sure Miss Fellows?"

"Yes; let's just fucking get on with it!"

DI Jones was a little taken aback by the vehemence in her reply, but he was also encouraged by it. This had gone better than he had expected. He was dealing with a strong character here; he hoped they still would be after the endgame had been played.

"We'll deal with the telephones straightaway. I think, if it's Williamson, that he is obsessed with you and that he will not be able to resist calling you again. Now that he has killed your friend he will want to know just how deeply you have been wounded by that, he will want to gloat."

"I want that bastard dead!" Amanda was angry. The police officers ignored the outburst; in the circumstances, such a reaction was to be expected.

"Where will you stay Amanda?"

WPC Walsh asked the question; it was a fundamental one in the circumstances. Amanda looked uncomfortable, her parents maybe, but that would bring them into this dangerous loop, friends? The same problem, she was lost for an answer.

"She could stay here if that would make sense; Margaret who had been both a fascinated and an appalled witness to the whole set of events since the discovery of Kate's body had made the suggestion. The police agreed that it was a good idea, surveillance was already in place and they now had a good inside knowledge of the building and its surroundings.

The decision was made and another figure arrived, he looked harassed, it was hardly surprising given the hard time he had gone through to gain access to the building.

He turned out to be a doctor, called some time ago by WPC Walsh but who had endured a terrible journey in the worsening snow and with the number of minor accidents caused by the weather and people not taking enough care when trying to get home.

**

It had been a bewildering couple of weeks for Margaret; things had always been so quiet in this neighbourhood. Now there had been two corpses in a matter of days, security doors were being breached, the whole situation was out of control and, as someone who took her duties seriously, she was considering her position on the resident's committee.

She looked around at the sea of men and wires as her flat was turned into some kind of operations centre that resembled the set of a James Bond film. If the man was out there he wouldn't come near this building any time soon. Perhaps that was for the best.

**

The telephone had been set up in the way suggested by the tall, plain clothed policeman. A police presence, female, would be here all night sitting by the contraption, monitoring, ready to spring into action if necessary.

Amanda had been given a sedative and was in the spare bedroom asleep. The man who had accompanied her had taken his leave and Margaret had no idea where he was now. He seemed a nice man; concerned for Amanda. Odd that Margaret liked him, she hadn't really liked any man since her marriage hit the rocks, ending in a painful divorce.

As Margaret tried to ignore the chaos and retired to her own bedroom, she wished that the doctor had seen fit to sedate her too. How could she sleep with all this nonsense going on in her flat? That, and the potential that a knife-wielding maniac might arrive at any time, didn't seem to Margaret to make much of a recipe for sweet dreams and a good night's sleep. Still, she couldn't complain, she had volunteered the use of her flat.

Margaret poured herself a scotch; she had taken the bottle and glass into the bedroom before she went to the bathroom, she had been as rattled as anyone by what had happened in this backwater. Until the last few days she had considered it an idyllic haven. She thought of Amanda in the next room; she was blameless in all of this. What had brought such pain and misery to her doorstep, or, more accurately, her home?

Outside in the main lounge area of the flat things were getting much quieter. She guessed that the majority of telephone engineers and police personnel had completed their work and headed home for the night. She wondered how they might sleep after the horrors that they had witnessed here today; perhaps it happened so often that they were now immune to it.

She had checked before retiring to bed, there were two patrol cars, parked in the heavy snow; Margaret didn't think that the murderer would return tonight but the police were taking no chances. There had been door to door enquiries in the building and neighbouring buildings already. Nobody had seen anything; it was a predictable outcome, people in this vicinity often left early for work and returned home late, and the worse for a few drinks in the main.

By now the only noises were the sounds of the gusty wind outside that pushed the snowflakes into ghostly white drifts and the almost silent clicks that indicated a cooling central heating system; she wondered about the police officer manning the telephone just in case of a call in the night, would she be cold; would she need something to wrap around her to keep warm? She drank the last of the scotch in her glass and decided that the police would know exactly what they were doing and would come prepared for such eventualities.

A couple of hours later, having failed to settle and been close to sleep only a couple of times. She slipped out of bed in the darkness and walked to the window where she gently pulled back the curtain to look outside. As a child she had done this all the time when it was snowing, she loved the way it painted everything with its pureness, everything looked beautiful; it seemed different tonight, the white shroud could be hiding anything. Would the maniac be out there now, watching, waiting for his chance to wreak more havoc?

She returned to the bed, shuddering at the thought that the flat, all the flats might be watched, she thought of Amanda. What if she had been Amanda's flat-mate instead of Kate; would the police now be investigating her death instead? Maybe it had nothing to do with Amanda at all, maybe Kate was always meant to be the victim; in a sea of what-ifs and maybes, she finally found the sleep she had thought she would not succumb to this night.

TWENTY SEVEN

The sedative had been slower to work than she might have imagined, but eventually sleep had overcome Amanda Fellows in this strange bed. Her terrible thoughts before sleep had come had been bleak, until tonight she was able to cling to the, however unlikely, hope that all of this was somehow in her mind. That she was not haunted by Alfred Williamson but by the memory of him. Perhaps it had been an adult reaction to a childhood trauma. That theory no longer had any credibility; her best friend's blood had been shed, her life snuffed out. Amanda was probably next and, when she considered the alternative potential victims she hoped she would be.

Her dreams were no less filled with foreboding, she saw herself, lost and alone walking through a series of long, dimly lit corridors. She looked like a small child again but knew it was her in the dream. In the far distance was a figure, dim and obscure; menacing. She felt waves of evil intent emanating from it.

Unlike her recurring dreams she did not want to find herself caught by this pursuer; this was different, the figure meant only to hurt her and to cause her pain. She was willing her dream-self to quicken pace, to sense the danger and put distance between herself and the menacing creature; it didn't happen. Nor too did the figure's pace quicken. It seemed merely content to follow; to stalk its prey. Time, it seemed to Amanda, was on its side.

Anyone in her room would have been dubious about the fact that Amanda had been sedated; she thrashed around beneath the duvet periodically and she murmured strange noises into the rapidly cooling night air in the bedroom. No one was there to hear, to offer help or to console her. This was one night when she really did not want to be alone but she wasn't in a position to be choosy about where she would lay down her head for the night.

Saying goodbye to Jim had been a terrible wrench for her, so convinced was she that he was her brother, she had felt as though she was losing him all over again. Panic rose up in her but what could she say to the people around her that wouldn't sound ridiculous? What, too could Jim say? The answer was that they could say nothing for now; people would just have to assume that Jim was her boyfriend; that seemed wrong to her, but it was the only thing for the time being.

In the still, darkness of the room, with the snow falling heavily outside, Amanda continued to wrestle with her demons, she was stalked through many places, she wanted to wake up but the chemicals of the sedative had bitten deep and her nightmare would be forced to continue for some time yet.

**

The trek back to the pub where he had acquired his bed and breakfast lodgings was almost a trial too far for the exhausted Jim Dowley. The snow was really quite deep now, even on the main roads where the gritting wagons had struggled in vain to keep back the white blanket, there was a fairly thick covering. Visibility was very poor and he was glad he was on foot despite the cold and the aching in his bones.

As he walked he tried to come to terms with the events that had beset him since he had walked out from his home and his marriage. Had he lost a wife and two children and gained a sister? He felt an affinity to Amanda and it wasn't a sexual one. Given that she was clearly very attractive did that add strength to the theory that they were related, or did it merely show loyalty to Jennifer?

Were there any real clues in his dreams? He wondered if he would dream this evening when he finally climbed out of his wet, cold clothes and clambered into a bed. It was only the thought of a bed, after sleeping in the cold cramped car the night before that kept him placing one foot in front of the other one.

He had no answers, he realised; just his instincts and he was so tired that he could barely trust them at the moment. Serious thought on the subject would have to wait until the following day. It was very late by the time he got to his lodgings and every part of his body and his soul seemed to hurt. It was doubtful if he would be down in time for breakfast tomorrow; his tiredness outweighed the hunger he felt, his dinner jettisoned in the horror scene flat.

He found his room and undressed. It was basic but in his current condition it looked like the Ritz. Leaving only the bedside lamp on he got into the bed, it was very cold at first, any heating having long ago shut down for the night and cooled. He sat there for a few minutes, slowly warming, staring at the television screen on the chest of drawers opposite which was blank.

In the morning the news programmes will be filled with reports on a terrible murder; a heinous crime that he had become a part of by association with a woman who believed herself his twin sister. He sighed at the magnitude of it all. The bedside light remained on but Jim Dowley could stay awake no longer.

TWENTY EIGHT

It was the cold that woke him. Bitter cold, biting into his old bones making them feel like they might crack right there and then. He wiped the back of his hand across his streaming nose and tried to get his eyes used to the darkness in the storage room beneath the bandstand in the park.

He was catching a chill at best, worse still it could be the onset of flu. He would have to overcome this or fight it; he couldn't allow himself to be thwarted now, not after coming so far. He was on God's errand and He would not allow Alfred to fail.

Alfred could have killed her this morning of course, but as he stood on the landing immediately above the floor below and saw her emerge from the flat, heard her exchanging pleasantries with someone inside, he had decided to indulge in a little fun, he could hurt her, make her suffer like he had had to suffer before he finally ended her miserable existence.

He wondered how much Amanda appreciated the trouble he had gone to, to leave her a little message on the wall of the flat. That had been an inspired afterthought; a gift from God, real horror story stuff. He smiled in the darkness.

She must be really upset, fearful for her life and grieving for the stupid little bitch that had so innocently opened her door to him this morning. It had just been so easy; as soon as Amanda was out of sight he had bounded down the staircase and knocked on the door, mindful that any delay would cause whoever was in the flat to doubt that it was Amanda who knocked gently on the door.

If she had screamed he might have had problems, but the girl had been half-asleep and he had managed to push the knife into her shoulder blade before she could show any real reaction, after that the shock of the blood and the sight of her assailant had struck her mute with fear whilst he continued his task. It was just so easy.

His hiding place was as comfortable as it could be given its position, but the cold had permeated and made him stiff and feeling his age. At least it was dry, that surprised him, but then builders had been so fastidious in the era when buildings like this one had been erected.

He was hungry, he hadn't eaten all day, the sheer adrenaline rush that he had felt when he killed the girl, coupled with the thought of what effect that would have on Amanda, had caused him to forget to eat; he had to eat soon, he didn't want to bring attention to himself.

Yesterday had been kind to him. No one took much notice of a stranger in the snow when all they wanted to do was to get in the warmth of a building or a car. Today might be different though, perhaps the snow had melted. Perhaps news of his exploits had travelled and people would now be so much more alert.

With a groan, and great difficulty, he managed to ease himself onto his knees. He began to pull on his coat which he had used as a blanket. It was difficult, such was the darkness, the cold and his aches and pains all contributing to his difficulties.

He began to push the small door beneath the bandstand open. He had been fortuitous in two ways, he had found it unlocked and, in November he guessed, so far correctly, that no one would be along to use the storage room until the spring at least.

The weight of the snow behind the door shocked him. He had to push with all his weight to open it at first. Panic rose in him as he considered the possibility that a park worker had noticed the door unlocked and locked him in. The feeling of being incarcerated he had known so well, washed over him and he felt nauseous, but just as his panic reached a peak the door had inched open a little.

He could see through the gap between the door and the jamb that it would soon be morning. Pushing the door again with an aching shoulder he edged it further open and marvelled at the winter wonderland that the park had become. It was still snowing, though there wasn't a great deal of light to see it by, just the distant orange glow of the sodium street lamps about three hundred yards away.

The snow was very deep and, here in the park, unspoiled by footprints except those of birds and small animals; how long had he slept for the snow to be this deep, he wondered, had he missed a day?

The thought of sleep reminded him of the dream he had been having when he was woken by the bitter cold. It had been years since he had remembered his dreams, probably something to do with his medication he reasoned. After this one he hoped it would be years before he had another.

As he started to walk through the snow, trying to keep under cover as much as possible, he thought about the dream again. It had started alright from his perspective. Amanda, the demon, had been there and he had chased her for a long time through dark and evil-looking places, caves and tunnels. Strange creatures had been in the caves with him, mutant creatures that mewled in the darkness as he raced by them.

Had he the time he would have sought them out and killed them, putting them out of their obvious misery, but he knew that to do so might mean losing sight of his quarry, Amanda. She was, after all, a demon and he knew from his research all those years ago that demons could be pretty bloody clever. The creatures in the darkness were probably put there by her to divert him from his primary aim.

He would not let her trick him, she fled from him like the frightened beast that she was. Knowing that with God on his side she could not defeat him; he would run her, it, into the ground and then he would banish the infernal creature to whence it came.

In his dream he had carried a knife, it looked like the one he had killed the bitch girl with, he recognised the serrated edge, it was ideal for ripping and tearing flesh as he now knew. Ahead of him, the demon woman stumbled and he began to close the gap with triumphant strides.

He towered over her as she looked up at him with fearful eyes. Time had been good to her he thought, she reminded him a little of Susan, that was probably just another diabolical trick to divert him from his task, the fear in her eyes certainly looked like the fear in Susan's all those years ago though.

In the dream, Amanda had pleaded with him, even as he dragged her by the hair a little way across the rough ground just to show his dominance over her, the power of his goodness over her evil.

He tried to tell her why she must pay for what she had made him do to Susan but she didn't appear to be listening despite the fact he must have had her total attention. This annoyed him and he had lashed out at her, then, still holding her by the hair, he pulled her face against his knee, enjoying the sickening crack of breaking bone.

The next time he looked into her face, her nose and mouth had both been bleeding. A hunger for revenge, rarely suppressed surged in him; this beast of hell had made him kill his beautiful wife with her strange charms and spells. She had bewitched him, but now she was powerless under his might. He raised the knife high above his head, ignoring the pain in his other hand as he continued to hold her by her hair. His moment of nemesis was at hand, he was about to thrust the knife into her exposed throat when he sensed somebody else in the cave, standing just behind him.

He turned to face this most unwelcome of intruders but took a step backwards at the sight of the monstrosity that confronted him. Another demon conjured by the evil woman who was at his mercy, at God's mercy.

The beast was huge, he struggled to comprehend what he was seeing, it had many legs and seemed to resemble a spider in some manner or form. The large claw, however, gave more the appearance of a lobster but the two heads were definitely humanoid.

This was bizarre, the first face he recognised, it was that of the old tramp who had frequented the small park outside Amanda's flat; but why? From the glazed expression in its eyes he guessed that it had either been drinking again or was actually dead. Was that possible?

He looked again at his protagonist, for that is what he had concluded it was. He focused on the other head. This one was much younger and he didn't recognise it at all. What he did recognise was that it looked at him malignantly, it meant him harm and he failed to understand its presence in this strange place, its intrusion into his dream.

Feeling threatened, he pushed the girl away. She was too hurt to go far he reasoned. He lunged at the strange creature holding the knife like a sword before him. God would protect him; this time it would be Saint Alfred that slayed the dragon. It didn't seem to matter in a dream that it was not breathing fire or wasn't remotely dragon like.

He struck the beast a blow to the body, twisting the blade at the same time, feeling the tearing of flesh and savouring his imminent triumph. He quickly realised that his effort had been largely wasted, no sign of agony, no scream of pain had been evident, for the first time he felt slightly fearful.

The 'dream Alfred' almost didn't see the huge claw as the beast threw it towards him with a speed that belied its cumbersome appearance. He managed to duck out of the way at the very last moment, the huge limb missing his head by inches. His fear helped him recover more quickly than the beast that seemed to be slightly off balance as a result of its attack. He flashed the knife wildly in its general direction.

The effect was shocking, the head of the beast that belonged to the old tramp simply fell off the neck that it had been waving around on and a thick green ooze pumped from the wound, the stench was awful and his dream-self gagged at the sight and the horror of the situation.

Despite this, and with rising excitement Alfred had roared in triumph; the beast was slain, he was victorious and now he would finish the girl, kill the demon. His win was short-lived; the beast merely swung the great claw at him once again, apparently oblivious to its injury which he had thought must surely be a mortal one.

The huge appendage struck him a glancing blow in the midriff and sent him sprawling, severely winding him. Suddenly the creature was looming over him, a fire burned in the eyes of the remaining head and Alfred again knew fear. The eyes burned with vengeance and anger; Alfred knew this, he had looked too many times into mirrors not to recognise it when he saw it.

It was quite clear that the creature meant to kill him; his time here was done, the demon had beaten him, the girl would live and he would fail. He watched in horror as the huge claw moved close to his throat and the great beast's remaining head moved so close to his own that he could feel the heat of its breath.

He knew he must fight, but his fear was starting to deny him his ability to do so. With a last and desperate effort he lunged upwards with the knife that he had managed to hold onto as he fell to the ground. The blade disappeared into the creature until only the handle was left visible.

He was engulfed in the surprisingly warm liquid that poured forth from the wound. This time it had been blood, red and familiar and he knew that, after all, he had won this strange battle. The creature backed off a little then fell to the floor, it did not move again.

His dream character was beside itself with triumph; now it was time for the demon girl, she had used her mightiest powers against him and she had been defeated.

Looking around him in the darkness of the cave he had not been able to locate her. Perhaps she had taken her opportunity to shamble off somewhere, but he knew he had hurt her. He looked around the cave; where would she have run to? He had been so close; wandered these dark tunnels, was he to be denied again? Would he have to search for his revenge for the rest of his days?

The question posed in his dream had remained unanswered by the time that the cold in his bones had awoken him, the darkness in the bandstand had scared him as he considered the prospect that the slain creature had only pretended to be slain and had stolen up behind him and torn the life out of him with its mighty claw. As the multitude of stacked deckchairs and the familiar feel of his coat swam into his consciousness he began to calm down.

Now he trudged across the park, hunger in his belly, and aches in his bones; he kept the undying passion to achieve his goal in his mind. The snow had abated a little and the grey light of dawn was trying to appear, that was unfortunate. His footsteps sounded very conspicuous as he crunched through the crisp snowfall, he felt exposed but there was no alternative. He had to keep up his strength, he had God's mission to perform and he would not fail.

Few cars moved in the snow covered streets that surrounded the park, and, at this time of the morning, he knew he was unlikely to encounter too many people, they would be doing their best to cling to their beds on a morning such as this.

As Alfred left the park and trudged through the lonely streets of the town, at times, it was easy for him to imagine that he was the only person alive, God's chosen one who had triumphed over the evil of the people, he hoped there was at least one more out there, one he had a destiny with and a destiny that he was desperate to fulfil.

The litter bin outside the fish and chip shop was covered in snow. The pickings would not be rich but would be diverse. Fish, chips, pies, sausages, curry, bread rolls. All would be soggy and cold, discarded by drunken idiots, probably, with more money than sense. It would not be a pleasant meal but the days since he had escaped the institution had taught him some important lessons. When hungry, food was food, no matter how unpalatable it may look or smell.

He ate what he could find and considered returning immediately to his hideaway in the park, just a couple of streets he thought, while the town was quiet. He trudged through the snow covered streets; now being added to again by a fresh blizzard. There were a few people about but no one paid him any attention really; just another down and out, just another loser in life's game.

Rounding the next corner he found what subconsciously he had been looking for. They were usually red but this one was white, such were the drifts of snow around it. He knew the telephone number off by heart now. She wouldn't be there though, not after last night.

He felt rising excitement as he thought of that strange machine that took messages, her answer phone at work. He began to dial the number. It didn't matter whether she returned to work next week or next month, when she did she would have a nice little message from her stepfather waiting for her. He was smiling as he heard the connection being made.

TWENTY NINE

Margaret was awakened by the sound of the telephone ringing; she opened her eyes and realised that it was still fairly dark. Who on earth could be calling at such an hour she wondered?

Slowly, the events of the previous evening came back to her. In the spare bedroom Amanda would be sleeping, or maybe the call had awoken her too. The telephone would be manned by the young policewoman; but what if the call was for her? What if something had happened to her mother?

Pushing sleep aside she climbed out of the bed and fumbled for her dressing gown in the semi-dark. Not bothering with her slippers she opened the door out into the main living area and took in the scene. Was this really her flat? It didn't seem like it.

Amanda was there looking absolutely desperate; her normally bright complexion had degenerated into an ashen, almost wraith-like visage. Even allowing for the sedative, Margaret had seldom seen anyone look quite so beaten as Amanda did right now.

The phone was still ringing and the WPC was gently encouraging Amanda to answer it. Margaret felt a pang of anger; it was her telephone for heaven's sake. Shouldn't she get first go at answering it? She remembered the call diverts that had been put in place the previous evening and thought, too, of the horror that had unfolded in this very building the night before.

If it was the madman who had done that on the other end of the line, did Margaret really want to speak to him? She decided that she did not and her anger subsided.

The WPC was holding Amanda's arm, steadying her for what might or might not be a terrible experience. Margaret could hear the conversation, she couldn't imagine herself in Amanda's situation and the whole scenario was simply beyond her comprehension.

"Try to act as naturally as you can in the circumstances Amanda; if it's Williamson he will expect you to be upset but try to act like you are alone."

Amanda nodded her understanding but looked like she might collapse at any moment. She felt sick and the dullness in her head would not be swept away. She had woken with a terrible thirst and was heading to the kitchen to get a glass of water. On entering the room the WPC smiled at her and she had tried to reciprocate, she was halfway across the room, right by the telephone, when it had rung. Was he watching her; was he really that omnipresent?

Amanda tried to do exactly as she had been instructed to; with trembling hands she reached out and lifted the receiver to her ear. Please let there be no one there, please let it be a wrong number she thought desperately but she knew it was him, she could feel it.

"Hello."

Her voice sounded weedy and came out in a strange high-pitched whisper. There was a long pause on the other end of the line as the caller seemed to be overcoming surprise that the call had been answered. She could hear breathing, she concluded that the caller didn't sound too healthy.

"Amanda is that you?"

She didn't answer at first; the tension down the telephone line seemed to crackle between the two ear-pieces.

"It is you Amanda isn't it? Did you like my little show of strength; did you recognise the craftsman? She didn't even get the chance to scream, she died a horrible death. Are you listening Amanda; are you imagining what went on in that room."

"Yes."

Her voice was even weaker than before, no more than a whisper.

"Amanda it is so good to hear your voice again. How are you feeling, shaken and upset I'd expect? That's as it should be."

"I'm fine."

This time her voice was a little louder but not much.

"Oh I don't think you are fine Amanda, I think you are trying to deceive your father. You were always very good at deception; all demons are good at trickery. You tricked me into killing your mother didn't you? No, don't answer that, I know you did.

Susan was a rival for my affections and so you forced me to remove her. You were like a cuckoo chick in the nest. You had to have it all didn't you?"

"That's not true."

Amanda's voice was once again a whisper, in her mind she was a child again, she was thinking back to the horror of that night. This was something she had tried to lock away in a safe place for so long and now here it was, again and again, assailing her, crushing her, making her feel guilt where there should be none.

Alfred Williamson, like a boxer closing in for the knockout, knew that all his blows were landing and that his opponent was beaten, he revelled in it and enjoyed her agony. Killing her flat-mate had been a master stroke.

"I would like the chance to explain to you Amanda, just why you are wrong about everything. I want to tell you face to face what you did to me, how your evil overcame me and forced me to do something I would never have done if you had not wheedled yourself into our lives."

Amanda said nothing; she felt unsteady, as if she might pass out at any moment. She knew she had to go through with this but she was not sure that she could. She willed her spirit to hold, tried to find courage from somewhere.

"Will you agree to meet me Amanda? Will you let Daddy tell you all about what you did to him? Can we speak adult to adult about old times; about what *you* did?"

"Yes, I'll meet you."

"What did you say Amanda; you were whispering, whisperers tell lies, even you know that."

"I said I'll meet you."

There was a long pause on the line. She could feel his shock at this development; he certainly hadn't expected her to agree to the meeting. Surely he was seeing this as a trap; he must know that the police had been all over the flat and all over her with questions. He wouldn't be so stupid. He had been missing, presumed dead and yet he was here, on the other end of the line, he was still killing people. He was surely too cunning to turn up to any proposed liaison with her.

When his response came, the excitement in his voice was very thinly disguised.

"I will meet with you tomorrow night by the bandstand in the park at eight-thirty. If there are any signs of police activity it will not happen and I will come for you and despatch you for your treachery. You have seen what I can do; you know I have God on my side and that you will succumb to His will through me."

"I'll be there, and I'll be alone; I have things I need to say to you as well!"

Amanda's voice finally sounded like it belonged to a grown woman and not a frightened child.

"I do hope you will show your father some respect."

"Fuck you, you moron you deserve no respect!"

"I wouldn't call that nice Amanda; perhaps I can tell you my version of what respect is when we meet."

"What you did to Kate; what you did to the woman you purported to love, was that respect?"

"That was you making me do it. I am just flesh and blood trying to do God's work; He will help me to redeem myself in His eyes by destroying the demon that possessed me. You must understand that I don't blame you entirely. Being possessed by demons is probably something that you were unable to prevent, but you are their way into this world of flesh and blood. I need to show you that, if there is any part of you left that is human. Then, I'm sure you will agree I will have to rid the world of your canker. You will thank me in the afterlife; your soul will be cleansed. With His help I will cleanse it."

Amanda tried to switch off her mind from the ramblings of this madman, tried to pretend that she hadn't just agreed to meet him at all. She just wanted the conversation to be ended, wanted space away from his warped view of life.

"Amanda? Are you still there?"

She didn't want to say anything more; she had taken all she could.

"I know you are. Please don't let me down, I would be so disappointed if you broke your word and didn't come on your own."

"I'll be there; alone."

She hung up. Perhaps it was easier to let him kill her as he wanted.

**

Amanda sat there ashen faced on the large settee. Immediately after the telephone call had ended she had dashed to the bathroom and been violently sick. Margaret had been so kind to let her stay the night, the last thing she wanted to do was to do something that would spoil her friend's flat.

After she had retired from the room, Margaret and the young policewoman exchanged appalled expressions. The conversation had been audible to the WPC through headphones but to Margaret, she didn't need to hear it to know that something terrible had passed between her friend and the perpetrator of the previous day's horror. How could this be happening; here in such a quiet neighbourhood and to a person as nice and kind as Amanda, and in her flat?

The call had been traced to a call-box in the town but, with the roads being treacherous and the snow continuing unabated, there was little chance of finding the caller. Footsteps were no sooner created than they were concealed once again as the rising wind pushed the snow into drifts.

PC Sean Craig and WPC Julie Walsh had just arrived. To Margaret they looked almost as shattered as Amanda did. This was a small and reasonably affluent, quiet town. In the last few days there had been armed robberies and murders, what was happening here, was the town twinned with Armageddon?"

"You did so well Amanda; you are so brave. There is no way I could have done that." WPC Walsh was trying to lift Amanda's spirits; it was going to be a tough task from the look of it. She continued to try though.

"You couldn't have been more convincing. I think his mania will be too much for him to not to try to meet you."

"I'm scared."

"Of course you are; it's only natural, everyone in this room would be scared in the same circumstances."

This was hardly an encouraging thought for her, she just wanted to go back to sleep and said so. She was shown back to the room that she had slept in the night before. This time a carafe filled with water and a glass was left on the bedside table.

THIRTY

The atmosphere in the operations room was tense. Detective Inspector Andrew Jones was directing proceedings; everyone in the room was patently aware of the shortcomings that this particular case had attached to it already and all were determined that they would not foul up again.

The mood was sombre, like the weather outside that threatened to make their task so much more difficult. DI Jones had not slept well at all and he was grumpy, the coffee machine was on the blink again, which, on any other day he might have seen as a blessing but not today.

He had been forced to justify the proposed operation with his superiors. The Blakeley killing was competing for resources and was high profile due to the old shopkeeper's position in the community. Jones had been forced to endure a lecture about finite resources and clearance targets. He knew it was their job to do this but he resented it nonetheless.

A psychologist had been brought in to try to profile the behaviour of their perpetrator. Why, for example, had he chosen to wait so long before trying to arrange the meeting with Amanda, given the length of time since the fire when he had, presumably, taken his opportunity to escape?

Also, now that he had arranged it, why the further day's delay? What business did he need to attend to in the interim period? Surely, after achieving her agreement to have a meeting he would want to get on with it. The psychologist presented a different theory.

The police team sat in silence as the bleak scenario was outlined to them by Professor Darren Grey.

"Alfred Williamson blames Amanda Fellows for everything that is wrong in his life. He blames her for the death of his wife, for his incarceration, he sees her as a demon. I have read the case notes; they do not make for good bedtime reading, this is the stuff of nightmares. That this man is out there somewhere is seriously bad news for society."

The professor paused for effect, letting the gravity of his assessment sink in to the team of officers, noting the worried looking faces that stared back at him though tired looking eyes.

"It is my view that he wants her to suffer. He feels he has suffered greatly at her hands and wants to exact a revenge that outstrips merely killing her. I suspect that is why Kate Harvey was killed. It is my guess that he had ample opportunity to kill Amanda but chose instead to inflict emotional pain on her by killing her friend first."

Again a delay, were there signs that his audience shared his view he wondered.

"This further delay is, in my opinion, designed to give her more time to suffer further. He gets a kick out of her torment. I also suspect that he is cleverer than we might think. You would be wise to assume that he will not expect Amanda to turn up alone. This is a man who escaped from a high security institution, kept himself alive and undetected and found Amanda Fellows."

"Also, he was able to get into and out of Amanda's apartment undetected and murder her flatmate without attracting any attention to himself. He must have been surveying the property for a while before making his move and again he did so as if he were a ghost. No one saw him, no one reported anyone hanging around and looking suspicious. He is shrewd, he is sly and, through his anger, he is driven."

"I suggest that he will be watching you as you make your plans to protect Amanda's welfare. As she walks into the bear pit, he will know what you intend to do. He might not show up at all, just observe and wait for a better chance, he may, of course, even try to get to her before the agreed time and place though, for the reasons I have already said, I think this is unlikely. You should rule nothing out, however."

There was an uncomfortable shuffling amongst the police officers in the room, a few coughs and clearing of throats. They were certainly not cheered by what they were hearing he thought.

"It is my belief that by now Williamson will stand out in any crowd. He will be unshaven and unkempt; he has been on the run for some time so he may be showing signs of malnourishment. I have seen the photographs that you have attached to your whiteboards and I would urge you not to look at these and memorise the face of the man that you see there. He will look nothing like this."

"I suggest he moves at night, rests by day, possibly another reason for the delay in meeting with Amanda, maybe killing Kate Harvey took a lot out of him. Maybe he needs to rest in between kills. This weather will be a mixed blessing to him. On the one hand it lends him stealth; people are less observant when they are cold, wet and miserable. On the other hand, he is not a young man any longer. If he is sleeping rough, which he surely must be, then the cold will be getting to him."

"He may also have injuries, disfiguring injuries. As far as we know, no one else escaped that fire from the wing in which he was incarcerated, it would be unwise to assume he just walked out of there uninjured. So, I would suggest that you are looking for an individual that would pass off easily as a tramp but who has some sort of obvious scarring. That would be unlikely to be someone you would miss, someone must have seen him. Someone must know where he is holing up."

Professor Grey surveyed the faces of his audience once again; he was quite sure he had not cheered any of them with his stark appraisal of the man they were seeking. In ordinary circumstances the news of the man's likely appearance might have given cause for optimism but with the weather like this it probably wasn't a great deal of help. It wasn't as though they could do an E-fit that they could show on the local news channels or run in the newspapers, so people on the street would simply not be as vigilant when all they wanted to do was get home.

"Thank you Professor; as always, your assessments are frank but fair." DI Jones had returned to front the gathering. He now addressed his team, trying to put on a positive air that he was not feeling.

"We have about thirty hours before this meeting is scheduled to take place. A lot of that time will be during the night-time hours when searching for Williamson is just not practical. You heard what the professor said; Williamson will be watching us. We have to try to make progress with what's left of today's daylight and tomorrow morning. We need to look at the park today, if we go tomorrow, he will surely see us and back off. We need, too, to speak to the homeless community, I know they are few and far between here but they do exist. Get out among them; see if anyone has seen Williamson, take the photographs anyway show them around. Even if he is unkempt there may be facial resemblance, eye shape, nose, chin, something."

The gathering disassembled to general muttering and disgruntled expressions. In this weather it was a thankless and nigh on impossible task, they all knew though, that this time they must not fail, a life had been lost already, no one wanted another murder on their patch, the town was starting to feel like Gotham City.

A team was despatched to the area around the old bus station where a number of old warehouse buildings were falling slowly into disrepair. The small number of homeless people in the town tended to gravitate to this part of the centre, using the warehouses for shelter and spending their days in the nearby shopping streets where they held out their hands and begged for change. It was a long shot but the police officers needed to feel that they were doing something other than watching the clock tick by until the scheduled meeting the following day.

**

They underestimated him; they thought he was stupid and easy to catch. These were the musings of Alfred Williamson who laughed in their faces, they could not stop him now, and God was still with him. How could they be so arrogant when they had already failed once to stop him with the resultant corpse of Kate Harvey their reward?

There had been other people in the room with the bitch when he had telephoned; he had still found it difficult to understand why she had been in her office at such an early hour, especially after what he had done to her friend. Maybe she was tougher than he thought, maybe, but she would not be tough enough.

Amanda had agreed too readily to meet him, it smacked of stage-management. When she answered he had been forced to think quickly; this was something he was getting better at all the time as he tried to stay one step ahead of her and the police at every point of his mission.

He had been tempted to rush into things but a cold detached reasoning, deep in his subconscious at first, had welled slowly to the surface during their conversation. Recognising its presence, he reacted accordingly; time was, after all, on his side.

He wanted that time to think, to assess and evaluate, he must avoid capture at all costs, at least until the deed was done, after that he didn't really care what happened, they could lock him up again and this time they could throw away the key for all he cared.

More likely, the police would gun him down, they were bound to be present somewhere when he met Amanda whether he went through with this rendezvous or not, he just needed to evade them for long enough to complete his task and kill her.

From his vantage point, high above the town he could observe the policemen who, through the still persistent snow, made their way through the park, scouring bushes, checking shelters and sheds. He laughed aloud at their stupidity, he could have waved at them and not one of the morons would see him.

The War Memorial was set in a carillon tower that stood some three hundred feet high and dominated the park and the surrounding area, watching over it all like some silent but mighty sentinel. A small but adequate museum containing artefacts from both of the World Wars, together with the stunning views over the town and surrounding countryside which was available from the viewing gallery at the top. It attracted many visitors, especially in the summer months.

Admission was free but a donation box invited contributions towards its upkeep. At this time of year, although it remained open, it attracted few visitors and, in weather such as this, fewer still. Only three others had braved the winding steps since he arrived there some six hours before. The last of these had been around three hours ago.

Earlier in the day he had moved his scant belongings from the storage area beneath the bandstand and had found an even better hiding place in the tower where he had stowed them. He had been tempted to try to catch up on some much needed sleep throughout the day but he resisted the temptation. Much of the time he had spent on the viewing platform, watching the developments below. It was crucial that he could anticipate what the police were planning so that he could thwart their pathetic efforts to capture him.

Alfred had seen Amanda a few times, accompanied, as she was, by a tall policeman, a man in plain clothes, presumably CID, and a WPC. Heads bowed against the wind and the snow they had made their way to the bandstand. Earlier two uniformed officers had checked the area for signs of him but, presumably, found nothing. His footprints, at least, would be long gone by now.

He sincerely hoped that Amanda would like the place that he had chosen for her to die, the park was a very beautiful place and the snow painted the landscape with an artistry that only nature itself was capable of. The red of her blood would be all the more striking against this most natural of white carpets.

The snow had finally stopped and the clouds retreated to allow the sun to bathe the vista in its light. The afternoon was slipping towards evening and it had turned very cold. Up here on the balcony, Alfred was finding it increasingly difficult to concentrate on the scene below. He knew he must keep going though, what the police did today was almost certain to dictate where they would deploy tomorrow. He was under no illusions, they would put at least one man, probably armed, right where he was now.

As he continued his vigil, the light finally slipped out of the day and he felt comforted as the police officers one by one sidled out through the plentiful gates of the park, their task no longer feasible. They probably figured that he would be as far away from the park as he could possibly be right now. As usual he was one step ahead of them.

He returned to his hiding place, it was a lot warmer than his previous one and was almost comfortable. He had found some hessian sacking in another storeroom area and he had laid these on the floor to act as a makeshift mattress against the hard concrete floor.

Alfred had no watch so he could only guess at the time but that was of no consequence, he was running this particular show. If he was early or late for his meeting with destiny it didn't matter a jot, the police would be on highest alert at the designated time. As long as he could work out where Amanda was and when she was there, he would hold all the cards in this particularly bloody game that they played. He slept well that night, his plan was nearing fruition and, at last, his beautiful wife Susan would be avenged.

THIRTY ONE

Jim Dowley had awoken a few times during the course of the day; he had barely managed to make it to the en-suite bathroom on the one occasion he had climbed from beneath the sweat covered sheets of his bed. He had slept right through the morning and he hoped that his host had not prepared breakfast in anticipation of him turning up to eat.

He was clearly suffering from some type of malaise, he felt feverish and light-headed and his thoughts came to him in a jumbled mess. Childhood memories were interspersed with memories of his time at university. There were snatches of memory relating to his marriage to Jennifer but he could make no sense of any of it. Each of the thoughts seemed connected but in such a loose way that he was not really able to order his mind to interpret them.

During the rest of the day he slept but, as before, his dreams were confusing and just added to his disorientation. The woman was in his dreams, she always was but he had no recollection of the previous day's events in the state he was in. Reality and fantasy had become as one for him.

He was having some sort of nightmare now though it made no sense to him at all. He was in some sort of laboratory, though it looked makeshift and was filled with clutter, old furniture mixed with trestle tables on which test tubes and pipettes served to give the impression of some underworld drug producing operation.

He looked at this strange world as if through a light-orange coloured liquid, perhaps he was wearing tinted spectacles, he couldn't tell, he was unable to see himself, just the things in the room. Periodically he saw a man, proud and tall and handsome as he worked at the trestle table, filling and emptying syringes into the multitude of lab equipment. What was this Frankenstein like scenario and why was it in his dreams?

The man would occasionally walk over to where Jim believed he was standing, or sitting, though it felt more like he was floating. He would feel vulnerable under the man's scrutiny, like a specimen in a zoo, something to be marvelled at maybe, or something to be pitied.

This strange world occasionally swam out of focus, adding to his feeling that he was somehow viewing the whole thing from some sort of liquid medium, and lending credibility to that floating feeling, what did it all mean he wondered. He tried to look around the room, to orient himself with his surroundings, but his efforts were useless, his body seemed not to want to obey his thought processes, as though his brain was not in control of his own body. How was this possible, he wondered, had he had a stroke of some sort, was that why he was unable to move?

**

He recognised the low buildings with their flat top roofs and their glass fronted sides. He knew where he must be but he just didn't understand why or how he had come to be here again and after all this time. Jim was in the playground of Smurthorpe Primary School; this was one of his earliest childhood memories.

Somewhere in his head he heard the ringing of a bell; turning he saw Mrs Pooley, a teacher who he particularly liked as she rang the little hand bell that signified that playtime was over. Around him the children formed into orderly lines ready to be readmitted to the school.

Inside there was fun to be had, a sandpit, musical instruments, some of which he and his fellow pupils had made using dried peas and plastic containers. His favourite thing though was the large mat that spread out on the floor on which was outlined streets and parks. On here you could place wooden houses, schools, garages and even a fire station. Then you could drive your wooden cars along the roads. All that was needed was a little imagination. He had it in abundance.

Why was he here though? Was he dying; is this what people meant when they said that their life flashed before them before they died?

In his dream he knelt down and played with his school chum Toby Wainscot. Toby lived in a big house, much bigger than his and his mother cooked brilliant cakes. A frisson of sadness washed over him in his dream, Toby had died not long after this time of mutual happiness. He had run out in front of a car when going to the mobile library with his Mum, she hadn't been able to react quickly enough and nor, unfortunately, had the driver.

Jim had been sad at the loss, his first, or at least he thought it was, he didn't understand life or death at that time. Toby just stopped coming to play, others took his place. Jim Dowley's life moved on and Toby was forgotten, until now, in this odd dream.

He wavered on the verge of consciousness once again, he knew he was sweating profusely, knew too that if he opened his eyes the room would be swirling around him. He was ill but too ill to help himself, sleep threatened to take him but that was all. Sleep not death, at least not yet anyway.

**

He was back in the laboratory, this time his orientation seemed different. He sensed rather than saw the man in the room as he continued being busy with his experiments or research, whatever it was that he was doing. Now he was able to see a very strange sight indeed. There was someone or something else in the room, something which floated in a tank of liquid, it looked orange, or maybe that was just his perspective.

Whatever was in there seemed tiny and vulnerable, he felt an affinity with it, he felt the same, tiny and vulnerable. There was more though, the feeling went deeper, he felt linked to the tiny creature in some way, as though it were a part of him. Perhaps he was looking into a mirror, it was possible but he thought that there was more to it than that.

As he continued to look movement attracted his attention, the man had walked into his field of vision and had approached the creature in the tank; he watched as the creature underwent scrutiny, he wondered again what it was and what the man was doing. Then, he tensed as the man turned towards him and walked towards him. Again he felt vulnerable under that gaze but he did not feel afraid. There was tenderness in the eyes of his beholder, no threat, just tenderness.

**

The fire was always so warm. It was a comfort but he sometimes found it too much. The other children never seemed to make any comment about it and so he kept his counsel. There were quite a few of them here in this place. It was not a bad place but there was an air of despair about it. None of the children seemed to be as happy as they should be.

They were gathered around the fire, sitting on the floor in a ring, the girl at his side was called Marie and he liked her best of all. She had always been there. The story that the kind lady was reading them was a good one, all about rabbits who were very naughty and tried to steal onions from an old man's garden.

He remembered this time; this was one of the last times that he had seen the girl called Marie. It was just after this story that she had stopped coming to hear the stories with him. It was just like Toby when he went to the school. Perhaps that was what happened when you made a friend, they just went away. Perhaps he should keep it a secret when he made friends so that they would not go away.

When the kind lady had finished telling them the story they were given some hot milk and a biscuit and then they went to their beds. He dreamed of naughty rabbits, he dreamed of good things, but, even then, he dreamed of strange things, strange places and a man who had love in his eyes when he looked at him.

**

He was in a nice house with nice people. He recognised the people in the dream, they had been to see him a few times in the place where the kind lady told the children stories. They were kind and he thought that they loved him, or liked him very much; he didn't really know the difference.

The nice man was holding something in his hands and Jim recognised it as a small plastic football and squealed with delight. He followed the man into a garden that was enclosed by fencing and shrubs and had a large grassed area. This was his favourite game, kicking the ball to the man. Who was the man; his father? He was never very sure but he liked to play the football game and the man smiled a lot and tried to make him smile too.

He remembered the day when he had played with the football and fallen over on the grass. There had been a big stone sticking partly out of the turf and he had cut his knee on it and he had cried a lot. That was when the kind lady put cream on it and then a plaster. She had told him a story about how it was important to be a brave boy when you cut your knee and he had been glad that she was there. Was she his mother? As with the man he was not sure in those days, she was just a kind person who helped him to stop crying.

He was happy here, in this house, he didn't know how he came to be here and he missed the lady who told the stories and his other friends, most of all though he missed the friend he called Marie. He hoped she would come to see him again sometime. He doubted that she would though, he dreamed about her sometimes and she always seemed to be running away from him. To the young mind of Jim Dowley this was all terribly confusing. Perhaps Marie didn't like him, and maybe that was why she stopped coming to listen to the kind lady's stories.

**

He was in quicksand, sinking, his legs felt heavy, and his heart heavier still, he was dying. Then he was free of it, just like that, dreams were like that, they made no sense really. Ahead of him was the mountain, he recognised it; he had been here in dreams before. The sheer rock had no flaws, no sign of the cave entrance into which the woman and the creature had disappeared, swallowed up by the stone. Had he dreamed it all? Of course he had, that was the whole point wasn't it?

He clawed at the rock with his bare fingernails, seeking purchase of some kind; some means of opening the orifice that logic told him was there somewhere. Should he try reciting magic words; 'open sesame' perhaps? It seemed he was not to be granted entry into the mountain, perhaps he needed his passport he thought crazily.

In his dream, day became night and once more day again. Even if he gained entry now they would be so far ahead of him that catching them, saving the girl from the beast would be nigh on impossible, surely. Nonetheless he persevered, his fingers bled where he had tried continuously to prise open the cliff face. Surely his endeavours deserved reward.

He had almost given up all hope when a great rumbling sound coupled with the movement of the ground beneath his feet had resulted in a small cave entrance, just big enough for him to enter by, opening in the rock face. By the dim light that shone in behind him he looked around, noting that he was in a huge open space from which a multitude of labyrinthine tunnels seemed to run deep into the mountain.

He looked around desperately for any clue as to which tunnel to choose. There were so many; had the creature known which one to take in pursuit of the girl? His instinct told him that it had, it didn't make his own choice any more obvious though and he stood there in a sea of indecision.

Closing his eyes and picturing the chamber, he opened them again and had just chosen a route when a large ground shift accompanied by a thunderous roar resulted in the closing of the cave mouth behind him once again. The darkness was total, he felt afraid and vulnerable and inched his way forward towards the tunnel he had decided to traverse downwards.

Progress was painfully slow, even when his eyes had started to grow more accustomed to the environment. The smooth rock beneath his feet was slimy and wet making his journey a treacherous one. The only sounds were the drip, dripping of water from the cave roof into the puddles below and the less frequent but disquieting sound of small creatures scuttling around in the gloom.

All sense of time was lost and he wandered uselessly in the tunnels for what seemed an age but might only have been minutes. He was truly lost and he would surely perish here in this cold and dreadful place as the girl had surely already done so.

The beast was upon him before he had even registered its advance, its eyes, at least on one of its faces, glowed with a dull green sheen that was filled with menace as it forced him backwards against the cold, wet cave wall. Huge pincers held his throat and he knew that they could finish him in a heartbeat. The grip on his throat tightened gradually and he tried to struggle against it, kicking his legs out into the dark and feeling satisfied as he made contact with it.

His chest was becoming warm with the blood that trickled from the wound in his neck; and then there had been nothing, a void, darkness and silence in equal abundance. He felt no fear, he felt nothing in fact. He woke.

**

The world had stopped spinning and his fever was subsiding. The sheets though remained wringing wet and he felt disorientated, thirsty and immensely tired. Where the hell was he for God's sake; where was Jennifer?

Slowly his thoughts gathered around him. He was in a bed and breakfast, he had left his wife and family and he had resigned from his job. Yesterday he had met a woman, the woman who he had shared his dreams with since he was a child, a woman who had been a girl, a girl who had listened to Beatrix Potter stories, had been his friend, who might be his sister, a girl who had once been called Marie.

He tried to see the time on his watch, it was too dark and he didn't have the energy to turn on the bedside light. Whatever the time, it was clearly the middle of the night and he had slept through the entire day, there really was nothing else for it but to return to sleep and wait for his malaise to pass.

THIRTY TWO

Amanda was in a state of flux. Her stomach churned with nerves and yet she knew she must eat and try to keep her strength up in these times of adversity. She hadn't really shaken off the effects of the sedative she had been given the night before. What the hell had it been? She reckoned it could have stopped a bull elephant in its tracks.

The police officers had done their best to be kind to her, they had allowed her to sleep for as long as they could but they had things they needed to arrange and they needed her cooperation to do it. WPC Walsh had been there as usual, did that woman ever go off duty? They wanted her to visit the park with them, to go to the bandstand where that madman Alfred Williamson had deigned that they should renew their acquaintance.

In the snow, the park had looked beautiful. It seemed unthinkable that someone was considering perpetuating a crime in such a setting. She had walked past this bandstand hundreds of times in her life. As a younger woman she had gone there with her stepparents to a picnic and listened to the various local bands as they had performed their repertoires on sunny Sunday afternoons.

The simple structure now looked forbidding, just seeing it made her shudder. Was he around now? Was Williamson watching her, tasting, smelling and revelling in her fear? She couldn't tell, she felt watched all the time, it could be Williamson, it could be her imagination. Perhaps he had no intention of meeting her here, just another psychological mind game to destroy her will.

She thought again of Kate, trying to draw strength from her anger, it didn't work; it just made her want to cry. Kate's next of kin were in town now and there were a lot of tears and recriminations. In her heart Amanda knew that Kate would still be alive if it weren't for her and her history. She found it hard to look them in the eyes though they seemed not to blame her.

DI Jones had explained what the plan was, where his men would be positioned so that they could adequately protect her. It seemed somehow unreal that she should be afforded police protection, that she should be the focus of so much attention.

The police officers would be in position hours before the meeting was scheduled, the reasoning being that Williamson would be on the lookout for their arrival. They would move in under the cover of darkness the next morning and stake out the park.

DI Jones was hopeful that they would be able to spot Williamson when he arrived at the park, negating the need to involve Amanda at all. He hoped that the man would be safely in custody long before the bandstand rendezvous. Amanda was doubtful, Williamson was canny, and she feared that the police would underestimate him yet again.

After visiting the bandstand, DI Jones had gone off to do other things, leaving her in the capable but no doubt exhausted hands of WPC Walsh. The police officer had insisted that Amanda must eat and had practically dragged her to a fish and chip restaurant. It had seemed at the time like the last thing on earth that she wanted to eat but now, as she wolfed down the large portion with bread and butter and hot, strong tea she marvelled at how right her chaperone had been.

Tomorrow was going to be, without doubt, the most traumatic day of her life. Today though was traumatic enough. Where was Phillip; or Jim, whatever his name was? She had not seen him since he left Margaret's flat last night. Had he found it all too much? Maybe he thought she was a little mad for suggesting that they were related. Whatever, surely he owed it to her to tell her that was what his thoughts on the matter were. Why had he just failed to try to contact her at all?

She tried to get things into perspective but it was difficult. The police had been around her all day, perhaps they had turned him away, wanting her undivided attention as they talked through the plans for the following day. Another possibility was that whilst she was out he had returned to the flat to find her gone and didn't know where she might be.

He had left his wife, left his job; what if in the cold light of the next day he had come to his senses and set about trying to reverse those decisions. In his position she suspected that this was exactly what she would do, who could blame him? Why did she feel she had a claim on his attention and his time? She concluded that she didn't, but a part of her was hurt nonetheless, she was in danger and he was all she had in the world.

Some of her fellow diners had been casting her sideways glances; she guessed it wasn't every day that a member of the public came into a fish and chip shop under police escort. WPC Walsh had simply had a strong cup of tea as she watched over her charge. The police were leaving nothing to chance, Williamson could be calling everyone's bluff, and he could strike at any moment. Amanda found that the thought did not put her off her meal, she ate every last morsel and could probably have managed even more.

As she left the restaurant and headed for the police car which would return her to Margaret's flat she had only one thing on her mind. Strangely it wasn't Alfred Williamson, it was Jim Dowley, the man she now regarded as her twin brother. Was he alright? She sensed he might be ill, but how could she know? She told herself to get a grip on herself as she climbed into the car.

As they drove away it started to snow again, the forecast was for worse to come, and Amanda wondered what could possibly be worse than this.

THIRTY THREE

The light had faded on another day and he felt that he hadn't achieved what he had set out to do. DI Jones was one of life's perfectionists, one of its greatest proponents of the art of worrying. His attention to detail had seen him rise through the ranks at a relatively young age, but inside he felt older than his years, he seemed to have lived a lot more than most people of his age.

He was sitting at his usual table in the Cambridge Hotel. The Cambridge was popular with the local police as a calling in point after a hard day's slog. For Andrew Jones it was a place where he could think outside the box, away from the office but not away from the job. Only when he made it to the small semi-detached bungalow that he had made his home did he consider himself away from the job, and even then he was away in the loosest sense of the word.

He wondered about the girl Amanda Fellows; she was being very brave about all this but did she have the guts to go with it? He wasn't so sure; the cracks were beginning to show in her fragile shell. He couldn't get away from the thought that if he could do his job better then she would be spared the ordeal that, tomorrow, she would be forced to endure.

His own world had been turned upside down in the last few days, what was a modest town with a low crime rate had erupted with armed robberies and murders, intruders who seemed to be able to literally ghost past his men, men he considered fastidious, to do whatever they wanted to do. Was he losing his grip on things; did his superiors think that?

When he drank, Andrew Jones was a beer drinker, real ales mostly. The Cambridge usually had a good selection of guest beers along with the staple fare and tonight he had tried the *Hobgoblin*. It was stronger than he would usually try, especially in the current situation but he hoped that the alcohol would lend him a different perspective on the events of the last few days.

Sometimes he felt that living and breathing the job, trying to anticipate every eventuality and nuance could result in mistakes. The most obvious things could be overlooked if you were in too close. He needed to step back, look in from the outside, much like the psychologist, Professor Wainscot, had done. It wasn't that the man had flagged up anything that he hadn't considered at some point already, it was just that it was refreshing to hear someone else coming up with ideas and suggestions, it lent a perspective to his own thoughts that were becoming jumbled by the pressure he felt he was under.

He finished his pint and nodded to Dave the barman who began to pull another one for him. What if they had this wrong and the man who killed Kate Harvey wasn't Alfred Williamson but someone pretending to be him. The fire at the institution had been devastating, how could the man just have walked out of there when no one else had, at least as far as the authorities were aware anyway. It didn't seem credible, what was it that drove the man after all these years to look for and find Amanda and then to torment her so?

He wanted to get inside the man's head but feared what he might find there. There lay madness, dark places that no sane person should visit, or was he kidding himself? Was it not possible that all men had those dark places, that all men at some time had contemplated even the darkest of deeds? Wasn't that the whole point really? If bad people went around with the word murderer or rapist tattooed on their foreheads then the need for a police force would be completely negated.

He wondered, yet again, whether he was calling the situation right. The top brass had sanctioned the use of police marksmen, it was a decision they could hardly refuse given the failed surveillance on Amanda's flat, not once but twice. Heads hadn't rolled yet but if it went wrong tomorrow they surely would.

There would be men by the park gates; not in uniform of course, armed men in the surrounding bushes on the approaches to the bandstand and a sniper at the top of the War Memorial. All would have contact with each other there didn't seem too much else he could put in place to ensure the girl's safety.

What though would be Williamson's approach, assuming it was him? He had murdered Kate Harvey with some kind of large knife, forensics had provisionally confirmed this, but was it dangerous to assume that he would maintain the same modus operandi? What if he procured, or already had, a firearm? If Williamson got a shot at his target and was a good shot, no amount of men crouching in the bushes could prevent a bullet from hitting Amanda.

Amanda, he had already decided, would be wearing body armour; it was the best he could do really. He collected his pint from the bar and paid for it using loose change from his pocket. There was a shortage of five pound notes everywhere at the moment. The Government were probably going to slowly take them out of circulation; it was playing hell with his trouser pockets though.

The door to the pub opened and a bitter breeze blew in to the snug little room. By the street lights outside he could see that the snow was falling heavily. That was another problem wasn't it? The snow would aid the police officers lying low in the park but, by the same token, it would lend an ally to their quarry. If visibility was as bad as at some times over the last couple of days, Williamson might just be able to amble up to the bandstand and do what he wanted to do before ambling away once again.

The thought chilled him. Should he call the whole thing off, was he playing Russian roulette with the life of a young woman in the name of clearing up a few crime statistics? He thought he wasn't but others would not see it that way if things went wrong.

DI Andrew Jones managed another couple of pints whilst wrestling with his conscience before leaving the Cambridge and returning home with an Indian take-away. Like others in the town, he would not sleep well this night.

**

Amanda suspected that even the sedative of the night before would have failed to work this night. By the time a grey light filtered through the patterned curtains of Margaret's spare bedroom she had slept only intermittently, often waking in the throes of a panic attack as if the very act of falling asleep could signify her untimely end.

During the night her thoughts had been of Susan Williamson, her poor stepmother on whose grave she still occasionally laid flowers. She had almost felt, once again, the sensation of the poor woman's blood all over her and she had almost vomited at the thought. Memories for so long suppressed in the name of self preservation were now vivid as if they had been formed only the day before.

Her thoughts were also of Kate, poor Kate who she had cared for so very much but never quite got round to telling her just how much. She was convinced now that this was the way of the world. One never quite got round to telling the bastards in life how much of a bastard they really were; and the ones that one loved how wonderful they were. It was a source of regret, but one she would have to live with if she was to survive this ordeal.

There were no guarantees about that though were there? She could sense the edginess amongst the police officers that surrounded her suddenly insular world. None of them expressed anything other than confidence that they would get their man and that Amanda would be fine but their eyes and their body language told a different story altogether.

Amanda was almost past caring now; her exhaustion was almost total and a part of her doubted if she would even be able to walk into that snow covered park and approach the bandstand to meet with her nemesis later in the day. He was winning and she knew it and she hated herself for being weak, for allowing this manipulating, psychotic bully to dominate her thoughts in this way.

Then there was Jim; he had not been to the flat, in fact he appeared to have made no attempt to renew his acquaintance with her at all. That was, above all, the reason for her despair and her sleeplessness. She had been so sure that he shared her view that they were related to each other. She believed and had convinced herself that he too believed that a psychic bond had somehow held them together over the years when all the odds were stacked against them ever meeting each other again.

Maybe she was clutching at straws, but she had thought that during the night she had recalled her early childhood. There were disturbing images, a creature in a glass tank of some description, but nice memories too, teddy bear sweet images, friendship and kinship. Could they be wishful thinking or were they real memories? They seemed to be real, long suppressed, like much of her early childhood memories, but real nonetheless.

The dull grey light slowly brightened though she suspected that the room was as bright as it was going to get this morning. She tried to imagine the world outside those curtains. Was it still covered in a blanket of snow? She suspected it was though the weather forecast had been just about the last thing on her mind in the last forty eight hours.

The little park opposite, she was sure he had been there watching her, learning her routines, reacquainting himself with her. Was he there now? With such a heavy police presence she doubted it but he was devious, he had come this far when the whole world had given him up for dead, now it could be her that ended up dead, just like Susan Williamson, just like Kate Harvey.

In the next room she heard the telephone ring and her stomach did a somersault as she contemplated the thought that she might have to speak to him once again. Since the call more than twenty four hours ago, the telephone had been relatively quiet. A couple of calls had come through from clients of Stark and Rutherford that had been fielded by the police officer on duty at the time. They had been given an alternative number to call and all seemed to be well.

She glanced at her watch and wondered who might be calling. It was ten past nine in the morning, it could be anyone. With her heart pounding she closed her eyes and waited for the bedroom door to open and her presence to be requested.

Moments later she heard the familiar voice of Margaret answering the telephone to either friend or relative and she breathed in deeply trying to slow her heart rate down. She guessed that this was how things were going to be from now on, life on the edge, grating nerves and sleepless nights, despite her attempts not to cry, a single tear escaped the corner of her right eye and tickled her cheek as it headed towards her neck.

If this was how life had to be then she needed to find strength from somewhere and soon. Right now she had no idea where that courage and resolve might come from, even the thought of avenging Kate seemed to make her weak with fear.

THIRTY FOUR

In his high tower, Alfred Williamson surveyed the world below with disdain. Up here he felt invincible. Nothing could stop him, of course, God was guiding him and he could not fail. He was cold and stiff from his exertions. During the day he had walked up and down the curving steps of the memorial to keep his circulation going and to ward off the biting cold.

Last night, long after he had retired to his hideaway and settled down for the night, he had heard footsteps on the stone staircase of the War Memorial. In his state of sleepiness he had wondered if the building might be haunted, perhaps by one of the war heroes it had been built to commemorate, but he had heard voices and seen torch-light through the slight gap in the door.

There had been two of them; uniformed police officers and they were discussing precisely what they planned to do the following day. One of them would deploy at the top of the tower, armed with a rifle, he was at pains to describe to his colleague just how things would be done and where his colleagues on the ground would be deployed.

Alfred listened with interest when it was mentioned that the deployment of men would be made early the next day, long in advance of the proposed meeting with Amanda, the rationale being that Alfred would be on his guard and looking out for traps but only later in the day. Fools, he thought, did they think he was that stupid? He had outwitted them on every level so far and it didn't look like that was going to change any time soon.

The policeman had even been good enough to tell his colleague exactly when he would be arriving at the top of the tower the next day. Although he had no watch, in daylight Alfred could make out the clock on the tower of the parish church. He would be waiting for the nice gentleman with a nasty little surprise.

It was ten to ten; the man would be here in ten minutes, dead in fifteen if Alfred's plan came to fruition. There was a problem though, the man would almost certainly have a radio of some sort, he had yet to determine exactly how he would deal with this but God would show him a way.

It was snowing again, though not as hard as it had been overnight. The pathways on the park were pristine once more, the overnight snow blanketing the previous day's footprints. For Alfred, of course, this was a further bonus. Having spent the night indoors he had left no tell-tale trail as to his presence or his whereabouts. The policeman entering the War Memorial would have no idea that he was already in there. Alfred was congratulating himself on his ingenuity when the first of the police officers came into view.

He watched as several men deployed to various positions surrounding the bandstand, most at a reasonable distance away, none of them too close. In his mind's eye he was already plotting a route to his destination. All was going well he thought, at least it had been until he spotted the two men that headed for the War Memorial. He looked at the wicked looking knife in his hand which was numb with cold.

Two of them, he had not expected this, was this the first hitch he had come across in his God inspired mission? Scampering down two flights of stairs, the higher stairs of which were wooden and, therefore, noisy to negotiate, he retreated to the little room where he had spent the previous night. Trying to control his breathing he had cowered down leaving a slight gap in the doorway to look through.

He gripped the knife more and more tightly as he heard the footsteps on the stone staircase get closer and closer, the voices that had been a murmuring sound that was indistinct were now becoming more audible and he strained his ears to listen.

The two men were clearly of differing ranks, one superior to the other was clucking like a mother hen, urging the need for fastidiousness, diligence, and for concentration. The other man sounded offended that such things were not considered to be something he would always do.

As he listened Alfred heard something that made his spirits soar. The police having some difficulties with their communications system. They were blaming the weather, the technicians, anything they could think of but the point was that it gave Alfred an opportunity, it solved his chief problem.

As he huddled there and waited he thanked God once again, it surely was a gift from the divine that such a thing was happening. He would send the police officers to meet their maker and their failure to contact their colleagues would be attributed to communications failure.

Things were set to get better for Alfred. The more senior officer, after spending some time out on the balcony above, descended the staircase alone. Had he just come up here to direct proceedings, perhaps to gain a birds-eye view of how his plan was progressing? Not very well thought Alfred; and now was he off to sit in his ivory tower away from the action? Alfred thought that that was exactly the scenario.

It was all going exactly to plan; in fact it was better than that even. He knew precisely where the police were deployed; on the other hand, the police would not have the faintest inclination as to where he would emerge from.

Now he must do what he had planned to do an hour ago, he had lost a bit of the element of surprise and would have to negotiate the wooden steps up to the top. But the wind was strengthening and he guessed that the sound of it would cover the sound of his footsteps to the policeman outside in the elements.

His progress was deliberately slow, the wooden stairs creaked from time to time but he was fairly sure that he would not be heard as he made his stealthy advance. Despite the cold, a thin film of sweat had formed on his brow and on his back, he could feel it as it trickled down beneath his clothes, he tried to close his mind off from it and to focus on the job at hand.

He was cold and he was tired and the adrenaline coursed through his bloodstream. He found, to his frustration, that he was unable to detach himself from what he was about to do in the same way that he had when he had killed Kate Harvey. Why was that he wondered? Maybe it was because the policeman was trained in unarmed combat, maybe it was the fact that he had a rifle, possibly a pistol too. Kate, of course, had none of those things, she was just a silly little girl who had got in his way and who he had despatched for his own amusement.

He could see the entrance to the balcony now, it was snowing heavily but up here, under the canopy of the balcony roof, that would not aid him in any way. He knew, of course, exactly where his prey would be setting up his position.

The view over to the bandstand was not on the doorway side of the building, he would be able to reach the corner of the building and, hopefully, peer around the edge. If the sniper was still setting up, which seemed likely to Alfred, he would most likely have his back to where Alfred stood. He would need to be quick, but he was confident that with God's help he could do this.

The wind and cold shocked his system as he silently climbed out onto the stone walkway that was the balcony with its views over the snow covered town and countryside beyond. Right now though he was not here for the view, the snow restricted it in any case. He tried again to focus totally on the job at hand.

His steps were small and careful as he inched his way to the corner of the building and, carefully, peered around the corner. He had been right, the hapless man, his next victim, was oblivious to his presence and had his back to him. Alfred looked at the man's exact position and then at the knife in his hand. This was going to be even easier than he thought.

With confident strides, the sounds of which were lost in the whistling of the wind, he covered the ground between where he stood and the policeman crouched. With a skill learned in the army during his National Service many years before, he cut the man's throat from ear to ear. There was a lot of blood but very little resistance. Alfred was surveying a corpse and a rifle that was meant for him within ninety seconds of his attack.

**

Jim Dowley woke with lucid thoughts for the first time since he had staggered through the snow back to the bed and breakfast room at the public house. His fever had passed, though the bed-clothes remained damp, he looked around the basic room he had rented, at the small and old-fashioned portable television set, the yellowed ceiling, the light with its tired looking shade, seventies probably, and the sparse but functional bedroom furniture.

He was desperately thirsty. How long had he slept he wondered. Certainly well in excess of twenty-four hours and his stomach told him so, it rumbled in a very empty sort of way and he recalled the Chinese meal that he had shared with the girl, Amanda, that had ended up on the floor.

Was that a dream? He knew he had been dreaming almost constantly and reality was something that had taken a back seat during that time but he was fairly sure that he hadn't dreamt that. He had met her, she did exist and her flat-mate had been murdered.

So what should he do now? Eating and getting a drink of some sort was a high priority but shouldn't he go and see the girl? He was pretty sure he recalled where she lived. Would she be there or would she be staying with her relatives? Crazily he thought about what she had said to him, he was her relative, at least she was convinced of it. He hadn't been there for her though had he? No, he had got sick and not been there when she needed him most.

He felt rotten, but not for one reason only; if he ate something, got a drink, then maybe he could focus on the rest of it and make some sort of sense of the whole thing, come up with a plan even. He struggled out of bed and went into the bathroom. He felt that after all that time in bed he should need the toilet but when he tried it was hardly worth it, he had probably lost so much liquid through sweating that he had become dehydrated.

He shaved and showered, feeling shivery and unsteady on his feet. The room was cool rather than cold and he suspected low blood sugar for his reaction. An hour later he made his way downstairs into the pub and ordered steak and ale pie with chips and a bitter shandy which he drank almost instantly before replacing it with a pint of the local bitter. It might not be the best thing for dehydration but it might just stop his nerves jangling quite so much.

The meal helped a lot; he was starting to think rationally again. He exchanged some banter with the landlord who noted his absence from breakfast for the past two mornings. He cited a dose of the flu and received the man's sympathy. He picked up one of the newspapers that were available to the patrons of the pub and looked at the headlines. He certainly hadn't dreamt the incident at Amanda's flat the other night. But what should he do next?

It crossed his mind that his absence from the scene during the whole of yesterday and much of today might be deemed out of the ordinary and wondered if this might lead to suspicion falling on him. Amanda, after all, had only just met him and the police were likely to be curious about the man who accompanied her home that evening. Why had he not gone to her side to comfort her, was he on the run maybe, after enjoying the kick of revisiting the crime scene?

Anything was possible he decided, but by the same token he also resolved that he must try to see her again and the sooner the better. Should he just get a taxi there now or maybe walking was best despite his weakened state. At least the fresh air might clear his head.

He looked out through the large picture window of the pub at the white blanketed landscape outside. There probably wouldn't be many taxis out and about in this weather in any case. He ordered a large brandy and drank it quickly, savouring the kick it gave to his system and then, with trepidation, he headed out into the snow.

He was shocked by the thickness of it; it had been a few years since the town had experienced a deluge like this as early in the year as November. It was difficult to walk in and he wondered within a couple of hundred yards whether he should return to the pub and call a taxi after all. Even if it took ages to turn up at least he would reach Amanda's flat in some sort of decent shape. An instinct told him to press on; a familiar feeling was starting to form in him. A feeling that time was not on his side.

**

The shadows were lengthening and the shortened day was drawing to a close by the time that Jim Dowley stood at the entrance to the street where Amanda Fellows lived. It was a snowscape, given its position off the main road; much of the freshly fallen snow lay undisturbed. He advanced with caution, mindful of the police car that was positioned right outside Amanda's building and the lonely police officer who held a vigil on the top step of the small staircase that led up to the front door.

With a heavy heart and a sense of dread he climbed the step and introduced himself to the police officer. He recognised the man and the recognition was clearly mutual. He explained that he was there to see Amanda and was told that she wasn't there. Where was she? The policeman wouldn't say. At that moment a figure, stooped against the cold and miserable weather approached the steps. Jim recognised her as Margaret, the woman who had allowed Amanda to stay with her on the night of Kate's murder.

Ignoring the policeman, he re-introduced himself and explained that he had come to visit Amanda but had found her to be out and he wondered where she might be. Margaret decided, possibly against her better judgement, to invite him in. The police officer shrugged his shoulders, what could he do?

**

"They're using her as bait in a trap to catch the killer."

Margaret tried to hide her disdain for what she considered to be utter folly as she recounted this simple fact to Jim. She placed a steaming hot cup of coffee on the small table which sat in front of the settee on which he sat; the same settee he had shared with Amanda, his sister, his twin?

The police officer who sat silently by the telephone, bored and anticipating nothing happening here looked up and looked slightly hurt at the disdain in Margaret's voice but did not make any comment. His job was to be invisible and to wait, just in case Williamson called to alter the plan. He supposed it wasn't impossible but the boredom overcame him nonetheless.

"Where is Amanda now?" Jim asked the question but he felt he already knew what Margaret's reply would be.

"I haven't a clue, they took her away sometime early this morning and I haven't seen her or heard from her since. I assume she's in protective custody of some kind. When I asked them they wouldn't tell me."

"Is she being pressured into this?"

"I don't think so. I think she wants to bring Kate's killer to justice."

"By risking her own life; what the hell is she thinking?"

"So it would seem; she was pretty determined I felt."

"Did you know about this man? Had she ever confided in you Margaret?"

"No. Amanda was a pretty secretive sort, not in a nasty way; she was always very charming to me and, in my experience, to others. I just got the impression she wasn't one for sharing her problems. It's fair to say that we weren't that close."

"You're talking about her in the past tense!"

"So I am; I don't know why, there's no reason."

"Let's hope you are right."

"Exactly; tell me Jim, how long have you been seeing Amanda? I haven't seen you around here before the other day, you seemed quite close."

Jim ignored the use of the past tense again.

"I'm not seeing Amanda." Should he tell her his suspicions, would it clarify or complicate matters? He decided he would.

"Amanda and I have just met after a number of years, we are quite sure that we are twins."

Margaret looked at him in a new light, her face screwing up as she examined him and compared him with some inner template she had for Amanda.

"Yes, I can see a resemblance," she announced eventually. Jim felt a shiver run down his spine, perhaps it was true, he was certainly coming around to the idea.

"I have to find her Margaret; she's in danger. I don't know how I know that but I do. I'm certain!"

"I think there is a rendezvous, tonight, in the park, it was just something I overheard."

The police officer by the telephone looked up and frowned. Was this going to prove a complication? Should he report it to DI Jones? He was torn and decided to wait and see what happened.

"Do you know what time; where? It's a big park."

"Sorry Jim, I don't know that. I am worried about her though, perhaps if you tell them you are her twin brother they will let you in on it."

Jim considered this for a moment and dismissed the idea. There wasn't time to go through all the necessary explanations. For God's sake he wasn't even sure that he was her twin brother at all, if he claimed to be and it was proven that he was not then he might find himself on some kind of charge.

"I don't think it would help to tell them that Margaret."

He drank the rest of the coffee and she offered him another. He declined, his heart was racing and he felt he had to do something but he didn't know what. How could he find out where she was; how could he warn her not to go? How too could he tell her about the dreams he had when he was wracked with fever?

Jim was beside himself with worry, he had placed an interpretation on his dreams and he didn't feel that this favoured the course of action that the police were taking on Amanda's behalf. He felt that the police operation was folly, they were not seeing things clearly; the words 'snow blind' came into his head and he wondered about why that was.

They could not be allowed to send Amanda, his twin sister, into a situation where they could not guarantee her safety but he didn't know how to stop them doing just that. If he couldn't stop them then he would have to find some other way of preventing Williamson from getting to her.

He thought once more of the two-headed monster in his dreams, the malevolent one, the one with the green eyes, the one that had held his very own dream character in its mighty claws, was this Williamson? He thought it was.

"Thank you for the coffee Margaret; I have to go." He didn't know where exactly, nor why he knew he had to, but he just knew he had to do something.

THIRTY FIVE

Despite everything that had happened to her in her short life, and she felt that a lot had, Amanda had never felt quite as wretched as she did today. For a start she felt like a prisoner, the day had been spent in a police 'safe house.' It was a bungalow in reality, which, in itself, seemed to be a security risk to her. Situated on the outskirts of town, the garden backed onto a railway embankment and having tried to get some sleep in the afternoon, she had endured a disrupted one on account of the trains that went past outside.

The snow was continuing to fall which, of course, served to slow the trains and any other form of transport and, as Amanda looked out of the large picture window in the sitting room she couldn't help thinking that the weather was somehow conspiring against her.

The white blanket made people invisible. Invisibility was surely Alfred Williamson's chief ally in the hours ahead. She remembered the joy she had felt as a child, and there had been precious little of that, at the sight of the snow. The simple pleasure of building a snowman with her friends, of making and throwing snowballs. Now the memory seemed impossibly distant and the snow ominous and portentious of her doom.

She had shared the building with two others during the night. The ubiquitous WPC Walsh, who seemed to be on a personal crusade to ensure both Amanda's protection and to keep her from brooding about what was happening to her, was one of them. PC Sean Craig was also present and had paced the room agitatedly since Amanda had roused herself, dressed and made coffee.

It was hard to concentrate on anything. Amanda's thoughts skipped between personal fears, at the thought of what was to come, personal guilt, at the thought of what had already happened and personal disappointment that Jim Dowley, who had touched her life so briefly, seemed to have disappeared.

In the corner of the room a television played uselessly to an audience that were not interested. A twenty four hour news channel showed footage of great sweeps of the country that had been blanketed in snow and told of multiple pile ups on motorways and major roads. Several train routes had been closed causing commuter chaos and businesses were counting the cost of absenteeism precipitated by staff not being able to get to their work premises.

It was all background noise, just filling that padded out the day, a hint of normality in a surreal situation. Amanda drank more of her coffee; she was high on adrenaline and the caffeine probably wouldn't help her, but she needed to be doing something with her hands.

"How are you feeling?" WPC Walsh couldn't think of anything else to ask her, she desperately wanted to keep Amanda's spirits high; she was full of admiration for the courage the young woman was showing.

"I've had better days." Amanda managed a thin smile.

"You should try to eat something."

"Maybe later, my stomach doesn't feel as though it could hold on to anything just yet."

"Okay but make sure you do; you'll need to keep your strength up."

Another thin smile from Amanda that was almost a grimace was her confirmation that she would bear this in mind.

"I admire you for what you are doing; you're very brave."

Amanda shrugged.

"When I read the case notes, the ones relating to Alfred Williamson killing his wife, it made me shiver. The medical notes too, he seems to have no remorse for what he did."

"He blames me, that's why. He won't feel guilt because he believes I forced him to do it."

"How can he justify thinking that?"

"I suppose you would need to ask a psychiatrist. He blames my presence in the family unit for diluting the attention he received from Susan; he sees that as a deliberate attempt by me to sideline him in the relationship."

"But you were only a child!"

"Yes."

"The inference is that he was unstable long before you were adopted."

"He most probably was, perhaps vetting procedures were not so stringent in those days. It wasn't something I considered at the time, I was too young. To me life was about watching children's television programmes, eating ice creams and fishing for tadpoles."

"You were happy there then?"

"I think I probably was, yes. I was too young to spot an undercurrent, my stepmother was very loving. I missed her when she wasn't there anymore but I couldn't work out what had happened."

"You were adopted again shortly afterwards weren't you?"

"Yes, there was no stability, it became normal for me to move on, to make friends and then never see them again."

"It sounds soul destroying."

"I suppose I was too young to know that I had a soul to destroy."

"That's a blessing at least."

"I have a brother."

Amanda didn't know why she said this but she felt the sudden need to talk about it.

"I didn't know, I thought we knew about your family."

"The records that you will have read about me won't make reference to a brother."

"I don't understand."

"My stepparents only told me a few days ago. I am one of twins, my twin brother was adopted elsewhere, and we were separated when we barely knew each other."

"But that's terrible, how could they let that happen?"

"Like I said before, I suppose that things were different back then."

"What happened to him?"

"I didn't know. Like I said, it was only recently that I discovered he existed. The man who was with me on the night we found Kate's body, I had only been reunited with him that very day. Although neither of us can be totally certain just yet, we both *feel* that we are related."

"My God that's amazing. What a day that must have been for you. Where is he now?"

"I wish I knew. Perhaps he can't cope with the idea that he has a twin sister after all these years."

"How did the two of you reunite; did you seek him out?"

"It's hard to explain. I suppose you could say we found each other."

"So the whole thing happened by accident?"

"On the face of it I suppose you could say that. I think it was something deeper though. I recognised him as soon as I saw him. It was the same for Jim even though we couldn't have seen each other for all those years there was a connection there right from the start."

"I've heard about something like that; a psychic link between twins, like one knows if the other one is ill or in trouble. Is that what it was like?"

"Yes, I suppose it might have been. In fact, given what is happening to me at the moment perhaps that is exactly why and how he found me. He may have sensed my trauma, somehow he came to realise that I was in trouble and he made a greater effort to find me. I hoped that he would be there to protect me but now I don't know where he's gone."

Amanda looked thoughtful for a moment; she had voiced aloud what her subconscious had been telling her all along through the strange dreams. That was it, Jim had been drawn to find her by the danger she was in. But, if that were so, where was he now when the danger was at its greatest?

**

The day was dying as the snow continued to fall unabated and the wind grew in intensity. An unmarked police car had struggled into the tiny cul-de-sac where the safe house was located and Amanda was being briefed once again by DI Jones who, she noted, looked haggard and stressed out.

"Remember Amanda, you will be watched at all times. I have armed police officers all over the park and plain clothed officers at all the entrances. If Williamson tries to get into the park we will almost certainly cut him off and arrest him. If, however, he somehow manages to gain entry, we have enough firepower in there to deal with him."

"Okay."

Amanda's voice was whisper quiet in the room, all eyes were on her. The time to leave and face her worst nightmares was upon her at last. She felt the panic move to another level.

Pulling on her coat she allowed herself to be led out into the bitterly cold evening. The snow flakes were huge and, in the garden where the snow had drifted there was easily eighteen inches of depth to it.

The car was an Audi A4, powerful enough to fight its way through the dreadful conditions. There were hardly any other cars on the road. Those that were, limped along at a snail's pace. Amanda gazed through the side window at the orange glow of the streetlights as they went slowly by. She felt sick to her stomach, the soup she had finally been persuaded to eat by WPC Walsh felt as though it might reappear at any moment.

No one spoke as the car crawled on its way, all the talking was done. DI Jones could see his reflection in the car window and he did not like what he saw there, the reflection was that of a worried man, a man who now doubted the course of action he was taking. The reflection did not lie; he hoped Amanda would not notice.

They were approaching the town centre now. It was eerie to see it under such conditions. On a more normal night the town would be full of cars, revellers; students, mainly at this time of the evening, would be moving from bar to bar taking advantage of the various 'happy hour' promotions offered by the town centre pubs. Buy one get one free; all drinks half price every bar had a different angle on the same theme and, at this time of year the students still had money in their pockets. Tonight though, the streets were empty.

"We are going to park a couple of streets away from the park Amanda. If Williamson is around and watching we don't want to scare him away before we get the chance to apprehend him." DI Jones' voice was grave as he addressed her.

"Yes alright, I understand."

Her voice sounded as weak as she was feeling and she tried to force herself to be brave.

"We have men on the route, some in parked cars some at high level on the buildings. The men on the rooftops are armed."

"I understand."

"I know this is very hard for you but try to imagine that they are not there as you walk. It's important that Williamson thinks you are keeping your side of the bargain and meeting him without involving us."

"I understand."

"You can still decide not to do this Amanda; it's not too late to pull the plug on the operation."

"No, I'll do it, I have to do it."

Amanda was well aware that DI Jones had only made the suggestion to ease his conscience should things not go to plan. Despite this she felt that if she didn't go ahead with this now then her life would no longer be worth living.

Pulling on her gloves and tightening the scarf around her neck she reached for the car door and, feeling sick to her heart, climbed out into the unrelenting blizzard.

THIRTY SIX

The day had dragged interminably for Alfred Williamson. Perched atop his tower watching the pathetic machinations of the local constabulary had been amusing at first but, as the cold and damp, got deep into his bones he had stopped seeing the joke.

The dead policeman had been useful to him though. After dragging the body right around the far side of the tower from the entrance, just in case some intrepid sightseer should climb the steps of the War Memorial, he had searched the body and the man's possessions for anything that might be useful to him.

The watch was a great find; it even fitted his wrist quite well. Although he could see the parish church tower from up here the weather had deteriorated such that he could no longer see the clock. With the watch at his disposal he would be able to time his move exactly. His plan was long formed and his confidence that he would complete it was total.

The flask which contained hot soup and the small *Tupperware* box that had chicken sandwiches and crisps inside had been an additional bonus for him. He had been feeling light-headed with the cold and lack of sustenance but the food, rationed throughout the day had really hit the mark and revived him each time he was feeling the effects of the tension and the conditions.

He wondered what was going through Amanda's mind now. Was she terrified; was she feeling or even being sick? He sincerely hoped that all of these things were happening to her; she deserved to suffer just as he hadn't deserved to. His mission would soon be over and then he no longer cared what happened to him. They could lock him away again or they could kill him, it really would not matter once he had disposed of the devil woman.

He glanced at the watch and, with rising excitement, noted that the time had come when he should make his move. Eating the last of the sandwiches to sustain him he began to descend the tower. First the wooden steps that led from the very top and then onto the stone spiral that would take him down to ground level.

His footsteps sounded reassuringly purposeful as he climbed down in the dim light afforded by the wall mounted lamps situated every sixth step. For nothing other than personal amusement, he counted the steps as he descended them, he was feeling light headed with the magnitude of what he was about to do. He had waited so long to do it.

At the bottom of the staircase he paused and looked carefully around the ground floor area. There was no evidence to suggest that anyone else was in the building, he was quite alone with the ghost of the dead police officer on the balcony high above.

He knew the route he would take, it had been easy to plan from the bird's eye view he had enjoyed for much of the last two days.

Bracing himself against the wind and cold he gently opened the door to the War Memorial and peered outside into the snowscape. The snow was a lot deeper than he had anticipated; the height of the tower had taken that particular perspective away. It didn't matter at all though; his plan would not be changed by a few flakes of snow.

Stepping out into the terrible night, he pulled the door closed behind him. The Memorial had been good to him, a safe refuge whilst he made his plans. He felt a shiver of sadness at leaving its safety. But there was no time for sentiment, no room for it in his ice-cold heart; he had a job to do.

He knew exactly where he was going though it was not easy in the dim light until his eyes began to grow accustomed to the conditions. He knew where each of the cells of police officers was hiding. It wouldn't take him long, even in these conditions, to reach the point where his chosen route would take him to where one of these cells would be.

His diligence had been thorough and he was fairly certain that each cell consisted of two officers, even he dare not hope that he would happen upon a single man in the snow covered bushes which he approached from an angle deliberately designed to be in a direction that the men would be unlikely to be maintaining a vigil.

He avoided the snow covered pathways, though with the depth of the snow it was a fairly uniform landscape over which he advanced.

Skirting a low wall which, in summer months prevented enthusiastic, bread throwing children from falling in the duck pond. He dashed, as best he could in the snow, across the short distance to the edge of the bushes in which he knew that less than twenty feet away police officers maintained their watching brief for him.

In this visibility, there was not a hope that he would have been observed during the short time he had been exposed. The snow, if anything, was worse than at any time since the blizzard had begun some days before. Alfred's confidence, already high, began to soar.

Here, in the shelter of the bushes, the snow was less deep, in some places it had failed to penetrate at all, the evergreen foliage acting as a barrier to its relentless onslaught. The noise of the wind was his ally. Any sound he may have made as he reached the shelter of the shrubbery was more than swallowed up by its thunderous roar.

He was less than thirty yards from the bandstand and he was confident that, should he successfully deal with the men that he could just hear talking ahead of him, he would be able to get to it without any chance of being observed by the other cells of police officers

This had been their error. In clement weather conditions their deployment might well have been flawless and Alfred might have had to abandon his attempt to meet Amanda, but, in visibility such as this, well, the police were committing a gross act of folly to let this go ahead at all.

Alfred slipped the knife out of his pocket. It felt robust in his grip, his confidence heightened as did his senses as he considered what he was about to do next. With his other hand, which still hurt him although the scar tissue was healing, he wiped a thin film of sweat from his brow. He listened carefully, trying to shut out the sound of the wind.

Just ahead he could hear voices and the scratchy reception of a two-way radio. So, had they managed to get their radio system working at last; would the man at the top of the tower be missed or would they assume that his radio was still not working properly? By now it hardly mattered.

He positioned himself behind a tree and carefully peered around its trunk to get some idea of what he would be dealing with. There were two of them, they looked tired, cold and fed up. Alfred considered that a bonus.

One of the men held a rifle; he really wouldn't want to be on the end of a bullet fired from that he thought. The man with the gun peered out into the whiteness in the direction of the bandstand, the other one, Alfred realised with some distress, was walking in his direction.

He shrank back behind the trunk of the tree, praying he had not been observed. Certainly the police officer's body language hadn't hinted that he had seen Alfred. Long seconds passed before he heard a hissing sound and realised, with some relief, that the man was urinating in the bushes on the other side of the tree.

He risked another look. The man was there for the taking, God had given him another helping hand. With lightning quick movements that belied both his age and his physical condition, he was behind the policeman in a moment and had drawn the serrated edge of the knife hard against the soft flesh of his neck.

Death was instant, blood gushed from the wound, staining the snow, and a hand across the man's mouth prevented him calling out in any way. At that moment the wind gusted harder and the moment in which Alfred was most vulnerable to discovery passed without incident. So far so good, he thought.

Alfred turned to the other police officer, his heart pounding in his chest. He almost laughed aloud in triumph as he saw that the man was straining his eyes to peer through the blizzard in the direction of the bandstand. He had heard and seen nothing and was a sitting duck. Stealthily Alfred began advancing on the man.

Killing the second police officer was almost as easy as the first. Alfred grabbed the man's hair with his bad hand and ran the blade across his throat with the other; the rifle fell to the ground next to the body, useless. The hard part was over and now he would be able to focus completely on what he had returned to this town to do.

Alfred allowed himself a moment or two to gloat. The police had thought how clever their plan had been. They hadn't counted on the resourcefulness of their opponent. Their surveillance points had one fundamental flaw, obvious from on high. Not one of their lookout positions was visible from any other one. In each case the bandstand would obscure the view for the other officers. All he had to do now was to walk in a straight line from his position in the trees. He was pleased to note that, even with an uninterrupted view such as this one was, he could hardly make out his destination in the blizzard. That would prove to be yet one more added reassurance as he went about his task.

A moment of doubt came over him. Just why was it so easy, was the girl safely at home? Had the police set up with the intention of leading him into a trap that had not been baited? A gut instinct, one he had learned to trust, told him that he should continue as planned, the girl would want this nightmare to end one way or the other. She would be there as she had promised.

Alfred Williamson was smiling as he began advancing on the bandstand.

THIRTY SEVEN

All the bravado that had been building inside her since Kate's death had seemed to drain out of her as she slammed the door of the Audi closed. Despite all the reassurances from Detective Inspector Jones she had never felt quite so totally alone.

The snow and wind made her shiver but that was only part of the reason. She was finding it hard to place one foot in front of the other as she advanced along the pavement towards the junction that would put her just a short street away from the entrance to the park.

It was eight-fifteen and she had begun the walk to the bandstand in the park, possibly the last journey she would make in her short and unhappy life. The visibility was terrible and she almost laughed aloud in her hysteria as she considered the men positioned on the rooftops who, supposedly, watched over her like guardian angels. They would be lucky if they could see their own feet in this weather.

Amanda pulled her coat tighter around her; it was in fact on loan, a much brighter colour than she would have chosen for herself but easier to see in the snow for the policeman who watched out for her. She had been tempted to point out the obvious, that it made her more visible to Williamson too, but it had seemed churlish and unnecessary.

The snow made strange whispering sounds as it landed as she strode through it with as confident a gait as she could manage in the circumstances. Reaching the park gate she saw the glow of a cigarette in one of the cars parked by the entrance, she guessed that this was one of her personal army of minders and tried not to look in that direction as she pushed open the gate, dragging a swathe of snow with it as she did so.

The park; though beautiful in its winter coat, was as forbidding as anywhere she had ever been and she had to fight down the bile in her throat as she was almost sick with the fear she was feeling. Around her there seemed to be a million places in which a maniac could hide. Only some of those shadowy places contained a friendly face, she wondered which.

In the daylight yesterday it had all seemed so straightforward but now at night, and now that things were real, she remembered nothing of where they were hiding. She shuddered at the thought of the task she had agreed to undertake; she could still turn back and, just for a moment, she almost did.

Despite her dread, her footsteps began to quicken, it was the adrenaline that coursed through her veins. Bizarrely, she remembered a biology lesson when she had learned all about the fight or flight response that animals adopted when threatened, she wondered where she fitted into this theory as her pace quickened still further.

She was stumbling through the deep snow towards the bandstand, towards her own funeral she thought crazily, but she could not slow herself down, some feral part of her had taken over, rational thought had been confined to the dustbin.

It felt like a thousand eyes were watching her; perhaps there were, policeman, small animals and birds and him, Alfred Williamson. She felt naked under their unseen observation. Her vulnerability felt total, in this kind of visibility she might not even get to the bandstand before Williamson was on her.

The wind whipped a snow flurry into her face, the cold snow like tiny needles on her cheeks. The cold penetrated her clothes easily and chilled her bones. She considered yet again DI Jones offer to call the whole exercise off and a part of her wished that she had taken that opportunity. Another part of her though knew that this nightmare had to reach a conclusion one way or another.

As she peered into the gloom she concluded that in normal circumstances she should be able to see the bandstand by now. Was she going the wrong way? Had she somehow become disorientated? She thought not but could not make out the structure despite of this.

How many times had Amanda Fellows walked through this park as adult and child? She could only guess but right now it was an alien and terrifying place. With sudden panic she wheeled around to look behind her, she had been sure she had heard footsteps in the snow behind her. Was it Williamson? Was he there with his knife; the knife that killed Kate? There was no one there, she was jumping at shadows.

She resumed her difficult journey, wading through this snow was taking it out of her, she was breathing heavily and, despite the cold, she was sweating. Was that fear, exertion or both? She didn't care any more.

When it appeared in the gloom it came as a shock to her, the bandstand was indistinct in the swirling snow but the very sight of it caused her spirits, which were already low, to drop like a stone. She stopped, swaying slightly in the snow as she gathered her mental strength for what she knew she must do.

Through the blizzard she tried to see if the structure was empty or whether a welcoming committee of one maniac would be there, waiting for her, waiting to introduce her to her destiny. It was hopeless, she couldn't tell.

On unsteady legs she continued her advance. There was a short series of stairs that led up to the bandstand, the one nearest to her at least showed no signs of footprints in the snow leading to it. She knew from memory that there were three more sets of such steps. The odds didn't seem very encouraging.

With nausea almost overwhelming her she mounted the bandstand steps and peered into the gloomy interior where it was more sheltered. There was nowhere to hide and she could see quite clearly that she was alone. She didn't know whether to laugh or cry at this revelation.

THIRTY EIGHT

The cold was almost too much to bear. Despite the coat, the gloves and the scarf, the thick sweater and the armoured vest she wore underneath it, the weather conditions seemed to be chilling her blood. She shivered uncontrollably.

Yet again she pulled at the sleeve of her coat and peered at her watch in the gloom. It was eight forty-five. Had they caught him yet? Or was this his idea of a joke, was he sitting in the warmth somewhere enjoying the fact that she was going through her own personal hell?

She tried to see out into the gloom. If anything the snow was worse than ever in the minutes since she reached the bandstand, was that possible? Again she looked at her watch; how long had she been here? She had no idea, she realised.

On this little island in the storm it was easy to imagine that she was on some remote planet, marooned and waiting expectantly for signs of life. Would that life, when it arrived, as she knew it would eventually, be friend or foe, angel or devil?

She tried again to penetrate the darkness and the swirling snow, turning right around so that she could survey, or attempt to survey, the whole three hundred and sixty degrees. Visibility was no more than about ten yards she decided. From here she could not even see the outlines of the trees and bushes in which her protectors were concealed and that, of course, meant that they could not see her either. She tried to push the thought from her mind.

In despair she sat on the low wooden bench that surrounded the perimeter of the bandstand, it was wet and cold but her legs had become increasingly unsteady and she feared she might fall down if she didn't sit.

Silently, she began to cry, no one could see, no one could hear, what did it matter anyway? The wind howled and the snowflakes danced a frenzied dance, mocking her, she no longer cared.

After a few more minutes she stood once more on unsteady legs. Enough was enough she had decided. Williamson was not going to come, the whole thing had been contrived to further undermine her and it had worked. She was bitterly cold and waves of fatigue washed over her. She was going to find the strength to just walk out of this park and abandon the whole thing.

As she started to take faltering steps towards the steps she had used to mount the bandstand she looked out into the swirling snow and halted in her tracks.

Had she seen something moving out there or was her imagination getting the better of her? She strained her eyes to see, struggled to find the exact spot where she thought she had seen something. With a gasp she realised that there was something out there in the murk.

She stood transfixed as she watched a figure emerge from the gloom, walking slowly but steadily straight towards the bandstand, towards where she stood, cold, afraid and vulnerable.

Was it him; Williamson? Had he somehow just walked right past the police officers and come to visit her here in this lonely place or was it a police officer coming to retrieve her, convinced, like she had been just moments before, that the maniac was not coming out to play tonight? Or, dare she hope? To tell her that Alfred Williamson was safely in police custody or, better still, dead.

Amanda stood there paralysed by her conflicting thoughts, unable to think, unable to move, waiting to either live or die.

**

It had been a long and difficult walk, or trudge was more accurate he supposed. Throughout the journey he had felt a mounting panic inside him and it wouldn't be quieted, he was obsessing on Amanda, or Marie as his subconscious thoughts still insisted she was called. She was in danger and he had to help her, but where would she be exactly? His mind refused to clarify things for him.

He put his hand to his forehead, there was considerable pain going on inside his head, like a particularly bad migraine, but he couldn't give in, he had to press on, she needed him he was sure of it.

What was it that Margaret had told him? They were going to use the girl, his twin sister, in some foolish plan to trap the man who had killed Kate Harvey. It was madness on a night like this but his instinct told him that the police had pressed ahead with their plan despite the weather. Perhaps Amanda had insisted, she had seemed a strong character, but was she strong right now? He thought she was terrified, he *felt* it.

When he closed his eyes, which was frequently as the cruel wind blew the icy snow into his face, it were as though he was in a waking dream. There was a structure of some kind, barely visible in the gloom and the swirling snow. In the structure, cold and alone, he thought he sensed her presence there. He tasted her fear as he saw these images in his mind's eye and his thoughts returned to the creature that had haunted his recent dreams. Was the human equivalent of that beast descending on her right now? Was that what the imagery in the dream meant?

If it was, then he knew he would face some sort of barrier that would prevent him from helping her. In the same way that the cave mouth had closed, swallowing up, as it had, both the girl and the beast but shutting him out. He felt that there would be an analogous problem for him to overcome if he was to go to her aid.

He turned into William Street, one of the old streets that bordered the park. From here it was about a hundred yards to one of the park gates. If he quickened his step he could make it quite quickly, the snow was less deep here, the street protected by the tall buildings.

As he advanced he became aware of something that he had not counted on. Someone was sitting in a parked car right by the entrance to the park. Of course there was, he chastened himself, if the police were laying a trap to catch a killer in the park then they would be taking every possible step to ensure that innocent civilians did not end up in the crossfire.

Feigning indifference he continued walking at the same pace and walked straight past the park gate and the man in the car who gave him a peremptory look but then returned his attention to the newspaper that he was reading by the internal light of the car.

He continued to walk until he was convinced that he was out of sight of the car and then, with an agility that surprised even himself, he scaled the snow-covered railings and entered the park amidst the tree cover that formed its perimeter.

He stood there for a moment gathering his thoughts, trying to get his breath back and closing his eyes against the pain in his head once again. He tried again to picture where Amanda might be. What was that damn structure in the snow? It wasn't particularly tall, come on man think! He demanded himself to concentrate but he still didn't get it.

As he squeezed his eyes tightly closed and tried to shut out all other thoughts he felt fear and anger well up inside him. He saw something else in his mind's eye, or was it someone else's mind's eye through whom he saw this strange world? Was he seeing the world through the eyes of his twin sister and, if he was, was she really seeing the figure that was shambling out of the snowstorm towards where she stood, cold and terrified?

He concentrated as hard as he could and, as he did so, the figure he was seeing in the snow began to change form. What had looked like a man now took on a spider-like form, on one of its two heads a dull green glow manifested itself from deep-set eyes and it shambled towards the structure in the snow. With a cry of despair he realised, finally, what that structure was, a bandstand. Probably some hundred yards away from where he stood concealed in the bushes and the shadows. Could he get there in time? He began his attempt.

THIRTY NINE

The legs on which she stood threatened to give up on her and deposit her on the bandstand floor in a heap. There she would wait for him and be at his mercy.

There had been little doubt in her mind from the first moment she saw the figure in the blizzard that it was him, Alfred Williamson, coming to mete out a revenge that only he felt was appropriate. Despite this she had been unable to run, her body had, quite simply, stopped obeying her conscious thought. She hadn't even been able to scream, though in these conditions it wouldn't have mattered in any case, there was no one who would hear her.

She had watched in stupefied silence as he slowly and deliberately climbed the steps to the bandstand and stood before her, he looked taller than she remembered. The look of triumph in his eyes chilled her to the core. He stood there for maybe thirty seconds, just watching her, perhaps waiting for some reaction that he could savour. She couldn't oblige, she was transfixed. Perhaps he was simply coming to terms with the fact that he had finally got close enough to her to speak or to kill or whatever else took his fancy.

Despite her fear she was able to think fairly lucidly. Williamson looked terrible. One side of his face was covered in a thick growth of beard, the other was distorted and shrivelled with no hair growth at all, this, she concluded, was obviously a result of his exposure to the fire at Carlton.

When he finally spoke, his voice was like a high pitched hissing whisper, she was reminded of a serpent, the analogy seemed appropriate.

"So Amanda, for once in your miserable life you almost did as you were told."

She looked dumbly on; she had nothing to say to him.

"It was too much to ask that you did everything I asked of you. It always was wasn't it?"

She still didn't react, she couldn't.

"Because of you Amanda, three men have died here. If you had kept the police out of this those men might be beside the fire watching the television with their families tonight. Instead they are dead in the snow; three more funerals to go with the others."

He took a small step towards her. She wanted to take a step backwards but her legs refused to work.

"You know Amanda, as the weather got steadily worse I feared that the police would call the whole thing off. I never in my wildest dreams believed that they would be as stupid as to attempt to use you as bait in a trap when they were hardly able to see past the ends of their noses. They must be really desperate to catch me."

Still nothing from Amanda, she was frozen with fear and despair.

"I can see you are afraid of me Amanda. You are right to be; though in a way you should be glad to see me tonight. I have come to unburden you of your guilt.

"Perhaps you don't see guilt as a burden but you should, even a devil, of which I know you are one, should recognise the existence of guilt. I am God's warrior sent to slay you and send you back to where you came from.

"You invaded my dreams, my mind, you got inside my head and you made me do things that I would never have done. I knew the difference between right and wrong and you took that away from me."

"You are truly mad."

Amanda's words were lost in the wind but Williamson seemed gratified that he had caused a reaction in her at last; he had been disappointed at the lack of terror in her expression. He took her almost inaudible words as a cue to continue.

"It was not me but you who killed Susan. Your friend Kate, you sacrificed her to protect yourself, you put the idea in my head, just as the policemen who lie dead in the snow were sacrificed by you to protect yourself. You must pay a price for that Amanda, the ultimate price."

Alfred reached inside his coat and produced the knife. Still Amanda felt frozen to the spot, even as he advanced towards her she failed to respond, perhaps she was resigned to her fate.

With less than three feet separating them she finally reacted. She turned and tried to head for one of the small staircases. She almost made it. Another couple of feet and she would have been away out into the blizzard. The snow that had been Alfred Williamson's ally throughout these last few days thwarted her, however. The drift that had encroached into the bandstand was wet and slippery and she had quite simply slipped and fallen.

The world spun around her as she came to terms with the reality that she had hit her head hard against the bench that surrounded the bandstand. How she wished that she had lost consciousness in that instant. As it was, dazed and useless she would have to witness Williamson's final triumph. She would be forced to look up into that distorted face as he ended her life here on earth.

The knife looked cruel and efficient as he held it before him like the High Priest in a black mass at the moment of ritual sacrifice. It was easy to believe that this distorted and demented creature was the devil incarnate.

All was lost, the police had failed and she would die, wet, cold and despairing in this snow-bound wilderness. Worse still, the bastard would probably get away with it. He had got in here like a ghost, who was to say he couldn't get out the same way he had come?

Amanda closed her eyes as her executioner knelt beside her and waited for the pain of the first of what she anticipated would be many stab wounds.

**

The pain in his side was excruciating. There was, on the whole, not much cause for the average financial consultant to attempt a three minute mile. He was out of condition at best and racing through snow this deep could do for him long before he reached the bandstand where he was now certain that an endgame was being played out.

How had Williamson got past the police; had they been complacent, believing that the man would not turn up on a night such as this? His anger fuelled his adrenaline which, in turn, somehow kept him going when he felt on the point of collapse.

Jim knew that as he continued his clumsy and disordered advance on the bandstand that at any moment he could feel the cold steel of a police marksman's bullet. There was no way in these conditions that an onlooker could tell the difference between him and any other person on the planet.

He marvelled at the irony of being shot trying to save the sister he didn't know he even had until a couple of days ago. He tried to push the thoughts out of his mind as he scrambled onwards. Perhaps the police had abandoned their plan; maybe there were no snipers out there in the dark.

He was in front of the bandstand before he had even realised it was there, he took the small steps two at a time. He knew by now who he would find there, he just hoped he was not too late to save her.

His spirits took a fall when he made out the scene in the gloom. The girl was lying prone on the floor; Williamson was on his knees beside her with a knife, a big knife, in his hand. Was he already too late? It was too dark to tell.

His noisy ascent of the little flight of stairs had not gone unnoticed despite the howling of the wind. Alfred Williamson turned slowly towards him and began to climb to his feet.

"What do we have here then; could it possibly be a knight in shining armour that has come to rescue this damsel in distress?"

He spat the words out, pure hatred in his eyes. He would not be denied his moment of triumph.

Williamson began walking towards where Jim stood, panting with exhaustion. The run had taken so much out of him he doubted he had the energy for a battle. He looked at the blade and was sure that he saw a dark stain on the blade, so he was too late then he thought.

The maniac's agility belied his appearance, his lunge at Jim caught him almost completely unawares, the blade caught his shoulder and the pain was excruciating. He fell to the ground and Williamson used his momentum to deliberately land on top of him, driving what little wind that Jim had left out of his lungs.

The knife, after being given a cruel twist, just for the hell of it, was pulled free of Jim's shoulder. Jim was left to look into the horror mask that was Williamson's triumphant face, the image was blurred, he realised he was crying with pain.

Despite everything, Jim thought fast, he brought his knee up hard and fast between his assailant's legs and was encouraged by the cry of outraged pain. Now he had to follow up his success with another small victory. He was, after all, not the one holding the sharp thing.

Pushing with his feet, Jim succeeded in toppling Alfred sideways onto the wooden floor of the bandstand, now; if only he could get to his feet he might be able to kick the bastard into unconsciousness.

It seemed a good plan but the slippery floor had other ideas, so too did the pain he felt as he tried to regain his feet, he fell back to his knees.

As if he were a man possessed, and Jim had just about enough time to consider this possible, Williamson had regained both his balance and his single-mindedness. Seizing his opportunity he swung the knife back towards Jim once again.

In a blinding white seizure of agony, Jim vaguely realised that the knife had penetrated him once again, this time a little way below the first wound. He could hear Williamson laughing, he had tried but he had failed; now he would die here in this lonely barren place. He slumped forward, falling onto his face.

The kill was at hand, the knife was raised high above Jim's neck, a cry of triumph was in Williamson's throat but it failed to emerge.

In the darkness, shapes were moving about, panic rose in Alfred, he had a job to do, and the girl must die before they got here. Climbing again to his feet he aimed a kick into the midriff of the stricken man and followed it with one to the head.

Amanda hadn't moved throughout the whole of the fracas, her body lay slumped on the bandstand floor her complexion the colour of the snow which lay all about her.

Alfred was worrying now, was he to be thwarted at the last after all he had been through, would God be that cruel to him? It would need to be a quick kill, a slicing of the jugular vein. The knife poised he grabbed her hair and pulled her head back exposing the pale flesh of her throat. Victory was to be his after all as he placed the tip of the blade against her skin and prepared to tear the life out of her.

"This is for Susan!" he whispered into the raging gale.

The gun shot sounded strangely distant, such were the acoustics in the storm. The bullet though had nothing distorted about it, it was accurate clinical and punched the life out of Alfred Williamson in an instant.

EPILOGUE

Four years later:

The memory of that night would stay with everyone involved, forever. How could it not; so many lives were changed?

For Jim Dowley recovery was a slow process, even now he had limited use of his left arm. His life though had changed for the better. He found he could relax again, he slept well, his drinking was down to social levels and his family life was better than it had ever been. His reconciliation with Jennifer and the children had been an emotional one but was probably the best day of his life.

There had been a third child, a girl and, with Jennifer's blessing, she had been named Marie after the twin sister that genetic testing had proved Amanda Fellows to be.

Jim started his own business and he was doing extremely well. He had a client base that rivalled that of the company he left behind. He was a genuine independent and got the best deal for the clients regardless of who was the service provider.

Amanda married Dave Sullington and they started a family, the twins born only a couple of days ago were beautiful. One was a girl, the other one a boy. It was lost on no one who saw them after the birth, that they shared a common feature with their mother and their Uncle Jim. On their chins were identical moles.

Neither Jim nor Amanda dreamt about each other any longer. It was as if the dreams had been like a gossamer thin thread that had held them together and now that they had finally been reunited they were no longer relevant.

On cold, winter evenings, Amanda often wondered about the old man who had died in front of her in the flat she shared with Kate Harvey. Just what was it that the man had wanted to say to her, why had it taken him so long to track her down and clear his conscience of whatever burdened it? She knew that she would now never know but she also knew that the curiosity would never go away.

Each year, on the anniversary of the old man's death she visited the churchyard and placed flowers next to the small plaque that celebrated the life and death of a once great man, each year the message was the same: 'To Dad may you rest in peace!'